Hagerstown

Also by William J. Hipkiss

Fasching

Normandie
Scandal on Pier 88

Hagerstown

William J. Hipkiss

To order additional copies of this book, contact:
Xlibris Corporation
1-888-795-4274
www.Xlibris.com
Orders@Xlibris.com
42324

CONTENTS

This book is dedicated to the
affectionate memory of
the Campbell Brothers,
Larry, deceased, Jack, deceased, Paul, and Ralph.

*In 1948, in Elmhurst, Queens, New York City, they were on the
cutting edge of the future.*

—Jack Willis

ACKNOWLEDGEMENTS

Elizabeth Catherine LaGrande, my wife and severest critic, has stood by me since the day we were married. Considering all the hair-brained schemes I've attempted, I find I must salute her efforts to encourage, advise, and love me for the last twenty years. I'm quite sure I could not have written three novels, after turning seventy years of age, without her help.

Paul Campbell promised me he would give the manuscript a final read through. I was sure that his scrutiny was what was needed, such was my respect for his wisdom and his intellect of old. If you find this novel something of interest, you owe much of it to my dear, oldest of pals, Paul Campbell. Truth be known, Sonny Campbell always wished he was the fifth Campbell brother back there in 1948.

Carol Peden who headed up the Muskegon, Michigan Civic Theater for many years, is presently quite ill. She has been steadfast in her appreciation of my stage career, such as it was, and now seems to be a fan of my writing as well. I wish us both many more years of reading and writing and look forward to the inevitable time when we are reunited with our theater friends who are no longer with us.

Kathie Boeschenstein, knows a dreamer when she meets one. More importantly she possesses the kindness to let him know that his dreams are now a reality.

My old standby copy editor, Claude Vernam, was at it again, trying to correct my miserable spelling and laboriously weeding out a sea of typographical errors. He has my never-ending gratitude.

Claude,
Thanks for all your help.
Bill Hopkins

PART ONE

The Fix

CHAPTER ONE

Sonny Campbell awakened at the usual time. He slowly sat upright with his legs draped over the edge of the king size bed. He rubbed his eyes and waited for his head to clear. His wife, Rochelle, remained in bed as he went into the bathroom and started the routine process of shaving. Before he lathered his face, he turned the small bathroom radio on. A newscaster was nervously reporting a downtown slaying, which was rare for the city of Hagerstown, Maryland. Murders in Washington County were commonly thought to occur at the rate of one per year. The murder of a celebrity like Archy Howell might be said to never have occurred.

He only half listened to the newscast until the sound of a very familiar name stimulated his ears into rapt attention.

> *. . . and Mister Vernon Lawrence identified his brother-in-law's body. The dead man's facial features had almost disappeared as a result of what appeared to be a double shotgun blast. Investigating Washington County sheriff's deputies at the scene were quoted as saying that Mister Howell was behind the wheel of a sedan and in a stopped position when the shotgun blasts were fired point blank through the driver's side open window. Death was almost instantaneous, causing the dead man's right foot to come off the brake. The vehicle then moved slowly forward down Plum Street, crossed to the left, and crashed into a telephone pole located on the northwest corner of Plum and Harrison. Howell's vehicle had some slight damage to the left front fender, the only real evidence of what must have been a collision.*

"Rocky, wake up. Something's happened to Archy Howell."

Rochelle Campbell lifted her head from her pillow and rolled over in the direction of the bathroom.

"What did you say? . . . Archy Howell? . . . I didn't hear the first part of what you said."

"Archy Howell's dead. Somebody took his head off with a couple of shotgun blasts. Listen." Sonny turned up the radio volume.

Rochelle exclaimed, "My God!"

> . . . Howell had been a first-baseman for the Hagerstown Suns. This 1982 season had been the best of his two years on the team—both in hitting and on the field. His performance had fallen off somewhat in the last six weeks. His family, a wife, Edith, and three children, have been notified of his killing. His wife's brother, who had been visiting Hagerstown, identified the body. Witnesses say the deceased had stopped in an all-night café around one A.M. after a night of heavy drinking with two other team members, one of whom was with Howell at the café. He apparently got into an argument there with a Negro man. Racial slurs ensued and the argument soon became a fist fight with the Negro getting the worst of it, causing him to flee the scene. Café employees summoned sheriff's deputies, but Howell managed to leave before they arrived. A statement was taken from Bucky Livingston, a fellow baseball player for the Hagerstown Suns, who had been seated with the victim when the fracas broke out. Two Negro customers, who had apparently witnessed the incident, had also fled before the deputies arrived at the scene. Howell wasn't reported seen again until his dead body was discovered in his automobile at Plum and Harrison. . . . More on this apparent murder of one of the Suns' star players as facts develop.

Anxiously, Rochelle asked, "Should we try to contact Edith?"

Sonny responded, "I don't think we should do that. I was very close to Archy and I may have to defend the person who did this. I see the possibility of a conflict of interest on the horizon. But she's probably frantic right now. We'll see. Maybe we'll go over there tonight . . . or better yet, tomorrow, after I've had a chance to sort this horrible thing out."

"But we're their closest friends. We've got to see if we can do anything to help her."

"Not yet, honey. If she calls us, maybe. Otherwise we give her time to let it sink in . . . give her time to calm down."

Sonny had put on a fresh white shirt and was tying his blue rep-striped tie. It had become a firm habit for him to be at his desk at the Public Defender's Office a good quarter of an hour before the business day commenced at eight thirty A.M.

"You want me to make you some breakfast?"

"I don't feel like eating anything. I'll call you from the office if I learn any more down there."

It was a bright sunny Friday, the end of the last week in June. As Sonny drove past Municipal Stadium on Memorial Drive he had to force himself to reflect on something other than the death of Archy Howell—first base would never feel the foot of the star player again. He brought to mind a day some eighteen years before in Baltimore when he sat on a bench outside of the Maryland State Public Defender's office. He would be interviewed by the Public Defender for a job.

Settling in Hagerstown had been a mutual choice of Sonny and Rochelle after they had visited Washington County while he was still employed at the U. S. Justice Department and before they were married. The idea of being a small-town lawyer first became his firm desire while he was still in law school. He perceived himself to be a hopeless idealist and was proud of his liberal leanings. Working for Robert F. Kennedy, considering what that Attorney General seemed to stand for, was an acceptable detour on the road to fulfilling Sonny's small-town-lawyer dream. Rochelle needed no persuading when it came to Sonny's view of life. She loved him unconditionally.

He felt confident that he would be appointed Deputy District Public Defender to fill a vacancy for Washington County, the northernmost county in Maryland on the Pennsylvania border. He had fallen into the habit of surprising old friends by telling them that Washington County was located exactly on the south side of the Mason Dixon line. His year's experience at the U. S. Justice Department under Attorney General Robert F. Kennedy made him the front runner above all other candidates for the vacancy.

By the time he got to Summit Avenue and had made a right turn, the specter of Archy Howell's head exploding from two shotgun blasts came back to the front of Sonny's brain. He turned left on Franklin Street and drove to his office building. It appeared that more office employees than usual had already arrived and were entering the building. Most were eager to get an early take on what had happened to Archy Howell.

Washington County had been named after the first U.S. President and been carved out of Frederick County by resolve of the Constitutional Convention of 1776. The public defenders for Washington and Frederick Counties and their staffs shared office space at 100 West Franklin Street. Sonny entered suite 102 and found a large cluster of Public Defender employees gathered around his secretary's desk.

She said, "Here he comes now. He was Archy's best buddy. He's got to know more than they said on the radio."

"I'm afraid you're wrong, Lori. I probably don't know any more than any of you do. I realize all of you are here early, but don't you think getting down to work might be a good idea now?"

The secretary for the Public Defender for Frederick County spoke up resentfully. "Mister Wilson doesn't expect me to start work until eight thirty. I'm going down the hall to get the morning paper. Maybe there's something more in there." She walked out of the suite briskly.

Sonny's secretary got his attention. "Two new defendant assignments are on your desk—one vehicular manslaughter and one aggravated assault."

"I guess they haven't issued any warrant for the Howell killing yet," Sonny responded. "Whoever did it has probably made his way to parts unknown by now."

"If you ask me, they should be tracking that guy he got into a fight with at Carmine's café last night."

"You're jumping to conclusions, Lori," he cautioned. "What seems obvious is wrong half the time."

"Bet you a buck I'm right this time."

Wilson's secretary returned with a copy of the *Hagerstown Herald-Mail*. "It looks like the paper's ahead of the newscast this time," she announced. She tossed the paper on Sonny's desk.

"Come on, Pat. You messed up my desk. What's new in the paper?"

"See for yourself . . . it's above the fold."

SUSPECT APPREHENDED AT SHARPSBURG GREYHOUND BUS TERMINAL

Chester Roosevelt, a custodian at Washington County Hospital, has been arrested at the Sharpsburg Greyhound Bus Terminal. Roosevelt was leaving the city at six thirty this morning with a bus ticket that bore a Chicago destination. It was learned that Roosevelt and the Hagerstown Suns' first baseman, Archy Howell, were in a physical scuffle at Carmine's café during the wee hours of this Friday morning. When Roosevelt was asked where he was headed on the bus, he remained silent. Washington County's Sheriff's officers were to seek a warrant at the State's Attorney's office sometime today, charging Roosevelt with first-degree murder.

Sonny picked up the newspaper and read the article at the top of the page, quickly the first time, and then slowly, picking out pertinent words—*custodian . . . bus-ticket . . . physical scuffle*. Sonny was instantly aware that Roosevelt was going to be a candidate for joining the Public Defender's small society of first degree murder suspects. It was rare that more than one murder was committed in Hagerstown each year, and rarer still that the killer could afford his own attorney. Lori had won her bet. When the arrest warrant for Chester Roosevelt had been issued by the State's Attorney, it meant that Sonny Campbell would have a new assignment on his desk by Monday, this despite the probability that he would have to reject the assignment because of his friendly relationship with the victim.

Sonny began reviewing the assignments now on his desk. The vehicular homicide was routine. It seemed that the defendant indisputably ran a red light and crashed into the driver's side of a car full of passengers that had apparently entered the intersection on green. That driver died at the scene. His three passengers escaped with minor injuries. Despite appearances, however, Sonny would have Walter Brock, an investigator whom he shared with Wilson, carefully review the witnesses' statements and the functioning of the traffic signal and hopefully discover some small defense which could provide a negotiating point with the State's Attorney.

The other assignment, aggravated assault, grew out of a domestic dispute that escalated into the husband's balled up fist coming in contact with the wife's face, and eventually wielding a butcher knife which he plunged one time into her shoulder.

Sonny buzzed Brock on the telephone and summoned him to his office. He explained what was needed in the two cases to which Brock sassily retorted, "You think I had to be told?"

Sonny just as sassily answered, "One of these days you're going to discover something you're not an expert in and you're not going to know what to do with it."

As Brock was turning to retreat to his desk, he said, "And I'll probably find some place in your anatomy for you to shove it."

Sonny snickered. He then removed a one-dollar bill from his billfold, paper clipped it to the top of the newspaper, and walked over to Lori's desk. He silently and gently placed the paper in front of her, and then returned to his office.

She tried to muffle a giggle as he walked away but was unsuccessful. He likewise could not resist laughing loudly all the way back to his desk where he made some notes in preparation for the arraignments of the two new defendants which were to start sharply at nine o'clock.

CHAPTER TWO

Rochelle and Sonny slept in on Saturday morning. Their alarm went off at nine o'clock. Sonny groaned. Rochelle laughed. "You can stay right here for exactly ten more minutes, Mister. I'll fix us some toast and hot tea." Again, Sonny groaned. Again, Rochelle laughed. "I take it you agree with my offer. Remember . . . ten minutes."

She returned to the bedroom with a tray. He was already on his feet. She poured the tea. He put marmalade on a piece of toast, which they shared.

Sonny spoke hoarsely, "You know, last week we made a date to see Archy and Edith at Smitty's after the game today. Do you think we should go over there and see her this morning?"

"I wanted to go over there yesterday. I think we're overdue."

"O.K. I'm going to get a jump on the case and go to the Detention Center to see my new client. It's a cinch I'll get the assignment." He didn't bring up the subject of the possibility of later having to recuse himself, even with Rochelle. "The sooner I talk to him, the better. I'll call you afterwards and we'll go over and see Edith."

Sonny drove to his office where he found Walter Brock who liked to catch up on his work on Saturday mornings. "I bet you want me to do something on that murder case, don't you boss?"

"Yep, now that you ask. Would you talk to the deputies in the sheriff's office and find out if a search warrant has been issued, and if it has, what is the result?"

"Aye, aye, sir."

It was only a three mile drive from Sonny's office to the Detention Center. Out of convenience, criminal defendants, waiting to appear in court for any reason, were held in the Detention Center.

Chester Roosevelt had the weekend to contemplate his predicament. He was to be arraigned on Monday. Sonny appeared at the Detention Center and checked in for visitation with the man now accused of nearly blowing Archy Howell's head off. After he signed in, he deemed it politic to go straight to

Sheriff Dick Shannon's office in the same building, and announce that he would be defending the Detention Center's most hated inmate, the killer of a local baseball hero.

"No surprise to us," said the sheriff smugly. "This guy is your typical black, below-the-poverty-line, uncivilized killer. You'd do well if you get him to plead guilty and throw himself on Judge Piercy's mercy and avoid the death penalty. You're lucky you got a liberal Democrat, Frederick County judge sitting as District judge on Monday in our fair Republican County," said Shannon.

"How do you sleep at night Dick Shannon? If you were a judge you'd be impeached on the basis of the racial prejudice your heart pumps constantly throughout your bloodstream," Sonny said in a voice that the inhabitants of the surrounding offices could hear.

"And how can you sleep at night, you defender of liberal causes? Every time you get one of **these people** off to go and do another crime, it makes me want to throw up," said Shannon.

"**These people** meaning poor and black and from the wrong side of town, right?"

The Sheriff came back with, "Oh, you've had a few from the white trash bin too, I remember."

"You'll have to excuse me now, Dick. I have some honest work to do. By the way, you don't happen to have any quick cure for nausea in that little bathroom of yours, do you?"

"Do I make you sick or are you anticipating that your new client is going to make you throw up?"

"We'll have to wait till we find out who really killed Archy Howell before we know who gets the last word here, don't you think, Dick?" Sonny said without much enthusiasm.

"You can't possibly think that, my friend."

"We'll see." Sonny left the sheriff's office with a frown on his face.

Roosevelt was waiting alone for Sonny in one of the prisoners' visiting rooms used for lawyer interviews and other special visitors.

"I'm William Campbell, the Public Defender, for Washington County, Mister Roosevelt."

The defendant rose from his chair. "I didn't do it."

"Stop. Don't speak until I ask you a question . . . understand?"

"But I really didn't do it. Don't tell me to stop talking. You've got to know . . . **I didn't kill that man.**" Roosevelt's speech was articulate and reflected at least a little bit of higher education.

"O.K., O.K. But it does me no good to hear that. Practically every defendant who's gone through my office has said the same thing. It never does any good to hear it."

"Mister Campbell, you're probably thinking that I'm just another typical Negro low-life criminal. I'm nothing of the sort. Just because I'm a custodian, most white people think I'm . . . well, they think I'm a person without morals or integrity. I may be poor and a little weird and have no family to speak of . . . but I've never killed anyone in my whole life. You're simply going to have to believe me."

"Forgive the pun, but I've got to tell you that the jury's still out on whether I believe you or not. Now, let me ask you a few questions."

"I'll answer all your questions . . . fully and truthfully."

"What was the dispute about in Carmine's café early Friday morning?"

"First of all, it didn't start between Howell and me. At the time, I wouldn't have known Howell from a circus clown. But I did know the guy he came in with. They were both drunk. The other guy had been a patient at the hospital where I worked. His name is Bucky Livingston. I'm sure he's on the same baseball team as Howell. I learned that Howell's a celebrity from the radio—the same time I heard someone had killed him."

"I wanted to know how the fight got started."

"I was at the lunch counter minding my own business when I heard loud voices coming from the booth area. I turned around and that's when I saw Howell for the first time in my life."

"How many people in the booth?"

"Just Howell and Livingston."

"Do you remember what the voices had been saying?"

"Just pieces. . . . Something about money . . . and something about who's fault it was about something. . . . When I turned around, Howell was just standing up and grabbing Livingston with one hand by the shirt collar and slapping him in the face with the other. Fool that I was, I quickly hustled to the booth and tried to break up what I thought was going to become an all-out fight."

"How many people in the café?"

"The white girl behind the counter. Besides me, there were two customers at either end of the counter. They were both black. As far as I know, neither of those guys turned around until Howell screamed at me to get the hell away . . . that it was none of my business. Again, I made the mistake of grabbing one of Howell's wrists—the hand that was doing the slapping. He let go of Livingston's collar and the two of us tumbled onto the floor. He hit me with his fists in the face three or four times. I'm no fighter. . . . Believe me I'm no fighter. . . . The counter girl was screaming a jumble of words during all this time. Then the colored cook came out from the back room kitchen area. He managed to separate the two of us. He yelled at me. *Chet, ya git yoself da hell out of heah, raaht now, ya hear?*"

I told him, "I gotta pay first."

He screamed back, *Neva you mind payin'. . . .* **Git out. . . . now! Ya hear?***"

"What did you do?"

"What would you do? I was too scared to do anything but scramble on out of there. On the way out, I heard the cook's voice saying, *We sorry 'bout dat Mista Howell. He won't be back in heah.*"

"That's how you found out that the man's name was Howell."

"I knew I'd never forget the name of Howell."

"Did you ever hear that name again?"

"First let me tell you that I usually don't get to sleep till mid-morning. I work the night shift at the hospital. I got home and turned on the radio like I usually do . . . WJEJ. About seven A.M. they started broadcasting the news that Archy Howell got shot."

"Where do you live?"

"I've got two rooms two blocks from the café. . . . I heard the news about Howell and I went into a crazy state of panic. I knew I would be their first suspect because of the café incident. I made a rash decision, as it turned out—to get out of town—bury myself in a large city where it would be hard to find me if I was right about being their first suspect and they started looking for me. I know what happens to a Negro once he gets into the system. I wasn't going to take any chances."

"And as it turned out you did the one thing that put you right into the system—try to run away."

"Ya got that right. As I was getting on the bus to Chicago I heard someone call my name out. I turned around and found three sheriff's deputies with guns drawn."

"One told me to step down off the bus stairs, put my bag on the ground, and my hands behind my head. Of course, I obeyed and I knew at that moment that my life had changed forever. From then on I knew there was only one thing I could be certain of."

"What's that?"

"That one day my life would end by a lethal injection."

"You sound like you've got some education."

"One year here at the Community College."

"Why only one year? You must be twenty, twenty-one years old."

"I'm taking the slow route to becoming a doctor."

"You didn't flunk out, then?"

"Hell, no. I got mostly good grades. I just ran out of money. I'm saving every damn cent I make at the hospital and wanted to start my plan up again in September. Now, that will all depend on you."

"Do you know anything about me?"

"No reason to."

"How old are you?"

"Twenty-one . . . twenty-two on October 31."

"Halloween."

"Yeah, trick or treat. No treat for me this year."

There was a knock on the visiting room door. A deputy spoke through the door. "You have a phone call, Mister Campbell."

"O.K. Unlock the door will you?"

There was a phone on a desk just outside the visiting room.

"Campbell here."

"This is Walt, Sonny."

"What's up?"

Brock spoke sadly, "I'm here in the building. It's worse than I imagined."

"What could be worse?"

"Their search warrant produced assorted shotgun shells in his apartment."

"No shotgun?"

"No shotgun, but one of the shells had pellets identical to the ones they found in Archy's head."

"Any more good news?"

"Isn't that enough? It'll probably convict him, along with his attempted escape to Chicago and the fight in Carmine's."

"But why no shotgun? Do you think he disposed of it?'

"More than likely."

"Is there anything else I should be asking him?"

"No. That's it, so far."

"O.K., call me again if you have any more bulletins. I'll be here for another half hour and then I'm going home."

The deputy let Sonny back into the lawyer's visiting room. Roosevelt was still seated with his elbows on top of a small table, holding his head in his hands.

Sonny asked, "What should I call you . . . Chester . . . or do you have a nickname?"

"My friends call me Chet."

"O.K., Chet. Important question for you."

"Go ahead."

"Do you own a shotgun?"

Roosevelt remained silent.

"What's wrong? Did I hit a nerve? Out with it. Do you have a shotgun somewhere?"

"I got rid of it. I thought it would put me further in the soup."

"You know, for a man who thinks he's smart enough to become a doctor your mistakes in this case are monumental."

"How so?"

"You tell me you didn't shoot Howell. You own a shotgun. You got rid of the shotgun. You got rid of the one thing that would go a long way to prove your innocence. Don't you realize that a forensic lab can do tests on a shotgun to see if it was fired recently? I sure hope getting rid of it doesn't mean it's gone forever."

"It's in a safe place."

"Why didn't you get rid of the shells?"

"Oh, jeez! I forgot I still had shells in the apartment."

"Well, my friend, with the help of a search warrant, those shells are now in an evidence locker at the Sheriff's Department. Where's this safe place where you put the gun?"

"I gave it to my partner for safe keeping."

"What partner? You mean business partner?"

"I'm afraid not. I mean my life partner."

"You're homosexual?"

"That will go against me too, won't it? I mean Hagerstown is about as straight a community as there is, isn't it?"

"Straight as an arrow. What's your partner's name?"

"Do we have to get him involved in this?"

"We do if you're still planning to become a doctor."

Roosevelt's silence was uncomfortable for both men.

"Come on, Chet. This is important."

Finally the words came out in a whimper. "His name is Howard Parsons. No one knows about us. Very few people know he's . . . different. He's a lot older than I am. He's white. He's on the custodial staff at the hospital with me."

"But you don't live together?"

"No."

"Do you own an automobile?"

"No."

"Well then, how did you get to the Greyhound Terminal?"

"Howard has an old Chevrolet. He drove me down there."

Sonny tore a sheet of paper from a small notebook. He handed it along with his ballpoint pen to Chet. "Here. Write down Howard's address and phone number."

"He doesn't have a phone."

"Just the address will do. Now, is there anything else you haven't told me that might be important?"

"Mister Campbell, I really can't think of anything."

"Are you right handed?"

"I'm left handed."

"Did anyone run a gunpowder test on your hands?"

"No, they didn't."

"O.K. I'll be back to talk to you just before you get arraigned. That'll probably be on Monday." Sonny pressed the buzzer on the wall and the deputy let him out of the visiting room.

CHAPTER THREE

The Howell residence was in a fairly upscale part of Hagerstown. That was never fully understood by Sonny and Rochelle because when they met Edith and Archy, their house was no fancier than the one that the Campbells lived in. Their middle class houses promoted, in part, the hard and fast friendship that developed between the two families. After all, the salary of a minor league baseball player was not very high. And at the time that the four of them first met at Smitty's Bar and Grill, the Campbells were on a frugality binge.

About three months before Archy's murder, the Howells moved into their present home. The explanation that Archy floated was that Edith came into a lot of money from the will of a rich relative who had passed away. Edith was silent on the matter.

Rochelle rang the front doorbell. A man, unknown to the Campbells, came to the door.

"Good afternoon. I'm the family lawyer, Douglas McNamara."

Rochelle responded with, "Good afternoon. We're the Campbells, close friends of the Howells."

"She's spoken of you. Come right in."

Edith was sitting on a mammoth couch. Her face was red with hint of dried-up tears. When she saw the Campbells, she jumped up and ran to Rochelle, embraced her tightly, and tears returned to her face.

"Oh, Rochelle, I don't know which way to turn."

Rochelle very wisely said, "Oh, Edith, you don't have to turn anywhere for the time being. Just surround yourself with loved ones, including us, and try to make some new sense out of your life."

"How can I do that? Mister McNamara says that Sonny's going to defend the man who killed Archy."

A profound silence descended upon the room.

Sonny said, "Mister McNamara's probably right. I confess I had thought about that as a possibility. And he's right. I have a huge conflict of interest that may never be resolved. Only time will tell. Only when whoever winds up defending Mister Roosevelt convinces a jury, and most especially you,

Edith, that he did not kill Archy. **I believe that Chester Roosevelt did not kill Archy Howell.** And until you believe that, I don't think our old beautiful friendship can be resumed. With your permission, Edith, we'll leave now."

Edith broke into full hysterical crying. She tried to speak. "I . . . I just . . . didn't know this would happen."

Rochelle said, "We understand, Edith. I have total confidence in what Sonny has said. Don't fret. We'll come back to you some day and I'm sure you'll welcome us. Come on Sonny. We've got to go now."

The Campbells left, unaccompanied, through the front door.

Sonny and Rochelle made it their business to see as many Saturday and holiday home games played by the Hagerstown Suns at Municipal Stadium as their work schedules permitted. Rochelle had found a teaching job at North Hagerstown High School in their first month in town. That was eighteen years ago. The Campbells lived off her salary until after Sonny passed the Maryland Bar and got his present work as Washington County Public Defender.

They found that they shared a keen interest in baseball and considered it their good fortune that in 1981, Hagerstown could boast of its professional Class A minor league team, the Hagerstown Suns. It was now the Suns second season in Hagerstown. It was their great regret that they had been unable to have children with whom they might share the baseball experience.

Saturdays were often special baseball days for the Campbells and the day after Archy Howell was murdered was no exception. On that Saturday they sat in their usual season seats to see the Suns play the Lexington Legends. Sonny had brought two beers from the refreshment stand. Rochelle had a box on her lap with four hotdogs with mustard and relish, which she had bought from a roaming vendor.

Rochelle said, "Seems weird not to see Archy warming up."

Sonny asked, "Who did they put in his place, I wonder?"

Rochelle looked at their program. . . . "Says here that it's the guy who used to play left field—Carl Huggins."

"Good! Huggins has got a great arm. Maybe he's the one we need to break the eight game skid."

Rochelle agreed. "Can't understand it. We were doing great until we lost all those games in a row."

Sonny's watch said it was almost one thirty. A singer would soon be singing *The Star Spangled Banner.* Sonny had already wolfed down one hotdog and was working on his second. Rochelle had barely begun to eat her first. Half of his cup of beer had disappeared. She still had all of hers.

A recording of the National Anthem played and a youthful, pretty soprano began to sing. Many of the spectators joined in. All the players faced the American flag in the outfield. Almost everybody put their hands or hats over their hearts.

Loud speakers paid tribute to Archy Howell. An umpire yelled, "**Play ball.**"

It turned out that Carl Huggins was the charm that was needed to break the skid. He fielded flawlessly and wracked up two homeruns The score was lopsided—ten to zero. The Suns bore Huggins off the field on their shoulders. The cheering was deafening.

Sonny said, "I haven't had so much fun since I played softball for the Air Force when I was a kid."

Rochelle joked, "I would have given my right arm to have seen you play softball."

As the crowd moved slowly out of the stadium, many Suns' fans were heard to shout praiseworthy phrases. *Howell was nothing compared to Huggins.—I had almost given up bettin' on this team.—We've waited a long time to see the Suns win a game like this.—Just you wait. . . . They'll fill the park next Saturday.—It's about time.—I'd like to buy that guy Huggins a beer.*

Smitty's Bar and Grill, located on East Antietam Drive, was conveniently near both Sonny's office and Municipal Stadium. It was not only a lawyers' hangout, but baseball fans by the dozens could be found there, especially after a Saturday game. Smitty's personality was such that both lawyers and baseball fans were attracted to him. He was usually on duty the entire business day for two reasons—to entertain his customers and to keep an eye on the cash register.

The Campbells preferred to sit at the bar. On the day after Archy Howell's murder, they sat near the far end of the bar and were engaged in a serious and sad conversation with the owner, Smitty himself. Smitty would wipe the bar occasional with a damp towel just to look busy while he talked to Rochelle and Sonny.

Smitty complained, "The thing that really pissed me off was that radio report when it first happened. That bastard newscaster said that *racial slurs ensued.* Any one hearing that would think that Archy gave that poor Negro a motive for killing him. It just isn't true. No one, and I mean, no one, was more tolerant of Negroes than Archy Howell. I never, and I mean never, heard him use the *N word* since I met him more than a year ago. If there were any racial slurs spoken in that café then it was the Negro calling Archy a *Honky* or something like that."

Rochelle agreed, "I never heard a racial word come out of Archy's mouth. It almost sounds like that someone was setting up that new client of yours, Sonny."

Sonny asked, "How do you mean?"

"I mean the motive thing—a reason for killing Archy—racial rage. Rage is certainly a motive for murder elsewhere in this screwed up country."

Sonny said, "O.K., O.K., don't start disparaging this country. Rage killings happen here, but this is still the greatest country in this crazy world."

Rochelle came back with, "The last hope on the globe, huh?"

Sonny answered, "The *only* hope on the globe. But you've got an excellent point, Smitty. It's what I imagine could make for a pretty good legal defense—no racial slurs and therefore no motive. Motive is terribly important in any criminal trial. You know, I can't tell you why I believe it, but I'm all but positive that this guy Roosevelt is innocent. . . . Don't you dare quote me on that, Smitty."

Smitty straightened up and folded up the towel. As he walked away, he talked over his shoulder, "If the State's Attorney is going to depend on Archy using racial slurs, then he's going to lose, big time."

Rochelle said, "Sonny, you better be listening to Smitty."

"I am, Rocky, I am. . . . But you know there's something else gnawing at me."

"What?"

"Who's Douglas McNamara?"

"That's been bothering me too."

Sonny was sure about his next statement. "Archy and Edith never mentioned anything about having an attorney . . . not even when they bought their new house."

Rochelle agreed, "Last thing on Edith's mind each month was making sure all the bills got paid, not hiring an attorney for anything."

"We've agreed not to see her again until this mess is cleared up. But, that doesn't mean I can't send Walter Brock over to that mansion to ask some questions. I think I've got to do that. I owe it to Roosevelt to see if there isn't anything there that will help his defense. Where and how did they really come into such a lot of money?"

"Their house is not exactly a mansion."

Sonny joked, "Compared to our humble cottage it's the Windsor Castle."

"I wonder what it would be like, Sonny, to live in a house like theirs."

"Are you jealous?"

"Jealous? In a few days her husband's going to be resting forever in his grave. No, I'm not jealous. I'd prefer to look out of our shabby front window and see my husband mowing the lawn."

Smitty came back and took Sonny's empty mug. He brought back a full frozen mug full of beer, moments later.

"Thanks, pal. Rocky has decided she's going to nurse hers till closing time."

Smitty laughed. "I'll kick her out right now if that's what she's up to."

Rochelle picked up her mug and drained it like a sailor. Soon she had her own fresh frozen mug of beer sitting in front of her.

Sonny asked Smitty, "Archy ever mention to you he had a lawyer for anything?"

"Only once. He made a call on that pay phone back there. He was on it for a good half hour. I asked him, was that his girlfriend? He denied the girlfriend joke and told me it was just his mouthpiece."

"When was that?"

"About a week ago."

"Was he upset after talking to the lawyer?"

"I would answer yes to that question."

"How so?"

"His hand was shaking when he picked up his glass. . . . 'Scuse me folks. I gotta get back to work." Smitty pushed his way past several employees behind the bar and started to wash glasses on this busy Saturday night.

Sonny said to Rochelle, "Looks like I better check out the lawyer angle."

She answered, "Like you said—you owe it to Mister Roosevelt."

The Campbells ordered a deluxe pizza. Sonny ate three quarters of it. Rochelle only nibbled on the rest. They got home at about seven o'clock in the evening on that baseball Saturday.

CHAPTER FOUR

It was eight o'clock in the morning on the Monday following the murder. Roosevelt was to be arraigned at nine o'clock that morning. Walter Brock reasoned that McNamara, the lawyer, wouldn't be up and around that early. He walked boldly up to the front door of the large house on Jefferson Boulevard and rang the doorbell. He had decided not to call in advance, preferring to catch Mrs. Howell off guard. A housekeeper answered the door and greeted Brock with a curt, "Yes?"

"I'm Walter Brock, official investigator with the Public Defender's office. I'm here to speak with Mrs. Howell."

"She's in seclusion."

"This is official business. I can get a subpoena before the business day ends today, if I have to."

"Wait right there. I'll tell her."

The housekeeper returned in a few minutes. "Come in. Mrs. Howell will speak to you." She led Brock into a sitting room and told him to have a seat. After ten minutes, Edith Howell, dressed in a robe and slippers, joined him, and sat down opposite him.

"Should I have my lawyer here with me?"

"I don't see why you would need your lawyer here. You're not a suspect."

"I fail to see what help I can give you."

"Just answer some routine questions."

"I hope I have some answers."

"When did you and your husband move into this house?"

Edith paused for almost ten seconds before she answered.

"About three months ago."

"The exact date, if you please."

"Let me see. Oh, I know. It was on my daughter's birthday, March 14th."

"Where did you used to live?"

"In Funkstown."

"How long did you live in Funkstown?"

"A little over a year."

"How much did you pay for this house?"

"Say, are you sure my lawyer shouldn't be here?"

"Like I said, you're not a suspect. How much?"

"Eighty-five thousand."

"How much did you pay for the house in Funkstown?"

"Nine thousand dollars."

"You must have come into a lot of money from somewhere."

"I'm going to call my lawyer."

"If you think you need him now."

"You said I'm not a suspect. Your questions sound to me like you think I am."

"Go call your lawyer."

"I'll answer your question. I inherited a lot of money from a relative who died."

"The name of that relative, please."

"Now, I'm going to phone Mister McNamara."

"How much does he charge an hour?"

She remained silent, got up from her easy chair and left the room. When she returned, she said sternly, "He says I'm to answer no more questions until he gets here."

"That's fine with me."

Edith Howell excused herself, explaining she would get dressed. "I'll tell Mary to make some coffee for you."

"Thank you." Brock picked up a newspaper that was lying on the coffee table in front of the couch.

McNamara arrived dressed in a suit, white shirt, but no tie. He entered the sitting room and blurted out, "What the hell do you think you're doing, Mister? Edith doesn't have to answer any of your questions."

"Mind your manners, lawyer. You're right. She doesn't have to answer my questions, not until I get a subpoena and we're sitting in my boss's office and he's asking her the questions at a deposition. Come to think of it, he's a lot better at this than I am."

Edith resumed her former easy chair. McNamara leaned over and whispered something in her ear. Then, she whispered something in his ear.

"I'll allow you to continue your questions, but I'm warning you, I'll object to any question that I find irrelevant."

"Fair enough."

The lawyer sat in an easy chair that matched Edith's.

"O.K., now where were we? Oh, yeah. You were just about to tell me the name of the relative you inherited all that money from."

"Objection! That question is not remotely relative to any aspect of your criminal case."

"I guess I'm the only one here who knows why my question is indeed relevant. But, to make you happy, Mister McNamara, we'll take the question into court and let the judge decide. Did Mister McNamara help you with the purchase of this house, Mrs. Howell?"

"You mean financially?"

The lawyer answered for her. "That's ridiculous. Of course, I didn't."

"I meant legal help at the closing."

This time Edith answered before her lawyer had a chance to object. "Yes, he did."

"So, he's not even a criminal lawyer, is he? Is your specialty real estate, Mister McNamara?"

"It so happens that it is one of the things I specialize in."

"Let me ask you—do you represent other members of the Hagerstown Suns' baseball team?"

There was a conspicuous silence. . . . "Mister McNamara? Do you help other members of the Suns buy their houses?"

Still no answer . . .

Finally, the lawyer said, "You're supposed to be asking my client questions, not me."

"But I'm learning a lot more when I ask you the questions, my friend. Your reluctance to answer my last question speaks volumes."

McNamara burst forth, "That's it. Your presence is no longer wanted in this house, Mister . . . whatever your name is."

"Isn't that up to Mrs. Howell?"

"I'm speaking for her now. . . . Leave! . . . Right now!"

"Mrs. Howell? Do you want me to go?"

She started to cry. "I guess I . . . Mister McNamara is speaking for me now. Please leave."

"Well, O.K., but you both will be singing a different tune when you're subpoenaed to a deposition. . . . Mister McNamara, you've now made yourself an intricate part of this case." Brock left the sitting room and went out through the front door.

Carmine's was located in the somewhat shabby part of Funkstown. It was probably the last place that Archy Howell intended to go before the fracas in the café broke out and before he changed his mind and wound up on Plum and Harrison.

Walter Brock sat at the counter. The white waitress confronted him and laid a menu within his reach.

"I'll take your order in a minute."

"I'm not eating."

She stopped and turned to face him. "What do you want, then?"

"To ask you some questions." By this time the half dozen café customers were all staring at the two as they exchanged words. "I'm an investigator with the Public Defender's office. This is official business."

"Are you working to get Chet Roosevelt out of jail?"

"You might say that."

"Good, 'cuz he didn't kill nobody."

"That's the way we see it."

"Let's go into the kitchen. How long is this going to take?"

"Five minutes."

"Good, 'cuz I gotta take care of my customers."

Brock left his counter stool and joined the waitress. The two went into the kitchen where the Negro cook was busying himself over the stoves.

The cook said, "I was heah dat night when Chet got hisself into dat fight. Axe me some questions, too."

"I'll do that. What's your full name?"

"Oscar Washington—after da first president."

Brock wrote the name down in his little book. "What's your full name, Miss?"

"Versie Dugger."

"How do you spell Versie?"

"V E R S I E. And my last name is spelled, D U G G E R."

Brock wrote her name down, as well.

Oscar said, "I'll take caah up front while you answer questions back heah, Miss Versie."

"Thanks, Oscar."

Oscar went out front to take care of the customers.

Versie asked, "What do you want to know?"

"Were you the only waitress in here that night?"

"Yeah."

"How many customers did you have?"

"Five, including Chet Roosevelt and Howell. Chet sat at the counter with two other guys, both colored. They sat on the ends. Chet sat in the middle. Howell sat in a booth with another white guy I didn't recognize."

"What happened?"

"Both the guys in the booth were loud and drunk. It started to get nasty. Howell got up and grabbed the other guy by his shirt collar. He slapped the guy's face with his other hand. I started to yell at them to stop."

"Did they stop?"

"No."

"Did either Chet or Howell say anything?"

"Howell said to Chet something like, *This is none of your business.*"

"What did Chet do?"

"I think he grabbed Howell's arm and they fell on the floor."

"Did anybody else get involved in the fight?"

"No. Howell had Chet down. He started punching Chet's face."

"That's when Oscar came out of the kitchen and broke it up. He yelled something at Chet and told him to get out."

"Did Chet obey?"

"Oh, yeah. Right away."

"Now, this is very important. At any time, once the fight started, did you hear anyone say or shout words like . . . *nigger* . . . *coon* . . . *Jigaboo* . . . *spade* or any words intended to insult colored people?"

"Oh, nothing like that . . . not one word like that."

"O.K., now, did anyone else get involved in the fight?"

"No. No one."

"That's all for now, Versie. Would you go out and send Oscar back here?"

"Sure."

When Oscar returned to the kitchen, Brock asked him only one question. "Did you at any time hear any insulting words about colored people that night?"

"You mean like, *nigger*. No suh. No suh. No woids lak dat."

"Thank you, Oscar. That'll be all for now."

Brock made some notes in his little book, said goodbye, and left the café. He drove back to the office and waited there for Sonny to finish his court activities.

Sonny addressed the court, "Mister Roosevelt pleads not guilty to the charge, asks for a jury and further asks the court to set a Preliminary Examination for as early a date as is convenient, your Honor."

Judge Piercy responded, "Very well, Mister Campbell. The plea is entered into the record and your client will have his jury. Let me take a look at the calendar and find an early date for the Prelim. . . . How does July 5 sound?"

Sonny looked at his pocket organizer, "Neither Mister Wilson nor I are busy on July 5, your Honor."

"Very well, gentlemen. We're all set for the time being. . . . Mister Roosevelt, do you understand what we've done here this morning?"

Roosevelt answered, "Yes, your Honor."

"Very well, we'll now take up the next arraignment."

A sheriff's deputy led Roosevelt through a door and eventually to his cell in the Detention Center. Sonny went back to his office where he found Walter Brock waiting for him. Brock was talking to Ed Wilson, Public Defender for Frederick County.

Wilson was speaking. . . . "Sonny should talk him into pleading, second degree, if the State's Attorney will go for it, and Roosevelt'll avoid the death penalty."

Brock got half his response out before Sonny interrupted. Brock said, "I'm not so sure he's guil. . . ."

Sonny interrupted the two men, "Well, I'm pretty sure he's innocent."

Wilson said, "Oh, come on, Sonny. Have you forgotten who you're talking to?"

Sonny responded, "Let's not go into details. I know what I'm talking about, this time."

"Plead the guy, Sonny. You'll save yourself a lotta grief."

Sonny didn't give up. He protested, "Since when are we in the business of saving ourselves grief?"

"Speaking of business, are you going to that criminal seminar in Memphis next month? The speaker's topic is *How to Save Time and Money With a Guilty Plea*."

"The speaker should be disbarred," Sonny insisted.

Wilson argued, "I think the Maryland Supreme Court is on our side on the subject."

Again Sonny protested, "That's ridiculous."

Brock spoke up, "We've got to talk Mister Campbell."

"Be right with you, Walt."

Wilson said, "Sometimes the law of ridiculousness is the only way to go."

"You're a first class bigot, Ed."

"But my record for plea convictions is one of the best in the state."

"But at what a human cost." Sonny went to his own desk where Brock was waiting.

"What did you find out?"

Brock answered, "McNamara's up to his eyeballs in some sort of intrigue."

"Intrigue?"

"When I asked him if he represented other Suns' players in the purchase of new homes, he refused to answer."

"That's not conclusive as to any wrong doing."

"If you'd been there and had seen the tension on their faces you'd agree with me."

"I trust your judgment. Stay on the McNamara angle. See if he's really up to something. . . . What about the *racial slurs* in the café?"

"I don't think there were any. The waitress didn't hear any. Neither did the cook. This afternoon I'm going to try to check with the two colored customers who sat at the counter. If they didn't hear any slurs, that leaves just the guy who was in the booth with Archy."

"Let me check that out. I'll go down to WJEJ and interview the newscaster. He had to get it from someone." Sonny handed the paper with Howard Parsons' name and address on it to Brock. "Parsons is an older white man and works on the hospital custodial staff with our boy. Don't be shocked. These guys are lovers and Roosevelt claims he gave his shotgun to Parsons for safe keeping while he was hiding out in Chicago."

"You know, boss, you're taking a big chance with this shotgun. Suppose it's been fired recently. That would just about cinch Roosevelt's conviction. You know you're eventually going to have to turn it over to the State's Attorney."

"But the opposite is also true. Not fired recently will go a long way toward proving his innocence. We have an obligation to discover the truth no matter what it proves. Gimme that address back and I'll go get the gun from Parsons. We'll first have our own forensics man tell us when it was last fired. I'll see you back here after I see Parsons. Right now I'm going to WJEJ."

Sonny skipped lunch. He found the WJEJ radio station on Haven Road. He spoke to the receptionist and discovered that a man by the name of Mark Eastern was the newscaster who covered the killing of Archy Howell the previous Friday morning. He had to wait a half hour till Eastern took a lunch break before he could interview him.

"I'm the Public Defender for Washington County, Mister Eastern."

"I suppose you're here to talk about the Howell killing."

"You got it."

"Not much I can tell you except for what I broadcast last Friday morning."

"That's precisely what I want to talk to you about—your broadcast last Friday morning."

"Oh?"

"I heard what you had to say that morning and there's one item I'm curious about. From whom did learn about the racial slurs you said ensued during the fracas?"

"The cook told me his name. Bucky Livingston."

"Was he the only one you talked to?"

"He had been the only white customer in the place. I got his address from a phone book and went over to see him."

"Why didn't you attempt to interview the two Negro customers?"

"There wasn't time. I had to get the story on the air."

"And the counter girl? Why didn't you interview her?"

"Same reason. But she was still acting hysterical. I figured Livingston would be more reliable."

"Was Livingston still drunk when you got to him?"

"He acted a bit hung over, but he was coherent."

"What did he tell you?"

"Essentially, that he and Howell were arguing and that Howell started to get physical with him. . . . That Roosevelt came over to break up the fight and that Howell said, *Get the hell away from here, nigger. . . . This is none of your business . . .* that Howell and Roosevelt tumbled on to the floor, all the while Howell calling Roosevelt nasty names of a racial variety and that the Negro cook came and threw Roosevelt out of the café."

"Is that it?"

"That's it and that's what I broadcast over the airwaves."

"Did you ever backtrack to the other witnesses to verify what Livingston told you?"

"I deemed Livingston reliable. There was no need to talk to anyone else."

"Thank you Mister Eastern. You've been very helpful. Now, how do I get out of here?"

"Follow me. I'll show you, Mister Campbell."

At three o'clock Sonny kept his appointment with Chester Roosevelt.

"My head is buzzing over everything we talked about this morning, Mister Campbell."

"You're sitting on a powder keg."

"Isn't it your job to get me off that powder keg?"

"Not for much longer. I've got to tell you something that you may not like."

"More evidence against me."

"Not that. Soon, I'm going to have to take myself off of your case."

"For God's sake why would you do such as thing? I like you, Mister Campbell. I really can tell that you're on my side."

"I am on your side, Chet. I believe you're innocent and I don't say that to many of the people I get to represent in here."

"Thank God! But why then must you desert me now?"

"I was a close friend of Archy Howell. I have a conflict of interest. I'll probably have to, what they call, recuse myself from being your lawyer."

"Who will be my lawyer then?"

"The Public Defender for Frederick County, Mister Edward Wilson."

"Is he as good as you are?"

"Probably. But I want to give you some final advice. If Mister Wilson tries to talk you into pleading to a lesser charge, promising you that the judge will be more lenient with you . . . or to First Degree Murder in order to avoid the death penalty, get in touch with me immediately. Even if the sheriff tells you you can't, act desperate. Write a letter to the judge if you have to. Send word with one of your fellow inmates who you know I represent. . . . You're innocent. I'll have a lot to say to Wilson and you if he tries that, you hear?"

"I still say I like you, Mister Campbell. I'll do everything you tell me to do. You're my only hope."

"Never give up your hope. You've got God and Sonny Campbell standing behind you."

CHAPTER FIVE

The funeral service for Archy Howell was held on the following Tuesday at Hagerstown's First Presbyterian Church. The Church was overflowing with friends and fans. He was buried at Hagerstown's Rose Hill Cemetery. At the grave site, the Campbells stood next to Smitty and opposite Edith who was seated on a folding chair in what appeared to be a section reserved for family. Douglas McNamara was nowhere to be seen either at the Church or the Cemetery. Edith avoided making eye contact with either Rochelle or Sonny.

Smitty asked, "Which one is the family lawyer?"

"Rochelle answered, "You mean that son-of-a-bitch, Douglas McNamara?"

"Is that his name?"

Sonny answered, "Yeah. He's not there. Why won't she even look at us. I suppose it wouldn't do any good to go over there and offer our condolences," said Sonny.

Rochelle responded, "This will sound kind of funny . . . and I don't even like to say it, but she acts like she's guilty of something. Oh, I don't mean guilty of anything in connection with Archy's killing, but something else . . . maybe something to do with their sudden good fortune."

Sonny said, "I wondered about that even before Archy was killed. They used to share practically their whole lives with us but never a word about that fancy house."

"And I'm sure that shifty eyed lawyer had something to do with it. By the way . . . where is he? Family lawyers usually attend their client's funerals."

"Good question. I think he has a lot to tell the world about Archy's murder."

Rochelle sounded angry. "Oh, let's leave. I can't stand to look at this scene . . . especially at that poor wretch of an Edith. She needs us but won't talk to us. And that bastard McNamara is the reason."

"Well, O.K. . . . You know, I really wish we knew more about where the money came from to buy that big house."

Smitty said, "You can go, but I'm staying. At least one of his best friends should speak to her."

Rochelle and Sonny left, feeling very guilty after hearing Smitty's remark.

Douglas McNamara stepped off his personal Lear Jet. Bad weather in Hagerstown had delayed his departure. He had planned to arrive in Las Vegas an hour earlier. The pilot assisted him with his luggage. The two walked briskly to the hangar area. A limousine was parked just outside of the Executive Air Systems offices. The pilot put McNamara's luggage into the boot of the limousine. McNamara handed him a fifty dollar tip.

The driver of the limousine needed no destination instructions. Twenty minutes later the long black vehicle discharged its single passenger in front of The Flying Eagle Casino, and its driver brought McNamara his two suitcases. Another fifty dollar tip exchanged hands. A porter from the Casino secured the luggage and greeted the passenger.

"Welcome back to Las Vegas, Mister McNamara. Go right up to the suite. Your associates are waiting for you there. I'll put your luggage in your usual room."

"That'll be fine." The lawyer gave the porter a twenty dollar bill and rode an elevator to the top floor. He unlocked and entered suite number 2230.

Four men, all dressed in sport clothes, were seated in comfortable chairs in a spacious room. A fifth man, very swarthy in complexion and wearing a pin-striped suit, white shirt and tie, sat opposite the four others. The five had been engaged in an earnest conversation. Room service carts with dirty dishes on them made the otherwise plush room appear unkempt.

"Well, the Irish shyster is back. You're more than an hour late, Dougie."

McNamara said, "Hello, Charlie. Bad weather in Hagerstown. We sat on the ground for more than an hour waiting for it to clear. You're lucky I'm here at all."

"We started without you," said Peter Smith. "Douglas McNamara, meet Felix Camino. Felix, this is our man in Hagerstown. As you already know, Mac, Felix is thinking of throwing his entire Mexican parlor operation in with us. We were just explaining to Felix how our operation works."

Camino stood and shook hands with McNamara.

"You better have a mighty good explanation for that mess you left behind you," said Charlie, a heavy set middle aged man smoking a cigar.

Peter Smith was handsome and slender. He stood and started strolling around the huge room. "Why is it, Mac, that nobody got killed in nineteen-

nineteen in the Black Sox debacle and we already got one corpse to our credit in a small town like Hagerstown, Maryland?"

"You can't lay any of that mess off on me, Pete."

Smith asked, "O.K., what happened?"

"Simple—the first baseman was threatening to blow the whistle on us. He had to be eliminated."

"Who'd you use?"

"An independent out of Detroit."

"Did he leave any traces?"

"Absolutely nothing. As a matter of fact they got some local spade under arrest for the killing."

"How'd you manage that?"

"Pure luck. The Detroit man followed the player for the most of two days—saw a lot of baseball. The Suns played a losing game that Thursday, and three players, including the first baseman, and the other two on our payroll, went out on the town. One went home for dinner with his wife and kids, leaving the whistle-blower first baseman and the third guy to wind up in a café at one in the morning to sober up on coffee. Those two got into a fight over the first baseman's threat to take the lid off. The black guy tried to break up the fight. Our loyal player, using his head, told the local media that there were racial slurs made by the now deceased . . . a perfect motive for the eggplant to blow Howell's head off a couple hours later. That's the way it now stands. The player's smilin' at the worms and the spade's in the Detention Center charged with homicide. One thing I don't get is why the Detroit man hasn't asked for his fee yet. You'd 'a thought that after a perfect job like he did he would even be askin' for a bonus. I haven't heard a word from him."

Smith, sounding relieved, spoke, "Well, we're a lot better off than I suspected."

McNamara sat down and asked, "How are we coming along with Felix, here? . . . Gimme a summary of what you guys have been talking about."

Smith reported, "Felix's Mexican parlors produce nearly a quarter of a million per week. We explained to him how much better he'd be doing if he joins our operation. . . . You could double your take, Felix. Our system is quite foolproof. When we want the Hagerstown Suns to win, we let 'em. When we need 'em to lose we contact Mac, here, right in the middle of a game if we have to, and he gives our players word to drop the ball. . . . We got fourteen illegal spots all over the country plus our legal betting lounge, here in Las Vegas. They all made us close to three million this past week. All these operations are on the same win-when-we-want and lose-when-we-want scheme, depending how the odds are going. The only danger is that we got to send all the bets through Antigua. That may one day be a wire wagering violation, big time. We work very hard on being careful who we let bet in the baseball gig.

Tomlinson, Valente and Greenberg had been in a huddle while Peter Smith was talking. Greenberg said, "Now, Mac, why don't you and Felix go downstairs and get acquainted over a couple o' drinks. And you must be hungry—get yourself something to eat. That was a long plane ride. We're going to talk the situation over up here. We gotta plan a guaranteed murder conviction of this black man they're holding. We gotta keep the heat off that Detroit guy you hired who could lead to us."

"I am hungry. I'll get me a filet and a bottle of wine and we'll be back here in an hour. . . . Felix, my friend, they serve a hell of a Margarita down in the lounge. You can watch me eat."

McNamara and Camino left the suite. McNamara's four partners started a methodical discussion on how to fix a jury.

Salvatore Valente, dressed in a pink sport jacket and forest green trousers, came up with a humorous introduction to their discussion, causing the other three to laugh uproariously. "If we can fix fifty baseball games we ought to be able to fix one small town jury."

Pete Smith warned, "It's gonna cost us some money."

Mark Greenberg snubbed his cigar stub out on a dirty plate on a room-service cart and said, "Two hundred grand ought to do it."

Valente asked, "Why that much? I'll bet that none of those jurors could earn that much money in ten years."

Greenberg defended paying the huge sum. "I'm thinkin' we gotta fix at least two of those hicks to guarantee a good result."

Charlie Tomlinson thought to make another important point. "Why stop there? Two jurors might not be enough. We need to guarantee this thing. We should make cozy with the prosecutor. We should pay to have him offer a sweet plea deal that puts this eggplant away for forty years or so. That black guy should take the deal just to avoid the death penalty. They do have the death penalty in Maryland, don't they?"

Smith knew the answer to that question. "Yeah. . . . gas."

Valente was genuinely curious. "What if his lawyer don't let him take the plea? What then? Some of these criminal defense lawyers are boy scouts, you know?"

"Are you kiddin'? If they can avoid the embarrassment of a first degree murder conviction on their record they'll jump every time . . . especially if the lawyer is a public defender. I know how it works, believe me."

Charlie smiled and said, "So we approach it from three directions—jury, prosecutor, and public defender . . . can't miss. You know, this really isn't much harder than fixin' a baseball game."

They all laughed again.

When McNamara returned, the plan was reviewed with him. His appraisal was favorable except for the public defender angle. He had the feeling that there was an air of incorruptibility in the Washington County Public Defender's office. He didn't bring that up with the others, however. He thought that you can't be sure of such things until you at least make the attempt.

Smith suggested, "Hey, you guys, how about an all night poker game? I feel lucky tonight."

McNamara said, "Count me out. I'm bushed. I gotta get some sleep. I'm goin' right back tomorrow."

Smith scolded him. "Oh, come on Mac. You can sleep on the plane."

"No. I gotta review some legal stuff on the plane. No poker for me tonight."

"O.K., then, but, I want daily calls on this black boy's trial. This is one fix we can't afford to screw up."

It was the Thursday following the death of Archy Howell. Edith greeted her lawyer at her front door. They went into the sitting room. "Oh, Mister McNamara, where were you on the day of Archy's funeral. And I tried to get in touch with you yesterday. I needed to talk to you."

"I was out of town on business. What's the problem?"

"You've got to tell me where all the money for this house came from."

"What did I tell you last Saturday?"

"I know, but I can't believe what you told me. I never had any relatives with that much money."

"Do you want to keep this house and not pay another cent on it?"

"For the sake of the children now I can't afford not to."

"Well, like I said, all you have to do for all of you to live here expense free for the rest of your lives is to never ask again where that money came from. That should be easy enough. That's what Archy would tell you to do. And to top it off, all three of your kids get a free education when the time comes. The money for that is already in your bank account."

"Will it be all right if I get advice from our pastor?"

"No! Absolutely not. I'm the only person you get your advice from. I'm your lawyer in this matter. Do you understand that?"

With trepidation, Edith answered, "I guess so."

"Whenever you're tempted to talk to somebody about your good fortune, you must get in touch with me first. Now, is that understood?"

"All I can say is yes and just count our blessings."

"Mrs. Howell do you think you could have your housekeeper make us some coffee? I haven't had any yet today."

"Of course."

Walter Brock sat unnoticed in his car a dozen yards down from Mrs. Howell's front door. On Wednesday he had made it his business to find out where in the Hagerstown area Douglas McNamara was staying. He discovered that the lawyer was a transient. No one in the Bar Association knew anything about him. He looked up his name in the Martindale Hubble national directory. He somehow wasn't surprised to learn that McNamara was a member of the Nevada Bar Association and supposedly practiced in Las Vegas.

He checked the registry of all the five star Hagerstown hotels near the Regional Airport and found that his quarry had been staying at the Howard Johnson's Plaza Hotel. On Wednesday he bribed a room-service busboy to find out if the lawyer was in his room. He wasn't. Brock entered the room with the busboy's help and did a quick search. On the dresser he found a receipt for fuel for a jet flight to Las Vegas for that very day. He went to the Executive Air Systems offices and learned that McNamara's personal Lear Jet was due back from Las Vegas on the next day at seven thirty in the morning.

On Thursday he was parked unobtrusively near the air strip for the Executive Air Systems. At seven twenty the expected Lear Jet landed ten minutes early. Brock followed the passenger shuttle back to the Plaza Hotel and parked in its parking lot to wait for McNamara. At quarter to nine, he observed him freshly dressed in different clothes come out of the hotel and get into his rental car. He followed the car to Mrs. Howell's house on Jefferson Boulevard.

Brock went to the Howell front door armed with two Notices Of Deposition, one for Edith Howell and one for Douglas McNamara. He pressed the front door bell button and heard some bells play the Big Ben tune. The housekeeper came to the door.

Brock knew that there was no chance that Edith Howell was going to come to the door if Brock told the housekeeper to announce to her who was out there. But there was no reason for the lawyer not to come. "I'm looking for Attorney McNamara. Is he here by any chance?"

McNamara had an angry look on his face. Brock said, "Today must be my lucky day. I just took a chance on your being here, Mister Lawyer. I have something for you."

"What's that?"

"Notices of Deposition for next Wednesday at the Public Defender's office at 100 Franklin Street, Suite 102, at one thirty in the afternoon. One is for you, sir, and one is for your client. You'll note that these are official court documents with sanctions for contempt if you fail to show. You're both to be there and promptly at one thirty."

"Damn you! You're like a fox terrier nipping at my ankles."

"Nice to see you again, Mister Lawyer." Brock did a heel spin, walked calmly to his car, and drove away.

Edith Howell gasped when she scanned her Notice of Deposition. "Oh, Mister McNamara, you're going to have to help me with this. Who's going to be asking the questions?"

"I assume it will be the Public Defender."

"My God! You know that he was my husband's best friend, Sonny Campbell."

"Don't fret. I'll file a motion demanding that he recuse himself. He'll have to comply."

On the day when Douglas McNamara was winging his way toward Las Vegas, Sonny Campbell was searching the streets of Hagerstown for the home of Howard Parsons. When he finally located it, Sonny was surprised to find that the address belonged to a neat little house that one would have imagined was occupied by someone other than a custodian at a hospital. Sonny presumed correctly that Parsons worked the night shift as had his lover and was at home during the day.

The yard in front of the house had hibiscus plants on either side of a path that led to a brass trimmed front door. Sonny flipped the door knocker several times. Moments later a man dressed in gold silk pajamas and a velvet maroon robe came to the door.

"Good morning sir. I'm William Campbell, Public Defender for Washington County. Here, let me show you my credentials." Sonny opened his black leather ID case and held it up for the man's examination. "Are you Howard Parsons?"

"Yes, I am. What do you want?"

"To ask you a few questions. May I come in?"

"Can't you ask your questions from there?"

"I prefer to talk to you inside."

Parsons opened the door wide and stood aside to let Sonny in.

"Go straight ahead to the living room."

"May I sit down?"

"Yes."

"I'm representing Chester Roosevelt. As you probably know Chester has been accused of murdering Archy Howell, a Hagerstown Suns baseball player."

"I've heard about the case."

"You're a close friend of Chester, aren't you?"

"You might say that. We work together at the hospital."

"He's told me that you're closer than that. Now, this next question is vital to Chester's defense so please answer truthfully. . . . Did he give you his shotgun to hold for him while he intended to go to Chicago?"

Parsons remained silent for a several moments.

"Come on, Mister Parsons. He told me that he gave the gun to you for safekeeping."

"All right. He gave me the shotgun."

"Do you have it here in the house?"

"Yes."

"I told Chester that I would be picking up the gun. Would you go get it?"

"Why?"

"We have to determine if it's been fired recently."

"And if it has, that won't help his defense, will it?"

"It depends on whether his fingerprints are on the trigger."

"If they were, they're not now."

"Why?"

"I wiped the gun clean."

"I wish you hadn't done that. Please, go get the gun."

Parsons left the living room and was gone for about five minutes. He returned with a shotgun which he turned over to Sonny.

Sonny broke the gun down and satisfied himself that the gun was not loaded. He examined the shell chamber carefully and gave it a sniff test. There was no odor of recent firing. He did the same with the end of the barrel. In fact, he reached the firm conclusion that the shotgun had not been used for months. He handed the gun back to Parsons.

"I thought you were going to take it with you. What should I do with it?"

"Put it back where you were keeping it. It's not the murder weapon. I'm sure of that. It's not evidence. Not yet it isn't. I have no obligation to turn over to the State's Attorney a gun which hasn't been used for months. If he discovers the gun on his own, then we'll be happy to agree to make it exculpatory evidence at the trial. In the mean time, don't let it out of your possession without checking with my office." Sonny handed Parsons a business card with his office address and phone number on it.

Parsons acted confused. "I'm not sure I understand all this. Don't we want everybody to know that Chet didn't use this gun?"

"Not yet we don't. The time will come when we'll let the world know that he didn't shoot a shotgun last Friday morning. The sheriff should have run a gunpowder test on Roosevelt. He didn't. That's a plus for us. Now, answer this question. Chet doesn't own a car, does he?"

"No, he doesn't."

"Did you drive him to the bus station?"

"Yes, I did."

"You realize, don't you, that if he is found guilty, they could charge you with aiding and abetting?"

"I never thought of that."

"You should have. You'll just have to wait and see what happens at the trial."

"You mean, there's going to be a trial? I've been thinking that they'd let him plead to a lesser charge." . . . Parsons put his head in his hands. "They just can't convict him of first degree murder. He didn't do it. I know he didn't do it. How could he have? Without a car? How could he get to Plum and Harrison without a car? Somebody in a car had to be following Howell. . . . Don't you see? It couldn't have been my darling boy."

Parsons began to cry. "The thought of him being executed . . . I can't bear the thought of that. I love him and he's not guilty. . . . Please, Mister Campbell, you've got to save him from that horror . . . I love him. I love him . . . I love . . ."

"Get a hold of yourself, Mister Parsons. We've all got to remain calm. I'm beginning to have confidence that he will not be found guilty. But we've got to avoid becoming hysterical. You just sit tight and leave it to God and the professionals."

"I'll try, but you've got to realize how hard this is for me. He's such a good and lovely boy. Please, do your best."

Sonny stood. "We'll all do our best."

Parsons showed Sonny to the front door. The two clasped hands and Sonny said, "You can be sure that a higher power than me has his eye on this mess. Have some faith, Mister Parsons."

CHAPTER SIX

Walter Brock stopped by Sonny Campbell's office. "I've got something I want to run by you, Mister Campbell. Let's say that we're right that McNamara has brought some kind of corruption to the Hagerstown baseball team. Let's also assume that somehow or other the State's Attorney gets wind of that corruption. So he investigates and the focus gets on Archy Howell as one of the guys who was involved. One thing leads to another. Remember that Bucky Livingston was arguing with Archy that night in Carmine's. What was the argument about? From what you've been telling me, Archy was a pretty decent man—a man with a conscience. Maybe his conscience was starting to squeeze a little bit and he wanted out. Maybe that's what he and Livingston were arguing about. Livingston would be a good place for our esteemed State's Attorney, Mister Winston Hathaway, to direct his investigation of the evil goin's on with the Hagerstown baseball team."

"Wow! How much we payin' you, lad? I think you got something there."

"I've got more. So you've recused yourself and can't defend Chester Roosevelt. Supposing Hathaway finds just one dirty baseball player. We know those guys don't make much legitimate money and the bad guy is not goin' to admit in open court that he's got a lot of cash hidden from whatever scheme McNamara has talked him into. There's a good chance that the bad baseball player may qualify for being defended by you for whatever offense he's committed."

"Let me stop you right there. Apparently you're unaware that fixing sports events is a federal offense—maximum ten years in prison and a 250,000 dollar fine. Even if we're right about this bit of corruption, under no circumstances would I be defending anybody on the baseball team who's committed a federal offense. My bailiwick is limited to Maryland offenses."

"You're right. I didn't know that it was a federal crime. . . . But the investigation still has to start locally. I understand that the only thing

Hathaway's got so far is a little damage to Archy's car and some shotgun pellets the ME took out of Archy's head. The State's Attorney can turn it over to the feds after he gets the goods on McNamara. His initial investigation will be doing triple duty—corruption in Municipal Stadium, and proving that McNamara had something to do with the Howell killing and therefore is in the middle of all this corruption, which would make Chester Roosevelt, who doesn't know McNamara from Adam, an innocent man."

"I agree that Roosevelt is innocent, but why else do you think so?"

"Well, for one thing, Roosevelt doesn't own a car."

"And you're going to have lunch with one of Hathaway's investigators and maybe just drop a hint about corruption in baseball games?"

"You got it, boss."

"You must be looking for a raise, Walter. If this puts Mister McNamara in prison and makes Roosevelt a free man, I'll see that you get one."

"My wife thanks you in advance."

Sonny complained to Ed Wilson, "I knew I was going to have to recuse myself from this case. For heaven's sake, I was Archy's best friend. I didn't have to have a Las Vegas lawyer tell me I had to recuse myself." He threw McNamara's *Motion to Order Recusal of Public Defender* on Wilson's desk. "Lori's typing up my *Voluntary Recusal* as we speak. You will soon be officially representing Chester Roosevelt."

Wilson said, "A recusal doesn't mean I can't ask you a question every once in a while."

"Just as long as it doesn't become public knowledge that I have my dirty hand in it."

Walter Brock stood nearby. "A two day trip in a Lear Jet to and from Las Vegas raises some interesting questions, don't you think?"

Wilson answered, "Especially right on the heels of the crime. It's like he was obliged to report in person to someone."

Sonny suggested, "But I don't think he did the shooting himself. I just can't picture him in his silk suit shooting a shotgun at anybody. But by the same token he could have hired it done. And the world knows that a hoard of criminals are bedded down in the fair city of Las Vegas. Mafia—fixing sports games—gambling—murder—sudden large increases in income . . . what does that all add up to? My friends . . . what I believe we now have in Hagerstown is a minor league Black Sox scandal. . . . Listen, you two. I'll make my contributions to Roosevelt's defense as the need arises. In the mean time,

Ed Wilson, I'll leave Walter to bring you up to speed. Remember. You're not going to plead this man to anything."

"I'll do what I think is best for the client, Sonny."

Joe Beyerly had worked as an investigator for the State's Attorney for twenty two years. He started playing tennis when he was eleven years old. He was considered one of the best amateur tennis players in the Washington and Frederick County areas.

Walter Brock was an excellent amateur tennis player, himself. But he had never been able to beat the great Joe Beyerly. Joe loved his status as a gifted amateur and he loved winning. He had played against Brock at least a dozen times and had always come away with the trophy of a pint glass of beer bought by his humbled opponent.

When another match was proposed by Brock, Beyerly didn't hesitate to agree to play him again. They met at the Hagerstown Tennis Club on a sunny Saturday morning when it was still fairly cool.

The scores of the completed match were not as lopsided as usual—3/6, 6/1 and 7/6, with Beyerly winning the tiebreaker. In the clubhouse, the two good friends toasted each with ice-cold pints of beer, Brock buying all the beer that morning.

Brock asked, "You goin' to the baseball game this afternoon, Joe?"

"Nah. Hagerstown has been playing pretty crappy ball for the last couple months. The bookies in Las Vegas are probably cleaning up. The world is not used to the Suns having a losing season—the first since they came here from the Western Carolina League. But we gotta be patient. They'll shape up. They got to. People are losing their shirts, bettin' on 'em."

"You don't know how right you are."

"What do you mean? You lost any money?"

"No, but I got an informant who insists that the fix is in this year."

"Who's your informant?"

"Can't tell you. But he's never let me down in the past."

"Come on, Walt. You got a civic duty to lead me in the right direction on a thing like this."

"I won't tell you who my informant is, but I'll give you the name of a person of interest."

"Out with it. If you're right and I score on an investigation of the name you give me, Hathaway will make me the head of his staff. Fixin' sports events for profit is a federal crime. But I would still get a feather in my cap by being the first to expose it in Hagerstown."

"The name is Bucky Livingston."

"My God! . . . Bucky Livingston! . . . Shush. Not another word. The feds have big ears and they'd like nothing better than to steal my thunder. If you're right, I'll let you win our next tennis match. I promise you that."

"Fat chance you'd ever do that."

Unknown to Bucky Livingston, Beyerly decided to check out the centerfielder's financial condition. Three months ago there was a sudden windfall—close to fifty thousand dollars in a new account, separate from Livingston's everyday checking account. At about the same time his skills on the ball field seemed to diminish dramatically.

Unlike Howell, Livingston had not bought a new house. But a review of his new account revealed that the money was being withdrawn from his savings account and disposed of rapidly. The man was living high on the hog. Beyerly telephoned Livingston and made an appointment to talk to him face to face. He told him it was in connection with the fight in Carmine's.

"Sure, but I can't tell you any more than I already said to the deputies."

"When is your next day off?"

"No game tomorrow."

"How about one thirty tomorrow afternoon at our office on Washington Street, Room 209?"

"O.K., but like I said, I won't be able to tell you much."

"O.K., Bucky. See you tomorrow." Beyerly hung up the phone on his desk.

"Listen, Mister Hathaway. Let me at least give this a try. He won't even suspect what my real purpose is."

The State's Attorney warned, "Look, if your questions tip him off to what you're up to, and you're wrong, you may find yourself facing a million dollar lawsuit. You haven't told anyone else about this, have you?"

"No, sir. Not a soul."

"You didn't dream up this wild scheme of baseball corruption all by yourself. How about your source?"

"I don't think he's told anyone but me. He's a pretty tightlipped guy."

"Let me tell you this, now, Joe. If this blows up in your face, I don't care how many years you've got invested in this office, I'll fire you on the spot, understand? A whole city of Hagerstown Suns' fans would attack this building and do away with all of us."

"I'll be careful."

"Damn! This thing gives me the jitters. . . . On the other hand if you're right, the federal authorities will probably want me to run for a U.S. Senate seat."

Rochelle and Sonny sat in their usual seats at Smitty's bar. Smitty had assumed his usual position in front of them with a damp towel in his hand and would periodically swipe the immaculate bar as if to put the finishing touches on a cleaning job.

"How come you two are not at the ballgame today? I've never known you to miss a Saturday home game."

Sonny said, "We're going to miss a lot of games from now on and I can't tell you why—not yet anyway."

"Why the mystery? Got something to do with Archy?"

"That's all I'll tell you."

"Some pal you are. I think you local government guys are too full of yourselves. Have you told Rocky here yet?"

"Had to. A man can't keep secrets from his wife, can they dear?"

Rochelle answered, "You better not."

"But she's the only one. . . . How about a couple pairs of hotdogs with mustard and relish. We'll pretend we're at Municipal Stadium."

"Be right back. Don't go away. I gotta find out more about this."

Sonny took a big swig from his mug of cold beer. Out of Smitty's earshot, he said, "He's not through grilling me yet. Trouble is, if I tell him that we refuse to watch fixed baseball games, the whole county will know about the corruption by tomorrow afternoon."

Rochelle protested. "If you tell Smitty not to say anything to anyone, he won't say anything. You know that."

"You're probably right, but I just can't take the chance. He tells one loose tongued person and it'll be in Sunday's Herald-Mail in the morning."

"Have it your way."

Smitty returned with two plates of hotdogs, with potato chips on the side. "God bless the guy who invented the microwave." Then he insisted, "Now, look bigwig, why aren't you at Municipal Stadium watching that ballgame?"

Sonny answered, "I told you Smitty, mum's the word. Now, let that be the end of it."

"I oughta throw you both out o' this place on your keesters."

"One more word about it and Rocky and I will walk out of here without any help from you."

"All right, all right. Can't have that. But when you do talk about it, I'd better be the first one you talk to."

"Deal."

Rochelle changed the subject. "When we leave your charming company Smitty, we're going to the Kiwanis Mason-Dixon Festival."

Smitty said, "Never went to that. What do they do there?"

Sonny answered, "Throw cow turds like a discus—women wrestle in the mud wearing T-shirts—men try to kill each other in demolition derbies—farmers milk pigs and other fun stuff."

"Ugh. Sounds awful." Smitty turned and blended back in with the help behind the bar. He started washing glasses.

Rochelle scolded Sonny, "If I knew you felt that way I wouldn't have suggested we go to the thing."

"I was just kidding. Let's get going. I don't want to miss anything."

They drained their beer mugs and waved goodbye to Smitty. It was raining quite heavily. Rochelle commented that the ballgame had probably been called due to rain. They scurried down the street to where Sonny had parked their car. As Rochelle sat in the car she tried to repair her dampened hair. By the time they had arrived at the fair grounds she felt that her hair never would be presentable again.

The rain had slowed to a drizzle. Sonny paid an attendant a three dollar parking fee and they proceeded into the fair grounds. By the time they found themselves walking through a myriad of exhibits, the rain had stopped altogether. They bought ice cream cones followed by caramel corn. They giggled their way past the cow chips being hurled through the air and stopped at the mud wrestling pit.

A few minutes later Rochelle spotted Bucky Livingston watching the wrestling. He had changed from his uniform into casual sport clothes after the game was called because of rain. He appeared almost as fashionable as the man he was standing next to. In a whisper, she drew Sonny's attention to the pair.

Sonny quickly grabbed his wife's elbow and turned her and himself away from the sightline of Livingston and his companion. "Well, I'll be damned. This is the first time I've ever seen Bucky outside of the stadium. And did you recognize the man he's talking to? Lawyer McNamara in the flesh. I don't think they've seen us, so let's walk away from them for a minute or two."

"He wouldn't have recognized me with this hideous wet hair even if he had seen us."

"Let me look at you. . . . You're right. I barely recognize you, myself."

"You want me to go over there and eavesdrop?"

"If you're willing to."

"O.K., here goes."

" . . . but why did the State's Attorney's investigator want to ask me all those questions?"

"Because you were the only white man at the café scene."

"Come to think of it, he didn't sound like he suspected anything was going on with the way we were playing."

"I'm proud of you, son. Talking about racial slurs gives their suspected killer a revenge motive."

"But, they're really were no racial slurs. I don't know what made me say that unless it was to give the newscaster a reason to suspect the black man was the killer and not me. Archy was slapping me around, too, you know. They might have thought I wanted to take out revenge myself."

"Well, whatever you told the cops got the guy arrested. Anyway, they more than likely have enough other evidence against him so that the scuffle was all they needed to convict him."

"But I'll be the only one at the trial who says there were racial slurs."

"I don't think there's going to be a trial. He'll probably plead guilty to something."

"You think he did it."

"I'm all but positive that he did it and like I said, he did it for revenge for being humiliated by Howell."

"I'd hate to be the reason for an innocent man to be executed."

"He's not an innocent man, Bucky."

"I hope you're right." The two men walked on and Rochelle went back to her husband and reported what she had heard of their conversation.

As Rochelle and Sonny lay in bed that night, the subject of Livingston and McNamara came up again.

Rochelle said, "I think I have a notion of how we can turn the incident this afternoon to Chester Roosevelt's benefit."

"What's on your mind?"

"If I were to call Hathaway and tell him what I heard, and then volunteered myself as a witness, we'd bring McNamara into the picture."

"I've thought of doing that myself, but Hathaway would think I had an axe to grind and was trying to help this office get Roosevelt off."

"But, that's exactly what we are trying to do."

"You gotta remember, I've recused myself. I'm supposed to stay completely away from Chester's defense and that means you have to do the same."

"Look, it was just happenstance that I spotted Bucky Livingston this afternoon. You had nothing to do with it. Let me call Hathaway, will you?"

"You should be the lawyer in this family, you know that? O.K., go ahead and call Hathaway. It really can't hurt anything. If he chooses to have you testify then so be it. And we need some way to inform him about McNamara."

CHAPTER SEVEN

State's Attorney Hathaway was on the phone to Sonny Campbell. "Your wife called me and told me she was witness to a conversation between Bucky Livingston and a man called McNamara. Do you know who this man McNamara is?"

"All I can tell you is that he was Archy Howell's lawyer."

"Why did Howell need a lawyer? He was just an underpaid kid who played minor league baseball."

"McNamara is now speaking for Edith Howell and was the Las Vegas lawyer who signed the Motion to have me recuse myself."

"Interesting. Las Vegas, huh? This lawyer is someone I better check on. Thanks, Sonny."

Hathaway pressed the cradle button that broke the connection. He dialed Joe Beyerly's interoffice number.

"Beyerly, here."

"Joe, can you come down here for a minute?"

Beyerly walked into his boss' office and sat down.

"Joe, we've had a major break in the baseball case."

"Can't wait to hear about it."

"Rochelle Campbell saw Bucky Livingston at the Mason-Dixon Festival last Saturday."

"No game Saturday—called because of rain."

"That's right. He was talking with another man."

"Who was it?"

"I called Sonny Campbell and asked him."

"He claimed it was a Las Vegas lawyer named McNamara, who's representing Archy Howell's wife."

"Wow! That is news."

"And it lends credence to the suspected corruption of baseball games in this town. Any time you combine Las Vegas and sports you must ask yourself if there's something funny going on."

"I certainly agree."

"Tell you what I'm going to do. I'm sending you to Nevada just as soon as you can get packed. You'll innocently ask around what the locals in Las Vegas know about this lawyer. What firm does he belong to? If he's not affiliated, then who does he hang around with and where? Try to place a bet on the Hagerstown Suns. If you win, where do you pick up your winnings? Before you leave here, get a photograph of McNamara if you can. Show it to Vegas taxi drivers. Check with limousine services. Maybe they'll know where he stays. See if he's got a criminal record. . . . Probably doesn't or he wouldn't still be practicing law. Check with the Las Vegas prosecutor and see what they have on him. . . . Listen to me. Telling you how to do your job. . . . Just go to Las Vegas and come back with as much info on this guy as you can. Understand?"

"Yes, I do, sir. How long should I stay?"

"Three or four days. Longer if you get on to something. And, please, Joe—no gambling except for a bet on the Suns. You should have no time for such frivolity, anyway."

"I'll get packed and take the next local plane to Chicago. My secretary will hook me up with an early flight from Chicago to Vegas. Anything else I should know?"

"I don't think so. Stay in telephone contact with me. Do you have my home number?"

"Yes, sir, I do."

"Well, off you go. Good luck with your snooping, Joe."

"Thank you, sir."

Beyerly left the Las Vegas airport building and got into the first cab of many that were lined up at the curb.

"Where to, sir?"

"Do you know an attorney in town by the name of McNamara?"

The cab driver answered with a sinister look on his face. "Not personally, but I know of him. I bet half the cabbies in town know of him."

"Where does he live?"

"Nowhere. But he stays at the Flying Eagle Casino Hotel when he's in the city, which isn't often. . . . What are you, a cop?"

"Nope. I'm his brother-in-law. His wife is my sister."

"What does she want—back alimony."

Beyerly laughed. "Something like that."

"Where am I going to take you?"

"The Flying Eagle Hotel."

"Right you are . . . But I don't think he's in town just now."

"That's O.K. Take me to his hotel, would you?"

The taxi ride was a short one. He got out of the cab and the driver turned his luggage over to a porter. "How long will you be staying with us, sir?"

"I don't know for sure. A few days I suppose."

"Just register at the desk. I'll see that your luggage is taken to your room." Beyerly gave the porter two one-dollar bills.

"Oh, thank you, sir." There was a hint of sarcasm in the porter's tone.

The desk clerk was typically unctuous. "Do you have a preference for your room choice—smoking or non-smoking?"

"No, but I would prefer to be on the same floor as Mister McNamara's room."

The request was met with stony silence. Then the clerk asked, "Are you a business associate of Mister McNamara?"

"Not exactly."

"I'm very sorry, sir, but that floor is reserved for our business residents only."

"But I'm . . ."

"I'm afraid there are no exceptions, sir."

"I'm disappointed."

"Sorry, sir. We have strict rules in this hotel about such things."

"I'll take a room on the floor below his, then."

"Very well, then. We'll give you room 2107."

"Would you just make out this credit card slip, sir. We'll settle up when you leave us. Do you know how long you'll be staying, sir?"

"No. A few days, I guess."

The clerk stapled the credit card slip to a blank room invoice and summoned a bell hop. "Show Mister Beyerly to room 2107."

A sullen faced boy in uniform picked up Beyerly's luggage and led the way to the elevators.

Room 2107 was spacious—two queen size beds, and a couch with matching easy chairs. The bell hop put Beyerly's two suitcases on racks and lingered a few moments waiting for a tip.

Beyerly took his billfold from his rear pants pocket, removed a ten dollar bill and tendered it conspicuously to the bell hop. "First some information. Tell me how to get to a betting parlor—one that features baseball games."

"Easy enough. Just ask any cab driver to take you to the Universal Lounge."

Beyerly let loose of the ten dollar bill and said, "Thank you."

"Thank you, sir."

"By the way. The porter at the entrance owes you a buck."

Downstairs again, the Hagerstown State's Attorney's Investigator sat at a small table and ate his dinner. At the entrance to the hotel he entered the first cab in a long line. "Universal Lounge, please."

"Right you are, sir."

Twenty minutes later they arrived at a large darkened building.

Beyerly asked, "Is this it? It doesn't look like much."

"It's not supposed to. That'll be seven and a half dollars."

Beyerly tipped the cabdriver two dollars. A single paneled front door with but one word, *UNIVERSAL,* painted on it opened automatically as Beyerly approached it. A well muscled attendant stood in a foyer just inside of the front door. "Good evening, sir. Are you here for the gaming?"

"Yes, I am."

"Would you sign the registry just inside this door and print your name under your signature."

"Why should I do that?"

"We like to get acquainted with our guests."

"I bet there are a lot of people by the name of Tom Jones on that list. That happens to be my name."

"Thank you, sir."

The space inside the building seemed huge. It appeared to have once been the inside of a warehouse. Electronic tote boards lined the walls. In between the boards were cages with clerks who accepted bets and paid off winners. Some four hundred patrons milled about the room and another hundred sat on benches reading newspapers and other sources of betting information.

Beyerly strolled the inside perimeter of the building, searching the tote boards for the following day's Hagerstown Suns game against the Lexington Legends. He spotted the game and placed a fifty dollar bet on the Suns to lose. He asked the teller in the cage where he had placed the bet, if there was a phone number he could call if wasn't in town to place a bet in person. "I can give you our number and our operator will connect you to our affiliate. They'll place your bet for you and we can settle with you here if you win when you're next in town. Can you give me a credit card number?"

"Sure."

The clerk gave Beyerly a *Universal* business card."

"Your credit card, sir?"

Beyerly wrote his credit card number on a business card and handed it to the teller.

"May I see the credit card, sir?"

The teller examined the credit card and compared it to the number on the business card. "Thank you, Mister Beyerly."

Joe glanced at the tote board and checked the odds against the Suns. After he laid a fifty dollar bet in cash on the visiting team, he didn't linger. He went to the foyer and asked the attendant to call him a cab. He asked the cab driver to take him to the nearest popular sports bar. "That'll be the *Outfield,* sir, about four miles from where we are now."

"Sounds good."

Ten minutes later, he paid the cabbie and entered the smoke filled bar. He took a seat at the bar and ordered a draught beer. A man seated next to him said, "The good thing about the beer in this joint is that they keep their bar plumbing clean—makes a difference you know."

"No, I wasn't aware of that. It stands to reason, though."

"Newcomer in Vegas?"

"Yep."

"What do they call you?"

"Jim. And you?"

"Elmer."

"Not much to do once the tables have taken all your money, Jim."

"I'm not worried about that. I set a limit for myself."

"Reach your limit?"

"Yep. Tell me, who runs the sports betting in this town?"

"It's a syndicate, of course. But us locals know who heads it up."

"Who's that?"

"It's an open secret. . . . Pete Smith, a big man in the mob, runs most of it."

"Does the name McNamara mean anything to you, Elmer?"

"I think he's one of the syndicate lawyers. Why do you ask?"

"He went to law school with me, twenty years ago. I heard he had become a big shot out here."

"Oh, he's a big shot, all right."

"Probably would deny knowing me after twenty years."

"Probably. And I have a suggestion for you. Don't be asking too many questions about McNamara or the syndicate. Those boys play rough."

Joe Beyerly drank two more beers, said goodbye to his new friend, Elmer, and took a cab back to the Flying Eagle.

By virtue of the difference in time zones, Beyerly calculated correctly that his boss would be at home. Hathaway's wife answered and called her husband to the phone.

Hathaway picked up the receiver. "Hathaway here."

"It's Joe, Mister Hathaway."

"I was hoping it was you. What do you have for me?"

"Quite a lot, actually. A man by the name of Peter Smith runs most of the sports betting in Las Vegas. I suggest you check with the FBI and see what they know about him. He heads up a gambling syndicate here. McNamara is one of the syndicate lawyers."

"You've been a busy boy out there, Joe."

"Just lucky I guess . . . like any whore would say if someone asked how she got her job."

Hathaway chuckled and asked, "Anything else?"

"Yeah, my hotel is called the Flying Eagle. It's part of a casino by the same name. I'm staying one floor below McNamara's room when he's in town and probably his syndicate's offices are on the same floor as his. I'll do some snooping up there when I get a chance."

"Good job, Joe. How about a bet on the game?"

"That's done, by all means. Fifty bucks on the visiting team. If I win, you can have your fifty bucks back. I'll split the winnings with you, which I think are going to be four to one according to the last figures on the tote board."

A good night's sleep had Beyerly all pumped up. While still in his underwear he looked up the number of the Clark County District Attorney.

"Good morning. This is Joseph Beyerly, investigator for the Washington County State's Attorney's Office in Maryland."

A pleasant female receptionist's voice answered, "Good morning, sir. How may I help you?"

"Could you make an appointment for me to meet with Joseph Libwire as soon as he might be free?"

"Let me look at his calendar for the day. . . . I see that he has twenty minutes at eight thirty this morning."

"I can make that, all right."

"May I tell the District Attorney what this concerns?"

"Sure. It concerns Peter Smith."

"Thank you, sir. We'll see you then at eight thirty."

Beyerly arrived fifteen minutes early. A receptionist greeted him and explained that the District Attorney had not yet arrived. "Would you have a seat, sir? Would you like a cup of coffee?"

"No, thank you. Nothing."

Twenty minutes later, the receptionist answered her phone. "I'll tell him. . . . Mister Libwire will see you now, Mister Beyerly. Right this way."

She showed the investigator into the District Attorney's office.

"Good morning Mister . . . Beyerly, is it? Sorry I'm late. How can I help you?"

"Good morning. . . . First, here are my credentials."

He showed his Official Investigator ID to the man seated behind a large desk. "We have an investigation going on in Hagerstown, Marylandactually in Washington County. Peter Smith's name has come up as a person of interest."

"What's the nature of the offense?"

"Fixing minor league baseball games."

"Wow! Do you actually have something like that on Pete Smith?"

"Nothing concrete, as of now. We were hoping you might have something against him or Douglas McNamara. . . . Or are you investigating him for anything, anything at all?"

"Sorry to disappoint you, Joseph. . . . May I call you Joseph?"

"I prefer Joe."

"I'm afraid Pete Smith's squeaky clean in this county, Joe."

"How about Douglas McNamara?"

"Sorry. Same thing. They're sports gamblers, but as you probably know, gambling is not illegal in the State of Nevada as long as a license has been approved. McNamara's membership in the Nevada Bar Association is also spotless."

"And in the case of Peter Smith, who you probably know is mob connected, there is an approved license? How is that possible?"

"Joe, I suggest you take that up with the federal authorities. We've had hearings on the matter of Pete's alleged mob connections. He came through the hearings with flying colors."

"Well, I find that astonishing. I'll take the questions I have to the F.B.I . . . see what they have to say. Thank you, Mister Libwire." Beyerly stood. "I'll probably be talking to you again."

Beyerly was not really astonished by Libwire's negative answers. After all, Smith was in the gambling business. He's managed to keep his coattails clean enough to have a license in Nevada. His illegal activities were being committed elsewhere—places like Hagerstown and probably other unsuspected locations abroad where it was possible to fix sports events. The murdering of Archy Howell may just be the tip of an iceberg. He thought, *All the more reason to push on. I must not be timid. . . . Just a little more careful on how I run my mouth. There's probably just enough room on Archy's slab for another corpse.*

CHAPTER EIGHT

A voice from the hall outside his room said, "Housekeeping. May I straighten up your room?"

Beyerly answered loudly, "Come in."

He heard a key turn in the door lock and the door opened.

"Good afternoon, sir."

"Good afternoon."

A middle aged woman, in a black dress covered with a white apron, pushed her cart of cleaning materials through the door. She went immediately into the bathroom. He went to the bathroom door and watched her as she busily went about her cleaning duties.

"Do you make good money on this job?"

"Pretty good, sir. I could use a raise, though."

"How'd ya like to earn a hundred dollar tip?"

"I never did that sort of thing, not since I started here two years ago."

"You misunderstand me. I don't want sex. I just want to borrow your master key for ten minutes. You can come into the room with me and make sure I don't steal anything. I just want to get some information from Mister McNamara's room. He does have his own room here, doesn't he?"

"Yes, sir."

"Here, look at my credentials. . . . See? . . . It's all on the up and up. You'll be helping the legal authorities and making some extra money at the same time."

"When do you want to do this?"

"Right now, if you're willing."

"Will you give me the money now?"

"Yes."

"Come with me. We'll use the stairs."

Together, they walked up one flight of stairs and then down a vacant hall to room 2215. The housekeeper turned her master key in the lock and entered the room. It too was vacant. Beyerly followed.

The first thing that struck his eye was a wooden clothes valet standing next to the closet area. A dark suit was hung neatly on the valet. A small desk had been placed flush to the wall opposite the closet doors. He went to the desk. He saw nothing on its top. He opened each drawer and found nothing but a telephone book, hotel guides, television instructions and a Gideon Bible.

He went to the closets and saw five suits hanging neatly on hangers. He started to search the pockets of each suit, intending to search all five.

"You won't find nothin' in them suits. When he comes home here at night he throws his clothes on one of the beds he doesn't use. I search all the pockets for papers and money he might have left in 'em. I put what I find in an envelope, write the date on it and put it on the desk. I never cheat him. Wouldn't dare. He hangs out with some very dangerous people. If he wants the clothes cleaned he hangs them on that wooden clothes butler. I search the clothes before I take 'em to the cleaners here in the hotel. The suit that's hanging there now he had on when he came home last week. He flew out of Vegas the next day and I haven't searched the pockets yet. I planned to do that today. I'll hang the suit in the closet when it comes back from the cleaners."

Beyerly started going through the pockets of the suit hanging on the valet. He found a few coins in a pants pocket. He found a small piece of paper in an inside breast pocket. It had a few letters and numbers written on it. *GREEN D. 3134256734.* There was nothing else in the pockets. He copied the letters and numbers into a small notebook and put the piece of paper back in the inside breast pocket.

He went through the dresser drawers and found nothing of interest. Likewise, a scan of the rest of the main room revealed nothing. In the bathroom, the medicine cabinet was almost empty, except for an outdated prescription bottle for kidney pills and some toothpaste.

Beyerly said to the housekeeper, who had been observing his every move, "I guess that's it. Let's go before someone finds us in here and we both get into trouble."

The housekeeper went first, making sure that there was no one in the hall. They used the staircase again to return to the twenty-first floor.

As soon as the housekeeper had closed the door to room 2215, a surveillance camera ceased to operate. It was disguised as part of a painting which hung on the wall opposite the door to the room. An alarm—both a flashing red light and a buzzer—went off in suite 2230 when the house keeper had turned her master key in the lock of room 2215. A television screen, visible only in the suite, came on simultaneously with the alarm. Peter Smith, and another member of his syndicate, had observed every movement made by Joe Beyerly in room 2215.

The housekeeper finished tidying up Beyerly's room and making his bed. When she left, he called his boss in Hagerstown.

"I think I may have something, Mister Hathaway. I had a housekeeper let me into McNamara's permanent room here in the hotel."

"What'd ya find?"

"A piece of paper with what I think is a name and telephone number on it. Write this down. *GREEN D. 3134256734.* I think the D stands for Detroit. 313 is the area code for Detroit. Have someone check in a reverse telephone directory and get a name and address for that number. Try to get me on this telephone when you have the results." He gave Hathaway the telephone number of the hotel. "That's all I have for now."

"You're doing fine, Joe. Keep it up."

"Call me when you match an address to that phone number. Am I authorized to fly to Detroit after I finish here?"

"Certainly. Don't want to kick a winning horse in the ass."

Beyerly had already left for Detroit when the Flying Eagle housekeeper failed to show up for work. After a Las Vegas police investigation was completed, it was concluded that the housekeeper, who had assisted Joe Beyerly in gaining entry to Attorney McNamara's room, would never be seen or heard from again. It wasn't discovered till much later that her corpse lay in a sandy grave some one hundred miles from Las Vegas.

Meanwhile, back in Hagerstown, the preliminary examination, set to determine whether there was probable cause to bind Chester Roosevelt over for trial for the first degree murder of Archy Howell, resulted in a decision which was favorable to the prosecution. The hearing lasted a half hour. The State's evidence consisted mainly of the dramatic testimony of Bucky Livingston concerning the happenings in Carmine's café. Expert forensic testimony established that the pellets in the shotgun shell discovered in the defendant's apartment were identical to those found in the upper body and head of the victim. Finally, there was the testimony of a sheriff's deputy concerning the details of the defendant's attempted bus trip to Chicago on the morning of the killing.

The defendant offered no testimony, his attorney contenting himself with the cross examination of the state's witnesses. This was not unusual.

Statistically, felony defendants were, nine times out of ten, bound over for trial with or without defense evidence, and Chester Roosevelt's case was no exception.

Joe Beyerly learned from Winston Hathaway, who used the reverse telephone directory technique, that the phone number obtained from a search of McNamara's suit led to a married man who lived with a wife and two children in Hamtramack, Michigan. Under intense questioning, the man broke down and confessed that he served as nothing more than a conduit for further contact with a second Detroit telephone number. The code word for passing on the caller's message was the mention of the name Green. The second Detroit number led to a man by the name of Constanza. The Hamtramack man said there had been two such code word transactions within the last month.

With his boss' blessing, Beyerly turned the Constanza information, as well as his suspicions of the fixing of baseball games in Hagerstown, over to the FBI. The Bureau decided to keep Constanza under close scrutiny to see where he might lead them and until a time when his apprehension would be useful.

On a crowded street, a week after Constanza was first discovered, he was cut down by one bullet to the back of the head. He was rushed to the nearest hospital and a brain surgeon and other specialists worked on him for more than ten hours. Miraculously, he did not perish. After surgery he was connected to life preserving hospital devices but remained in a deep coma. His assailant was never caught.

Beyerly had left Las Vegas two hundred dollars richer, having collected his baseball winnings from a teller at the *Universal Lounge.* As Joe was flying to Detroit, Peter Smith was reexamining the video tape of Beyerly's intrusion into McNamara's room 2215. Joe was seen searching the suit hanging on the clothes valet and writing something in his notebook. The piece of paper with the name Green and the Detroit telephone number on it caused a furious Peter Smith to call McNamara to find out how he could misplace such an important item. Thus, the game-fixing criminals discovered the hit man's identity on the same day as the FBI. The Bureau's surveillance of Constanza was not diligent enough to prevent an assassination attempt on the hit man. It was a mob hit man's bullet that almost took the life of a fellow hit man on a crowded Detroit street.

Sonny Campbell spoke to Ed Wilson at the top of his voice. "Both Howell and Livingston had mysterious increases in income this year and their performance on the field had just as mysteriously deteriorated."

"You gotta admit, the Suns have been on a winning streak lately."

"Yeah, ever since Joe almost blew the top off the whole operation. The game fixers are running scared. . . . Archy, normally a fine and decent person, gets killed after a violent argument with Livingston. I knew Archy about as well as anybody did. That man had a conscience. The fight with Livingston was probably because he wanted to get out of fixing ballgames. Edith Howell is either lying about inheriting money from a dead relative or has been kept totally in the dark. McNamara does all of her talking for her. Poor kid is probably terrified and doesn't even know why. Some guy in Detroit, probably the one who killed Archy, gets shot in the head and lies on a hospital bed in a coma. He probably won't ever talk."

"That's just the point, the guy in Detroit won't ever talk, so how can I prove he killed Howell and that it wasn't Roosevelt? Look, the evidence they got against our hospital custodian is very compelling—more compelling than the scenario you're trying to lay on me."

"Say what you will, but I'm expecting you to give Chester a first-class defense . . . and none of this business of talking him into pleading—even to a lesser offense."

"It's my case and I'll do what I think is right. . . . Get off my back, will you?"

"You're hopeless, Ed Wilson. When did this idea of pleading practically every black defendant to something without regard for the Canons of Ethics get started? Remember? *To pursue with zeal his client's cause.*"

"I interpret that particular Canon to include the circumstance, where it seems appropriate to plead to a lesser charge . . . and sometimes even to First Degree Murder, to avoid the death penalty."

"Even where there's a strong indication that your client's innocent?"

"Sonny, in this case there's a strong indication that he's guilty."

"The thing I don't get is that your type of lawyer seems to apply that reasoning almost every time it involves a black defendant. Just once, I'd like to see you defend a Negro until the jury foreman stands up and announces a verdict. *Plead 'em—don't defend 'em* seems to be your credo."

Wilson turned and left Sonny hanging on those last words, which amounted to an accusation against too many of the country's public defenders.

Sonny yelled after Wilson, "You know I'm right."

Two weeks after the attempted assassination of Constanza, the investigation of McNamara's involvement in the fixing of minor league baseball games took on major federal proportions.

CHAPTER NINE

"Jesus, Dougie, you've gotten yourself into a mess over there—all that has to happen is for that guy in Detroit to snap out of his coma, mumble a confession to the feds, and were all suddenly a loaf of toast." Peter Smith was talking to Douglas McNamara, payphone to payphone, in an excess of caution."

McNamara answered, "That's why we have to keep our original plan alive. That bullet in his head is what kept him from ever asking for his fee. It would be, oh so nice, if he died and we could be sure that the authorities never found out I hired him to whack Howell. But we can't ever be sure of that guy dying. He could even talk in his sleep some day and the jig is up for all of us."

"I'm working on a plan to snuff him right there in the hospital."

"It better be a good plan. You get caught trying to pull something like that off and we might as well move to China."

"I know that. Who do you think I am, some two-bit hoodlum or something? I won't move on Mister Constanza until the plan is letter-perfect. In the mean time, you set Hathaway up so that we're sure he's going to offer Roosevelt a plea at the right time. . . . And just to be sure the deal goes through, have the Public Defender ready to make the spade accept the deal. Report to me just as soon as you got everything in place, O.K?"

"O.K., Pete."

Winston Hathaway found himself in what he deemed to be a dangerous quandary. Now he had a call from McNamara himself who wanted to have a talk. It wouldn't hurt to talk to the lawyer and it might hurt a lot to refuse to talk to him. McNamara suggested in a commanding voice, "How about dinner at Lakos Restaurant? Say, this Saturday night at nine o'clock?"

"I'm busy then."

"O.K. . . . next Saturday, same time, same place?"

"You're a persistent man, Mister McNamara."

"Say yes, and I promise you won't regret it."

"We'll see how much I'll regret it. I'll be there at nine o'clock, a week from this coming Saturday."

"As I said, you won't regret it."

After hanging up his receiver, Hathaway thought to himself, *Regrets have a way of smelling bad right from the beginning. Heaven help me. I shouldn't even talk to that man on the phone, much less face to face.*

The Sterling Life Insurance Company advertised that its doors would be open for business in a month. The FBI devoted that month to surreptitiously placing bugs on all the telephones and in inconspicuous places in the State's Attorney's and Public Defender's offices and on Edith Howell's, Bucky Livingston's and Douglas McNamara's telephones. The making of dinner plans for Hathaway and McNamara would be intercepted at the *Sterling* offices by a female FBI agent who posed as a secretary during the business day. Other Bureau personnel would man her ear phones during the rest of the twenty-four hours on business days, and all day and night on weekends.

By the beginning of the third week, the Bureau had an agreement with the authentic Gibraltar Life Insurance Company. The phony *Sterling* offices would act as a branch of *Gibraltar*, which would have one of its real sales representatives on the *Sterling* premises every day to close or reject all walk-in applications for life insurance.

Business was never very brisk at the Sterling Life Insurance Company. Of course, the *Gibraltar* man handled all the interviews. This allowed the FBI agents to vigorously carry out their investigative chores.

On the Saturday evening when Hathaway and McNamara were to have dinner together, agent Alan Jones arrived at *Lakos Restaurant* at eight thirty. He asked to see the manager.

"How may I help you, sir?"

Alan showed the tuxedoed manager his credentials. "Do you have a reservation for two this evening for a Mister Hathaway or a Mister McNamara?"

"Let me check." The manager walked to the reservations station and checked a list. He rejoined Alan and said, "Yes we do, sir. Table twelve for two at nine o'clock."

"Where is table twelve?"

"Follow me, sir."

Alan followed the manager to a table. He nodded to the maitre d', who was standing nearby being brought up to speed by the manager, and said, "Give me a few minutes at this table and then forget you ever saw me."

The agent removed the top from a salt shaker. He dropped a small round device into it, screwed the top back on and shook the shaker until the device fell to its bottom. The whole procedure lasted less than a minute. Alan then went out to his car and tuned into the salt shaker bug. He could hear occasional faint voices get louder, then dimmer, as they passed the table. Satisfied with the reception he leaned back in the car seat and waited.

Douglas McNamara was speaking to State's Attorney, Winston Hathaway. Alan was listening in his car and agent, Maggie Howe, was monitoring and taping their conversation at the Sterling Insurance Company offices.

"I've eaten here before. For a small town, the food here is superior."
"Best in town."
"I bet you can't afford to eat here on what they pay you."
"I do all right."
The maitre d' had accompanied the two men to their reserved table. "I can strongly recommend our special, tonight, gentlemen."
McNamara said, "Oh? What is the special?"
"Choucroute Garnie."
Hathaway said, "I've had that here. It's excellent." He glanced at McNamara who nodded.
"We'll both have that."
McNamara asked the maitre d', "What wine do you recommend?"
"Graves Superiour."
"Sounds good."
The conversation continued as they waited for their wine and food.
McNamara spoke first. "How much do they pay you?"
"Twenty-four thousand dollars a year."
"Well, let's get right down to business. If I were to propose that you could make three times that amount in a lump sum from one transaction, which is perfectly legal—something which you do routinely practically every day—would you find that an attractive proposition?"
"Sounds like a bribe . . . I may have to turn this over to federal authorities."
"I said the quid pro quo is perfectly legal."
"How could it be and still be worth that much money?"
A waiter brought a bottle of iced down wine in a silver bucket to the table. With an exaggerated flourish, he opened it and poured wine into the pre-set wine glasses.

"That's more information than you need to know right now."

"O.K. What is this perfectly legal thing that you want me to do?"

"Oh, no, I'll tell you when the time is appropriate. There's no great hurry. We're only here to discuss whether this sort of thing would be attractive to you. If it is, then when the time comes, I tell you what it is and you'll decide what you want to do about it. If you do it, you get paid. If you don't, you're back to your twenty-four thousand a year."

A different waiter brought them their dinner.

"If I tell you what I want you to do now, you're liable to shoot your mouth off, tell everybody I tried to bribe you, and we've got a big scandal on our hands. You do this thing in advance of getting paid, then you don't dare say you were bribed because you've already acted and you'd be guilty too. Anyway, it's not illegal. I keep telling you that. You've got to believe me. You've probably done it a hundred times in your career."

The waiter served their dinner for two out of a silver tureen.

Hathaway said, "At least the dinner smells good. I'm not so sure about your proposal."

"Let's drop it for the time being and enjoy this food. Like I said, there's no hurry."

The three agents at *Sterling* had just played back a tape of the Hathaway-McNamara *Lakos* dinner conversation. Alan said to Maggie and Tom, "Boy, this guy is slick. There's not a word of provable bribery on that tape. Since what he's asking the State's Attorney to do has been done many times before and, according to McNamara, is not illegal, we'll probably not even know if and when Hathaway has accepted the deal. At this point we've got zilch. We may never get more than zilch. We simply don't know what we're looking for."

Tom protested, "I wouldn't say that. You gotta ask yourself, what do prosecutors do? They prosecute. What big time prosecution does Hathaway have that McNamara might be interested in? Chester Roosevelt, that's who. If the mob ordered Constanza to kill Howell, then they gotta make sure that that poor Negro is the fall guy. Why? Because they have no guarantee that Constanza won't come out of his coma. If he does revive, then Hathaway will learn that he belongs to us. He'll tell him that McNamara hired him to kill Howell. How do they make sure that Constanza won't testify? They pay Hathaway to make a deal—to offer an attractive plea to Roosevelt—some deal he can't refuse. And if Constanza does wake up, Hathaway has already put himself in the soup. He's chosen Roosevelt as his killer, and made the deal."

Maggie exclaimed, "Of course, that's it! Roosevelt's plea is McNamara's insurance policy."

Tom said, "But let's not forget what our assignment is in this town. We're here to investigate the fixing of baseball games. It may be a by-product of our investigation that we find out who really killed Archy Howell, but that's far from the end-all. We've got to map out our strategy for our assigned duty."

Alan was enthusiastic as he spoke. "I see it this way. Let's try this on for size. . . . Why kill Howell, anyway? He's having an argument with Livingston in the café. It's pretty violent. What's it about? Howell wants to defect, that's what. . . . His drunken conscience is bothering him. . . . Livingston likes his new found wealth so he makes an emergency call to McNamara who makes an emergency call to Constanza. Constanza makes a private jet flight from Detroit to Hagerstown where he is met by McNamara in a rented VW. Constanza drops McNamara off some place and drives to Howell's home where he finds all of the house lights on. He hears loud voices. The garage door opens. Out comes Howell in his car and drives away followed by Constanza. Constanza chooses Plum and Harrison to stop Howell in his rented VW and then **Bang, Bang**—Howell's face is gone and so is Constanza."

Maggie then spoke, "Your timing is awfully tight, but professionals like Constanza are used to tight schedules. We've got to start somewhere. How about one of you check with the private-jet flights from Detroit to Hagerstown for the week preceding the killing."

Tom responded, "If we score on that one we're well on our way."

Alan added, "We'll follow that with an intimidating interview with Bucky Livingston."

Tom was filling in for Maggie on the ear phones. It was eight forty-five A.M. On a panel on her desk a red light started blinking, indicating that the telephone in Public Defender Edward Wilson's office was active.

"This is Attorney McNamara. How are you today, Mister Wilson?"

"Ah, Edith Howell's lawyer. I'm just fine, Mister McNamara. How may I help you today?"

Wilson threw a switch under his keyhole desk which activated a recording device on his telephone.

"I just heard a mysterious click. I assume you're recording what we say today. You may regret throwing that switch, Mister Wilson."

"I doubt it. What do you want?"

"I want to meet with you."

"Why?"

"I want to meet you some place and make a proposition that may or may not be attractive to you."

"Why can't you do that right now . . . on the phone?"

"Because you're recording our every word. . . . Let's say we have lunch together . . . nothing fancy. . . . Let's say the hotdog stand across the street from your building . . . at noon sharp. And please don't be wearing a wire. I'll have to check on that before we have our conversation."

Alan asked fellow agent Tom Hillenbrand, "Can you get over to the hotdog stand near 100 Franklin Street, order a hotdog, and place a bug on the operator's cart before noon?"

"Sure. Hotdogs are high on my gourmet list."

McNamara ordered a bratwurst and Hathaway a hotdog. While they waited, McNamara casually ran his hand down Hathaway's shirtfront

They didn't linger long enough at the stand for Maggie to make out much useful information. The last words she heard through her earphones were, *You're defending Chester Roosevelt, aren't you?*

"Yes, I am. Who do you represent besides Mrs. Howell?"

"Let's just say that I am . . . a sort of Friend of the Court."

"That's a crock."

"I've taken the trouble to investigate your record on pleading your so-called clients to lesser charges. You seem to have a penchant for doing that."

"That's part of the duty of a public defender."

"Duty?"

"Certainly. Unless a defense lawyer has built a solid defense for his client he should persevere to get the prosecutor to offer a plea deal. Why should you be asking me these questions? You're a lawyer. You should know all this already. Are you an ACLU character, or something?"

"Nothing like that. But I'm curious. When was the last time you found yourself vigorously defending a Negro client in a courtroom?"

"If you've been investigating me, you probably know when that was."

"I believe it was more than a year since you gave a Negro his right to a courtroom defense. Am I right?"

Wilson threw the rest of his hotdog in a trash can. His body language showed great hostility. "Look, you bastard. This conversation is over. . . . What the hell are you here for? You want something. What is it?"

"How would you like to earn the magnificent sum of ten thousand dollars for simply doing what you normally do?"

"You're kidding?"

"Not in the slightest."

"And how would you like to be brought up on bribery charges?"

"Oh, come on, Mister Wilson. You're doubtless going to do what I ask anyway and without any reward from me. I'm just trying to assure myself that the Roosevelt case will not be an exception to your normal routine. We don't even have to talk again. Just wait for Hathaway to make the offer . . . point out the advantages to your client to accept the offer and look for a cashier's check for ten thousand dollars in your home mailbox after he pleads."

"I'm going back to my office. Know this, Mister McNamara . . . you are skating on very thin ice. All I have to do is report this conversation to the State's Attorney and suggest he charge you with attempted bribery."

"What conversation? We just talked about my great admiration for the work you're doing."

They had circled the block. Wilson hurried through the front door of his office building. McNamara went back to the hotdog stand and ordered another bratwurst.

Alan said to his two colleagues, "I believe we can reconstruct the conversation they had on the basis of just the one phrase you did hear, Maggie, *Are you defending Chester Roosevelt?*"

Maggie responded, "Yeah. When you put that phrase with the Hathaway dinner conversation you have a perfect insurance policyno one would ever think to accuse Constanza, dead or alive, of the killing if Chester Roosevelt has pleaded guilty and he's sitting in a prison cell. Now, which one of you guys is going to interview Bucky Livingston?"

Alan answered, "Both of us. Two serious FBI faces are sure to scare the shit out of good old game-fixin' Bucky Livingston?"

CHAPTER TEN

Wilson almost burst into Suite 102. He had a look of anger on his face. He went into his office and sat down at his desk. For the next ten minutes he did nothing but just sit there. The look of anger turned to one of deep thought. After sitting without moving he picked up the phone and buzzed Pat, his secretary. He had forgotten that she was out of the office, probably eating her lunch somewhere. He flipped through his Rolodex, stopping at the State's Attorney's information card. He dialed Hathaway's number and waited for someone to answer. A female voice came on the line. "State's Attorney's Office."

"Is Mister Hathaway there? This is Ed Wilson calling."

"No, sir. He's signed out till one o'clock."

"Would you tell him to return this call when he gets in?"

"Yes, sir."

"Ed Wilson? I'm returning your call. What can I do for you?"

"Winston . . . about the Roosevelt case. Are you thinking of offering a plea in that matter?"

"Not yet, I'm not. But it's within the realm of possibility."

"Have you thought about the fact that Roosevelt doesn't own a vehicle of any kind? He'd need a car or some kind of a vehicle to get to Plum and Harrison and do the killing."

"We're looking into that. He may have had a friend drive him down there."

"You mean follow Howell down there, don't you?"

"Yeah, I guess so. Look, it's too early to talk about a plea. I'll get back to you later. Racial fury may persuade me that it's second degree and not first. That would take the death penalty off the table."

"We're looking into that, ourselves."

"We'll get in touch later, Ed. I promise that. . . . I've got to be in court in a couple of minutes so I gotta hang up now."

When Wilson heard the click of Hathaway's telephone he felt a sense of relief. He may be in for a windfall and not have to do anything out of the ordinary to get it.

He left suite 102, now with half a smile on his face, replacing the anger that was there when he had come in.

Maggie turned to Alan, took off her ear phones, and said, "Like they say in politics, *It's the economy, stupid.* That was public defender Ed Wilson talking to Winston Hathaway. I think they were both feathering their nests."

It was raining all that Friday morning and the scheduled Suns game at Municipal Stadium was canceled. The federal staff of three at the Sterling Life Insurance Company, calculated that Bucky Livingston would be at home not expecting to play baseball that day. Alan and Tom took the elevator to the tenth floor of Livingston's luxury apartment house. His apartment didn't have an ordinary apartment buzzer. It had a brass doorknocker, which when lifted caused bells to play the Big Ben Clock melody inside the apartment.

An almost beautiful youthful woman came to the door.

Alan said politely, "We're here to see Mister Livingston."

"Who are you guys? Mormons or somethin'? I can tell you right now. . . . He don't want to join no church."

Tom asked, "Is he at home?"

"I'll go get him for you. Who do you want me to say you are?"

"FBI." They both showed the woman their federal ID.

The women turned pale and appeared to be frozen in her tracks.

"I . . . guess I should . . . invite you in. . . . Come in. He's in the bedroom."

Livingston came out of the bedroom dressed in his underwear covered by a bathrobe. "You want to talk to me? What about?"

The two agents showed Livingston their credentials.

Tom Hillenbrand answered, "First, may we sit down?"

"Sure. Can I get you something to drink?"

Alan Jones asked, "Would a cup of coffee be too much trouble?"

"Shirley, make some coffee, would you?"

"Sure, honey."

The two agents sat side by side on the living room couch.

"Well, what do you want to talk to me about?"

Alan asked, "Do you know someone by the name of McNamara?"

"Oh, you mean Archy Howell's lawyer. . . . I met him once when Archy was still alive."

Tom asked, "But not since Archy got killed. . . . Is that right?"

"That's right."

Tom stated matter-of-factly. "I should tell you. . . . It's a felony called obstruction of justice to lie to federal investigating officers."

"What are you investigatin'?"

"The fixing of minor league baseball games," Tom answered.

Shirley, who had been standing in the doorway to the kitchen, turned and went back to the stove where she had been preparing the coffee.

Livingston was silent for an awkward thirty seconds. Finally, he spoke, "I heard the rumor."

Alan said, "I'm afraid it's not a rumor, Bucky. You seem to have come into a substantial amount of money lately. Am I right?"

"Oh, yeah. I won a ton of money at the crap table in Vegas a couple o' months ago."

Tom asked, "Did the casino keep a portion of it for taxes?"

Another moment of silence filled the room.

"I was so excited, I don't remember."

Alan sounded reassuring. "We can always check on that. The casinos are very efficient about that sort of thing."

"It sounds to me like you guys are accusing me of something. I'm going to call a lawyer."

"Who's your lawyer?" asked Tom.

"Mister McNamara. He's the only lawyer I know."

"And we haven't accused you of anything . . . and you're not under arrest."

"Just the same, I'm not goin' to answer no more questions without a lawyer here."

Alan said, "And we're not going to ask you any more questions, so you're safe, for the time being, Bucky, my lad."

"Well, get the hell out of here, then."

The two agents stood and left the apartment.

Shirley's voice was high pitched and she sounded terrified. "You better call that lawyer right away."

"Can't you see I'm dialin' the phone?"

Livingston had extracted a business card from his billfold. Douglas McNamara had written a local phone number on the card. A messaging service answered the phone.

"Mister McNamara, please."

"This is his answering service. May I take a message?"

"Tell him to call Bucky Livingston. It's urgent."

"I will tell him when he calls in."

"Thanks."

Maggie reported Livingston's attempt to contact McNamara to the two agents when they returned to the *Sterling* offices.

Alan joked, "That was one scared baseball player, Maggie. Sorry you're going to have to stay on the microphones until Mister Las Vegas returns Bucky Boy's call."

"One of you guys is going to have to relieve me every hour or so. Remember your promise."

They didn't have to wait long. Forty-five minutes later the call came through. Maggie turned on the tape recorder and the speaker phone switches.

Shirley answered Livingston's phone. "Bucky's residence."

"Is he there? This is Attorney McNamara, returning his call."

"Oh, yes. I'll go get him."

"Mister McNamara. Jeez, am I glad you called back so soon."

"Calm down. Is there a problem?"

"I'll say there's a problem. Two FBI men were here asking me questions. They asked about you."

"Like what, about me?"

"Did I know you? And on top of that they asked about fixin' baseball games."

"That is a problem for you. What did you tell them?"

"I dummied up . . . refused to answer any more questions without a lawyer."

"I'm going to tell you something now, Bucky. And listen carefully because I want you to tell the other guy exactly what I'm telling you. Understand?"

"What do you want me to tell him?"

"That all deals are off. Understand? All deals are off. I want the three of you to play your asses off starting with tomorrow's double header at Municipal Stadium."

"But . . ."

"It's over. No ifs, ands or buts. Get it? And don't try to call me again. I'm not your lawyer any more. Goodbye."

Both games of the double header, played in Hagerstown by the Suns the next day, were won by the home team with scores not seen in Hagerstown during the 1982 season—nine to one and twelve to zero. Shocking to the fans were the next six games which were also won by the Suns. These victories did not escape the attention of Rochelle and Sonny Campbell.

Right after checking the standings, Rochelle exclaimed, "Looks like we're back in the baseball business, dear husband. We're going to drink gallons of beer and eat dozens of hotdogs this afternoon. Good thing we've got season's tickets. There won't be an empty seat in the Stadium."

"We could probably sell those tickets for a hundred bucks apiece," responded Sonny gleefully.

"Me thinks I smell the FBI in town. What do you think?"

"That was the plan. That's why we pushed Walter Brock in the direction of Joe Beyerly. Joe probably did his usual masterful investigation and turned the results over to the feds."

"And Mister M. is probably speedily on his way to the protections of the Mafia dons in Sicily right about now," Rochelle joked.

Sonny asked, "What time does Smitty open up on Saturday?"

"At eleven o'clock sharp."

"Oh, yeah. Now we can tell him why we were skipping Saturday games," he declared.

"Oh, I think he could guess what the reason was a long time ago. Smitty's a pretty smart cookie, you know? Remember when he made reference to what you government people know and what the general public doesn't," she emphasized.

"One of the smartest bartenders I ever ran into. And like you once told me, I bet he never spread any rumors about what he suspected."

"It's almost eleven. I can't wait to talk to our favorite bartender."

"What time do the concessions open at Municipal Stadium? I'm really hungry."

"One o'clock, I think," Rochelle answered.

"Let's get down to the bar. I want to hear what Smitty has to say."

Smitty presented his case to the Campbells slowly and deliberately—like he was giving a closing argument to a jury. "My first clue was what probably bothered the two of you . . . their sudden move from the wrong side of Funkstown to the house on Jefferson Boulevard. They did that without telling anybody it was going to happen and why it was going to happen. And it seems to me that right after they moved, the Suns started playing three hundred ball. Up until then they were playing seven hundred ball. . . . Then there was that half hour phone call to his lawyer—what's his name—McNamara? That phone call visibly unnerved him. I could tell. And he wouldn't tell me what was the problem. . . . Listen, you two. Archy Howell used to bring all of his problems to me, and I mean all . . . like I was his father confessor or something. Why did he hide that one from me, if it bothered him so much? And that fight in Carmine's with Bucky Livingston wasn't the first time those two argued. Just before he got murdered, the two of them came in here after a game and they argued like hell. I couldn't hear what it was about, but they never, and I mean never, used to argue about anything."

Sonny interrupted him, "How'd you know they argued in Carmine's?"

"Because the radio newscaster was in here last week shooting his mouth off. He told me that that's how the fight really got started. . . . It wasn't with the Negro guy. He was trying to break it up, when Archy turned on him. That was not the Archy Howell we know. I can't imagine him fighting with anybody . . . physically, anyway."

Rochelle said, "Me neither."

"And the clincher was when you two stopped going to the home games on Saturday. By the time you stopped going I had already figured out there was something rotten in Denmark. But you don't have to worry about me spreadin' rumors around town about my suspicions. I figured that you were keepin' your mouths shut so I better do the same."

Sonny said, "You know something, Smitty. You're really a hell of a guy."

Sonny was sure he recognized the man seated to his left at Municipal Stadium. "You must have a reserved seat the same as we do."

"Yeah. I watched this team lose twenty-eight out of thirty-six games in the last three months." The man then whispered, "Somebody must have shoved corn cobs up their asses a week ago." In a normal tone he then jokingly said, "They're playing like their old selves for a week now."

Rochelle said, "They sure are."

Sonny stood and excused himself. "I'm going to the refreshment stand. Can I get you anything, sir?"

The man handed Sonny a ten dollar bill. "Three redhots with catsup and onions."

"You bet." Sonny left.

"Isn't your man the public defender?"

"He sure is."

"Which one is he? Wilson or Campbell?"

"He's Sonny Campbell. He's public defender for Washington County."

"Is he defending that nigger who killed Archy Howell?"

Rochelle was silent for an awkward interval. Then in an angry tone, she said, "I beg your pardon."

"Don't get mad at me. I understand that somebody has to defend those black hoodlums."

"I'm not angry for that reason you racist bastard. For the rest of the afternoon I would prefer that you not talk to either one of us, especially not my husband. If he had been here to hear you use that bigot's badge of cowardly prejudice, he probably would have knocked you right on your racist's ass. Now, excuse me. I'm going to the lady's room to throw up."

Sonny returned with two cardboard trays loaded with hotdogs. He handed the tray with three hotdogs in it to his neighbor. As he handed the man his change he asked, "What happened to my wife?"

"I'm not supposed to talk to you." The man stood and started pushing himself down the row of other fans without excusing himself. He almost dropped the tray of hotdogs.

"Why not?"

Over his shoulder, the man said, "Ask her."

While he waited for Rochelle to return, Sonny hailed a uniformed black man who was selling beer. "Two beers."

"Comin' up, sir."

Sonny held a cup of beer in each hand with the tray of hotdogs between his feet until Rochelle returned. After she was settled in her seat he turned to her and in an almost inaudible voice asked what her conversation with his neighbor had been. In normal volume, making sure that the surrounding fans could hear her, she told him all the details, including a word for word repeat of her speech to the man.

Sonny's response was, "Well, he probably won't be coming this way again. And now that our team is playing decent baseball again, he won't have any trouble selling his reserved seat ticket to someone."

"Answer a question, will you?"

"If I can."

"Would you really have knocked him on his ass if you had heard him use that word?"

Sonny thought for a moment, then answered, "I don't know, honey. He was a pretty big guy."

"You bastard. Don't make a liar out of me."

The Campbells were on their way home from Municipal Stadium to their home in Beaver Creek.

"So, how long can I expect my hotshot husband to go around sulking about his team losing today's game by one run?"

"I'm not sulking. You tell me how those guys can win eight games in a row and then blow a three run lead in the ninth inning and lose."

"It was inevitable that their winning streak had to come to an end, sometime. Why not, when the great Sonny Campbell was in the stands expecting them to stretch their winning streak to nine?"

"Rocky, they were winning by three runs at the end of the eighth. There's such a thing as momentum, you know."

"You should have sent a note to the Suns' manager about momentum."

"Don't make fun of me. I see this game as a disaster."

"Like I said, you're sulking. I'll go to next Saturday's game by myself, if I have to."

"What kind of a dinner do I get tonight?"

"Spaghetti. I can have it on the table in fifteen minutes."

"Sounds good. Any beer in the fridge?"

"Plenty. You can have spaghetti, salad, warm Italian bread and butter and a beer orgy."

"Speed it up, will you? You got my mouth watering."

When they got home, there was an unexpected telephone message on their machine.

> *"Sonny, this is Edith. I know this call is a surprise. Would you return this call? I simply have to talk to you. Don't let me down. I have to talk to you. I'm scared."*

"Edith? Sonny Campbell, returning your call."

"Let me call you back on my satellite phone. I think the FBI has tapped this phone."

The Campbell phone rang just moments later. "Edith?"

"Yes."

"What's this business about the F.B.I?"

"They were here, this morning. There were two of them. I felt like they were giving me the third degree, or something."

"They probably were. Did you answer all of their questions?"

"I tried to. I didn't have honest answers for them most of the time."

"But you didn't lie, did you?

"No! I didn't lie. I just didn't have answers for them. I didn't know what they were talking about."

"Give me an example of a question you couldn't answer."

" . . . For instance, where did we get the money to buy this house?"

"How did you answer that one?"

"All I could say was that Mister McNamara showed up at our house in Funkstown one day and told us that I had inherited a lot of money from an anonymous relative who had died. The money was mine, provided I didn't tell anyone about it. . . . Oh Sonny, I haven't told anyone about it until this morning. I told the FBI men about it. . . . Did I do the right thing?"

"You did exactly the right thing."

"And another thing. I've been trying to reach Mister McNamara since last Friday. He was staying at the Howard Johnson's Plaza. They told me he checked out of there. Since Friday, I've called every hotel in town. He wasn't at any of them."

"Did you tell them that?"

"Yes."

"What did they say?"

"One of them just laughed. The other one said, *We're not surprised to hear that.*"

"You said you were scared on your phone message. What are you scared about?"

"That I have all that money in the bank and it might not really be mine . . . that maybe Archy was doing something crooked and maybe that's why somebody killed him . . . that maybe somebody is going to kill me."

Sonny knew he was about to tell the biggest lie he had ever told anyone in his entire life.

"Edith, honey. I'm going to tell you something, now—something you must never tell any one else till this mess is cleared up. You know that Archy was my best friend. The reason he was murdered was because he was working undercover for the FBI here in Hagerstown. This man McNamara is closely associated with a gambling syndicate in Las Vegas. Archy had to accept that money in order to convince McNamara that he was the real thing—a crook working for the Las Vegas Syndicate—that he was one of the players on the Suns who was willing to drop the ball, strike out in tight spots and anything else that would make it look like he was playing ball with McNamara.

Unfortunately for the syndicate, Archy had a conscience. When he got drunk his conscience took over. That's why he got into a fight with Bucky Livingston in that café that morning and that's what got him killed."

"But Sonny, what do I do . . . ?"

"Shush . . . Let me talk."

Edith didn't finish her question.

"The FBI is now in Hagerstown. That's because fixing any sport for gambling purposes is a federal offense. And that's why McNamara is no where to be found . . . not yet anyway. And that's also why the Suns were on a long overdue winning streak. The fixing of baseball games in our town is over."

Rochelle announced that dinner was ready.

"Just a few more minutes with Edith. She really needs our help, honey."

Edith said, "Is that Rocky? Oh, tell her I'm so sorry I've been treating her so badly. Can you explain to her all this ugliness? Can I call her and have some girl talk, like we used to have?"

"I'm sure you can, Edith." He covered the mouthpiece on the telephone and whispered that he had just told Edith that Archy was working undercover for the FBI" Rochelle nodded her head in approval.

"What do I do with the money in the bank, Sonny?"

"Leave it there. Don't touch it. It may be that it will become evidence in a federal case against McNamara and his syndicate. But if there are convictions, the money is going to be yours to keep. Consider the source. It's simply an expense that those bad guys had, which they have no claims on anymore."

"But what do I do with this dinosaur of a house?"

"I recommend that you sell it and put the money you get in the bank with the other McNamara money you're going to use for the kids' education."

"Good thing that Archy had an insurance policy. We can live on that till I get a job."

"I can help you get a job, Edith."

"Maybe I'll buy back the house in Funkstown. I see there's a *For Sale* sign on it again. The kids loved that house."

"Good idea."

"I'll let you go now, Sonny. Tell Rocky that I still love her. I'll call her tomorrow after church."

"I'll do that. Bye, for now."

"Bye. I still love you too, dear Sonny."

Rochelle was sitting in a straight-back dining room chair. "I only heard part of what you told her. Sounded like you were lying your Irish ass off."

"I was. I have no doubt that Archy, all by himself and in a weakened moment, went for an offer from that smooth talkin' McNamara. But that doesn't mean that Edith knew anything about how that money got into their bank account. Let's just say I was repairing some undeserved damage to that woman's future."

"Come here, you big lug."

They embraced. The kiss was unusually long.

CHAPTER ELEVEN

Ever since stabilizing surgery was performed on Mario Constanza in July at the Henry Ford Hospital, Department of Neurological Surgery, in Detroit, Michigan, he lay in a near vegetative state in an intensive care unit. The medical consensus was simply stated. *It would take a near-miracle for him to emerge from his neurological netherworld.*

But in August there occurred a dramatic twist in the hit man's condition. He awoke from his coma and began speaking, non-stop.

A twenty-four hour police guard stood duty just outside the only door to the intensive care unit. One of the two guards then on duty left his station and telephoned his local precinct.

"Constanza woke up. He's chattering like a magpie. Better bring a tape recorder down here and notify the feds. He's talking about some stuff that I think they are going to be very interested in."

"This is FBI agent Kevin Freedlund. I am present in an intensive care unit of Henry Ford Hospital, Department of Neurological Surgery, in Detroit, Michigan. Present also is Agent Charles Pampe. The date is August 15, 1982. Mario Constanza, who emerged from a vegetative coma approximately two and a half hours ago, now appears fully conscious and indicates that he wishes to give testimony in the case of the United States of America vs. Peter Smith, Douglas McNamara, Charles Tomlinson, Mark Greenberg and Salvatore Valente. . . . Mister Constanza, did you understand my preliminary remarks?"

"Yeah. But I want you guys to know that the only reason I'm giving this recorded statement is I'm being accused of something I never did."

"You mean, you were never hired by a certain Douglas McNamara, to murder a certain Archy Howell in Hagerstown, Maryland on the last Friday in June of this year?"

"Those names sound familiar, but I'm not sure . . . oh, I got the contract to kill some guy, all right, but I didn't kill him."

"Did you get paid in advance to kill someone?"

"No, I never got paid and after the poor sap got killed by someone else I didn't expect to get paid."

"How do you know he got killed by someone else?"

"Because a guy on the radio said that somebody blew his head off."

"You were in Hagerstown then, when Mister Howell got killed?"

"I followed the poor bastard, whatever his name was, for almost two days . . . watched him play one whole baseball game. . . . Watched him and two of his buddies get drunk together. . . . Saw the black guy run out of a place and down the street for parts unknown. . . . Saw the mark leave the place and drive away. I couldn't tell you what he looked like today."

"Did you follow him?"

"Naah. My car was pointed the other way. I decided to put it off and try the next day. But then I heard the guy on the radio say he was killed and I decided to beat feet and come back to Detroit."

"Did you ever talk to McNamara again?"

"I told you, I'm not sure I know anybody by that name. But I knew I wouldn't get any money. I just lay low. Went out one day to get some booze and cigarettes and something hit me in the head and then I woke up here. They tell me I've been out for a couple o' months."

Despite diligent efforts to keep secret the emergence from a vegetative state of a mysterious patient under police guard at Henry Ford Hospital, the nation's news media somehow gained access to the amazing story of a modern miracle.

In Hagerstown, Ed Wilson's secretary, Pat, was the first in the Public Defender's office to speak of the shocking news of another possible suspect in the murder of Archy Howell. She walked into Sonny Campbell's office and threw a copy of the *Hagerstown Herald-Mail* on his desk.

"I wish you wouldn't do that, Pat. It's very annoying."

"You'll forgive me when you read the lead story above the fold."

SUSPECT IN HOWELL MURDERCOMES TO IN DETROIT HOSPITAL

The news that a Detroit man, Mario Constanza, who awoke from a comatose state after more than two months, is talking once again is a dramatic twist to a story that is fascinating the medical world. In another shocking event, it was revealed that Constanza is a suspect in a murder plot that occurred in Hagerstown, Maryland in June of this year. More shocking still, was more reliable information that an assassination attempt on the hit man himself was made last July, but was unsuccessful when brain surgery at the Department of Neurology, Henry Ford Hospital in Detroit, left him alive, but in a coma.

Reliable sources say that Constanza was cooperative when interviewed by the FBI just hours before he again lapsed into a coma.

Because Mario Constanza's emergence from this vegetative state is considered a near-miracle, doctors say it shouldn't raise false hopes for relatives of similar patients. But at the same time, a thread of hope can sometimes sustain families faced with the devastation of seeing someone they love in that condition. One doctor was heard to say, "No love lost on this professional killer, however."

"I'll be damned," said Sonny to Pat. "But Joe Beyerly is the hero. He tracked Constanza down for the State's Attorney. What we need is a copy of that FBI interview, to get Chester out of this mess. Maybe Joe can get it for us."

Sonny was happy to find Ed Wilson working at his desk in his office. "Have you seen the latest on your defense of Roosevelt?" He showed the newspaper article to Wilson.

Wilson read the short article. "I won't be impressed until I see the FBI interview in black and white."

"Write to them and explain your dilemma. They'll probably have an agent bring it to you during the trial as a kind o' surprise witness, like in Perry Mason."

"You still think there's going to be a trial?"

"Now, more than ever. Come on, Ed. You can't ignore this new revelation. This guy can't talk, but the FBI interview will speak for itself."

"How the hell could I get it in. It's not a deathbed statement."

"You file a motion and ask the judge to consider it a death bed statement, that's how."

"Now you're grasping at straws."

"No, but I have more faith than you do that somehow the truth will out. Let me ask you a question. How do you and Hathaway expect to seat a jury when the whole of Washington County has read this story about Constanza and are doubtless in a quandary as to who killed Archy?"

"We'll have our jury, because at least half of those people will believe that their State's Attorney knew what he was doing when he charged Roosevelt in the first place."

"But it was his own investigator who uncovered the identity of the hit man who is probably the real killer. He's now stuck with his first choice. . . . But you're not. You should be excited as hell that you've got another suspect to sell to the jury. Reasonable doubt, my friend. Reasonable doubt."

"I told you. There won't be another suspect until I see what that FBI report has to say."

"Which means you're bound and determined to avoid another trial and hope to plead Chester Roosevelt guilty to some lousy deal that Hathaway will offer you."

"Why don't you get the hell out of my office? You've recused yourself from representing Roosevelt and Judge Piercy has signed an order to that effect. If I get any more static from you on how I'm handling Roosevelt's defense, I'll file a motion to have you held in contempt of that order. . . . I swear I will."

Sonny left Wilson's office without saying another word.

"But Mister Campbell, they found the real killer. I read it in the newspaper."

"Maybe that man is the real killer, but you're still the one who's been charged, Chet. I know you understand what I'm talking about because I remember you telling me when I first met you that once a Negro gets into the system he never gets out."

"Does that mean you've given up on me?"

"I'm not your lawyer anymore. I have no choice in that. I was too close to the man who got killed."

"That's only because they won't let you be. I know that you believe I'm innocent. How can you give up on me?"

Sonny put his head down and the room became silent. He thought to himself. *To pursue with zeal his client's cause . . . he's still my client no matter what that order says. . . . He's my client, because I say he is. I just can't turn him over to a bigot like Wilson and forget about him. Now I've got twice the reason to pursue his cause with zeal, where I can.* "Chet, I have not given up on you. I'm going to have to work in the background, but I'm going to work every angle I can think of. In the mean time, don't forget what I asked you to do if Wilson tries to get you to plead. If he does, you get me down here, come hell or high water, you understand?"

"*Yessah, boss. I understands.*"

They were both laughing as Sonny pressed the buzzer to alert the deputy that he wanted to leave the visiting cell.

Ed Wilson wrote a letter to the Detroit FBI office and requested, in very polite language, a copy of the interview that agents took from Mario Constanza after he awoke from his coma. Three weeks later he received a large registered envelope containing the interview consisting of questions and answers given by the hit man. A letter accompanied the Q. and A.

Office of the
Federal Bureau of Investigation
DETROIT, MICHIGAN

September 24, 1982

Dear Mister Wilson,

I have your request for a copy of the Q. and A. taken of Mario Constanza on August 15, 1982. Enclosed is a copy of same, sent to you on the condition that you retain it in your possession until needed for official purposes. We request that it be destroyed when your need for it expires.

You will note that Mister Constanza resolutely denies killing or attempting to kill anyone. I'm sure this comes as a disappointment to you. For that we are indeed regretful.

Sincerely yours,
Robert H. Johnson
Robert H. Johnson,
Agent in Charge

Wilson thought, *Well, what do you think of that turn of events, Mister Campbell? Kind of puts your man smack back in the middle of our murder, doesn't it?*

During the lunch hour, he placed the letter neatly in the center of Sonny Campbell's desktop. He wished he could see Sonny's face at the precise moment that he returned from lunch and found the letter. He didn't really expect that he would come rushing into his office to admit defeat on the issue of his client's guilt. Henceforth, he would give Mister Campbell the silent treatment.

He couldn't help but wonder, now, whether he could expect anonymous recompense for persuading Roosevelt to plead guilty to a lesser included offense. He must continue hoping that Hathaway will forever think that Mario Constanza killed Archy Howell. That would be a sufficient reason for Hathaway to offer a plea deal and to put some money in his own pocket.

"I don't care what the damn FBI interview says." Sonny was furious. "Since when do we believe a seasoned hit man when he denies that he filled a contract he had to murder somebody, somebody whose name he says he doesn't even remember. Oh hell, he doesn't even remember what Archy looked like."

Sonny was sharing information and private thoughts with the only person he could trust to never reveal them to anybody, not even to the best of her friends. Rochelle responded in what she believed was truly a sensible manner. "But aren't you missing the point? Just suppose Constanza wakes up again and persists in denying he killed an unnamed victim. Ed Wilson could never get what's in that interview or even a courtroom statement into evidence in a million years—not when it's about an unnamed victim. The judge would have to find it irrelevant. Wilson couldn't even mention it in his opening statement. Piercy would declare a mistrial and he would be correct in doing so."

"Like I keep telling you, you should be the lawyer in the family."

At a summit meeting in San Francisco of the gambling syndicate, Peter Smith tried to reassure Douglas McNamara that he would see to it that Mario Constanza would not live to see the inside of a Hagerstown courtroom.

"I hope you know what you're talking about. How easy it would be for Hathaway to make a deal with him if he wakes up again to testify against me. And you've got to worry about that too. If he says that it was me who made a contract with him to kill Howell, a jury would ask themselves why. Then Hathaway would hook me up to our little gang here and the whole thing will blow up in our faces. They'd draw a straight line from Hagerstown to Las Vegas, take one look at the stats and see how suddenly the Suns started to play three hundred ball. Then they haul Edith Howell, along with the other two, into court with their fat bank accounts, all of them having had the same clever lawyer, and we can trade our thousand dollar suits for some with black and white stripes."

"He'll never wake up again. I told you that. The plans are already made."

Charlie Tomlinson interrupted, "And we're not using any more Detroit hit men. We found a fat ugly nurse who has constant access to the intensive care room where they have the Wop bedded down, and . . ."

Salvatore Valente said nastily, "I'll let that slide, Charlie. You ever call me that and I'll cut your damn dick off."

"All it meant on Ellis Island was *With Out Papers*. You got no sense of humor Sal."

"You heard me. And you can bet your last nickel, I meant it."

Charlie continued, "Anyway this gal has been a nurse for thirty years. She's married to a made guy in Detroit. We paid him a twenty-five grand bonus to have her come aboard. She guarantees she'll have a poison med bottle made up, and switch labels from a real med bottle, and somebody else will unwittingly put the bad stuff in his feeding tube and he'll be dead within three hours. This'll happen in the nighttime and she'll be able to retrieve the plastic med bottle and it will be in the hospital incinerator before morning. The stuff won't show up in an autopsy either, so she tells us."

McNamara grumbled. "Sounds too simple."

Mark Greenberg was consoling. "You're too cynical, Dougie. You gotta have some faith."

"I'll have some faith when I'm walking around a free man five years from now."

Mark responded, "The fat nurse knows what happens to people who rat on the mob. He'll probably not wake up to testify again anyway. The doctors say that it was a miracle that he woke up the first time . . . one in a thousand odds. And your plan to fix a plea with the State's Attorney and the Public Defender will back us up just fine. The jig will go to the poky for a long time, not you."

Pete warned, "We'll all communicate with each other only when essential through the manager of *Universal* for the indefinite future."

O.K., no sense in worrying about it anymore tonight. I think I'll get some drinks and see a little of San Francisco. For some reason I don't think I'm going to miss Vegas—too much stress and strain back there."

Pete tried to joke. "Splittin' up is the only way to go. So we'll all say so-long, now. My strong advice to all of you is, *Don't take any wooden nickels.*"

No one laughed.

PART TWO

Federal Trial

CHAPTER TWELVE

It was the middle of September, the time of Rosh Hashana. Sarah Greenberg was devoutly Jewish. She had lived in East New York all of her life. That part of Brooklyn was mostly populated with Jews. The smarter children in her particular neighborhood went to Thomas Jefferson High School. Her only son, Mark Greenberg, was one of them.

After high school, he went on to Law School at New York University but flunked out in his first year. His despondency over that stumbling block was mostly due to the disappointment that his poor legal scholarship inflicted upon his mother. In fact, despite his later, hugely successful criminal ways, his mother continued to be his conscience. He found it very difficult to communicate with her, but sent her a substantial financial stipend each and every month.

In September 1982, he found himself in desperate need of avoiding arrest by the federal authorities. It occurred to him that he hadn't been back to East New York for more than twenty years. Either his mother would throw him out or she would welcome him with open arms and cry like a baby—more likely the latter.

The apartment doorbell rang. Sarah Greenberg put down a large wooden stirring spoon, wiped her hands on her apron, and went to the door. What she saw through the peephole in the door, confused her at first. The grotesque and elongated features of a man's face that bore resemblance to the face of her only son made her gasp.

"Open the door, Mama. It's your son, Mark."

Sarah anxiously undid the four assorted locks on her door, and let her son turn the knob to let himself in.

He was carrying two large suitcases. She thought, *Is he coming or going? When did he come back to the city? Dear God, I hope he's coming to stay.*

Once inside, Mark stood there in front of her without saying a word. Sarah said, "I must sit down."

She turned and walked slowly into the living room and sat in a cushioned straight-backed chair next to a small table that bore a lamp and a box of

Kleenex. She pulled one tissue from the box and tried, unsuccessfully to dry her eyes. Finally, she broke down and wept uncontrollably.

"Oh God, Mama. Don't cry. I'm here to stay with you for a little while, if you'll let me."

"Come here, son."

He went to her and kneeled beside her. Awkwardly, she took his head in her lap and kissed him furiously on his hair and face.

Then suddenly, in a sarcastic tone, she said, "You should come to me now, after all these years, and tell me you're going to stay with me for a little while? What's the matter? Are you being chased by the police or are some of your fellow criminals after you?"

"You want me to go?"

"I want you to stay. What are mothers for?"

"Have you got an extra room?"

"Yes, but it's got a sewing machine in it."

He laughed softly. "I'll make you a new dress. That one looks a little old."

"Old is comforting. New is irritating. When old becomes new it breaks my heart—all over again. What are you doing here?"

"*Rosh Ashana and Yom Kipur*. I want to atone for my sins."

"You think that's possible?"

"Cook me a *Sederim* and we'll find out."

"You and I would be eating alone."

"Just like old times."

She looked into his eyes and saw tears. He stood and turned away, going back to his suit cases. He picked them both up and asked, "Where should I put these?"

"Underneath the bed in that room over there."

He went to the room, opened the door, and suddenly realized that it was his own room from his childhood.

Hathaway was getting more nervous with each passing day. Finally, he called Ed Wilson and asked him if he was prepared to make a deal at the pre-trial scheduled for the following week.

"See if he'll plead straight up to First degree, if I eliminate the death penalty. That should look pretty good to him right about now."

"Second would look a lot better. Your case against him has more holes in it than a Chinese checkerboard. Remember that little surprise package in Detroit that could surprise the world all over again any day, now, by waking up and coming clean."

"Oh no! If I agree to Second, the next thing you'll come back with is manslaughter."

"No. I really think I could talk him into Second."

"Talk to him . . . then call me back."

"I'll do that yet today."

"Goodbye, Ed."

"Talk to you later, Winston."

A federal grand jury brought in a True Bill stating a finding that there was probable cause to bring several charges against the *Minor League Wagering Team,* as the defendants in the game-fixing conspiracy came to be nicknamed. All five principals were charged with one count each of conspiracy to violate the Wire Wagering Statute and a second charge of racketeering. Peter Smith was charged additionally with an attempt to violate the civil rights of Mario Constanza. Douglas McNamara was charged with soliciting the violation of the civil rights of Archy Howell. Salvatore Valente was charged with first degree kidnapping under the federal statute. The racketeering charges were dropped. Trial was set for several months hence. The trial date could change at a pretrial hearing which would be held to handle housekeeping details.

Chester Roosevelt had no difficulty in communicating with his fellow inmates. In the course of a typical day he talked openly with inmates in nearby cells by shouting when necessary. Guards paid little or no attention to what was said to one another by these half-crazed prisoners who had nothing better to do than talk all kinds of jail nonsense.

"Leroy. . . . Leroy. . . . I need you to tell your lawyer something. You're going to see Mister Campbell, today, aren't you?"

"Yeah, man. He wants to go over my whole case with me today."

"Tell him that they want me to make a deal, will you? This is important, man, so don't forget. Say, **they want me to make a deal.** O.K.?"

"Good as done, Chet."

"I got your message." Sonny and Chester Roosevelt sat opposite one another in a lawyer's visiting room. "When did he pass on Hathaway's proposal?"

Roosevelt answered, "Late, yesterday afternoon. He started out with a bunch of gobble de goop about why I should plead guilty to first degree murder. . . . My God! First degree murder! . . . Tell that judge I did something I didn't do just because Hathaway would take away the death penalty? He might as well leave the death penalty where it is if they want me to spend the rest of life in a place like this."

"What did you tell Wilson?"

"Just what I told you. I won't do it. . . . That's it. I won't do it."

"Let me say that I would have told him exactly the same thing. God knows, it's not the way I would ever practice law. I still believe, more than ever, that you didn't do this thing. And it's my opinion that the only reason he wants you to plead is for **his** benefit, not yours. He's either too lazy to go to battle for you, or too frightened to do it, or has gotten into the habit of pleading his clients, not defending them. And I would say these things if he were sitting right here in this room. Now, what was his response to your refusal to plead guilty?"

"He started singing a different tune. As it stands now he wants me to beg Mister Hathaway for a second degree plea and tells me that that way I would some day get out of prison after I serve out a long sentence, or that I might even get a parole and get out earlier."

"How do you feel about that?"

"I'm not going to do that either. **I didn't kill Mister Howell.** Only God and you seem to understand that. I would end my own life before I would plead to even a misdemeanor. I hope that's what you expected to hear when you came down here."

"Exactly, except for the suicide. And let me tell you, Chet, you are a proud man with the right kind of ideals. I believe you have the courage to stand up for trial no matter what the charge turns out to be.

"I will never change my mind. Even if the good Mister Hathaway reduces the charge without me begging him to do it. **I will never play his game, never, never, never."**

"We don't need to talk any more. I will sleep better tonight, Chet."

"And I'll include you when I start to pray tonight."

Wilson called the State's Attorney back. "Winston, he won't plead to anything you have to offer and I'm just as disappointed as you are. I think I know why. I asked the deputy in the lawyer's visitation room if he had any recent visitors and found out what I suspected. Sonny Campbell, in violation of a court order, spoke to my client today. I believe he is responsible for Roosevelt being so unreasonable. And my secretary is right now preparing a motion to have him be held in contempt of a court order. It won't do any good, I suppose, because Roosevelt seems to be resolute in his non-cooperation."

"Sorry to hear the bad news, Ed. Nothing will help the situation now. Better get back to work. We both have our work cut out for us now."

"I haven't given up, Winston. I just can't believe that a man like Roosevelt really would face death when he can accept the offer of a lesser punishment."

"That may be the mistake in thinking that we're both making."

Joe Beyerly was about to leave for lunch, when his secretary's phone rang. "He's just leaving for lunch Mister Libwire. I'll see if I can stop him. **"Joe, Joe. You're wanted on the telephone, line five. Mister Libwire, the D.A. in Las Vegas."**

Joe picked up the receiver and pressed the line-five button. "Mister Libwire. How in the world are you?"

Just wanted to give you a heads up, Joe. Are you going to be free any time tomorrow afternoon?"

"Sure, the whole afternoon, if it's business."

"I'm sending a detective from this office to interview you about the work you did at McNamara's hotel when you were last out here."

"What time does his plane land in Hagerstown."

"One forty-five in the afternoon."

"I'll pick him up at the airport. Tell him to look for the best looking man in the waiting crowd. He can't miss me."

"I always thought you were full of yourself, Joe. I'll tell him to look for you. Wear some bib overalls, and he'll find you. Or do you guys all wear overalls up there?"

"Will a pin striped suit do? Not many of those in this little town."

"His name is Dave Marra. You should wear one of those welcome signs."

Five years earlier, Peter Smith had quietly and secretly purchased a small villa in Jamaica, anticipating just such a predicament as he was now facing. He inconspicuously flew coach class from San Francisco to Montego Bay on the day after the baseball-fixing conspirators last parted company. He was dressed like a typical tourist and carried his own bags to the Hertz counter where he had previously arranged to rent, for an unlimited time, the smallest vehicle available.

His villa was located half-way between Ocho Rios and the airport at Montego Bay. He had made no previous effort to hire a house boy or cook. His plan was to make his presence in Jamaica as inconspicuous as possible. He would suffer the inconvenience of doing his own cooking and housekeeping for the indefinite future.

He saw to it, while still in San Francisco, that the telephone in the villa would be made operational on the day of his arrival in Montego Bay. His first undertaking was to call a previously determined number of a nearby grocery store to order provisions including an ample supply of assorted liquors. A grocery store delivery was made within an hour of his telephone call.

Part of his plan to be unnoticed was to make no long distance phone calls during his tenure at the villa in Jamaica. He would stay in touch with the outside world by use of a sophisticated radio that long ago he had installed. The short-wave radio would allow regular communication with the manager of the *Universal Lounge* in Las Vegas. He spent what was left of that first day, drinking rum and Seven Up. He was sound asleep by nine o'clock, Eastern Standard Time.

Sonny addressed the court politely, "Your Honor, in defense of this claim of contempt of court, I wish to advise you that it was the defendant Roosevelt himself who requested urgently that I come to see him. When I got down to the visiting room I learned why. The public defender now has the duty, which was formerly mine, to protect the defendant's rights and to pursue his cause with zeal—and I quote the Canon to that effect. Mister Wilson is attempting to apply unreasonable pressure to get Mister Roosevelt to accept a plea offer of the State's Attorney which the defendant deemed to be oppressive. . . . And retrospectively I find myself agreeing with him. On the contrary, my refusal to talk to Mister Roosevelt would have run contrary to the duties any lawyer might have toward any one in legal trouble."

Judge Piercy interrupted, "It's sort of a Good Samaritan rule that you believe you should abide by. I mean it makes you a volunteer when my Order forbade you to do that very thing."

"Even God approved of what the Good Samaritan did for a person in distress."

"You have a smooth tongue, Mister Campbell, and some day it's going to get you into a heap of difficulty."

"I'm in a heap of difficulty now, your Honor, but my difficulty doesn't even approach the level of difficulty that defendant Roosevelt is presently trying to rescue himself from."

"You mean that the mere fact that Mister Wilson is exerting his best efforts to make his client follow his advice, is a difficulty from which Mister Roosevelt needs to rescue himself?"

"Exactly that, your Honor."

"Well, Mister Campbell you've come mighty close to be contemptuous of my Order. But I don't see where you've done any harm. In an excess of caution, I'm going to amend my Order to include the phrase, *that he shall not intentionally be within a conversational distance of defendant Roosevelt.* Do you understand what my Order now forbids?"

"Yes, your Honor. I do."

"Court adjourned."

Charlie Tomlinson, although, like the others had not yet been arrested, was now a named defendant in a federal indictment. He was also a defiant man. He did not believe that the FBI could possibly have any evidence that would ultimately prove he was a part of any conspiracy. He had meticulously avoided to openly do any act that would tie him into furthering the claimed conspiracy. As far as he was concerned, anything in the indictment to the contrary had to be false.

"I'm not going to hide from anybody. Bring 'em on. My lawyers will make them look foolish."

Federal authorities accommodated Tomlinson's invitation to *bring 'em on* almost immediately after he made his defiant speech. He was arrested by U.S. Marshals when he disembarked from a private airplane the morning after he said goodbye to his four compatriots in San Francisco. He was hostile to everybody he encountered, from the Marshals who put handcuffs on his wrists behind his back, to the jail attendants who took his fingerprints at the Baltimore County Detention Center. The BCDC is the oldest detention center in the country and living conditions for the inmates there are deplorable. For Charlie, those conditions were insufferable.

He retained the services of two lawyers who had superior reputations in the field of sports wagering fraud. His earlier calculation, that his lawyers would make the federal authorities look foolish, was to miss the mark at the very first stage of the proceedings against him. Bail was set at two million dollars. Bail through a Baltimore bonding company was readily provided for the still defiant Charlie Tomlinson.

The two guards at Mario Constanza's intensive care room at Henry Ford Hospital were still on duty. They were relieved by other guards every eight hours. All the guards had become familiar with all regular official visitors to Constanza's room. Some visitors came and went without being stopped or searched. One visitor, a nurse, married to the Mafia member, saw her chance to place a tainted bottle of nutrients into Constanza's intensive care supply cupboard sometime in the middle of the night. Unknown to her, a fellow nurse, a young man, discovered the original nutrient bottle without a label in a waste container that was scheduled for burning. A full nutrient bottle without a label was a conspicuously rare item in the Henry Ford Hospital, especially on the intensive care floor. The nurse possessed the wisdom to report his discovery to the head intensive-care nurse who reported it to one of the police guards who, in turn, reported the incident to the FBI.

An emergency behind-the-scene investigation was conducted of all persons who had access of any kind to Constanza's room. The investigation revealed the identity of the nurse's Mafioso husband and brought the nurse under close scrutiny. The cupboard in Constanza's room was examined and its contents removed. The bottles were subjected to analysis. The nurse was detained pending the outcome of the analysis, which, of course, revealed the slow acting, but fatal poison.

Salvatore Valente did not make the mistake of immediately seeking the help and protection of any of the Mafia cells in the country. In 1982, Paul Castellano was then the head of the Gambino family in New York City. He was still three years away from being assassinated in a plot masterminded by John Gotti. Castellano and Valente grew up together in Hell's Kitchen. There was a strong sentimental attachment between the two. Valente knew enough about mob protocol to first check out the political status of the Gambino family. He needed to know where his friend Paul stood in its hierarchy. He was one of a few who forecast the violent killing of Castellano in 1985.

Valente contacted Castellano. He explained he was being sought by federal authorities and outlined the baseball game-fixing scenario. He proposed that if he could depend on Castellano's protection he would seek to stay close to John Gotti for the indefinite future and warn his friend Paul of any danger presented by the *Teflon Don*. Castellano, who trusted very few of his minions, agreed readily.

Gotti, who was told that Valente was on the lam, suggested to the fugitive that for the time being he could live with Vinnie Pasterino, a less significant member of the mob. This lasted until Valente was recognized on a surveillance tape of the Gambino family coming and going to the Bergin Hunt and Fish Club, in Ozone Park in Queens, N.Y.C. He was followed and abruptly arrested a week later.

The conspirators were now falling like bowling pins. The BCDC in Baltimore, Maryland, had another temporary inmate. Judge Samuel Zavitz set Valente's bail at two million dollars. The Fleetwood Bonding Company of Baltimore provided bail within an hour of his arraignment.

The FBI was diligent in its search for the remaining members of the *Minor League Wagering Team* who were at large. They considered every possible person and hiding place, including childhood friends and relatives. The agent who one day knocked on Sarah Greenberg's apartment door, actually felt sorry for the nice old lady.

"Is that you Mark?"

"Yes, Mother."

Although suspicious of the peculiar use of the word *mother*, Sarah unlocked the four locks and opened the door. The agent shoved his credentials into Sarah's face. She didn't scream or show any other verbal form of distress.

"I knew this day would come. He isn't here. I never know when to expect him. You better come in and sit down. It may be hours."

Shortly after midnight there was a loud knock on the door. The agent undid the locks and opened the door. Mark Greenberg was already running down the hall, having not heard his mother ask the familiar, *Is that you, Mark?* The relatively young agent took chase. He caught up to Greenberg in the first stairwell going down and wrestled him to the stairs. Greenberg hit his head on the sharp edge of one stair and later had to be treated for a deep gash to the forehead. Now he sat in his mother's favorite straight backed cushioned chair with a towel around his head and muttered, "This is where I was born and this is where I almost died. Hey, Mister FBI . . . You got a cigarette?"

"Sure." Greenberg was handed a cigarette and the agent used his Zippo lighter to light it for him. "You better enjoy this. You got a long flight to Baltimore ahead of you and they don't allow smoking on this particular plane."

"Yeah. Like I said, this is where I was born and this is where my life will change forever."

Sarah Greenberg sat on the couch and didn't cry. "As far as I'm concerned your life changed forever twenty years ago."

Mark Greenberg had traveled a different route, but wound up at the same destination as did Charlie Tomlinson and Salvatore Valente—the BCDC in Baltimore, Maryland. He was arraigned at the United States District Court, Baltimore Division. Judge Samuel Zavitz, was an avid baseball fan. "Given what you're charged with and your alleged assault on this nation's pastime, Mister Greenberg, I'm tempted to set your bail at a prohibitive amount, but the law will not allow me to do that. Your bail is set at two million dollars. Now we have a trio of apparent experts who probably can bring us all up to speed on the game of baseball. I look forward to the schooling."

There was no way of knowing how many of the world's population knew that the National Security Agency was listening to every word spoken on earth, into telephones, radio receivers, television sets, and other communication devices. It was as if there were millions of amateur ham-radio enthusiasts all over the globe equipped with ear phones that intercepted all the spoken words that moved along wires and through the air, to be transmitted in turn to the N.S.A. facility at Fort Mead, Maryland. Not that it was from mouth directly to ear, but there were computers, which would pick up the raw data and then send it to other computers that looked for key words like *nuclear* or *Fort Benning* or *kidnap* or *oil facility* and the like, then save them to be filtered again by operators who would separate the wheat from the chaff, and if lucky, they would glean valuable intelligence from the billions of words collected.

In late January 1983, the words *Universal Lounge* made their journey through the filtering process and wound up on someone's desk at N.S.A. This led to an expert N.S.A. clerk's identification of Federal Court records and the name of Peter Smith, at large from a pending criminal case in Baltimore, Maryland. The raw intercepted message was produced by a radio in Jamaica.

A team of five FBI agents was sent to the popular tourist spot to methodically search the island with electronic eavesdropping equipment. In the morning of the fifth day after their arrival in Jamaica, one of the agents hit pay dirt. Peter Smith had radioed another member of his syndicate to inquire about the status of the federal case against him and the others. Forty-five minutes after he had turned his radio equipment off, he was apprehended in the living room of his villa. His name joined a list of his fellow conspirators at the Baltimore County Detention Center on the same day of his arrest.

Like them, he spent little time at the wretched BCDC. He was soon freed on bail of two million dollars of his own money. Bail was set by Federal District Judge Samuel Zavitz, who would preside over the trial of all members of the *Minor League Wagering Team.*

Sonny Campbell sat alone in Smitty's bar. Rochelle was visiting her mother in Durham, North Carolina.

Smitty asked, "Where's Rocky?"

"She's visiting her mother."

"It's none of my business, but what happened to her father?"

"Lost to cancer ten years ago."

"That kind of thing is always sad, Sonny. I know. I lost my father that way. Have you read this morning's paper?"

"Just the explosive headlines."

"How come it didn't come out earlier?"

"I think the Baltimore District Court has been keeping this thing under wraps. They didn't want this scandal to blacken the name of Hagerstown's favorite sons, no pun intended, until they absolutely had to. You know how vicious the news media can be."

"But why now? Why did the paper come out with this trash now?"

"Somebody must have leaked the story."

Smitty, wet towel in hand, had just opened the front doors of his establishment. "I'll wager you miss the baseball season. . . . Don't fret. Only three months to go before it begins again. . . . Oh shit, I shouldn't use that word around my friend, the public defender."

"What word?"

"Wager."

Both men laughed.

"The paper didn't give many details."

Sonny said, "The details will be in tomorrow morning's paper, probably all over the country. After all, who would have imagined that minor league baseball games would ever be fixed? It's going to be a media feeding frenzy."

"Bet you've got the details. You do, don't you?"

"Oh, I suppose it won't hurt anything if I tell you what I've heard. But do me a favor, will you? Not a word to anybody till tomorrow afternoon and the nation has had a chance to read for themselves."

"Mums the word."

"The feds got 'em all except McNamara now. A guy by the name of Peter Smith was picked up in Jamaica last week."

"Worry not, my friend. They'll find McNamara, bye and bye."

"He's got no family. If he had, they'd already have him. Most people can't resist contacting their spouses or their children when they're on the lam."

Smitty took another swipe at the bar, just in case he missed a spot the first time. "Like I said. They'll find him. He's probably got an irresistible girlfriend in some secluded rendezvous hideaway. Where they got those guys stashed, anyway?"

"They're not. They're all out on bail. Two million dollars each. So far, they're going to be tried together by Judge Samuel Zavitz in the U.S. District Court, *Ballamore* Division."

"You pronounce that like a native."

"What?"

"*Ballamore.*"

"Sometimes, when I'm not concentrating."

"That almost takes care of all the bums at the top of this scheme. What about Livingston and Black? Players are a part of this slimy conspiracy, aren't they?"

"Both of them pleaded guilty to one count of criminal conspiracy to violate the Wire Wagering Statute. That's been under wraps, too. The rumor is they made a deal with the U.S. Attorney and they're gonna testify against the big guys."

"Will they go to jail?"

"No. They get no jail time. This is a first offense for both of them. No jail is part of the deal. And they each have to donate the money that McNamara paid them, or what's left of it, to the Y.M.C.A. Black has to sell his new house and throw the proceeds into the pot. For some reason Judge Zavitz really doesn't like Bucky Livingston. Bucky only has about thirty five thousand left of the McNamara money. He'll be ordered to sign an I.O.U for fifteen thousand, payable to the Y, and the note can't be discharged in bankruptcy by the terms of the order. One thing's for sure. None of them will ever play professional baseball again."

"When do they get sentenced?"

"Some time after the feds pick up McNamara, which should happen in the near future."

"This is like reading the *Ballamore Legal News*."

"There's no such thing."

"Whatever. Don't be so damn serious all the time. What happened to the famous Campbell sense of humor. You miss Rocky, don't you? How are other things downtown?"

"Not good. I thought that when Constanza woke up and they took his statement, he'd a' given Chet a perfect defense by confessing. I saw an FBI letter last week that said Constanza *resolutely* denies killing Archy. I guess we gotta hope and pray that he wakes up again and this time comes clean."

"You're just being lazy. You have no right to have a perfect defense fall into your lap. You gotta work for it, son. You gotta work for it."

"I know that. It's just that now I don't know where to start, since Piercy has put the kybosh on my ever talking to Chet again."

"Can't you pick Joe Beyerly's brains? I understand that's how they got Constanza's name."

"I've almost forgotten about Joe. But that's a good angle. I'll talk to Walter Brock on Monday. He's got an in with Joe."

"And I haven't heard anything about those other two Negroes who were in the café that night—not since the killing happened. You know, it always seems to work out that way. Our Negro friends suddenly turn invisible when the chips are down. I'm surprised that even a guy like you doesn't seem to realize that. Go talk to those guys will you?"

"I'll get Brock to do it. I'm under orders from Judge Piercy not to pursue Chet's defense personally, at least that's how Wilson interprets Piercy's Order. . . . I need another beer."

Smitty brought the beer. "It looks like it's gettin' pretty busy. I better get back to work. See you next Saturday, if not sooner." He disappeared into the accumulating crowd.

Joe Beyerly stood in the crowd waiting for Dave Marra to disembark. Only one passenger was well tanned, and Joe surmised that that must be Marra. He was wrong. "Are you Dave Marra?"

"No, sir."

Another man, a little farther back in the disembarking line laughed loud enough to attract Joe's attention.

"It was the guy's suntan, wasn't it? Can't blame you. Any detective would have gone for the suntan. You Joe Beyerly? I'm the real Dave Marra. I stay indoors most of the time in Las Vegas."

"I'm embarrassed," said Joe. The two men shook hands.

"Follow me to the baggage carousel."

"No luggage, Joe. I'm not going to be here overnight. My flight home leaves at nine o'clock."

"Well, let's go to my car, then. It's not far."

They drove to the State's Attorney's building on West Washington Street, a few doors down from the courthouse.

Dave Marra made himself comfortable in Joe's office.

"You want a cup of coffee, Dave?"

"Nothing, thanks."

"Well, let's get down to business, then. What do you want to know?"

"First, let me tell you that we're expecting you to come out to Vegas to testify. We're charging Peter Smith with first degree murder. We found the housekeeper's grave in the desert. We had a tip from the inside. Our man has been in place in that syndicate's entourage ever since you went out there and asked about Smith and McNamara. He actually saw Smith kill the housekeeper with his own hand. Some of his boys did the burying. But we'll need you, in an excess of caution, to explain your part in the deal. Hope that meets with your approval."

"You know, don't you, that Smith was arrested in Jamaica a couple of weeks ago."

"To be honest with you. We were waiting for that to happen before we brought our charges."

"When do you think you'll want me."

"Oh, probably in six months or so. You know how criminal dockets can get all jammed up."

"Same problem here. We gotta guy, in a way connected to your case, whose been waiting in the Detention Center for two years to go to trial."

"Who's that . . . connected to Peter Smith?"

"Chester Roosevelt. We charged him with killing one of the players who were helping to fix games."

"You mean, Archy Howell. We've been following that case closely. I know about Roosevelt."

"I'm not surprised."

Joe then gave Marra as complete a narrative as his memory could muster, about how he got into McNamara's hotel room with the housekeepers help. "I guess I broke some search and seizure rules. Will that bring me some trouble?"

"Not a chance. You're a State's Attorney investigator, after all, and Libwire understands what an investigator must resort to at urgent times. Don't worry about search and seizure or breaking and entering or anything like that. By the way, did that piece of paper you found in McNamara's suit pay off?"

"How'd you know about that?"

"We saw it on the mob's surveillance tape. Speaking of tapes, you realize, of course, that I'm recorded this interview."

"And without my permission."

"You might have said no if I asked for your permission. You see, Las Vegas sometimes breaks laws too."

Both men laughed.

"Well, that's it, Joe. I'm going to get some dinner now. Care to join me?"

"Better than that. Have dinner with me and my wife. I'll call her and we'll pick her up and take you to a dandy place to eat. You'll love it, I promise."

"Sounds great."

After dinner at LJ's steak house the three talked over drinks until it was time to take Dave Marra to the airport. Marra thanked Joe and was gone back to Las Vegas as quickly as he had come.

CHAPTER THIRTEEN

Douglas McNamara was hiding in Stratford, Canada. In his life's journey he had met and fallen in love with an actress. That was in Chicago, some eight years ago. After a month he had abandoned her. She was still in love with him, but not *vice versa*.

He had decided that the best way to handle his desperate situation now was to travel inconspicuously to Stratford and surprise his ex-lover. On arrival he checked in at the Victoria Inn, an older well established inn near a park. He had kept track of where she was performing and noted that she had spent the summer at Stratford doing repertory. It was October and nearing the end of the Stratford Festival Season. He checked the brochure he had obtained in the lobby of the Inn. Merideth Ostrowski was appearing as Ophelia in Othello at the Avon Theater in downtown Stratford, one of four theaters that composed the Stratford Festival complex.

He cased the theater before the performance and discovered through which door the players would exit. After the final curtain he hurried himself to the exit and stood alone on the sidewalk. After a brief wait he saw her with a group of several actors coming through the door.

She spotted him immediately. "Douglas. Douglas. Is that really you?"

"Yes, Merideth, it's really me."

She left the other actors and approached him slowly in a state of disbelief. "It's a shock to see you here."

"I hope, a pleasant shock."

She walked to where he was standing and stood, staring him down silently. "I don't know what to say to you."

"You're doing a pretty good job so far."

"Why? But, why? I thought I'd never see you again. Are you staying here tonight?"

"Yes, at the Victoria Inn. Where do you live? Do you live alone?"

"I'm staying with two other girls."

"Let's have a drink. Is there a place you like particularly?"

"This is my dinnertime, believe it or not. I never eat before a performance."

"Well, then. Let's go to my place and get you dinner in the dining room and me a drink."

"How could I say no to such an offer? I happen to be almost broke as we're standing here."

"It's a beautiful night. Let's walk."

"That sounds wonderful."

Twenty minutes later they were strolling through the park and towards the Inn.

She ate her small filet like a starving wolf. "This is the same wine we used to drink in Chicago. Isn't it *Frankenwein?*"

"You always had a good memory. I used to wonder how you could remember all those lines. . . . By the way your performance was exquisite tonight."

"Thanks. Does that mean you fell in love with me again?"

"I never fell out of love with you."

"Why did you leave me then?"

"The Chicago authorities were after me. I didn't leave you by choice. I escaped—one step ahead of the fuzz."

"But never even a phone call. Not one word from you for all those years . . . until now. Never mind. I've got you back again. I do have you back again, don't I?"

"Indeed, you do. From this moment on."

They woke up in his bed to the sound of a thunderstorm. "Damn! I wanted to look for a house to rent for us today."

She responded with a giggle. "You're serious, aren't you? About us, I mean?"

"Damn right, I am."

"I wouldn't mind the rain."

"Then I don't want to hear any complaints today."

He rented a small, but elegant house, for eight-hundred-fifty dollars, Canadian, a month, paying the first and last months in advance. The first two months were delightful for both parties. But the Festival season was over and Merideth was no longer in a spotlight. Gradually the bloom came off the rose. Merideth had become less attractive to him off stage than on. He became disenchanted, just as he had in Chicago eight years before. He discovered that his mind couldn't shake the thought of the indictment that was waiting for him in Baltimore. Boredom caused him to make his first mistake. He telephoned the *Universal Lounge* in Las Vegas. The telephone there was, of course, tapped and traced by the FBI.

On the same day of his phone call, two agents flew to Stratford. A reverse directory gave them the address of the soon-again-to-be ex-lovers. This time the alienation might have been permanent, were it not for another need for Merideth's help that occurred months later.

McNamara submitted to arrest without protest. A lack of convenient flight connections caused a delay in their journey to Baltimore. Douglas McNamara's name was added to the so-called *Minor League Wagering Team* roster in the Baltimore County Detention Center the next day. After processing, he was arraigned and released on two million dollars bail, which his lawyer took care of through the Fleetwood Bonding Company of Baltimore.

Rochelle said with a giggle, "Well sweetheart, we got 'em all now."

"No, we haven't. There's a killer on the loose out there, that is if Constanza told the truth in his interview. I've decided to run the risk of contempt of court and track down those two black men who were in the café that night. I've got to start somewhere. Business at the office is very slow and I've got plenty of spare time on my hands. One of those guys may have seen something I can use."

"When are you going to start this secret investigation?"

"Right away. I was going to have Walt Brock do it, but I'm too involved now not to keep my own hand in it."

"Let's see. This is Thursday. Why don't you wait till Saturday and invite me to go along. That'll give you sort of an alibi—that it's not you doing the investigation, it's your wife."

"You're just full of legal mischief, aren't you?"

"You've told me often enough that it should be me that's the lawyer in the family."

"All right. We'll start together on Saturday. Our point of departure will be Smitty's."

"What happened to *no drinkin' on the job*?"

"You won't be drinking anything, my dear. Nothin', you understand? You're the one who's working this caper, not me."

"Deal. Not a drop for me until I'm finished working."

Sonny drove. Rochelle talked. "The reason this will probably work is that it was Walter Brock who did the interview of the waitress and the cook the first time. They both wouldn't know either one of us from a load of coal."

"You're right, but I still want you to do most of the talking. I'm not too good at playacting. You, on the other hand, should have an Academy Award for some of the theater I've seen you pull off."

He pulled up directly in front of Carmine's café. "How's that for parking Karma?"

They took seats at the counter. Versie Dugger was on duty. She slapped two menus down in front of the Campbells. "Be right back, folks."

Rochelle responded, "We're in no hurry."

And they purposely showed that they were not in any hurry. In fact, they wanted to be the last people left at the counter during this busy lunch hour.

Moments later Versie was back with two glasses of water held adeptly in one hand, and silverware for two held in the other. "I'll give you a couple of minutes with those menus."

After another brief interval, she was back. "O.K., now, what would you like to have today?"

"I want two B.L.T.s with lots of mayonnaise and a large glass of milk," answered Sonny. "A B.L.T. for me, too, light on the mayo and a small coke."

Versie scribbled their order quickly into her pad. "Comin' up."

It took ten minutes for Oscar the cook to prepare the sandwiches. Versie brought them to the Campbells and went back to the far end of the counter for their drinks. Rochelle and Sonny ate slowly. He ordered apple pie *a la mode*. She had no dessert. By the time they had finished their lunches the counter was almost vacated.

Rochelle blurted out, "Were you on duty last June when that guy got murdered?"

"Hey! That guy wasn't murdered in here. He was shot with a shotgun downtown, somewhere."

"We heard a black guy killed him."

"I beg your pardon, madam. A black guy didn't kill him."

"There were some black guys in here that night, weren't there?"

"Oh, some of our regular customers are black. The guy they're holding is black. His name is Chester Roosevelt and he's a sweetheart. Wouldn't hurt a fly. Neither would the other two guys. Timmy and Bobby have been coming in here for years. Just like Chet. Chet used to be a busboy in here."

Rochelle said, "Seems like they always pick on the Negroes in this town."

"Not just here. Anywhere in this country, if it's a choice between a Negro and a white man, the police will pick the Negro most of the time. This time they really got the wrong man. If you ask me, it was that Bucky Livingston they should have nabbed. He's the one that was causing all the trouble in here that night."

Sonny asked, "Doesn't he play on our baseball team?"

"Yeah. He used to come in here a lot. Come to think of it, I haven't seen him in here since that night. Scuse me folks," she said, as she totaled their bill. "I'm due for a smoke break. Here's your tab."

While she was gone, presumably outside in the cold for an habitual cigarette, Oscar the cook came out from the kitchen to tend the cash register.

Rochelle picked up the tab and the two went to the register. Oscar quickly took up a position behind it. "How was everyting, folks?"

"Fine. Say, do you know either Timmy or Bobby who come in here a lot."

"Shur do, ma'am. Dey's Timmy Aadams and Bob Haading. Nice black fellows. Dey in some kinda troubles?"

"Not at all. I'm sure they're very nice fellows."

On the way out, Sonny left a two dollar tip for Versie Dugger.

They drove home to Beaver Creek. Sonny quickly pulled the Hagerstown phonebook from under a kitchen counter. "That's Timothy Adams and Robert Harding, right?"

"I think that would be it."

He leafed through the pages. "Yeah, here's a Robert Harding."

He wrote the name, address and phone number on a small piece of paper. Then he found a Timothy Adams and did the same. He handed the piece of paper to Rochelle. "You better do the honors? You seem to be on a roll."

She dialed the Adams number. "Mister Adams, I'm Rocky Campbell and I'm representing Chester Roosevelt today. You know him, don't you?"

"Yes, ma'am."

"Right. Are you busy today? Chet wants me to talk to you for a few minutes."

"Ya know where my house is?"

"Yes, I know where you live."

"Ya got a car?"

"Right. See you in twenty minutes."

It was decided that Rochelle would talk to Timothy Adams all by herself. His address was in Funkstown. He was married and his wife came to the door. Sonny stayed in the car."

"Hello, I have an a appointment to talk to Timothy Adams."

"What's your name?"

"Rocky Campbell."

"What you want to talk to him about?"

"Chet Roosevelt."

"Come on in."

Rochelle took a few steps and found herself in a tiny living room. A few moments later Timmy Adams joined her. They sat side by side on a threadbare couch. Rochelle had a yellow legal pad with her, ready to take notes.

"I'm Rocky. Chet wants to know what you saw and what you did the morning he got arrested for killing that baseball player."

"He didn't kill nobody."

"How do you know?"

"I knows Chet. He didn't kill nobody."

"Did you see the fight in Carmine's?"

"Tweren't no fight . . . Jes a little scuffle. I kept my back to it, drinkin' my coffee."

"Did you hear anybody say *nigger* or *jig* or *spade* or bad words like that in Carmine's?"

"Weren't no words like dat spoke in der dat night."

"How did the scuffle end?"

"Oscar broke 'em up and chased Chet out da place for his own good."

"What did you do?"

"He didn't have to chase me out. I know when to get away from a scuffle between one of ours and a white man."

"You left too?"

"Yes, ma'am."

"Did you see where Chet went?"

"Round da corner towards his house."

"You know where he lives?"

"Yes, ma'am."

"What else did you see."

"I saw a car parked right out front wid a driver in it. And den I saw another car dat looked like it was following Chet."

"What kind of a car?"

"One of dem little cars, kinda all banged up. It had funny stick lights comin' out the side each door. I never saw dem kinda lights before. They pointed out when the car made a turn to follow Chet and den went back down again when the car straightened out."

"Is that the last you saw of Chet, running around the corner and towards his house?"

"Yes, ma'am."

"Thank you, Mister Adams. That's all I have today."

"Yes, ma'am. Say hello to Chet when you sees him again."

"I'll do that. Bye for now."

"*Mox Nix,*" said Sonny as they drove home. "The G.I.s corrupted the German expression, *Es macht Nichts* to *Es mox nix,* in the early fifties. They may still do it, for all I know. Well anyway, the turn signals on German cars back in the thirties, forties and some in the early fifties, were finger-like sticks about eight inches long just ahead of the front doors. They were lighted at night, one on the left and one on the right. They would flip out when you operated them from inside the car. The Americans called these devices *mox nix sticks.* There's supposed to be a joke in there someplace."

"I didn't know what the hell Timmy was talking about. But he did say he saw those lighted sticks when the banged-up car was making a left turn to follow Chet. And as I said, he confirmed there were no racial slurs in the café when the fight broke out."

"Let me take the next one. You still got Harding's phone number?" Sonny said as they walked up the path to their front door."

Inside, she handed him the small piece of paper with Bobby Harding's number on it. He dialed the number.

"Mister Harding?"

"He don't live here no more. Lives in Mississippi."

"Where does he live in Mississippi?"

"Columbus."

"Do you have his phone number in Columbus?"

"Yes, suh."

"Let me write that down."

Sonny wrote down and then dialed the number. A woman answered.

"Mister Harding, please. This is Sonny Campbell, friend of Chester Roosevelt in Hagerstown."

A man came on the line. "Who's that?"

"Hello, Mister Harding. This is Sonny Campbell. I'm calling you from Hagerstown. Chet Roosevelt asked me to call you. . . . It's about that fight in Carmine's café back in June."

"What about it?"

"Chet wants you to tell me what you saw and heard that night."

"I ain't seen nothin' or heard nothin'."

"You must have seen something."

"Nothin', I told ya."

"Don't you want to help Mister Roosevelt? He's in big trouble."

"I don't want no trouble. If I tell something' you want ta hear you're goin' to haul me back up to Maryland. I don't want to go back up there."

"If you tell me something I want to hear, I'll come down there."

There was a long silence. Then Harding spoke again.

"What you want ta know?"

"Did you hear any bad words describing black people in the café that night? Words like *nigger* or *jig?*"

"No, suh."

"I know you left the café. What did you see when you got outside?"

"A man sittin' behind the wheel of a car parked out front."

"Anything else?"

"Nother car drivin' up to the road the café's on—one of dem Vws. I was already past the corner so I ran the other way—away from Carmine's."

"Why'd you do that?"

"I lived that way."

"Did you see Mister Roosevelt anywhere?"

"He must o' turned down at his corner by the time I got out there. He lived around the corner and down a couple blocks."

"That's all for now, Mister Harding."

"You gonna come down heah to get me?"

"No sir, I'm not. Good bye, Mister Harding."

"Not so good, huh?"

"Not bad. About the same as Adams, only he saw what must have been the same VW which had to have circled the block."

"I think that was a good day's work, don't you?"

"I guess so."

A month later, the *Minor League Wagering Team* and the six lawyers they had hired to defend them, attended a pretrial conference at the Federal District Court in Baltimore. It was decided there that all five defendants would be tried at the same time. Surprisingly, that was the choice of the defendants which the U.S. Attorney consented to.

Judge Samuel Zavitz would preside over a jury trial in Baltimore, which he scheduled to commence on July 7, 1984. Back in Hagerstown, Chester Roosevelt still languished in the Detention Center waiting for the state trial to begin. Several more attempts to get him to plead to some lesser charge were made at a series of pretrial conferences scheduled by Judge Piercy's office. It was the judge's hope that Roosevelt would see the light and decide to plead. Piercy abhorred the notion of having to preside over a death penalty decision, the first of his twenty-five year career on the judiciary.

A joint private meeting of the six trial lawyers and the defendants in Baltimore resulted in an amazing defense strategy. The most eloquent of the six lawyers would give the opening statement for all five of the defendants. This was intended to show the jury a solidarity among all these men who would be identified as honest businessmen whose actions were simply misapprehended by the federal authorities. The jury would be told that these businessmen had embarked on a unique and innovative plan to form and own their own minor league baseball team. Out of necessity, they would send Mister McNamara out across the country to recruit members of existing minor league teams to join their new team which was to have become operational in the 1984 season. When a potential member was discovered, he was paid a handsome signing bonus and their commitments would be kept secret from the owners of the teams for which they were playing. All this kind of activity was illegal, of course, but that fact was irrelevant in planning and presenting the opening statement. This scheme emboldened the five defendants and all agreed to testify on their own behalf. They were simply adventurous, however reckless, businessmen who had innocently blundered into an ill-advised enterprise.

"After all," said Charles Hitesman, the lawyer chosen to give the opening statement, "all we need is for one juror to buy this cock-and-bull story and we'll at least get a mistrial. I personally think that we'll get them all to find you guys innocent beyond a reasonable doubt."

Peter Smith blustered, "My God, you've got balls, Mister. I suppose you're going to make me the CEO. of this phony minor league corporation."

"Of course. You're the CEO. of the *Universal Lounge*, aren't you? And that's another perfectly legal enterprise."

Paul Peach had been the operational manager of the *Universal Lounge* for more than seven years. Now he had a huge responsibility added to his regular job description. Under detailed instructions, surreptitiously communicated to him from Peter Smith, Peach found himself in his personal limousine speeding toward Charlotte, North Carolina.

After pleading guilty to a one count violation of the Wire Wagering Act, Bucky Livingston had moved to Charlotte and was working as a waiter in a small café called the Bowl and Spoon. He was having great difficulty going back to a life of relative poverty, after having briefly enjoyed a life of relative luxury in Hagerstown.

Peach spoke to his limousine driver. "Park in the lot. I'm going in and have a bowl of soup and talk to him a little bit."

"Yes, sir."

Peach entered the shabby café. The imitation leather covering on the booth and chair seats were, without exception, cracked beyond mending. There was an air of dirtiness about the place and patrons were smoking with impunity.

Still standing, Peach asked the cashier, "What kind of soup are you serving tonight?"

"Split pea with ham."

"Have that waiter bring me some soup to go, would you?"

She hailed a young waiter. "Yes, sir. . . . Bucky, would you take care of this customer, please?"

Livingston finished waiting on a table, then walked to the cash register. "Yes, can I help you?"

"Bowl of pea soup to go. Are you Bucky Livingston?"

"Yes, I am."

"What time do you get through here."

"In a half hour."

"How much is the soup going to be?"

"Dollar fifty."

Peach handed him a five dollar bill. "The change is your tip. I'll wait for you outside."

Livingston looked at Peach's expensive suit and heard his commanding voice register in his ears. Then he glanced into the parking lot and saw the limousine. "You want something from me? I don't do that sort of thing."

"I'm a friend of Douglas McNamara."

"What? I don't know that bastard anymore."

"You will. Bring the soup with you when you come."

Confident that Livingston would meet him at the limousine, Peach turned and left the café. He said over his shoulder, "See you in a half an hour."

"Hand the soup to the driver. Get in here boy and sit down. I'm not going to shoot you."

Livingston obeyed.

"How's life treating you, son?"

"Shitty. Rather be playing baseball in Hagerstown."

"Like to have another taste of the good life, would you? You're going to give testimony in Douglas McNamara's federal case, aren't you?"

"Yeah."

"He's getting railroaded, you know."

"Look. He paid me that money to throw baseball games. That's the long and short of it. How is he getting railroaded?"

Peach instructed his driver to drive around town for a little while. As they were leaving the parking lot, Peach started talking again.

"This time you're in for a lot of money, Bucky, my lad."

"What the hell are you talking about?"

"And the alternative is that you could meet the same fate as Archy Howell if you don't think that a quarter million dollars is attractive."

"Jeez! Really? A quarter million dollars?"

"Yes."

"I don't believe that."

"It's true."

Peach then outlined the conspirators' defense in the simplest of terms.

"So you see, all you have to do is convince that jury you liked the idea of joining the forming of a new type of minor league baseball team. You wanted to become a charter member. You signed up and received your fifty thousand dollar signing bonus. Now, would that be so hard for you to do?"

"Hard and dangerous. I already got burned once because of you guys."

"You expect a quarter million dollars for something that isn't dangerous? Where's your spirit of adventure? You don't want us to think you're a coward, do you?"

"I'm not a coward."

"Show us."

Livingston remained speechless. . . . "When would you pay me this quarter million, before or after I testify?"

"After."

"Regardless of what I say?"

"We're not going to buy a pig in a poke. But if you come down on the right side of this thing, you'll get a quarter million dollars."

"And this is not a sting? You're not with the government?"

"Don't be ridiculous."

"Yeah, the government is through hurting me now."

"Now, you're making sense."

"Are the others going to do it?"

"If you do."

"I'll do it then."

"Good boy."

"I'm not a boy."

Peach's effort with the other ex-Suns player was successful on the same terms. His calculation that *once a crook-always a crook*, was born out, probably because both of these young men had fallen on such poverty stricken conditions. He reported back to Peter Smith through the lawyers Smith had hired. "Hurrah!" said Smith. I'm getting more confident by the day. You'll see. We'll beat this thing yet."

Chester Roosevelt was not so joyous or confident of victory. For the first time he was paid a visit by his lover, Howard Parsons.

"Don't cry, lover. I still love you. But I wish you had visited me sooner. You realize you haven't seen me for more than two years. At first it almost drove me nuts, you not coming. But then the time seemed to all run together, until I got used to not having you in my arms every day."

"And you're telling me not to cry. How do you think I feel? I feel nothing but pain in my heart. . . . One thing, I want you to know. I promise you that I have been faithful to you. I will be faithful to you forever."

"Until I'm gone. Until the gas gets me, you mean?"

Parsons began to cry again, this time hysterically. Despite the glass partition that separated the two, they both stood up and placed hands opposite one another on either side of the glass.

Parsons said, "You know I love you, but I can't bear to stay here any longer. Forgive me, darling boy. I've got to leave you now. I'll come every week from now on. . . . I promise I will."

Parsons stood and left, exiting through the front door of the detention center all the while thinking, *Could he tell? Could he know that the reason I wasn't here was because there is someone else. But I don't love this other man. It's just sex. I've got to have that. How can I come to this horrible place every week? I can't, knowing that my beautiful Chester will never be mine again.*

CHAPTER FOURTEEN

None of the six attorneys representing the five defendants in the case of conspiracy to violate the federal Wire Wagering Act were licensed to practice law in the State of Maryland. Those who intended to appear in the Federal District Court would have to apply to gain temporary admission to the Maryland Bar. Their sole purpose was to represent the members of the *Minor League Wagering Team,* a name that seemed to have stuck to the group of violators.

It was decided among the *Team* and their six lawyers that only five would apply for admission, one for each defendant. Peter Smith's lawyer, Charles Hitesman, would lead the team of five and give the opening statement. Charles Tomlinson had to give up one of his two attorneys because that one had a suspended license in his background. Maryland was very particular about whom it let practice in its proud state. However, the remaining attorney had a pristine background and proved to be up to the task demanded by Mister Tomlinson.

So, five trial lawyers and five defendants, all dressed in slick and very expensive suits, assembled at three tables that stood in a straight line most distant from the jury box. The single U.S. Attorney's table was, out of long established tradition countrywide, closest to the jury.

Only one pretrial motion had been brought by the defendants—none by the U.S. Attorney. Three months before the trial was to commence in Baltimore, Charles Hitesman brought a motion for a change of venue. He argued that since the defendants were sole owners of a sports betting parlor located in Las Vegas, the State of Nevada was the only venue that this court could consider proper. The U.S. Attorney countered with the ultimately prevailing reasoning that since the actual alleged game fixing was committed in Hagerstown by the three baseball players, the District Court, Baltimore Division, was undoubtedly where jurisdiction should lie.

On the first Tuesday in August, the first day of trial commenced. Sarah Greenberg and Merideth Ostrowski, the only parties who were related or close to any of the defendants, had come to watch the trial. They were not yet acquainted, but sat next to one another in the first row behind the defendants' tables. There were only three dozen other onlookers, six of whom were members of the news media.

A U.S. Marshal acted, as was customary, as the bailiff. "*All rise. Oyez, oyez, oyez. . . . Draw nigh and listen. U.S. District Court, Baltimore Division, is now in session. . . . The right Honorable Samuel Zavitz presiding.*"

Judge Zavitz entered the courtroom directly through a door that opened behind his large leather chair. As he sat, he said, "You may be seated."

A rear door opened and a sixty person jury panel paraded into the courtroom. All took seats in the last four rows of churchlike pews.

The judge spoke in stentorian tones. "Ladies and gentlemen, I welcome you to the U.S. District Court, Baltimore Division. The exclusionary rule shall be in effect. Before we take the next step, I ask that any persons in the courtroom who know that they are going to be called as a witness in this case retire to the hallway."

Two youthful men, sitting together, stood and went out to the hall.

Judge Zavitz continued, "We are about to enter upon what we call the *voir dire.* Simply stated, we're about to ask you some questions about your personal views, attitudes and vital statistics, so that it can be determined if you're qualified, or whether we want you to act as jurors in the criminal case we have before us. I realize, of course, that that sounds intimidating, but I assure you that the attorneys and I will be respectful and gentle with this questioning process."

The bailiff called out sixteen numbers and the jury box was filled with sixteen candidates, some of whom might ultimately be seated as actual jurors. As one seat would be vacated because of the questioning process, another would take that seat. The questioning lasted for two days, largely due to the large number of defendants and the nature of the case, gambling being such a popular pastime in the world.

"Ladies and gentlemen of the jury. Sixteen of you have been chosen to listen to the evidence in this case. The law prescribes that only twelve will decide on a verdict. When all the evidence is in, the bailiff, by blind draw, will pick four of you who will be excused from further participation and thanked for performing your civic duty. Mister Bailiff would you swear the jury, please?"

The jury sworn, Zavitz then went into a long description and dissertation of preliminary instructions that would prepare the jury for what they were about to see and hear. "Now we are ready to hear opening statements. Mister Lacey, are you prepared to give your opening statement?"

Anthony Lacey, U.S. Attorney for the District of Maryland, stood and answered, "Thank you, your Honor, I am."

"Proceed."

Lacey walked to a podium that faced the jury. "Ladies and Gentlemen. I'm Tony Lacey, U.S. Attorney for the District of Maryland. It is now time for the government to give you details of this bizarre case of the fraudulent fixing of minor league baseball games. That's right, minor league baseball games! . . . Some of the defendants are charged with more serious crimes—more about that later. Now, when I have finished with this opening statement, the defense lawyer will be given the opportunity to talk about his defense. I'm told that only one of these defense lawyers will speak. But he may postpone his opening statement until after I have presented all the evidence I have for you. That's entirely up to the defense."

Lacey then proceeded to tell the incredible story of the Hagerstown Suns and the delinquency of three players who deliberately played inferior baseball to insure critical losses that would financially benefit the *Universal Lounge* betting parlor and other illegal parlors throughout the country. Most of the activities that promoted the conspiracy were committed by Douglas McNamara, but it was alleged that the other four knowingly agreed to, planned and benefited from, his criminal activities. Lacey emphasized the fact that these activities, while not rising to the fame of the 1919 Black Sox scandal, in many ways were even more reprehensible, since the scheme was such a blight on America's principal pastime and was intended to be an ongoing enterprise. He underscored the effect the conspiracy already had on the morale of Hagerstown citizens and especially how it broke the hearts of young fans who followed the Suns' games religiously. An integral part of the scheme ultimately involved the more serious crimes of kidnapping and violations of the civil rights of persons who unwittingly became a part of the game-fixing scenario.

When Lacey had finished his opening statement, Judge Zavitz then turned his attention to the defense table. "Is the defense going to speak now or will you reserve your opening until the U.S. Attorney has rested?"

"We will reserve," said Hitesman.

Zavitz said, "We will then take a half hour recess after which I will expect Mister Lacey to call his first witness."

"Well then, everyone is in his place. You may call your witness, Mister Lacey."

"The prosecution calls Joseph Libwire, District Attorney for Clark County, Nevada."

The witness was sworn and identified himself. He remained standing.

"As District Attorney, working primarily in Las Vegas, Nevada, did you have occasion to investigate the case of a Flying Eagle housekeeper who went missing in 1982?"

"Yes, I did."

"Did you ever find the lady?"

"Yes. We found her body buried in the desert."

"Did you ever discover the responsible party or parties for her death?"

"Yes. We think we know what happened to her."

"How's that? What do you think happened to her?"

"The Flying Eagle Casino has a video surveillance system. If I may, I'll show you a piece of a video tape taken on the day she went missing. Your Honor?"

"Hearing no objection from the defense table you can go ahead with your video tape."

A large video television screen was set up for easy observance by the jury. The tape, which ran with the date and exact time on the lower right hand corner of the screen, started running. Mister Libwire stood to the right of the screen with a pointer in his hand.

"The lens of the camera is located over the hotel entrance and shows the area from the front door to the elevator door. Keep your eyes on the elevator. The housekeeper, with a man holding her arm is about to get off. . . . there she is." Libwire used his pointer to focus attention on the housekeeper, her uniform covered with a raincoat, and the man holding on to her right arm. "She's not yet struggling. Now they are walking toward the front door of the hotel and she starts to struggle ever so slightly. The man turns his head toward her and appears to say something. She immediately assumes a placid, cooperative attitude. There is another camera on the outside of the entrance and shows the area where cabs and other autos pick up hotel guests." He pointed to a Negro porter who was opening the back door of a limousine. "The man, whom you will recognize as Salvatore Valente, still holds on to the housekeeper's arm, puts her forcibly into a limousine and says something to the porter."

"Is that porter available for testimony?"

"Yes, he is. We flew out here together."

"Is the man who holds on to the housekeeper's arm in this courtroom?"

"Yes, he is."

"Now, please note that the time is four twenty. And please understand that the date you see is the last time anyone observed the housekeeper in the hotel. Now, Mister Libwire, please point to the man we see on television if he is indeed somewhere in this courtroom."

Libwire pointed with his wooden pointer to one of the defendants sitting approximately in the middle of the group of five.

"You mean the man dressed in the black suit?"

"Yes, sir."

The judge interjected, "Would Mister Valente stand up?"

"Thank you, your Honor."

Valente stood up.

The judge asked, "Is that the man?"

"Yes, sir."

Lacey said, "Your witness, Mister Hitesman."

Hitesman stood and was now almost face to face with Libwire.

The judge said, "Take the witness chair, Mister Libwire."

Hitesman spoke directly to Libwire who was now sitting, "Just one question, Mister Libwire. Do you know what transpired in an upstairs room, just minutes before the two people got off the elevator?"

"No, I don't."

"I have no other questions."

Lacey said, "We call Mister William Johnson."

Libwire left the court room. Moments later a young Negro man entered. Johnson went directly to the witness chair and was sworn in.

Lacey asked for his name and address.

"William Johnson. 8953 Manhattan Avenue, Las Vegas, Nevada."

"Thank you, Mister Johnson. Where do you work, sir?"

"As a porter, usually at the front door, at the Flying Eagle Hotel and Casino."

"Mister Johnson, we, in this court room, have just witnessed a video surveillance tape in which you appear along with Mister Salvatore Valente and a housekeeper who used to work at your hotel. Have you seen that video tape?"

"Yes, sir, I have."

"It appeared on the tape that as Mister Valente was putting the housekeeper into a limousine, he said something to you. Do you remember what he said?"

"Yes, sir," he said, *Caught her stealing a lot of money from the syndicate's room. We're going to get it back.*

"Did you ever see that women again?"

"No, sir."

Lacey turned to Attorney Hitesman and said, "Your witness."

Hitesman stood in place and asked the witness, "Is it possible that Mister Valente recovered the defendants' money and then dropped the lady off at the apartment where she lives alone?"

"I know she lives alone, so I guess it is possible."

"Then it's also possible that someone else knows where the woman got to, isn't it Mister Johnson?"

"I guess so."

"You know so, don't you?"

"Yes, sir."

"I have no other questions, your Honor."

Johnson left the witness chair and the courtroom.

Judge Zavitz said, "Gentlemen, may Mister Johnson and Mister Libwire fly back to Las Vegas?"

A collective *yes, and yes, your Honor* was emitted from the two lawyers facing the front of the courtroom. "Call your next witness, Mister Lacey."

"Yes, sir. We call Mrs. Edith Howell."

The bailiff went into the hall and returned with Mrs. Howell. The judge ordered the witness to be sworn. Lacey started the questioning. "State your full name, please."

"Edith Howell."

"Where have you lived for the past two years?"

"Hagerstown, Maryland, my whole life."

"Have you recently changed your residence?"

"Yes. I and my children now live at 36 Jefferson Boulevard, in Hagerstown."

"Are you the wife of Archy Howell who was killed in June of 1982?"

"Yes, I am."

"Did your husband used to play baseball for the Hagerstown Suns?"

"Yes."

"Do you know Defendant Douglas McNamara?"

"Yes."

"When and how did you meet him?"

"He came unannounced to our house in Funkstown, that's a suburb of Hagerstown, in March of 1982. He said he was a lawyer and that a relative of mine had died and left me fifty thousand dollars and had established a college trust fund for my three children."

"Did he tell you who the dead relative was?"

"No. He said that the terms of the will were that the relative remain anonymous.

Later, in June of 1982, Mister McNamara came to our house on Jefferson Boulevard and woke us all up with his ringing of the doorbell. The housekeeper came and got me and I went downstairs to talk to him. He told me that he had heard on the radio that Archy was dead from a shotgun wound. He thought I might need him."

"What time was that?"

"Six forty five in the morning."

"How was he dressed?"

"In a suit and tie."

"At six-forty-five in the morning? Did you know where he was staying?"

"At the Howard Johnson Plaza at the airport."

"How much of a drive is that to your house?"

"About a half hour."

"Did he tell you what he was doing up at six-forty-five in the morning, five-forty-five if you give him a half hour to shave and get dressed in his suit and tie, and another half hour to drive to your house?"

"No. I never thought to ask."

"Did you ever imagine that Mister McNamara was responsible for the shooting death of your husband?"

Charles Hitesman jumped to his feet. "Objection! Calls for an opinion."

"Sustained," pronounced Judge Zavitz.

"Did you ever find out that Mister McNamara hired a hit man from Detroit to shoot your husband to death?"

Again Hitesman shouted, "Objection, your Honor. That's blatant hearsay at its best."

Lacey commented gratuitously, "I agree. I guess anything in the *Hagerstown Herald-Mail* newspaper would be hearsay."

Judge Zavitz scolded, "Watch your step Mister Lacey. There'll be none of those backdoor shenanigans in my court."

Lacey responded sheepishly, "Sorry, your Honor."

"Move on then."

"Did your husband and McNamara have a social relationship?"

"At first they did. They used to go out drinking together for a few weeks right after we first met Mister McNamara. I asked what they would talk about, he being a lawyer and all, and Archy knowing nothing about legal stuff. But after about a month or so, right after we bought the house on Jefferson Boulevard, Archy began to complain to me that he didn't like him any more."

"Did Archy ever say anything to you about Mister McNamara being in Hagerstown to recruit players for a new minor league baseball team?"

"Objection . . . hearsay."

"I'll allow it. You may answer the question, Mrs. Howell."

"But your Honor . . ."

"I said I'll allow the answer, Mister Hitesman."

Mrs. Howell answered, "No."

"Did you keep track of Archy's performance as a baseball player when he first joined the Hagerstown Suns?"

"Yes."

"How'd he do?"

"He was their star player."

"Objection. . . . Opinion."

"Sustained. Jury will disregard the question and the answer."

"Anything happen to his performance for the Suns after Mister McNamara came on the scene?"

"Objection. Calls for an opinion."

"Sustained."

"Did there come a time when you felt you needed to speak to Mister McNamara, but that he was no where to be found in Hagerstown?"

"Yes. I had received a call from someone who identified himself as an FBI agent. He said he wanted to ask me some questions. I thought I should have an attorney present when he came to interview me. I tried to call Mister McNamara at his hotel at the airport and they said he had checked out the day before. Then I called every hotel in Hagerstown and he wasn't staying at any of them."

"When was this?"

"I remember it was when the Suns were finally having a winning streak."

"How long a streak?"

"Oh, seven or eight games. It was the talk of the town."

"How were they doing before the winning streak had started?"

"Objection. . . . Relevance."

"Overruled. I think I know now where Mister Lacey is going with this line of questioning."

"The Suns were performing miserably."

"Thank you, Mrs. Howell. . . . Did the FBI ever come to your house to visit you?"

"Like I said, this all happened close to the end of the Suns' winning streak. When the FBI man came, I had to talk to him without a lawyer present because I couldn't find Mister McNamara."

"Probably because he heard the FBI was in town."

Hitesman stood, and ran up to a spot before the judge. He almost screamed. "**I object to Mister Lacey's gratuitous statement.**"

"Sustained. Mister Lacey, you know better than that. We'll hear no more of that kind of thing."

"Yes, your Honor. I have no more questions of this witness at this time."

Hitesman said, "Defendants have no questions."

Edith Howell took a seat on the prosecution side of the courtroom. Judge Zavitz said, "Mrs. Howell, there's no need for you to stay in the courtroom if you don't care to. None of the lawyers have indicated that they will be calling you to the stand again."

Edith said, "I prefer to stay."

Zavitz said, "Call your next witness, Mister Lacey."

"We call Mister Bucky Livingston."

The Bailiff brought Livingston in from the hall and after seating him in the witness' chair, swore him in and asked him to state his name.

"William Livingston, but my friends call me Bucky."

Attorney Lacey asked, "May I call you Bucky?"

"Yes, you can."

"Where do you live?"

"Charlotte, North Carolina."

"Do you have an address in Charlotte?"

"6452 Oak Street."

"Phone number, in case we need to get a hold of you?"

"I don't have a phone. Can't afford it."

"Do you work there in Charlotte?"

"I work at the Bowl and Spoon."

"Did you ever work and live in Hagerstown, Maryland?"

"I was a minor league baseball player on the Hagerstown Suns."

"Did you lose that job?"

"Yes, I did."

"Why?"

"Because I pleaded guilty to one count of conspiracy to violate the Wire Waging statute."

"Were you guilty of that charge?"

Livingston was silent for a few moments. Then he took a deep breath and answered, "No . . . I don't think I was."

A wave of mumbling and assorted comments was heard spreading over the heavily populated courtroom."

Lacey was somewhat surprised, but the answer to his next question stunned him.

"Then why did you plead guilty?"

"Because I didn't have a real lawyer and the public defender who was supposed to be looking out for my rights, talked me into it."

The courtroom reaction to the witness' answers grew louder.

"But you must have known whether you were guilty or not, with or without a real lawyer, as you call him."

"This public defender seemed to be working for the State's Attorney."

"Your Honor, do I have permission to treat this man as a hostile witness?"

"Not yet. We'll see just how hostile he gets as you proceed."

"Mister Livingston, did you and I have an understanding as to how you would testify here, this morning?"

"You said I should tell the truth."

"Will you tell the truth from this point on?"

"I've been telling the truth so far. Why would I not continue telling the truth?"

"We'll see. Did you ever accept money from McNamara?"

"Yes, I did."

"How much money?"

"Fifty thousand dollars."

"What was your understanding about the purpose of that money?"

There was another brief silent interval before Livingston answered.

"It was a signing bonus for a new minor league baseball team that McNamara and some friends of his were getting together."

Lacey went back behind the prosecution's table and whispered something to the FBI agent who was seated there.

Judge Zavitz inquired, "Mister Lacey, are you going to continue?"

"Your Honor, the witness' last answer comes as a total shock to us and is contrary to anything he has told us before this trial started. May we have a one day adjournment, so that I may confer with Mister Livingston?"

"Mister Lacey, I can understand your consternation. But I frankly cannot justify an adjournment at this time. There are two sides to this case and I'm bound to follow the rules as I understand them. Continue the questioning now, or turn the witness over to Mister Hitesman."

Lacey bent down and whispered something else to the FBI agent. Then he straightened up and announced, "I have no more questions of this witness."

The judge said, "In light of this apparent recent development, we'll have a brief recess. I want all of the lawyers in my office, right now. The rest of you people including the jury, will keep your seats."

"Gentlemen, I've seen this sort of thing happen before. Now, I'm not saying that you defense lawyers have been up to anything shady, but I'll tell you this much. If I ever find out that any of you have been involved with this witness to persuade him to recant the story he gave to the U.S. Attorney, those of you who are so involved are guilty of suborning perjury and will spend more time in prison than your clients if they are found guilty. Do you all understand?"

Collectively, all the defense lawyers answered with the word "yes".

"Now, let's all get back in there and hope nothing more like this happens again during this trial."

"Gentlemen at the defense table, the witness is now yours."

"We have no questions, your Honor."

During the recess that followed, Agent Toliver, who was attending the trial to assist at the prosecution table, asked U.S. Attorney Lacey, "Do I have your permission to talk to that bastard?"

"Can't do that, Tony. Not now, anyway. I'd be accused of trying to intimidate him at the least or attempting to suborn perjury at the worst."

Toliver said, "I'll have the Bureau quietly look into this immediately. I'll wager, forgive the expression, that some money has changed hands again."

"That's all we can do for the time being."

Toliver again spoke. "The big question now, is what Black's going to say. Nothing says that we can't ask him before they get on the stand, is there?"

"No. I just won't call him until tomorrow. You'll talk to him after the close of business today."

There was a hint of sorrow in the voice of Agent Tony Toliver as he spoke to U.S. Attorney Tony Lacey. "The guys at the Bureau tell me that that bastard, Black, is going to say exactly what Livingston said—that the big money he got was a signing bonus for joining the new so-called minor league baseball team that McNamara and his hoodlum friends were organizing. You know, when I heard Hitesman's opening statement I couldn't believe my ears. It was like someone was telling the jury that UFOs were real. We gotta hope there's someone on that jury who knows baseball and is smart enough to teach the rest of them that that's not the way it works—that such a scheme is simply a hoax that was manufactured by the defense attorneys because they just don't have a real defense."

"But Tony, some jurors are capable of believing anything that comes out of a smart lawyer's mouth. The odds are in favor of at least one juror buying Hitesman's bullshit. That's all they need—one juror, and they get a mistrial. And a retrial would produce the same result and we couldn't afford to spend the money to take the case any farther."

"Well, then, what are you going to do?"

"I'm going to have to prove the hoax with what we got left. It's obvious that I can't take any more chances with Black. He is an unknown quantity as far as smarts is concerned, and might convince a juror or two to feel sorry for him."

"Keep a stiff upper lip. For what it's worth, I think you're sharper than any of those defense attorneys. Go get 'em chief."

"It's a warm fuzzy feeling to have a one man cheering section, but I gotta admit, I'd prefer to have twelve more on the team."

Sonny Campbell asked his wife, "Can you get the day off tomorrow?"

"I think so. I haven't taken a personal day off in more than a year."

Sonny and Rochelle were having dinner at a McDonalds.

"Joe Beyerly called me at the office yesterday and said he was going to appear as a witness in the McNamara case in Baltimore tomorrow," continued Sonny. "I really should be there and I think you would like to hear what he has to say. And next month he's going to Las Vegas to testify against Peter Smith who's charged there with killing that housekeeper who let him into McNamara hotel room."

"Boy, Joe is really in demand. Maybe you'll buy me a decent dinner in Baltimore tomorrow. I'm getting kinda sick of eating Big Macs, aren't you?"

"Love 'em. Loved 'em ever since I got back here from Germany thirty years ago. I could hardly think of anything else but a nice big hamburger on the plane coming home. That's how homesick I was after nearly three years over there."

"And now you're homesick for German beer, aren't you?"

"Can't get it in this country. What bears a German label is not the real thing. We make them pasteurize it before we import it."

"How about seafood at Bookbinder's? We haven't been there since we left D. C."

"Another good idea, Rocky. I'll call right now and make a reservation."

CHAPTER FIFTEEN

On the following morning, Sonny and Rochelle took seats on the prosecution side of the courtroom. They sat next to Edith Howell.

"Your next witness, Mister Lacey?"

"Yes, your Honor. We call Mister Joseph Beyerly."

Joe Beyerly had been listening through the door at the courtroom entrance. When he heard his name, he opened the door and stepped inside. He was met by the bailiff, who accompanied him to the witness stand.

The witness was sworn by the bailiff, who asked him to identify himself.

"Joseph Beyerly, official investigator for the State's Attorney for Washington County, Maryland. I live at 6352, Downing Lane, Hagerstown, Maryland."

"In the course of your duties as an investigator, did you receive an assignment from your State's Attorney to check on a lawyer named Douglas McNamara?"

"Yes, I did. Winston Hathaway is the State's Attorney, and he gave me such an assignment."

"What was the purpose of the investigation?"

"Mister McNamara was suspected of being connected to the murder of Archy Howell, a baseball player who played for the Hagerstown Suns."

Charles Hitesman calmly stood and said, "Objection, your honor. The question is prejudicial. There's nothing in the record of the case we're trying here that would suggest that Mister McNamara should be suspected of being connected to Mister Howell's killing."

"I see no prejudice in this witness' testimony. He's merely describing the nature of his assignment from the man he had to answer to. Your objection is overruled."

"How did you commence your investigation?"

"I determined where Mister McNamara was staying in Hagerstown."

"What did you learn?"

"At the Howard Johnson's Plaza Hotel, one of the airport hotels."

"Did you find Mister McNamara at his hotel?"

"No, but I found evidence in his room that showed he had taken his Lear Jet to Las Vegas on the very day I found that evidence."

"What did you do next?"

"I got permission from my boss to fly to Las Vegas."

"What did your boss expect of you? What were you supposed to explore in Las Vegas?"

"Oh, the usual things. Does he have a criminal record; what firm does he belong to; what kind of reputation he had; what was he really doing in Hagerstown; what was the connection between sports betting and minor league baseball?"

"Objection . . . relevance and hearsay."

"Sustained. There's little in Mister Beyerly's stated mission that so far has anything to do with the issues we're trying here. The jury is instructed to disregard that part of Mister Beyerly's answer."

"Did you go to Las Vegas?"

"On that very day."

"What is the first thing you learned about Mister McNamara when you got to Las Vegas?"

"Found out where he lived."

"Where was that?"

"The Flying Eagle Hotel and Casino."

"Where did you stay when you were in Las Vegas?"

"The Flying Eagle Hotel and Casino."

"And after checking into the hotel what did you undertake as the next part of your investigation?"

"I asked the bellhop where a sports betting parlor was located, one that featured baseball."

"Did you learn where one was located?"

"The *Universal Lounge* had baseball betting."

"Did you go there?"

"Yes."

"What did you learn?"

"That I could place a bet on the Hagerstown Suns."

"Did you place a bet on the Suns?"

"Yes. I bet fifty dollars of government money that the Suns would lose that day."

"Did you win or lose?"

"I won two hundred dollars."

"Meaning that the Suns lost? . . . What else did you learn at the betting parlor?"

"That I could also make a bet on the Suns when I wasn't in Las Vegas. The teller there gave me a *Universal* business card and told me that their operator would connect me to an off shore number. My bet would be taken on that number, but I'd settle on the *Universal* number."

"Objection. . . . Hearsay."

"Sustained. The jury will disregard any conversation Mister Beyerly had with the *Universal* teller."

"Where did you go next?"

"To a popular sports bar called the *Outfield*."

"Did you learn anything at the *Outfield?*"

"That defendants Douglas McNamara and Peter Smith along with others, were members of a syndicate that owned and operated the *Universal Lounge*, and that both of those defendants were mob connected."

"Objection. . . . That last statement has to be hearsay."

The judge nodded. "I agree. The objection is sustained. The jury will ignore any reference that Mister Beyerly just made to the mob."

"What did you do after learning whatever you learned?"

"Took a cab back to the Flying Eagle Hotel. It was time to go to bed and get some sleep."

"What did you do when you got up in the morning?"

"I called the Clark County District Attorney."

"What did you learn?"

"That Peter Smith and Douglas McNamara were . . ."

"Objection . . . Hears . . ."

"were squeaky clean."

Hitesman appeared somewhat embarrassed. "Withdraw the objection."

"What did you do following consultation with the District Attorney?"

"Returned to the hotel and planned my next move."

"Which was?"

"I waited for housekeeping to come to my room to clean and straighten. Then I offered the housekeeper one hundred dollars to let me into Mister McNamara's room."

"Did she accept that deal?"

"Yes, I showed her my credentials and we went up one flight of stairs to room 2215 and she went into the room first to see if he was there. He wasn't. We both went in and I quickly searched the room."

"What did you find?"

"In a suit that he had worn on the day Archy Howell was killed and he had returned to Las Vegas from Hagerstown, I found the telephone number that turned out to be that of a mob hit man in Detroit."

"Objection! How could the witness know anything at all about what suit he was wearing when he returned to Las Vegas and who the telephone number belonged to in Detroit? Your Honor, would it be possible to warn the witness that he can't just go on and on, especially with something like that statement about the mob. I respectfully ask that his comment about the Detroit hit man be stricken from the record and that our jury be told to ignore it."

"It's too late now, Mister Hitesman. Mister Beyerly? Can you straighten this mess out?"

"Sure. The housekeeper told me about the suit and I used a reverse directory on the Detroit telephone number. The F.B.I had a record on the hit man, Mister Constanza, and the nation's media picked it up—called it a miracle when he came out of a coma after someone shot him in the back of the head, execution style."

"Satisfied, Mister Hitesman?"

"No, indeed! Now I have to move for a mistrial."

The Judge said, "Denied. But I will instruct the jury to ignore all the witness' comments about the hit man. Go on with your questioning, Mister Lacey."

Mad as a hornet, Hitesman said, "Please note my exception to his Honor's ruling."

"So noted. We'll let the appellate court figure this one out."

"Shall we proceed, Mister Lacey?"

"Certainly, your Honor. What did you do after your experience in Detroit?"

"Went home to Hagerstown . . . thought I learned enough about Mister McNamara."

"Objection. . . . The witness is not answering. . . . He's volunteering information that he thinks will get Mister McNamara convicted of the charge."

"I believe you're right, Mister Hitesman. Objection sustained. Stop your editorializing, Mister Beyerly."

"Yes, your Honor."

The judge responded, "I think it's time for a half hour recess, to let things calm down."

Sonny Campbell spoke to his wife with some anxiety in his voice. "I don't know whether a conviction will hold up on appeal. The judge sort of let things get out of hand. We'll see." All three, including Edith, were eating hotdogs and drinking Coca Colas, which Sonny bought from a vendor outside of the courthouse.

Edith said, "I think Mister Beyerly was wonderful, a lot smarter than the defense lawyer. How old is Joe, anyway?"

Rochelle said, "Around thirty-five, I think. I gotta admit, Joe twisted that defense attorney around his little finger. I thought he was wonderful too."

"Is he married?"

Sonny answered, "His wife died about five years ago. They didn't have any children."

He looked at Edith and smiled. "He was wonderful, wasn't he?"

When all the onlookers were seated calmly and comfortably in the courtroom, the bailiff came in and sang out his signal that the court was again open for business.

The Judge came in and told everyone to take their seats.

"Are we ready to resume with Mister Beyerly's testimony?" Lacey answered, "Yes, your Honor. He's all ready to go."

"Proceed, then."

"Mister Beyerly, what happened next with your investigation of Mister McNamara?"

"I got word from the Las Vegas District Attorney that they were investigating the disappearance of the housekeeper who had let me into McNamara's room."

"Do you know if the lady was ever found?"

"You probably already heard . . . in a grave, somewhere in the desert. I guess I got out of Las Vegas in the nick of time . . . to avoid the same fate."

The Judge said, "This time **I'm** going to object. Mister Beyerly, I know you're not just stupid. On the contrary, you're as clever as a fox with your gratuitous phrases. Do it again and I'll hold you in contempt. You are an embarrassment. Yes, I'm mad. I'm furious. Now let's get going with no more of your nonsense."

After consulting with the FBI agent who was assisting him at the prosecution table, Tony Lacey said, "We are prepared to call our next witness, your Honor."

"Then you are finished with Mister Beyerly?"

"Yes, your Honor."

"Any cross, Mister Hitesman?"

"No, your honor. You've stricken all of the answers of Mister Beyerly, that were asked on direct."

Joe Beyerly left the witness stand and joined Sonny, Rochelle and Edith in the courtroom pews.

Judge Zavitz said, "Proceed."

"We call Mary Catalino."

The bailiff left the courtroom and returned with a middle aged, rather heavyset lady with bleached blond hair.

"You may swear the witness," said the judge.

The bailiff requested that the lady raise her right hand and swear to tell the truth.

The judge asked, "Your name please."

"Mary Catalino."

"Address?"

"Women's Division of the Detroit House of Correction."

The U.S. Attorney, Tony Lacey, started the questioning process.

"Why are you imprisoned at the present time?"

"I pleaded guilty to attempted murder."

"Whom did you try to murder?"

"Mario Constanza."

"Is it Mrs. Catalino? Are you married?"

"Yes, I'm married."

"To whom?"

"Vito Catalino."

"Where does he live?"

"Jackson Prison, in Michigan."

"What is he in for?"

"First Degree Murder."

"Did the two of you used to live together as man and wife?"

"Yes."

"Where?"

"Ozone Park, New York City."

"What brought you to Michigan?"

"Vito's imprisonment at Jackson Prison."

"How is it that you came to try to kill Mario Constanza."

"I'm a licensed surgical nurse and was working at Henry Ford Hospital, Department of Neurological Surgery in Detroit. That's where Mario Constanza was lying in a coma after brain surgery. He got shot in the head. My husband is what the New York mob calls a made man. He carries a lot of weight even though he's in prison. He told me that I had to kill Constanza, and let me know that a man named Art Ferris would tell me how I was going to do it."

"Did you talk to Art Ferris?"

"Yes. Ferris called me and I met him at the Red Fox Restaurant on I-96 in eastern Michigan."

"Do you see Art Ferris in this courtroom?"

"Yes."

"Would you point him out?"

Mrs. Catalino pointed to Peter Smith at the defense table.

"You mean the man sitting at the far end of those tables?"

"Yes."

"Is that the man from whom you got your instructions on how to murder Mario Constanza?"

"Yes."

Lacey said, "Would the defendant at the far end of the tables, please stand up."

Peter Smith reluctantly stood up.

Edith turned to Rochelle and whispered, "Looks like we've got a whole gang of murderers in this case."

Lacey again consulted with the agent who whispered back to him for several minutes. Lacey then announced, "No more questions of Mrs. Catalino."

"Cross examination, Mister Hitesman?"

"Yes, your Honor."

"Go ahead, then"

"Mrs. Catalino, did Mister Lacey put you up to this absurd accusation of Peter Smith?"

Lacey jumped to his feet. Objection! Mister Hitesman should not be heard to demean my character and in effect accuse me of suborning perjury."

"I agree. Unless you have a basis to accuse Mister Lacey of suborning perjury you're not to do so with such a question. Do you have such a basis."

"No, sir. Only that my client denies ever meeting Mrs. Catalino."

"That's not good enough, Mister Hitesman. Objection sustained. Any more cross, Mister Hitesman?"

"No, your Honor."

A U.S. Marshal came to the witness stand to collect Mrs. Catalino. He placed shackles on her ankles and handcuffs on her wrists behind her back.

The Judge seemed to speak to everyone in the courtroom, "Ladies and gentlemen, we can't always predict how much time we can spend each day on a trial like this one. I find that we have other urgent business in this courtroom in a matter that is unrelated to our trial. I'm going to adjourn until tomorrow. The jury will check in with the bailiff in the jury assembly room at quarter to nine in the morning. We'll start again in here promptly at nine o'clock. Court is adjourned till then." He then pounded his gavel once on its pad.

As the audience filed out of the courtroom, Edith Howell spoke to Joe Beyerly.

"I wonder if I could ask a favor of you, Mister Beyerly? Are you driving back to Hagerstown now?"

"Yes, I am, Mrs. Howell."

"Please, call me Edith."

"And you should call me Joe."

"Rochelle and Sonny are staying in Baltimore for dinner. Could I hitch a ride with you? I took the Baltimore bus here yesterday. I don't drive."

Rochelle whispered to Sonny, "And Cupid had nothing to do with it."

"Have you lived in Hagerstown all your life, Joe?"

"Yup. My wife did too. Do you know that I lost her to cancer?"

"I heard that. That must have been tough on you."

"Worst thing I ever experienced."

"Do you live alone now?"

"Yes."

He took his eyes off the road long enough to look at her.

"Edith said, I don't know what I'd do if I didn't have the children."

"There are times when I really wish we had had kids."

"It has its down side too, you know?"

"I suppose so."

They rode in silence for about five minutes.

Finally she spoke, "Joe, I might as well be blunt. I find you a very attractive man."

"Really? I never thought of myself as attractive."

"I'll bet Spencer Tracy never did either."

"What's so attractive about me?"

"For one thing, you never seem to say anything that isn't either funny or very, very intelligent."

"I knew it couldn't be what I look like."

"That's where you're wrong. You're the type of man that I do like to look at."

This time, the interval of silence was even longer. He broke the ice.

"I find you a damn good looking women, Edith."

"You're not going to say I remind you of your wife, are you?"

"Not a chance. She was a totally different type."

"Did you go to college?"

"No. I got all my smarts in the Army. Battlefield commission in Korea. They wanted me to go to OCS, but I shied away from that."

"Why?"

"I thought the competition would be too great."

"I find that hard to believe. The way you made a fool out of that defense lawyer today tells me there aren't many men around who have more native intelligence than you do."

"Are you hittin' on me, Edith?"

"You're damn right I am, Joe."

"If I stopped at the next motel would you jump out of this car and run away?"

"I'd run into the motel and sign us up, that's what I'd do."

He rolled over in the bed and made an animal-like sound. "What do you think? Is this going to turn into something?"

"You mean is it going to last? Don't you think it's too soon to say?"

"Probably. But I see no obstacles on our horizon."

"And you're a poet on top of everything else."

He insisted, "You're going to have to talk me out of stopping at the next motel."

"This could get expensive. But it's nice to know you're thinking about it."

"I'm thinking that where we are will do just fine." He rolled back to where he had started and stroked her hair.

She pulled herself up to him by putting her arm around his neck. She kissed him gently at first, and ultimately with much passion. "I could stay here forever."

"Gotta eat sometime."

"Please. You can't be thinking about food."

"I'm thinking that we have to stop someplace for dinner, a bottle of wine and maybe some *crepes suzette* for dessert."

"But that's gonna be hours from now, right?"

"Yeah. . . . Hours."

Walter Brock was refused a tennis match with Joe Beyerly three times in a row. "O. K. O. K. You're going to play with your woman again. I suppose

I should be happy for you. I must say she's a beauty. But is she any good on the tennis court? I bet you're just carrying her most of the time."

"Not true. She's better than you are, I'm sorry to inform you."

"Boy! Do you know how to make a guy feel good. . . . How about this? I find a good female player and we play doubles sometime."

"That would be just fine. Call me, when you're ready to have your ass whooped again."

Rochelle played tennis like Martina Navratilova. The idea of taking on Edith and Joe was appealing. Especially since she very much approved of their relationship. Walter Brock picked her up on Saturday morning and all had agreed to meet Sonny at eleven o'clock at Rocky's Pizza Parlor for beer and pizza for the five of them.

The players gathered at eight o'clock in the morning. The match would be played inside the tennis club building. The tennis turned out to be furious. The scores were fairly even until the last set when Rochelle Campbell turned on the steam. The Brock-Campbell team took the set, six to three. They had won the day, much to the chagrin of Joe Beyerly.

Sonny had a pitcher of ice cold beer waiting for the four players on their arrival. Three large pizzas with assorted toppings were ordered.

"When you think about it, there are more conflicts of interest at this table than at a middle-east peace conference," said Joe. "Sonny has a major conflict because he was pals with Archy, Walter, because he works for both public defenders, Rocky, because she's married to Sonny and eavesdrops on conversations that Edith's lawyer has with players on the Suns."

"McNamara is hardly my lawyer any more," said Edith. "He'll be lucky if he ever practices law again. You know Joe, you've got the worst conflict of all . . . on the tennis court with your arch rival, Walt Brock."

Rochelle lifted her beer mug and declared, "Here's to conflict. May it all be resolved through public drunkenness on this fine day."

The four others joined in a chorus of, "Hear! Hear! . . . Hear! Hear!"

"Who'd have imagined two years ago that these two love birds would have gotten together?" asked Sonny. "When can we expect bells to ring for you two, anyway?"

Beyerly complained, "Come on, Sonny. Leave it alone, will you?"

"Sorry. Guess we shouldn't rush things."

Edith joked, "That's not my position. The sooner the better, sez I."

"Drop it, you guys," responded Joe. "What happened in Baltimore last Thursday, Sonny?"

"Not much. They introduced corporate papers and financial records and stuff like that, which I imagine was very boring. They got a Mafia turncoat to tell how Salvatore Valente was hanging out with John Gotti's boys and was really a member of the mob and was a reason why the *Universal Lounge* never should have gotten a gambling license."

Walter Brock asked, "What I want to know is how the hell did they have a hearing in Nevada on Mafia connections and miss that one?"

Rocky answered, "Payoffs, dear boy. Payoffs."

Sonny had heard of one other witness who testified on Thursday. The man explained how there was a direct TV connection from a painting in McNamara's room to the gambling syndicate's suite where activities were recorded on tape. "That's how that poor housekeeper was identified by the defendants," said Sonny. "And they spent all of Friday arguing if the recorded FBI interview of Constanza could be admitted as evidence like they do under the death bed statute."

Edith asked, "And . . . how did it turn out?"

"I'm afraid we lost that one, folks."

"What's scheduled for next week?" asked Rochelle.

Sonny answered, "Well they don't have trials on Mondays. They'll resume on Tuesday morning. I'm pretty sure that the U.S. Attorney is about to rest his case. So we can probably expect Hitesman to start shooting his mouth off some time on Tuesday."

"I'm sick of talking about this. Somebody change the subject," said Edith. "Let's ask Walt how the Roosevelt case is coming along."

"Not much is happening. I think they're waiting for the federal case to end and see whether that jury finds McNamara guilty of killing Archy. If they do they'll call it, *Violation of Archy's civil rights,* and then Sonny's favorite defendant, Chester Roosevelt, will win his case without lifting a finger."

"He's not my favorite defendant," said Rochelle. "I just don't like the way the system has gotten into the habit of screwing Negroes, once they get into the system, innocent or guilty."

Joe said, "What . . . you don't think Roosevelt is guilty?"

"No, I don't think he's guilty, but that's beside the point. Let's say, for the sake of argument, that McNamara actually did hire a hit man to kill Archy. . . . And the hit man did do the murder and it starts to look that way to all reasonable persons associated with Chester's defense. Chester is already in the system, and everybody involved on the prosecution side, including the cops and even some judges, will knock themselves out to see that the black man gets convicted, despite McNamara's obvious guilt."

Edith said, "But, Rochelle, if it's the other way around—that is if Roosevelt really did do the murder, and McNamara gets convicted, then justice isn't served that way either and it has nothing to do with race."

"You're still missing the point. It's because Chet is black that nobody will take McNamara's obvious guilt into consideration and push for the black man's acquittal. They'll just go ahead and let Chet get the gas. And that's the way Chet's case seems to be going. Let's pray that Constanza wakes up and confesses to the murder before they have a chance to convict Roosevelt. That's the only way justice will be served for this black man."

Brock said that it was time for another subject change. "Have you checked the standings lately? Our Suns are one game out of first place. Greensboro loses one and the Suns win one and it's tied."

"Just think," said Brock. "If Archy hadn't gotten murdered the Suns would probably be in last place."

An awkward silence descended on the table. Everybody stared at Edith. Sonny hailed the waitress. "Two more pitchers, please—ice cold, if that's possible."

Edith said, "That's all right dear friends. I'm through grieving over Archy. I've got a new man now." She took Joe by the hand and squeezed it, which caused Joe to slightly blush.

Rochelle asked, "Where are the Suns playing this afternoon?"

Sonny answered, "Fayetteville. The Suns should beat them. So let's hope that Greensboro loses."

Rochelle asked Edith, "How are the kids getting along without their father?"

"Pretty good. Every once in a while, one will tell me he or she misses Daddy, especially the boy."

Rochelle asked, "Has anybody seen those commercials on local TV about this place? They got a half dozen people to say that Rocky's makes the best pizza in the world."

"That may be so," said Joe. "Would someone pass me that last piece. Should we order another large one?"

"I'm all for another," said Walter Brock. "By God, I think it is the best pizza in the world."

The waitress placed two pitchers of beer on the table. Sonny ordered a large deluxe pizza.

"Yes, sir. That'll be about twenty minutes."

All were surprised to see Vernon Lawrence, Edith's brother, come into the dining room with his wife and four children. "Hi gang. What's the matter? Wives and girlfriends refuse to cook today?"

All those at the Campbell table laughed.

Edith said, "Forgot how to cook is more like it. The truth is that we come here because the place has the same name as Rocky's nickname. What you doing in town?"

"Here to visit Margaret's mother."

Margaret Lawrence spoke up. "In my case, I simply refuse to cook. They all prefer the pizza in this place to my cooking, anyway. Why should I bother?"

"We understand, Margaret. Sit down there, next to us. We're going to stay a little while longer."

With Joe's help, Vernon Lawrence moved a table to join with his sister's friends. His family pulled up chairs and sat down.

Vernon said, "Well, what's up with this gang?"

"Playing tennis," said Sonny. "All except me."

"And talking about the Howell murder, of course," said Rochelle.

Edith asked, "You know, I know some stuff about all the conspirators except Charles Tomlinson. He seems to remain in the background, and so far I haven't heard anything bad that he's done."

Joe answered, "Nothing except be a member of the syndicate that fixed minor league baseball games. Isn't that enough?"

"Oh, you know what I mean. He didn't kill or kidnap anybody. He wasn't hanging out with any Mafia characters. He sits there at the table and looks as innocent as a lamb."

Lawrence interrupted, "You know, I've been following the federal case very carefully. There was an analysis on TV, just once, that gave the background of the five defendants. Tomlinson was once a Warrant Officer in the Army, believe it or not. They didn't describe how and where he went wrong. But I guess he was a pretty good officer. Flew small rescue aircraft in Korea, including helicopters."

"Jeez!" exclaimed Edith, "That's amazing. Maybe he was just a silent and innocent partner in the syndicate."

"Not possible, honey," said Joe. "Those guys were all splitting millions. He had to know what was going on."

Sonny protested, "Even without the fixing of games, they were making millions. We'll probably find out that he killed the housekeeper, or something, before Lacey gets through presenting his case."

Joe said, "I happened to know who killed the housekeeper, and it wasn't Mister Tomlinson."

"Who was it?" asked Rochelle.

"Can't tell you."

Edith said joyfully, "I told you Tomlinson is a good guy."

"You're being too kind, Edith," said Rochelle. "I believe that all those bastards should spend the rest of their lives in prison."

"Who can get the day off when Hathaway gives his opening statement?" asked Sonny. "I've got lots of personal days and nothing on my calendar that Wilson can't handle."

Joe answered, "Can't do it, Sonny. Too much on my plate."

Edith said, "I'll be there for both of us, honey."

Rochelle said, "Count me out, husband. They'd have my scalp if I'd take another day off. Summer school is over and the regular school year starts some time next week. We don't know when the defense will give his opening statement, so I can't plan anything for the next week or so."

Walter Brock said to Sonny, "It's up to you, boss. But it doesn't really make sense for both of us to go. . . . Let's say you go and you tell me all about it when you get back."

"That makes two of us who can go," Sonny concluded. "Edith and me. Don't worry Joe, I won't lay a glove on her in Baltimore. . . . Well, folks, the beer is gone and the pizza is gone and there's a Baltimore game that will start on TV in about a half an hour. Time to go home."

The Campbell gang all said goodbye to Vernon Lawrence and his family and left Rocky's, where they make the best pizza in the world."

CHAPTER SIXTEEN

At six thirty, on Sunday morning, the day following the pizza feast at Rocky's, a young boy riding his bicycle tossed the Sunday edition of the Hagerstown Herald-Mail onto Edith Howell's front porch. She was up early out of habit and heard the paper hit the porch. Dressed in her nightgown and bathrobe she went outside and picked up the newspaper.

The headline over what appeared to be an important bulletin caught her eye.

HIT MAN WAKES FROM COMA

Henry Ford Hospital, Detroit. Neurology Surgeons announced early this morning that a so-called hit man, Mario Constanza, who last year awoke from a bullet-to-the-head-induced coma for a brief eighteen hours, has again awakened from his vegetative state. Doctors had concluded that the first awakening was a miracle. They now say that they can hardly believe it has happened again.

The case has particular legal significance inasmuch as Constanza is a potential witness in the "Minor League Wagering Team" case presently being tried in a federal court in Baltimore, Maryland. FBI agents interviewed Constanza in an out of court setting when he awoke the first time. The District Court, Baltimore Division, in a motion filed by the defendants in the case, ruled that the interview could not be used as evidence since it was done under non-judicial circumstances.

When interviewed by this reporter, FBI agent Kevin Freedlund was heard to say, "This time we are leaving little to chance. We will take the man's testimony, with all attorneys, Judge Zavitz, the jury, court reporter and even the bailiff present in a large hospital room where Constanza will be hooked up to his essential intensive care apparatus. The attorneys will be warned to be gentle in handling the questioning process. What this man says will probably determine the outcome of all charges in the "Minor League Wagering Team" case.

Edith waited until after Sonny's church let out, before she called the Campbells. "I'm sure you got your newspaper already."

"We just got home. He's reading it now. That headline was enough to make me almost faint."

Sonny, yelled from the kitchen table, "Who is it, Rocky?"

"Edith is on the phone, honey. Wants to know if you read the paper."

"I'll be right there."

"Hello, Edith. You got Joe with you? . . . Did he explain what that article all means?"

"Yes, he's here. I think I understand what it all means. What we want to know is when are they going to have this out-of-court session at the hospital?"

"As early as the court is open again—probably bright and early tomorrow morning."

"I don't see how the public will be able to attend . . . in a hospital room."

"I don't know either, Edith. You and I should go over there anyway. Today, if you can get away. Those court people are undoubtedly arranging for a plane to fly the jury and all the essential people to Detroit. Maybe they'll squeeze us in somewhere. You're a special case because it's your husband who got killed. It won't do any good to call anybody on a Sunday. I wouldn't know who to call, anyway. We may have to arrange our own flight to Detroit."

"Can you pick us up? Joe says he's going with us. He can smooth it over with Hathaway. He's upstairs right now packing a bag. I'll pack as soon as I hang up. . . . Oh, Sonny? Hurry will you? I want to be sure we can get into that hospital room and hear him speak. If he killed Archy, I want to be among the first to know it. Do you understand?"

"Of course, Edith, honey. I'll be at your house in forty-five minutes."

Sonny, Edith and Joe checked into the Pontchartrain Hotel at four o'clock in the morning. They had arranged their own flight from Baltimore to Detroit on Sunday afternoon. Sonny was able to contact the U.S. Attorney who in turn contacted Judge Zavitz. Because Constanza's potential testimony bore heavily on the question of whether he killed Edith's husband, the Judge granted permission to Edith, and the close friends who accompanied her, to be squeezed into the large operating theater area where the testimony would be taken.

All three went immediately to bed and managed a couple hours of sleep. With written instructions from U.S. Attorney Lacey, they first obtained a government pass with all three names on it.

After an hour of confused organizing, the out-of-court session finally got underway. Edith Howell stood closest to the gurney on which Constanza lay with a number of tubes and wires attached to his propped up body. Everybody in the room stood, with the exception of the jury, Judge Zavitz and the court reporter. The latter two sat at a small table with a stenographic machine standing next to it. There was barely enough room on the table for essential paper work.

The five defendants stood at the foot of the gurney. An attorney stood behind each defendant. Two doctors stood near Constanza. The entire jury sat in the upstairs swivel chairs of the operating theater.

The bailiff spoke first, making his sing-song salutation just as he would if he had been in a real courtroom. He identified the location and spoke of the unusual circumstances that brought the court to Henry Ford Hospital.

Judge Zavitz said, "Ladies and gentlemen, let's get underway immediately. Make yourself as comfortable as possible. Mister Bailiff, would you swear the witness?"

Constanza was sworn in and attorney Lacey started the questioning.

"Mister Constanza, I can well imagine that this setting with all these good people surrounding you and staring at you must be somewhat disturbing."

"I know what's going on here. Get on with it, would you, before I pass out again." He then entertained everyone with a little chuckle. Some of the people in the room joined in and also laughed.

The Judge said, "Let's have order here. I suggest that everyone pretend that we're back in the Baltimore court house. Proceed."

"I take it, then, that you feel up to what's about to happen here?" asked U.S. Attorney Lacey.

"Yeah, I feel up to just about anything after that long nap I took."

"Are you acquainted with Attorney Douglas McNamara?"

"Yeah, we've met. That's him standing right there."

Lacey said, "Let the record show that the witness has identified defendant Douglas McNamara, standing at the foot of the witness' bed."

"How many times have you met Mister McNamara?"

"Once."

"Where did you meet?"

"In the Caucus Room restaurant downtown."

"Detroit?"

"Yeah."

"What was the purpose of your meeting?"

"To arrange the details of how I was going to whack some minor league baseball player."

"You mean, to murder someone? How did you know that that's what you were going to discuss?"

"McNamara called me on a very private number that I reserve for that kind of business."

"What is that number? Can you remember it?"

"Oh yeah, it was my life's blood. . . . 3134256734."

"Can you say who the minor league baseball player was?"

"Oh, yeah. His name was Archy Howell. I say *was* because he's dead now."

"Can you remember what he looked like?"

"Of course, I do."

"Did you kill him?"

"I told you the last time. I didn't kill the man. I only agreed to kill him for the sum of twenty-five-thousand dollars."

"Would you explain that, please?"

"O. K. It came down like this. I got the contract from McNamara to kill Howell for twenty-five-thousand dollars. I would be paid after the job was done. I never got paid anything because somebody else killed him. I heard that on a Hagerstown radio station on the morning when he got it in the face with a couple of shotgun blasts. When I heard the news on the radio, I left Hagerstown in a hurry. That town is in Maryland. I drove straight back to Detroit. Is that enough? I'm feelin' kind of tired."

"Mister Hitesman here, is a lawyer representing Mister McNamara today. He may have some questions for you."

The judge asked, "Mister Hitesman? Any questions?"

McNamara whispered something to Hitesman who addressed the court, such as it was constituted. "No questions, your Honor."

"This court is now adjourned," said the Judge. "Would the doctors attend to Mister Constanza immediately and would everybody in this room leave as swiftly as they are able."

Within five minutes the only persons left in the room were the two doctors, three nurses and Mister Constanza.

Edith, Joe and Sonny had their lunch at Stouffers in the Northland part of Southfield in Detroit.

"This is certainly a nice place," said Edith.

"Yeah, pretty fancy for the likes of us," said Joe.

"But not expensive, for what they give you," Sonny added to the chorus. "Look, we deserve to celebrate. This time our man in the coma remembers

McNamara's name and Archy's name and all the details of the contract that was offered him. . . . And it was all admissible evidence. We now can say we got those guys by the short hairs."

Edith seemed confused. "What do the newspapers mean when they say that what Constanza would say would determine the outcome of the whole *Minor League Wagering Team* case?"

Sonny explained, "Think about it for a minute, Edith. Whether Mister Constanza killed Archy, which the lying bastard probably did, or McNamara just gave him the contract to do it, either way it still connects him to the game fixing case. Why else would McNamara want someone like Archy dead? It's because he found out that Archy was going to tell the whole nasty business to the feds—that McNamara had recruited him to fix games. And since McNamara is tied in with the other four at *Universal*, they're all guilty of fixin' baseball games. Now that Lacey's got iron-clad evidence against him, all five of those bastards better try to make deals and plead guilty to at least the betting violations. In the case of Smith, Valente and McNamara, those three are in even deeper. You should just wait and see. This trial will come to a screeching halt now. The next thing you'll hear is that all five are standing before Zavitz and begging for mercy."

"Sonny's right, honey," said Joe. "As the song goes. *You can't have one without the other.* Constanza kills a baseball player or just agrees to do it, it follows that McNamara's also guilty of having recruited the victim to fix baseball games . . . and his four buddies are guilty by association."

"I think I understand. How soon do you expect to see them asking for deals?"

"Just as soon as their lawyers think the climate is healthy enough to plead," answered Sonny.

She asked, "How much prison time do you think they'll get?"

He answered, "Depends on which of them the judge is dealing with. Of course, murder is the worst and a contract to murder somebody is far worse than kidnapping. And Peter Smith actually instructed Mrs. Catalino on how to kill Constanza. Valente, McNamara and Smith will get the longest sentences. The authorities got nothin' extra on Greenberg and Tomlinson so those two'll get the lightest sentences . . . maybe even probation and a fine."

"What? Probation and a fine? You might as well send them on a vacation to Tahiti," she exclaimed.

He scolded, "Don't be so cynical, Edith. The law is the law. You said yourself that you hadn't heard anything really bad about Tomlinson."

Edith came back with, "And you said yourself that we've got these criminals by the short hairs. As far as I'm concerned they're all guilty of killing my ex-husband—or, more politely, violating his civil rights. McNamara was only the man who made the contract with Constanza—the guy they all chose to get the job done. They're all conspirators, aren't they? Well, they're all guilty of agreeing to do anything to make their conspiracy work. Killing Archy was one of those essential things."

"I've got to admit, you've got a good argument. But I've also got to tell you, honey, the court isn't going to look at it that way. They're going to have to follow the law."

"Then, the law is an ass."

"You're in good company there, too. Wish we had Oliver Wendell Holmes here to settle this thing."

Joe interrupted,

"Come on, you two. Next thing you know you'll be duking it out in the alley."

Edith heaved a sigh of disgust. "I can see I'm getting nowhere with you, and you're a lawyer. . . . Let's drop the whole thing. I'll just ask Tomlinson and Greenberg if I can go to Tahiti with them."

The laughter of all three seemed to settle the friendly disagreement.

CHAPTER SEVENTEEN

The *Minor League Wagering Team* stopped having their periodic meetings when the five of them got indicted. They met through their lawyers.

Charles Tomlinson was angry. He spoke to his two lawyers. "I don't care what his damn lawyer says we should do. McNamara was responsible for this whole thing coming apart. He caused the Hagerstown investigator to go to Las Vegas and stick his nose into our telephone betting service, and if the shamus hadn't found the phone number in that Irish bastard's suit pocket, none of this trouble would have happened. Besides, I'm the only one who isn't staring down a more serious charge—well, maybe Greenberg is pretty clean, but my taking punishment for the rest of those guys, I won't stand for. And now you two guys tell me that I should consider taking a plea on the Wire Wagering charge. You people are starting to piss me off too."

"I think it's time for you and us to go our separate ways. We've talked it over and we're going to file a petition to withdraw as your attorneys."

"Jeez, you shysters stick together. File your damn petition. I'll defend myself from here on in."

Douglas McNamara had a different approach to his legal problems. He would simply say yes to all the advice his lawyer, Charles Hitesman gave him. He anticipated weeks before that the advice would include getting the U.S. Attorney to offer a deal. But he realized that the attempted murder charge complicated matters. Any deal would include a long prison sentence for that charge alone, which he had no intention of ever serving.

He went back to wooing Merideth Ostrowski. She was still very much in love, despite the criminal accusations leveled against him. He thought she would do anything he asked her to do.

The second miraculous awaking of Mario Constanza changed the thinking of practically everyone involved in the *Minor League Wagering Team*. McNamara envisioned a guilty verdict. if the Constanza testimony were introduced at the trial. It would be a slam dunk. He perceived that the only way to avoid such a consequence was to agree to any offer of a deal from the U.S. Attorney, even if it involved pleading guilty to the original charges. That way, he could buy time. He would then not show up in the Baltimore federal court at the appointed time for sentencing. He would, by the time the slow moving wheels of justice demanded his appearance, be well on his way to Argentina. Perhaps he and Merideth would even be settled there. They'd be living with false identities in some remote place not easily discoverable. He would have smuggled most of his considerable wealth into the country upon entry. From the beginning of their flight, no one but he and Merideth and a pilot would know about these details. Anyone else, who by chance did discover anything that would lead to exposing their false identities or location, would be eliminated as the occasion demanded.

He was well aware that Tomlinson had been a pilot during the Korean War and had maintained his flying skills through the years. He called Tomlinson's lawyer and obtained a list of telephone numbers for places his former partner might now be located. Conveniently, the receptionist at the Radisson Plaza Lord Baltimore Hotel in Baltimore advised that he was staying there. After several abortive attempts over a period of a week, he finally got his old friend and partner on the line.

"Charlie, there's something I've got to discuss with you face to face before you do something foolish like make a deal with the U.S. Attorney."

"Oh, yeah. What could be so important? You got a plan to get me off, or something?"

"Yes, I do. Just you and me. Not the others. After, all, I got the best lawyer."

"Ya got my ear—and probably the ear of the FBI. This phone is probably bugged, so don't tell those bastards what your plan is."

"I'm calling you from Chicago. I can take my Lear Jet to Baltimore at any time. When will you be available?"

"I ain't goin' no place. I'll look for you today, if that's possible?"

The door opened and there stood Charles Tomlinson with one finger to his lips. He pointed to his ear and silently mouthed the word *bugged*. Tomlinson went out in the hall and whispered, "Let's take a walk."

When they were several blocks from the hotel and felt safe from any surveillance, McNamara took Tomlinson's hand and shook it. "Long time no see, Charlie, outside the courtroom, I mean."

"What ya got on your mind, Dougie boy?"

"Argentina."

"Argentina! What the hell does that mean?"

"You and I are going to Argentina instead of prison."

"Jeez! I can see the wheels spinning in that criminal brain of yours."

"You still fly planes, don't you—still a pilot?"

"Yeah."

"Jets, like my Lear Jet?"

"Yeah."

"I've been saying yes to every suggestion my lawyer, Hitesman, throws at me. He's now working on me to plead to attempted second degree murder and one count of Wire Wagering. I'm even going to do that . . . to buy time to fill out my scheme for an escape to Argentina. I plead, you plead and we both get a sentencing date some time way down the road."

"And what do we do while we're waiting?"

"I know the best man on the globe when it comes to forging identity documents . . . including passports. I plan to have a lady, Merideth, with me from now on. The three of us, maybe four, if you've got somebody you're really fond of you want with us, become new people from the time my jet takes off and then forever in Argentina."

"That's your first mistake. Some smart FBI guy finds out your plane is missing and they follow up on that until they find us down in Argentina. . . . Jeez, you're dumb. Why didn't you think of that?"

"Have you got a better idea?"

"It so happens, I do. I know pilots all over the world. I know one in Chile. Chile's near Argentina, isn't it?"

"Next door, I think. What can he do for us?"

"I can fly us to Chile in your jet, with our phony passports. We'll be over Mexico in short order and nobody there will give a damn about flight plans. We stay in Chile while my friend flies your plane back to the U.S., let's say Texas, for instance. Then we drive to Argentina and he takes a commercial flight back to Chile and picks up his life where he left off. And we start our new life in Buenos Aires or somewhere. They find your plane in Texas, but Texas is a dead end. They still think we're hiding somewhere in the U.S. They won't have the slightest idea that you're in the capital of Argentina screwing your broad."

They crossed the street and entered a large park.

"Charlie, you're a genius."

"We would still have to worry about what the aerometer showed for miles flown."

"I can fix that. We determine the extra miles flown, then have some expert roll the aerometer back."

"And I'll bet you know of such an expert."

"So happens I do. . . . O. K., let's do it that way. And to cover our tracks, I'll buy a second hand car and the three of us will drive to, let's say Dallas, where I'll have instructed my pilot to have planted my plane. You'll fly us to Chile from Dallas."

"You gotta have insurance when you buy a car."

"I got people who can do that for me."

"And you've just created a witness who will be found and put the FBI on the trail of the used car."

"I'll get a phony driver's license when I get the other documents, and I'll buy the insurance myself."

"That may work."

"Stop your doubting. This is all going to work. I'm assuming you've got plenty of money to live on. I'm not going to carry you."

"When do I meet this Merideth you talk about?"

"On the day she picks you up in the used car. . . . You hungry? There's a guy pushing a cart over there. Want a hot dog or an ice cream or something?"

"Nothing. How do you manage to keep your weight down? I swear you eat and drink three times what I do."

"You know, gambling is not legal in the city of Buenos Aires. I don't think that you and I will wait long to get into business of the sort we're used to."

"Jeez. You really do have a criminal mind."

"It's all I know. You're no Sunday school teacher yourself, you know? . . . O. K., mums the word. Don't try to contact me, at least on that hotel phone of yours. You say they've got that bugged."

"Oh, yeah, you got that right. I hope your contact with me this morning on that phone won't get us into any trouble."

"I think I chose my words carefully."

"We'll know you didn't if they bust into your bedroom down there and you're in a clinch with your Merideth."

McNamara's limousine looked quite out of place on Thirty-ninth Street in Hell's Kitchen in New York City.

In the ample rear seat area, he turned to Merideth and said, "I should have some misgivings about having Bobby park this limo on the street. But he's armed and was a former Green Beret and can take care of himself, to say nothing about the car."

Bobby held the door open and the two got out. The forger's shop was a converted bedroom on the fourth floor. His name, Alphonse, was probably just as false as the documents he created.

"We've brought the passport photographs, Alphonse. Will they work for the driver's licenses too?"

"They usually work for both the passport and the license. Let me take a look at them."

The photos changed hands.

"Oh, yes. They'll do fine. . . . What's the lady's name going to be?"

She answered, "Elizabeth Lucile Quinn." He was writing it all down.

He asked her to spell Lucile.

"L U C I L E"

"And you, sir. What's your name to be?"

"Thomas Edward Quinn."

"Are you to be married?"

"Yes."

"Common address?"

"Yes."

"Which is?"

"88-38 53rd Avenue, Elmhurst, New York."

"You said that there was to be a third set of documents."

"Shoot."

"Anthony Phillip Wilson."

"He's the heavy-set man in the photo?"

"Yes."

"His address will be . . . ?"

"9024 43rd Avenue, Seattle, Washington."

"I'll look up the ZIP codes. Have you got the money with you?"

"Yes. There's thirty-thousand dollars in this envelope. When will this stuff be ready to pick up?"

"On this coming Sunday afternoon, at four o'clock."

"Anything else you need from us?"

"No. That's it." Alphonse walked the two visitors to the door.

The used car lot had some shiny, almost new-looking vehicles for sale. Merideth wasn't particular about her purchase. She told the salesman to write down the automobile details that were essential to buy a full coverage insurance policy. She returned to the lot with the policy and the purchase of a small sedan was completed. She drove to McNamara's rather large home in Glen Ellyn, a suburb of Chicago. He had left the garage over-hanging door unlocked. She clicked a remote switch, the door opened and she drove in. She clicked again to close it.

McNamara's regular pilot was instructed to rent a single plane hangar in Dallas for three months, and to place the Lear Jet in the hangar. The key to the hangar was turned over to the proprietor of the hangar to be picked up by McNamara only. The pilot was to fly commercial back to Las Vegas. There he was given three months salary and told to go and blend into the scenery somewhere.

An expert used car dealer, who was proficient in changing odometer readings, would be employed to change the digital distance on the Lear Jet's aerometer to reflect that it had been flown to Dallas/Fort Worth, Texas and not all the way to Chile and back.

By use of a computer and without any negotiation, a house in the suburbs of Buenos Aires was purchased for the asking price. The place was bought in the names of Thomas and Elizabeth Quinn. McNamara decided that the Quinns would buy a small unobtrusive looking car, once they were established in their new home. Mister Quinn would grow a full beard.

Anthony Phillip Wilson would be left to his own devices, but was asked to stay in touch with Mister Quinn. On November 14, 1984 Charles Tomlinson received a phone call. The voice on the other end of the line uttered a short phrase, "Mister Tomlinson?" The voice sounded familiar. "Your shirts are ready. You may pick them up at any time."

On November 15, the five members of the *Minor League Wagering Team* all pleaded guilty to assorted charges. Their bail was continued until December 20, the date of sentencing. On that date, Mister and Mrs. Thomas Quinn were attending an Asado, an Argentinian barbeque, in their new neighbor's back yard.

CHAPTER EIGHTEEN

The first tapping of silverware on glass by several hundred invitees, signaled that the newlyweds should kiss one another. Both smiling parties stood and obliged their audience. Their embrace was unusually long. They both were aware that this ritual would be repeated many more times before the evening came to a close.

Joe Beyerly took Edith Howell by the hand and raised it on high. From the audience came a combination of hoots, hollers and applause. There also came a chorus of demands for speeches be made by the newlyweds, but in keeping with tradition, the speeches would come later.

Sonny said, "You know, if I were a woman I think I'd cry. I really would."

Rochelle whispered, "Well, I have no such compunctions and I am crying." She wiped her eyes with her dinner napkin.

"They both look beautiful, don't they?"

Rochelle responded, "If a man can look beautiful, Joe fits the bill. Nothing really need be said about the bride . . . but she is radiant."

"Too bad I have to give them the bad news . . . that Tomlinson and McNamara never showed up for the sentencing. They are now fugitives and hundreds of bail bondsmen are looking for them, to say nothing of the FBI agents and U.S. marshals. Their bail totaled four million dollars so there's much incentive for the bondsmen, who are probably tripping over each other, to find those bastards."

"But they were both pretty high profile people in Las Vegas. It shouldn't be that hard to find them," Rochelle suggested.

"What the bail bondsman, who pledged the money should do, is to persuade Joe to take a leave of absence and hire him to track these guys."

She continued, "Would Winston Hathaway permit such a thing . . . that is, give him a leave of absence and then let Joe come back to work for him once he finds the fugitives?"

"By that time, Joe would be such a national hero, Hathaway would be begging him to come back, and probably with a raise in pay."

"But Edith would have to give up her honeymoon."

"Postpone is a better way to describe it. And just think of what a honeymoon they'd have on the couple hundred thousand dollars the bail bondsman would pay them . . . maybe even more than that."

Rochelle looked glassy eyed. "Hmm. Why don't you quit your job and put on your tracking shoes. I've now got thousands of dollars dancing around in my head."

"Because I'm not the genius at investigating that Joe is. But he's not the lawyer that I am."

"I guess I can't argue with that."

Rochelle had been the maid of honor and Sonny the best man at the wedding. They were entitled to hitch a ride with Edith and Joe back to the church to retrieve their car. Edith's parents had driven the Campbells to the reception at the country club.

The men sat in front, the women in the rear.

"Joe, you're probably the best investigator in the state of Maryland," said Sonny.

Joe responded incredulously. "Is that so? Hagerstown's own Dick Tracy, am I?"

Rochelle backed up her husband. "It's true, Joe. You are the best in Maryland."

"What are you two up to?" asked Edith.

Sonny explained, "Tomlinson and McNamara didn't show up for their sentencing. They're now federal fugitives. Four million dollars in bail money is out there somewhere."

"So, what are you thinking Joe should do about it?" asked Edith.

"Just listen to what Sonny has to say, then you can make up your minds."

"So, speak Mister Campbell," Joe said.

"Just imagine if Joe Beyerly found those two fugitives. . . . Think of the money the bail bondsman would have to pay him . . . thousands . . . it's traditional."

"And what about my job with Hathaway?"

"Hathaway would want you to take a leave of absence. . . . And he would want you back after you found those guys . . . probably even give you a raise."

"And what about our honeymoon?" asked Edith. "We've already paid for two weeks in the Bahamas."

"What about a two hundred thousand dollar honeymoon? All you need is a little patience," answered Sonny

"And we just throw away our trip to the Bahamas?" she responded.

"I'll tell you what. Rochelle has spring break coming up. And I've got some time coming. We'll buy your Bahamian trip from you and pay the travel agency the difference for any adjustment that our schedule may cause."

Edith was now very interested in what was being proposed. "You think Joe can actually make two hundred thousand dollars if he finds the fugitives?"

"Positive."

"Oh, Joe. Just think of what we could do with that amount of money."

Joe said impatiently, "All right, all right. I'll ask Hathaway for an indefinite leave of absence. But who's going to talk to the bail bondsman? He's got something to say about this scheme, you know."

Sonny said, "I'll take care of that. I can honestly say you've got a head start on the search . . . that there's nobody who knows more about this case than you do."

Joe insisted, "Do that first. Then I'll bring the whole deal to Hathaway and see what he says about a leave of absence."

"Thata boy. And we'll send Edith a postcard from the Bahamas."

Rochelle asked Edith, "What's your honest opinion, Edith? Do you want Joe to undertake this thing?"

"Two hundred thousand dollars is a lot of money. I say yes."

"Where'd you park, Sonny?"

"Right out in front of the church."

"That's going to be a good deal for those two," said Sonny.

"Yeah. I wish it were you."

"Remember, he's the best."

"And all you ever wanted to be was a small town lawyer."

"That's still true. When we get home, I'm going to outline every thing that Joe has already done in this case. I don't want to miss anything when I talk to the bail bondsman in Baltimore."

"What you should understand, Mister Fleetwood, is that Joe Beyerly knows more about McNamara and Tomlinson than any other human being on earth. He, practically single handedly, broke the case. He knows their habits, their skills, their likes and dislikes, and where they are likely to think of going. Give him an exclusive contract and you'll have them both behind bars in a month."

"You are probably unaware that an applicant to become an agent must have one year's experience as an employee of an insurer and he also must pass an examination given by the insurance commissioner."

"I know that and so does he. We also know that both of those requirements can be waived by the commissioner, which in Joe's case will surely happen, right?"

"You drive a hard bargain, Mister Campbell. All right, have him come to Baltimore and drop by here. I'll arrange the proper waivers and bonding. I've heard of the famous Joe Beyerly. He has an excellent reputation. Instinct tells me I'm making the right move here."

"Mister Fleetwood, I guarantee you're making the right move. Joe will have your quarry before a judge before you can say Jackie Robinson."

"Very funny, Mister Campbell. I'll still keep my fingers crossed."

On Monday afternoon Sonny telephoned Joe at his office.

"It's a go, Joe. Do you think you can find Fleetwood's Bailbond Office in Baltimore?"

"I better be able to find his office, that is if he expects me to find his two fugitives."

"He'll take care of all the paperwork for you. I guess your reputation marches out in front of you by a mile. Congratulations!"

"Thanks, Sonny. Couldn't have done it without you."

"You're very welcome, Mister Bounty Hunter."

The four sleuths held a strategy meeting at Sonny's house that very night.

"When was the last time anyone saw McNamara and what was he doing?" asked Rochelle.

"In court . . . at the guilty pleas. He was the last one to get arrested, wasn't he?" asked Rochelle.

Sonny answered, "Yeah, they picked him up with some woman in Stratford, Canada."

Joe said, "Looks like I start with that woman. Does anyone have her name?" The question was met with silence.

"You can get her name from the FBI agents who arrested McNamara," said Sonny.

Joe joked, "I wish I could have this team with me until I catch up with those two bums."

"I'll go with you if you split what you make off this caper with me," said Sonny.

"No deal."

"Hello. This is FBI agent Gene Gillespie speaking."

"This is Joe Beyerly, investigator for the State's Attorney for Maryland. How are you today, Mister Gillespie?"

"I'm fine. What can I do for you today, Mister Beyerly?"

"Well, I'm investigating the whereabouts of a pair of fugitives in a case you've got going in Baltimore."

"You must mean Douglas McNamara and Charlie Tomlinson, don't you? I've heard of you Mister Beyerly and the great job you did in busting our case open for us."

"Yeah, McNamara's the bird I'm looking for just now. He may have arranged a murder here in Hagerstown. You apprehended him in Stratford, Canada, didn't you?"

"I did indeed. I and another agent."

"And he was with a woman at the time?"

"Yeah. Merideth Ostrowski. We almost charged her with aiding and abetting a federal fugitive."

"Why didn't you?"

"Because we figured she got duped by McNamara . . . knew nothing about his being a fugitive."

"Have you got a photograph of the woman, by any chance?"

"Sure, we do. I'll send you one . . . care of the Maryland State's Attorney's office, Hagerstown, right?"

"Right. When did you last see her?"

"She was at McNamara's arraignment . . . sat down front . . . next to Mark Greenberg's mother."

"What's the mother's name?"

"Sarah Greenberg. . . . Lives in East New York. That's in Brooklyn. I'll send the address and phone number along with Ostrowski's photo and her last known address and number."

"That's very kind of you, Mister Gillespie."

"Think nothing of it, Mister Beyerly. All part of the job."

"Well. So long for now"

"Call me if you need anything else from us."

Winston Hathaway's secretary held up a brown envelope and waved it in the direction of Joe Beyerly as he arrived for work. Hathaway was enthusiastic about granting a leave of absence for Joe which was to start in a few days. **"This is for you, Joe . . . from the F.B.I,"** shouted the secretary.

Joe opened the envelope immediately. A letter accompanied a photograph of Merideth Ostrowski.

Dear Mister Beyerly:

At your request I enclose a photo of Merideth Ostrowski. The address of Sarah Greenberg is 20-25 Sheepshead Bay Avenue, Brooklyn. 11223. Her phone number is 718 535 4971.

The last known address of Ostrowski was 3086 Meadowbrook Avenue, Stratford, Canada. N5A 2M5. Her phone number was 519 435 6798. That's the place where we picked up McNamara.

As ever,

Gene Gillespie
Gene Gillespie

He turned back to the secretary and asked, "Jean, would you try to get a hold of Sonny Campbell and ask him if he'll have lunch with me today?"

Jean said, "Gotcha."

Minutes later Jean got Joe's attention and said, "You're on for lunch with Sonny Campbell at Dino's."

Joe showed Gillespie's letter to Sonny. They were working on a large pizza with green peppers and mushrooms. Sonny read the letter and said, "This will give you a good start. Both of these women might be helpful."

"Should I start with Ostrowski. She's one of McNamara's girlfriends. Greenberg is Mark Greenberg's mother. I doubt if she'll be much help."

"Maybe one will lead to the other."

"Yeah, maybe the two talked to each other in the court room."

"When does your leave of absence start?"

"In a few days."

"I guess we won't be seeing much of you after it starts."

"Guess not. This search will probably take me all over the world."

Sonny raised his mug of beer and said, "Well, good hunting."

"Thanks pal. I won't come back till I got 'em both. What you got going in my absence?"

"Chester Roosevelt wants to see me about something. I'm going over to the Detention Center when we finish here."

"How's he holding up?"

"Not bad. In a way, he's depending on you, along with every one else, only more so. He's convinced that Constanza is lying and that he murdered Archy."

"Good theory. Good as anything else I've heard."

"Well, you've got to nab McNamara and we've got to beat the truth out of his hit man. You'll hear a sigh of relief all the way in France or in whatever country you find Mister M. . . . Roosevelt still has me on his team. He did not kill Archy, as far as I'm concerned."

"He's lucky to have you, still pluggin' for him."

"Well, I better be on my way. Since you're soon gonna be a very wealthy man, I'll let you get the tab."

"Another incentive for me to succeed."

CHAPTER NINETEEN

Chester Roosevelt sat patiently waiting for Sonny. The prohibition against Sonny's communicating with Chester had been relaxed. Chester had almost become a forgotten man. No trial date had been established. The unspoken reason was the existence of Mario Constanza. The judge was not going to rush to a trial where reasonable doubt was a foregone conclusion, only to discover after an acquittal that Roosevelt was guilty after all. Ed Wilson was content to leave things as they were and refused to raise the issue of a speedy trial. He feared that there would be a conviction and then a later confession from Constanza that would be meaningless. The existence of these opposing forces caused the trial process to be mired down.

"I didn't think you were going to come this time. I thought you might have given up on me, Mister Campbell."

"Never. I don't believe you killed that man, Chet. Other things have been occupying my mind."

"About my case?"

"In a way, yes."

"May I ask what things?"

"Mister McNamara didn't show up for his sentencing. Joe Beyerly has been assigned the job of finding him. I just had lunch with Joe. He's already got some leads. He brings him before Judge Zavitz and McNamara confesses that he put out a contract on Archy Howell, and your chances of an acquittal go up astronomically. It's called reasonable doubt. Once a jury smells a theory that somebody else killed Archy, they're bound to set you free."

"That's the best news I've had since they put me in here."

"I feel the same way, Chet."

"You've got to promise me that you'll keep me posted on every thing you hear about Mister Beyerly's progress."

"Now, the message you got to me said that you have something urgent on your mind. What is so urgent?"

"I haven't seen or heard from Howard Parsons for over two years. The last time he was here he promised emphatically to visit the following week. He also said that he had been faithful to me. I find that hard to believe. Now, I don't expect that you should play the cupid role in this romance. But could you find out if anything has happened to him? I dream that he's dead or badly injured or something. Could you at least find out if he's safe and sound? I'd be very grateful to know."

"I'll do my best to find out what his status is. In the mean time, you must keep your chin up. With the help of God and your own instinct, I'm sure you'll come out of this on top. I have other matters to attend to now, so I'll say so long for the time being."

Joe Beyerly picked up Lancaster Highway in Pennsylvania and then it was on to the Pennsylvania Turnpike. It wasn't long before he was entering New York City and on to Brooklyn. He had decided to talk to Mark Greenberg's mother before he tackled the more serious business of Merideth Ostrowski. When he arrived in the Sheepshead Bay area of Brooklyn, he pulled over to call Sarah Greenberg from his car.

"Mrs. Greenberg, this is Joseph Beyerly from Hagerstown, Maryland. It's extremely important I talk to you about your son's case. I'm just minutes away from your apartment house."

"But I don't know who you are. Can you identify yourself?"

"I'm the chief investigator for the State's Attorney in Hagerstown. What I want to talk to you about can't possibly hurt Mark. It might even help him, if you and he cooperate."

"Well, if it could help Mark I guess I'll talk to you. Come on up."

"Did you drive all the way here from Hagerstown, Mister Beyerly?"

"Yes, I did. It was a pleasant drive."

"How can I cooperate to help Mark?"

"You attended the arraignment in Baltimore, didn't you?"

"Yes, I did."

"And you sat next to Merideth Ostrowski, didn't you?"

"Yes."

"Did you talk to her?"

"Yes, briefly."

"Did you find out from her that she had a relationship with one of the defendants?"

"With Douglas McNamara, I believe."

"That's right."

"Did she tell you that they were living together at the time of the arraignment?"

"I think she implied that."

"How so?"

"She mentioned they had driven to Baltimore from Chicago together."

"Did she mention what part of Chicago they were living in?"

"No."

"Did you see the car they were using?"

"No, but she mentioned it was parked outside and their driver was in it. I sort of thought it was a limousine. . . . Oh, one more thing that might be important. She told me they were not going to be in Chicago much longer. Now, you haven't told me how this will help Mark."

"Well, you know that McNamara and Tomlinson didn't show up for their sentencing?"

"Yes, I know that."

"That makes them fugitives. It's been my experience that when a coconspirator helps in the apprehension of one of his escaped comrades that he will often have part of his sentence knocked off."

"I must tell Mark that. Maybe he knows something about where they are. I'm sure he'll be in touch with you if he does."

"You already have been of some help, Mrs. Greenberg. You seem to be a fine lady. I really hope we see each other again." Joe stood and handed Mark Greenberg's mother his business card. She showed him to the door.

The next day found Joe again on the Pennsylvania Turnpike. When he reached the Queen's Expressway he stopped for something to eat. After lunch he drove on to the Gennesee Expressway to Highway 7 which took him into Stratford, Canada.

He drove straight to the Post Office. There he inquired whether the former inhabitants of the Meadowbrook Avenue house had left a forwarding address.

"May I ask for what purpose you want this information, sir?"

Joe showed the clerk his official ID "It's part of an investigation my office is making."

"A Merideth Ostrowski has left a forwarding address for a suburb of Chicago in the U.S. The address is 396 Red Oak Avenue, Glen Ellyn.

The other inhabitant, a Mister Douglas McNamara, left no forwarding address."

Joe then drove to the Meadowbrook Avenue address. The house was still vacant. He used his skeleton key apparatus to open the back door. The inside of the house was as clean as a whistle. He examined every room. He found nothing of significance. After his search of the house was completed he went outside to a back yard. There he found two large garbage cans, both empty. As he was about to leave the property, his eye caught what appeared to be a scrap of white paper at the bottom of one of the cans. His arm was not quite long enough to pick up the scrap. He found a stick and turned the can on its side. He scraped the piece of paper to a spot within reach. The scrap turned out to be a business card. The business was located in Detroit.

That evening, he passed through the Windsor-Detroit tunnel, and drove into the city. He examined the business card he had found in the Meadowbrook Avenue house.

Used Cars Bought and Sold
Mileage Not an Option

Samuel Martin Sussman
13253 Martin Luther King Boulevard
Detroit, Michigan 48242
Phone: 313 785 2549

Mister Sussman's used car lot was a shabby affair. Joe parked his car close to the entrance of a small building, which must have served as an office and washroom and little more. A sign on the office door announced that the business was open. Joe decided to wait for Mister Sussman to appear. Twenty minutes later a 1979 Plymouth baring dealer plates pulled up and parked. A man in a wrinkled gray suit emerged from the car and walked over to where Joe was parked. "Looking for a good ride and a good price, sir?"

Joe responded, "Can we talk?"

"That's what we're here for. Talk and bargain is what I always say."

Joe got out of his car. "What do you mean by *mileage not an option* that appears on your business card?"

"High or low, we can always make adjustments."

"Where do you make the adjustments? I don't see a garage around here anywhere."

"It's a good thing you don't look like a cop. With a remark like that I'd kick you out of here on your keester if you did."

"I'm not a cop. Search me if you want."

"My garage is down the street. It's full up just now. There's always a truck or car in that garage. You got a vehicle that needs adjustment?"

"Maybe. Depends on what you charge."

"What kind of a vehicle do you have?"

"1983 Chrysler limousine."

"How much of an adjustment?"

"Five thousand."

"Fifty cents a mile, ought to do it. By the way who told you about me?"

"Douglas McNamara, remember him?"

Sussman took several moments. "Can't say that I do."

"You wouldn't tell me if you did."

"You're right. Gotta look out for my customers. When do I see the vehicle?"

"I'll bring it in next week sometime."

"Is my price all right?"

"Could be lower, but I'll pay it."

"What's your name?"

"Charlie Hamersham."

"O. K., then. See you next week sometime."

"Right."

Joe was quite sure he had seen recognition in Sussman's eyes when McNamara's name was mentioned. Outside of that small crumb, the meeting with the used car dealer was not very helpful.

Sussman called the Glen Ellyn telephone number he had on file. The phone had already been disconnected. No replacement number was provided by the operator.

Joe returned to Hagerstown. The next morning he drove to the Executive Air Systems office. There he asked to examine the records of incoming and outgoing flights from and to Las Vegas for 1984. He found what he was looking for and copied the information down. McNamara's most recently employed pilot was a Michael Larro who's Hagerstown address was 9563 Peach Tree Lane.

No one was home at the Peach Tree Lane house. The neighbors said its inhabitant hadn't been seen for six weeks. Joe opened the front door with his special key apparatus. The living room floor was littered with hundreds of pieces of mail. He sat on the floor and examined each piece. In twenty-five minutes he found nothing of interest.

He went next door and spoke to a neighbor. He showed the neighbor his State Investigator credentials and handed her his business card. "Would you please notify me on that number if Mister Larro returns to his house? Be discreet about it, if you will. He doesn't have to know you're calling. If I'm not there, leave a message." He left exactly the same message with the man who lived on the other side of the Larro house.

That afternoon he called the Motor Vehicle Bureau in Las Vegas. He identified himself as a State Investigator in Hagerstown.

"How do I know that you are who you say you are?"

"Call back collect and ask for the State's Attorney's office then ask for me, Joseph Beyerly." He gave the clerk Charles Hathaway's number. He waited with Hathaway in his office. The phone rang. The operator spoke, "A Mister Kraft calling you collect from Las Vegas, sir."

"Accept the call, operator."

"Go ahead, sir."

"This is Winston Hathaway, Maryland State's Attorney."

"Mister Beyerly, please."

"One moment." He handed the phone to Beyerly.

"Joe Beyerly, here."

"What can I do for you today, Mister Beyerly?"

"Would you check on the registration of a 1983 Chrysler limousine. It should be in the name of Douglas McNamara or *Universal Lounge.*"

"Here it is. 1984 plate number HN 24854. Registered to McNamara, himself."

"Thank you. Now, do you have a list of limousine operators in the Las Vegas area?"

"Yes. There are about one hundred and forty of them, current for 1984."

"Could you fax the list to this office?"

"Yes, I would. You'll have the list in five minutes. But, I might add, almost everyone in town knows that Larry Bastion drives for Mister McNamara."

"Thank you, Mister Kraft. Don't bother faxing the list."

Joe spoke to Winston Hathaway. "McNamara was so well known in Vegas that Mister Kraft gave me his limousine driver's name off the top of his head."

Joe called the FBI office in Las Vegas. "Agent William Tyson, please."
"Tyson here."

"This is Joe Beyerly, State's Attorney Investigator in Hagerstown, Maryland. Agent Tom Hillenbrand recommended that I talk to you. We're seeking to locate a federal fugitive named Douglas McNamara."

"I'm very familiar with the case, Mister Beyerly. McNamara is well known in these parts. What can I do for you?"

"I've determined that the regular driver of McNamara's limousine is a man named Larry Bastion. We need somebody out there who will pick Mister Bastion's brains . . . find out anything he knows about the whereabouts of the fugitive. I might suggest that there is the identity of McNamara's pilot of his Lear Jet, a man named Michael Larro. That might help. If you could find out where the jet plane now is located, that would also help—also the present location of the limousine, 1984 registration HN 24854. Any questions you might have of me just contact the State's Attorney's office here in Hagerstown."

"We'll do our best, sir."
"Thank you, Mister Tyson. Bye, for now."
"Bye."

The next day, Joe's phone rang. His secretary, Jean announced, "Agent Tyson on the line, Joe."

"Joe Beyerly, here."
"This is Agent Tyson reporting back to you, Mister Beyerly."
"Well, that was quick. You guys really get down to business, don't you?"
"We considered your request urgent, sir."
"Did you get anything worthwhile out of that Bastion fellow?"

"Probably not enough to suit your purposes. Not that he was tight lipped. He just didn't know very much. I'll highlight what we've got here on the phone and follow up with a written report."

"That'll be fine."

"Well, the last contact he had with McNamara was at the time of the guilty plea. He worked his regular shuttling tasks for him until three days after the plea and then he was sent back here to Las Vegas. Then something out of the ordinary happened. He was instructed by phone to drive all the way from here to Baltimore and pick up Charles Tomlinson at the Radisson Hotel and drive him to McNamara's home in Chicago. Tomlinson didn't say a word to him the entire trip, except *thank you* and a few other niceties. He brought two large suit cases along, which he was asked to bring into the house in Glen Ellyn. McNamara abruptly discharged him in Chicago and gave him three months salary and thanked him for his service. He was told he could keep the limousine and papers were prepared transferring ownership. He drove back here and has been operating as a limousine service ever since. The vehicle has never been out of his possession since his return."

"How about McNamara's Lear Jet? Anything on its location?"

"The Lear Jet is in Dallas, Texas, in a locked hangar. We're assuming that you will find your two fugitives somewhere near Dallas. The location we got mostly from the pilot's pals in Las Vegas. We found that Larro's got a big mouth. The fact that McNamara fired him seems to have loosened his tongue."

"That's certainly a ton of information. Thank you, Mister Tyson. Look forward to reading your report. Talk to you again. Bye for now."

Joe received Tyson's report the next day. He reviewed his recent discoveries in his mind. *Tomlinson, carrying suitcases, got together with McNamara three days after the guilty pleas. They got rid of the limousine so Sussman, the used car salesman, wasn't hired to work on the car. That leaves the Lear Jet. You can't bring a Lear Jet down Martin Luther King Boulevard to Sussman's garage, so Sussman had to travel to wherever the plane was. They had to have a car so they probably bought one inconspicuously. Merideth Ostrowski would have come in handy to buy the car. Changing the air mileage on the plane means that they expect the plane to be tracked down, but wanted to hide the distance it traveled away from Dallas. Gotta talk to Michael Larro. If I don't miss my guess, the three of them flew somewhere quite distant from Dallas. . . . Probably drove from Chicago to Dallas. Sussman's mileage adjustment will tell us how far they flew.*

CHAPTER TWENTY

Joe's investigation remained almost nonproductive for a week. Then a pleasant break came by way of two phone calls from Michael Larro's neighbors. Larro had come home!

He got a hold of a sheriff's deputy whom he knew well and the two hurriedly drove in a marked sheriff's vehicle to the Larro home.

Joe rang the buzzer and was greeted at the front door by a youthful, trim and handsome man who appeared shocked by the sight of the deputy and Joe holding his official ID in his face.

"Mister Larro?"

"Yes."

"May we come in? We have a few questions for you."

"I don't know. Should I call a lawyer?"

"If you think you need one. Have you done anything wrong lately. I really think you don't need a lawyer . . . not yet, anyway."

Silently, Larro stepped aside and let the two men in.

"May we sit down?"

"Of course."

"To begin with, I have to ask you whether you are still employed by Douglas McNamara?"

"No. He let me go a couple o' months ago."

"Where was it that he let you go?"

"I was in Las Vegas. Say, are you sure I don't need a lawyer here?"

"Well, we can charge you with obstructing justice and then you will need a lawyer. Do you want to go ahead and answer my question?"

"I guess I better. He told me to fly to Dallas and rent a hangar there for three months. I would receive three months salary and then I was to get lost. I should leave the key to the hangar with the proprietor to be picked up by McNamara only. I did as I was told and flew commercial back here. A couple days later I received three months salary in the mail. I took off for a much needed vacation in Cancun, Mexico."

"Have you heard from either McNamara or Tomlinson since?"

"Nope. Not a word."

"Mister Larro, I suggest you don't leave Hagerstown without notifying my office." Joe handed Larro his business card. "Now, all that wasn't so painful, was it? You don't need to show us out."

Back in the State's Attorney's office, Joe called FBI agent Tom Hillenbrand. "Tom, I think I'm on to something. Do you think you can get authority to accompany me to Detroit, tomorrow. What I suspect is that Tomlinson, McNamara and his girlfriend have somehow flown out of the country from Dallas, Texas in McNamara's Lear Jet. To put us off their trail I think he got a used car salesman to go to Dallas to adjust the air mileage on the plane. I've talked to the salesman and he's pretty slick. I think, however, with a little federal intimidation he might come clean. We've got enough evidence already to arrest him on the spot if he doesn't cooperate."

"Sounds fascinating, Joe. I'm pretty sure I can get the authority. Any idea where they went?"

"That'll depend on the mileage adjustment that this guy, Samuel Sussman, made on McNamara's Lear Jet. Call me back and confirm your authority. I'll arrange our plane tickets and car rental."

"You got it, Joe."

On the plane, Joe further outlined his plan. "If we find out how much Sussman adjusted the jet's mileage backward, we take that amount and divide it by two. That'll give the number of miles they flew the plane away from Dallas. We get a map of the world and get a hold of one of those big protractors and spike it on Dallas and extend the curve to match the distance they traveled. As we sweep it around the map, we'll hit water most of the time But where it hits land, that'll show us the possible places where they might have flown to."

"Ingenious, Joe."

"Sussman holds the key. We've got to use your expertise in interrogation to break him down."

"We can have some fun with this if we do it right."

Joe and Tom drove their rental VW to the used car lot on Martin Luther King Boulevard. The sign on the door said the lot was open. Joe said, "I hope that sign means what it says."

They parked near the office door, got out and entered the office. Samuel Sussman was sitting at his shabby desk and fairly leaped out of his chair when he saw and recognized Joe. Sussman glanced outside and asked, "Is that what you call a limousine?"

Joe answered, "No, Mister Sussman. And I'm not what you think I am either." He showed Sussman his official ID. "And I'd like you to meet FBI agent Tom Hillenbrand."

Sussman paled and sat back down in his desk chair.

Tom said, "Before I place you under arrest, Mister Sussman, I want to give you the opportunity to mitigate your crimes by coming clean on one of them."

"I'm not saying a word until my lawyer gets here."

Tom responded, "Oops, I'm afraid there goes any mitigation right down the toilet. Go ahead, call your lawyer. We've got all the time in the world."

Sussman's hand was on his telephone receiver. When he heard Tom's short speech he removed his hand from the phone and asked, "What do you want to talk about and how much mitigation are you offering."

"A free ride on everything if you give the right answers."

"Whew! This must be a hell of a case you two are investigating."

Tom brought out a picture of Douglas McNamara and showed it to Sussman. "Do you know this man?"

"Maybe."

Tom said roughly, "There goes five percent of the mitigation, right there. We know you know him and what you did for him in Dallas."

"If you know everything, why don't you arrest me?"

"There's one specific we got to get from you. Give it to us and you're a free man . . . for the time being anyway . . . until you roll back another odometer on a car or a plane."

"What specific?"

There's a short answer to that question.

"Which is?"

"How much did you take off McNamara's Lear Jet in Dallas?"

"Jeez. You do know it all."

Joe shouted, **"How many miles, Sussman?"**

"Don't shout. I gotta look it up."

Sussman pulled back a top drawer and shuffled through some papers. "Here it is. Exactly 9724 miles."

Tom asked, "Where'd you get that number."

"From a guy named Tomlinson who was standing right where you are. He came in with McNamara."

"How much did they pay you?"

"The usual. Fifty cents a mile. 4,862 dollars."

Joe said, "That's what I call comin' clean. Like Tom said, you're a free man till you roll another odometer. Then we'll come down on you like white on snow. Letting McNamara or Tomlinson know we've been here would be a bad move. You'd be guilty of obstructing justice and wind up in the same place those guys are going, understand?"

"All I understand is I'm a free man, right?"

Tom answered, "I said it, didn't I. You can bank your crummy business on it. Goodbye, Mister Sussman."

"Get the hell, out of here. You made me crap my pants."

It took the better part of the afternoon to locate a large world map. Using the scale printed on the map, an FBI technician used a large protractor with a representative distance of 4,862 miles between it's two arms. One arm had a sharp point on it's end which Tom placed on Dallas, Texas. Joe swept the other arm slowly around the map, noting all the countries that were touched by the point of the other arm. The European continent was too far. England and Ireland were too close. Buenos Aires was too far. Santiago, Chile was right on the money. Chile became their working target.

"What do you know about Chile, Tom," asked Joe.

"Pacific Ocean on the west side and the Andes mountains on the east. Skinniest country in the world. Santiago's a pretty lively city. It's been a police state for years, thanks to our CIA. Perfect place to land a Lear Jet. Probably have to pay the police off. Wanna take a trip down there, Joe?"

"Don't have any choice, do we?"

"My wife will probably have deserted me by the time we get back."

"Ditto."

Joe was home in time for a sirloin tip roast for dinner. Edith didn't spare the trimmings. He had called her from Tom's office and told her about the trip to Chile.

"It's a good thing I love you, you clever man. I don't think I even know where Chile is."

"I'll tell you all about it when I get back. By the size of that roast we should have invited about ten guests."

"Oh, no. I've got you all to myself tonight. And don't plan on getting much sleep, my dear."

"I'll sleep on the plane."

"Now, be serious for a moment. Do you think you're getting close to those guys?"

"Seriously, I think I am. They're either in Chile or in a country nearby. But Tom and I have some heavy duty investigating ahead of us."

"It'll have been worth it, if you catch up with them. Think of all that money you'll get."

"You know something? The money will be nice, but I haven't been thinking about it much. Too wrapped up in what I'm doing, I guess."

"That's the kinda guy you are, and I love you for it. Let's go to bed early, O. K?"

"No, argument there."

The next morning he was up at the crack of dawn. He drove to Tom's office. Tom was waiting for him. He drove to the airport. He parked in the long term parking area. They were on a plane headed for Chicago within the hour.

They sat in the Santiago departure gate area at O'Hare airport. "You know Joe, now that we're about to make a forty-five-hundred mile trip, I kinda hope your theory about the protractor and all that stuff was right."

"I haven't let you down yet, have I?"

"By golly. I wish I were perfect like you."

Joe said, "Let's review what we've got here."

Tom asked, "Do we know what day they took off from Dallas for Santiago?"

"I think we're close. The sentencing date was September 24. Neither one of them was there. But three days later, Larry Bastion delivered Tomlinson and his luggage to the Glen Ellyn House. I have to presume that they left Chicago the same day and drove to Dallas. They either drove straight through or took two days to make the trip. That brings us to either 28 or 29 September. Sussman had already rolled back the mileage on the Lear Jet so they could feel free to fly out of Dallas and land in Santiago on either of those two days. They probably prearranged with a Chilean pilot to fly the plane right back to Dallas and lock it up in the hangar for the authorities to find. That pilot turns himself right around and flies commercial back to Santiago on either September 30 or October 1. The fugitives have already left for parts unknown—that is unknown by everyone with the possible exception of that pilot. If he had been their Chilean contact he may have arranged their exit from the city. We've got to learn the identity of the pilot."

"How about this? We call my Dallas office and have them get the passenger manifests for all flights from Dallas to Santiago on September 30, October 1, and, for good measure, October 2. . . . There's a phone right over there on that wall that I can use. . . . Then, we have them call our Consular Office in Santiago and ask that they contact the Chilean police state authorities and request that they check the manifests for anyone employed as a pilot who might have reentered Chile on the critical dates. There cannot be many pilots' names on those manifests . . . probably only one. Depending on the degree of cooperation that we now enjoy with the Chilean police state, we request that the pilot be picked up and held for questioning. You know that our CIA practically created the fascist police state that now governs Chile. We shouldn't have a problem."

Joe said with a sense of urgency, "Make the call. They're going to announce our flight any minute now."

Tom went over to the nearby bank of telephones. He spoke on a phone for about five minutes, then returned to where Joe was snoozing in his chair. "Hate to wake you up pal, but they're about to call our flight."

"I was half dreaming about your plan. Did you get through all right?" Tom nodded his head. Joe gave Tom a compliment. "You sounded to me like you knew what you were talking about. And you know, I did a little research myself last night. I'll tell you what I found when I looked up on my computer what the visa situation in that country is. As a foreigner you need a valid passport to enter. They will issue you a tourist card for a fee, good for ninety days. We'll check the authorities' tourist cards files to see if they left Santiago. If our two boys stayed in Chile we'll have to track them down there, with the pilot's help. Maybe even the authorities will lend a hand when they see your FBI credentials. If they left Chile they would have to have surrendered their tourist cards. We may be able to glean false identities from those cards if we're given a chance to examine them."

A loud speaker called their flight for Santiago. "Come on, Tom. Let's line up. I want to get aboard and get some shut eye. We have a lot to do when we get off this plane."

When they disembarked in Santiago and had cleared customs, Tom called the U.S. Consular office. A contact gave him the name and telephone number of an English speaking Chilean official who by this time was supposed to have examined the critical Dallas to Santiago manifests. He called the official's number and received some good news. A Chilean citizen, the only pilot whose name appeared on the manifests, was being confined in a cell awaiting an interview by Tom and Joe. The two American investigators would have to pay a fee for the service performed in apprehending the pilot, but the entire matter was conducted with a spirit of cooperation.

The U.S. Consular Service had made available a Spanish speaking employee who would be present for the interview with the pilot. They took a taxi to the central Chilean police station where they were greeted at the entrance to an ancient gray building by the man from the Consular Service

"Which one of you two guys is Agent Hillenbrand?" Tom extended his hand. "I'm Peter Gallegos. I take it this is your comrade, Mister Beyerly."

"Yes, I'm Joseph Beyerly."

"They've got your man in a holding cell in the back of the station. Follow me and we'll see what he has to say. I'm afraid he's not a very happy man. He's been screaming for a lawyer, but that doesn't mean much in this country."

The two investigators followed Gallegos into the building where a uniformed policeman introduced himself as police chief and led them to a bank of cells. In one cell, a disheveled looking man sat on a metal cot wringing his hands and was obviously complaining about something in Spanish. He looked up and when he saw the group of visitors he leapt to his feet and directed his Spanish complaints to all who stood outside his cell staring at him.

Tom spoke, "He probably speaks English, if you've got the right man."

"You're damn right I speak English. What the hell's this all about, anyway?"

The police chief spoke politely. "Señor Beyerly, if you wish to ask the prisoner some questions you may do so."

"Tom, would you hand me those photographs? . . . Sir, what is your name?"

"Ask the police chief, here. I've already told him what my name is."

"Como se llama?" The police chief almost shouted.

"Raul Hernandez."

Joe showed the prisoner two photographs, one of Tomlinson and one of McNamara. "Do you know either of these men?"

Hernandez shook his head in the negative.

The police chief spoke again. "Señor Beyerly, would you and your compatriots please excuse yourselves to the front office. I wish to speak to Señor Hernandez privately."

The three Americans left the cell block. As soon as a door closed behind them, a single loud voice could be heard. In the office area Joe asked, "What's that all about?"

The Consular officer answered, "Our country has paid a considerable amount of money to the present police government of this country to purchase, so to speak, their respect and cooperation. I think what we are witnessing is one of the benefits of money well spent."

When the shouting from the cell block subsided, the door opened and the policemen invited the Americans back in.

"Señor Beyerly, you may ask Señor Hernandez again if he knows the men in your pictures."

"Without being asked, Hernandez said, "I know both of the men. Mister Tomlinson has been my flying colleague for more than fifteen years. He is presently living in my home, here in Santiago."

Joe asked, "And the other man?"

"I also know Mister McNamara. He is now using the name of Thomas Quinn. He and Mrs. Quinn are presently traveling by bus by way of Mendoza through the Andes with the intention of settling in Buenos Aires, Argentina."

Tom asked, "What name is Tomlinson using?"

"Anthony Wilson."

Joe asked, "Mister Hernandez, did you recently illicitly fly Mister McNamara's Lear Jet to Dallas Texas?"

"Yes, I flew across the border undetected, landed in Dallas and placed the plane in a private hangar which Mister McNamara's map directed me to. I locked the hangar door and flew commercial back here. The police chief here has the hangar key along with my other private possessions."

Tom asked, "Did you receive compensation for flying the plane to Dallas?"

"Yes, I did."

"How much?"

"Ten thousand, U.S."

"Where is that money?"

"With Mister Tomlinson, for safe keeping."

Joe asked Tom, "Do you have any more questions of Mister Hernandez, Tom."

"I don't think so. I think that's all."

The four men left the cell block and went to the police chief's office.

Joe asked the police chief, "What happens to that man now?"

The chief answered, "We all take him home and collect Mister Tomlinson for you. Our courts will approve Tomlinson's extradition to your country. Incidentally, Argentina has an extradition treaty with your country also . . .

if you ever catch up with that other fellow, McNamara and his wife. In the mean time we will hold Tomlinson in a cell until your people file the essential extradition papers."

Tom asked the chief, "What's the best way for us to get to Buenos Aires?"

"By plane. Automobile is too dangerous to the uninitiated. The bus is safer and it attracts less attention than renting an aircraft. Still, you have nothing to hide, do you. I'd fly if I were you. I'll assist with the renting of an airplane and expert pilot. Now, let's drive to Hernandez' home and pick up your man, Tomlinson. We'll take an official police vehicle to scare the fugitive into submission."

The flight from Santiago to Buenos Aires was frightening. It was the first time that either of the investigators had flown through a dangerous, fog shrouded mountainous area. While refusing to communicate their fears to one another, both Joe and Tom had visions of crash landing in the snowy Andes and having to wait to be rescued.

Their fears were unfounded. They were safe and sound when they disembarked their small plane at Buenos Aires. By telephone from Santiago they had arranged for indefinite lodging in Buenos Aires.

The following morning they went to a real estate office in their rented car, and inquired after recent house purchases by anyone by the name of Thomas Quinn. The name showed up in the records. They then stopped at a police station, and, by prearrangement, rode with two police officers in their patrol car to the modest home that McNamara had purchased weeks before under the name of Quinn. There was a second hand Ford Thunderbird parked in the driveway. Joe, Tom and the two officers went to the front door and flipped the brass door knocker a couple of times. Merideth Ostrowski came to the door. When she saw who her visitor were, she screamed, **"Douglas."** McNamara came running and saw the two officers flanking Joe Beyerly with their guns drawn.

"Oh, my God! Beyerly! I should have known I couldn't outwit you. Will you give us time to pack a few things? Nothing like receiving unexpected guests."

The Baltimore Federal Court was filled to capacity, mostly with members of the media. Charles Tomlinson and Douglas McNamara stood in the front of the courtroom with their heads bowed and lawyers at their sides. Judge Samuel Zavitz was speaking. "I hesitate to say that you two should be given some moral credit, so to speak, for not resisting extradition from Argentina, gentlemen. But for the swift and artful action of Mister Joseph Beyerly, the total bail for the both of you, the huge sum of four million dollars might have been forfeited. I have before me an affidavit, signed by FBI agent Thomas Hillenbrand, stating that he provided some small amount of technical assistance in the apprehension of the two of you in Buenos Aires and Santiago. Mister Hillenbrand further states that practically all of the critical planning and investigation was provided by Mister Beyerly. However, in the spirit of fairness, it is ordered that Mister Beyerly, and or, Mister Fleetwood, the bondsman in this matter, shall reimburse all actual expenditures advanced by the U.S. government for technical assistance, the details of that reimbursement to be worked out and agreed to by Mister Beyerly and Mister Fleetwood.

"It is further ordered that from this day forward the two fugitive defendants shall be held without bail until the date of their sentencing.

"It is further ordered that the date of sentencing shall be December 7, 1984 at ten o'clock in the morning. Now that date will forever hereafter commemorate more than Pearl Harbor Now, it is my understanding that there is to be an arraignment of a Merideth Ostrowski on the charge of aiding and abetting a federal fugitive, immediately following these proceedings."

U.S. Attorney Lacey spoke. "That's correct your Honor. Miss Ostrowski is currently being held without bail and I will, under the circumstances of her apprehension, be moving that his Honor continue to order her held without bail."

"We'll get to that matter in a few minutes, Mister Lacey."

CHAPTER TWENTY ONE

Pop . . . pop . . . pop. Champagne bottles popped incessantly for five minutes as the Country Club celebration got underway. Joe Beyerly didn't really want the party to take place. He was an inherently modest man, but his wife Edith insisted.

Sonny and Rochelle Campbell approved as well. After all it was Sonny's idea that Joe would be the most desirable person to track down the fugitives. Sonny's prophesy proved correct. The bad guys were brought before Judge Zavitz in record time. It would now be up to Ed Wilson to fashion a part of Chester's defense through the admission of Douglas McNamara that he had hired a hit man to kill Archy Howell. The problem of that hit man's denial that he did the killing would be a sticky one, but Sonny planned to work on a Constanza confession. Even if that didn't work, the mere fact of the McNamara hiring of Constanza might be enough to convince a jury that there was reasonable doubt that Chester did the murder.

But this was a night to celebrate, not to be contemplating the misery of Chester Roosevelt. Rochelle asked Joe to dance, not expecting that he would accept. But he did. He was very fond of the beautiful Rocky Campbell and he knew that his equally beautiful wife Edith would not be jealous. That aside, the music the orchestra was playing was a waltz and Joe could waltz as well as he played tennis.

The Beyerlys made a major decision after they received Joe's substantial compensation for the capture of Tomlinson and McNamara. They would not reveal to anyone, except the IRS, of course, the amount of money he received. However, all in attendance at this night's celebration knew that the party cost the Beyerlys a small fortune. Joe and Edith would never have been able to afford it prior to their windfall payment by the Fleetwood bail bonding business.

Ed Wilson stood with a group of lawyers discussing their hero, Joe Beyerly. Never before, in the history of Hagerstown, had such a dramatic event occurred. And it had been a dangerous adventure to boot. Flying over the fogbound Andes in a small plane, on his way to capture a man who could kill if he thought he had to, and dealing with the Chilean police state had to be a touch-and-go situation even if you had an FBI agent as your partner. Joe would be talked about for decades. He was a genuine hero.

Ed Wilson also talked about his defense of Chester Roosevelt. "Now, I've got a chance for an acquittal. There would be no deal, no matter what Hathaway may offer."

Joe was back working for Hathaway, his leave of absence having come to a logical conclusion. Hathaway was as proud of Joe as the rest of the world. He was well aware that Wilson was now holding a much stronger hand in the Roosevelt case than he held. The time for plea offers had disappeared. And, of course, the possibility of windfall money from McNamara for making a plea offer, had disappeared as well.

Ed Wilson's secretary, Patricia Erickson, stared at Joe Beyerly dancing with Rochelle Campbell. *And to think that I practically ignored Joe Beyerly all those years he worked for Winston Hathaway. It's not just that he's a bloody hero and a wealthy man, he's really quite an attractive man physically. Oh, well. Such is life . . . nothing but missed opportunities. Somewhere there's got to be a man out there for me. After all, I'm a damn good looking woman.*

There was an unlikely guest standing across the dance floor, with a very handsome young man. Edith said to Sonny, "I haven't the slightest idea who that man is standing next to that beautiful youngster over by the champagne table."

"You gave Rochelle and me the option of inviting twenty-five guests of our own choice. I invited Howard Parsons, over there. He was Chester Roosevelt's lover at the time Archy was murdered. I didn't know that he was going to bring his current little fancy boy with him. And now I'm going to have to report to Chet that he's been betrayed by Parsons. It's going to break Chet's heart. It's really sad."

Edith responded, "I never have understood how you could be so sure that this Roosevelt fellow is innocent of the murder. Maybe I can fathom it now that we know that McNamara hired a hit man to do it, but you didn't know that way back when."

"Edith, I pride myself with knowing innocence when I see it. I wasn't with Chester Roosevelt more than ten minutes before I became positive he was innocent. I still feel that way. By the same token, I'm almost positive that Mario Constanza is lying when he denies doing the job. I'm going to work on Constanza and maybe I can get him to admit his guilt."

"Oh, Sonny, you're never going to get Constanza to admit he did it. He's beat death once, with the help of his surgeons, and he'd have to be a fool to take a chance with the death chamber by admitting he's guilty of committing murder."

"I'm going to see if I can convince Hathaway to take the death penalty off the table in a trade for Constanza's confession."

"I have my doubts that that's ever going to happen, either."

"We'll see, Edith. Dance with me, will you. I want to see if I can do these modern dances that the kids do."

"What makes you think I can do modern kids' dances?"

"Because I've seen you do it. Come dance with me."

She agreed and both of them acquitted themselves on the dance floor quite well.

Howard Parsons' companion spoke softly. "Isn't this going to get back to Chester Roosevelt?"

"I want it to. I don't have the guts to tell him myself . . . or even visit him again, for that matter."

"I better never reach the conclusion that you're still in love with that killer. You do love me, don't you?"

"How many times have I told you I love you?"

"Yeah, but it's always when I'm in your bed. I wish that some time you can tell me you love me when we're doing our laundry together, for instance."

Parsons laughed. "We're about due for a trip to the coin laundry. I'll tell everybody in there that I love you madly."

The party lasted till one in the morning. The Campbells, the Brocks and the Beyerlys went to Sonny's house for coffee. After they had settled in, Walter Brock got into a mild argument with Sonny about the CIA's role in setting up fascist governments to defeat Communism.

Sonny said, "This country has been empire building for decades—trying to emulate England. Don't you remember Guatemala and the United Fruit Company when Allen Dulles was running the CIA. Don't you remember when the people in that country voted to have a Socialist government . . . that's not a *Communist* government . . . but a *Socialist* government? Allen Dulles' brother, John Foster Dulles was on the board of directors of the United Fruit Company. That company had systematically acquired vast mounts of acreage in Guatemala and was taking home huge profits to the U.S. When the Socialist government threatened to nationalize the United Fruit Company acreage, Allen Dulles hired a bunch of hoodlums to overthrow those in power. . . . Dulles called those thugs a revolutionary force, which, of course, was completely untrue. It reminded me of the Nazis in Spain back in the thirties. When the attack on the government turned out to be laughable and failed, Allen Dulles got his brother to send in U.S. bombers and fighter planes to supposedly give aid to what he called a legitimate revolt. Well, of course, the Socialist government was no match for U.S. air power and it collapsed."

Walter Brock retorted. "Sonny, you sound like a Communist to me."

"Walt, you were not listening to me. I said it was a Socialist Government in Guatemala, not Communist. And if you talk sympathy for the Dulles brothers in that deplorable situation, then, to me you sound like a fascist."

Rochelle interrupted. "Hey, you two. Cut it out. We had a wonderful party tonight. Don't ruin it all with political talk."

Sonny responded, "All right, honey. But I just can't understand why you let yourselves get fooled by what the CIA is doing."

"I said, cut it out. One more word about the CIA and I'm going upstairs."

"O. K., O. K. I'll shut up."

Joe joined the conversation. "I can say something good about the CIA. Without them and the established police state in Chile, Tom and I probably wouldn't have come back with Tomlinson and McNamara."

Rochelle complained. "You too, Joe? Please, please, please. Stop with the politics."

Joe answered, "Only because you're threatening to go upstairs. We can't have that now, can we?"

Later, Rochelle came into the living room with a tray full of coffee, cream and sugar. "Help yourselves, folks." The political talk died a natural death.

Walter Brock asked, "What's the rumor on when they're going to start the Roosevelt trial?"

Sonny answered, "No word yet. Not even rumors. Ask Ed Wilson on Monday. He must know something."

Joe asked Brock, "You been doing any more investigating, Walt? I'd love to know what your defense is going to be . . . aside from the reasonable doubt defense that Douglas McNamara has handed to you on a silver platter."

Brock answered, "You don't get a word out of me. You should know better than to ask me to divulge our defense. If I told you and people found out, we could both lose our licenses."

Edith complained, "Are you guys going to talk shop for the rest of the night? If you are, I'm going to go home."

Joe joked, "Not without me, you're not."

Brock suggested, "How about baseball? That's a nice neutral subject."

Joe complained, "But this is football season. Baseball doesn't start again till next spring."

Brock was fixing himself a cup of coffee. "Professional football hasn't been the same since our beloved Colts moved to Indianapolis. I grew up with those guys. Johnny Unitas was my all time hero. How did we ever let 'em get away . . . shame on Baltimore."

Joe offered an opinion. "I hear the Suns are going to have a practically whole new squad. I guess they don't want to take any more chances on game fixin' like we had in1982."

Sonny said, "You gotta be kiddin'. You're talkin' nonsense. With the *Minor League Wagering Team* under wraps and the two left over game-fixers suspended, we're going to have a team as pure as the driven snow."

"Yes, but will they be able to play good baseball? I still think we're going to have to recruit a few stars to replace those criminals," said Rochelle.

Sonny looked over at Edith. She was weeping softly into a tissue.

Rochelle said, "Oh, Edith honey, I'm so sorry I said that. We all know that you'll never really be able to replace Archy. . . . I mean, we know how much you love Joe. . . . But Archy was a special guy. . . . Oh, hell, everything I'm saying seems to be wrong. Oh, I'm so sorry I said anything."

Sonny looked around. Joe had disappeared. "I guess Joe's sorry you said anything too, Rocky," he said.

Sonny didn't want to talk to Chester Roosevelt about Howard Parsons, but he had promised that he would find out the man's status. He was quite surprised to see Parsons at the country club with that handsome young man. Roosevelt sat with his head in his hands and was quietly weeping. "I'm sorry Mister Campbell. You probably don't like to see grown men cry. I can't help myself. That man meant everything in the world to me. I thought he felt the same way about me. Thinking about him helped sustain me in this place all the time I've been in here. Did you find out who the boy was?"

"Sorry, Chet. I didn't speak to either one of them."

"Even now, I'm willing to forgive him if he were to come back to me. . . . I know. I know. What's there to come back to? . . . Before long I'll probably be sitting in front of an all white jury and they'll be sending me to my creator."

"Now that's just nonsense, my friend. Your chances of an acquittal are getting better all the time . . . even if you do draw twelve white people. And whatever else you might think of Ed Wilson, he's a damn good lawyer. He's got a lot to work with now that we've got Constanza in a position to testify that he was hired to kill Howell . . . even if denies actually doing it."

"But what do I do if they do set me free? Do I go looking for him? What if I find him with that boy? What if he tells me that I mean nothing to him anymore? . . . If that happens I might as well have been gassed to death."

"Now, you're talking like a damn fool. Don't make me lose respect for you. You should be thinking about just two things right now . . . getting free is one . . . and going back to school to become a doctor is the other. No person in the world is worth throwing your life away for. Please Chet . . . please don't make me lose respect for you."

"I guess you should leave now. You just don't know how much Howard meant to me. I'll think about what you said . . . about going back to school and all. Maybe, just maybe, that'll get my mind off of him."

Roosevelt stood, "Now, please leave me. I can't stand the thought of you not respecting me anymore."

Sonny stood also. "Thata boy, Chet. Start right now on a new set of ambitions. He's just not worth throwing all the old noble ones away."

They shook hands. "I'll try very, very hard to do as you tell me. I always have done that, haven't I? You're like a father to me now."

"Bye, Chet. Let me know through the grape vine when you want to talk to me again."

"God bless you, Mister Campbell."

Ed Wilson walked into Sonny's office without knocking. "Well, I thought you should know . . . I've got a trial date in the Roosevelt case . . . six weeks from now."

"It's about time. Anything I can do to help? . . . Not that you need any help from me."

"You're wrong. You can help me. I know you've been talking to my client, despite the judge's order to stay away from him. I also know that he respects you. He doesn't respect me. It would help me a great deal if I knew you weren't badmouthing me. It would help me even more if you could persuade him that he should have just a little respect for me. If I decide to put him on the stand, I want respect for me to be apparent to the jury. Would you do that for me?"

"Already have. But I'll keep what you asked in mind and keep working on him. . . . Anything else?"

"I guess not. But I wish we could call a truce. I know you don't like me . . . think I'm a bigot and all that. I want you to know that I'm working on that. Your advice many months ago seems to have stuck in my brain."

"What advice?"

"To defend your client with zeal."

"I learned that in law school, didn't you?"

"Probably. But I guess I forgot it. Anyway, it's back in my brain."

Sonny got up and came around his desk. He took Wilson's right hand in his and said, "Truce, old friend."

Wilson echoed, "Truce."

"What have you got to lose?" said Sonny to Mario Constanza who was still confined to a hospital bed. "I'm sure I can fix it so you'll get no more time than they already have scheduled for you for accepting the contract from McNamara to kill Howell."

"That's right. What have I got to lose? I'll tell you what I've got to lose . . . the truth, that's all. Listen to me, pal. I didn't kill the baseball star. Get it? I didn't kill that punk, you hear me this time?"

"I'm starting to believe you. But that leaves me with the sixty-four-thousand dollar question. Who did kill him?"

"That nigger, that's who. You investigator guys usually know what you're doing. Why can't you settle for what you got? It was the black guy, I tell you."

"No, no. I'll never believe that. Goodbye, Mister Constanza. I don't think I'll be bothering you again."

Sonny tossed and turned and got little sleep that night. He thought over and over that a clue as to who committed the murder had to be staring him in the face. But it wouldn't come . . . it just wouldn't come.

The convenience of Sonny Campbell and Ed Wilson sharing office space had new meaning. Wilson desperately wanted to know what Sonny knew about what happened in Carmine's on the morning of the Howell murder. Now that they had drawn a truce, he felt he could approach his old adversary. He asked for Sonny's cooperation who now felt quite comfortable in sharing with Wilson what Rochelle had developed many months before.

"I'm sure you already know that Constanza was in his rental car outside the café when the scuffle took place. When he came out of his coma the first time, he told the FBI that he saw Howell leave Carmine's and drive away. He decided not to follow him and would make his murder attempt the next day. When he heard on the radio that Archy was shot dead he simply went back to Detroit. What Rochelle and I found out was that the two Negro customers who scurried out of the café, saw Constanza parked in his car. One of them, a Mister Adams, also saw another car turn and apparently follow Chester Roosevelt running around the corner. He described the car as an old VW with *Mox Nix* turn signals. Do you know what they are?"

"Sure do. I was stationed in Germany in the early fifties. Have you or Brock tried to locate that VW."

"Yeah. I thought you wouldn't mind if I put Brock on it. He had no luck. It was probably just a coincidence that he thought it was following Chester."

"At one o'clock in the morning? I doubt it. I'm going to accept that the VW was following Roosevelt."

"Well, let's both go down and talk to Roosevelt and see what he has to say about VWs at one o'clock in the morning."

"All right with me. I've never asked him about the car that was following him."

Wilson drove. On the way to the Detention Center, Sonny divulged that Roosevelt was a homosexual and he had seen his lover that morning to get him to drive him to the Greyhound Station. He hadn't thought at the time to ask him what kind of a car his lover had.

They had called ahead and requested that Roosevelt be waiting for them in an attorney visiting room. The accused murderer seemed nervous when both attorneys entered the room. He stood and said, "I never thought I'd see both of you in here at the same time."

When all three were seated, Wilson said, "We have some questions to ask you, Mister Roosevelt. On the night of the murder we know that the café cook threw you out of the place. I guess you ran out and down to the nearest corner. We have a witness who claims he saw a VW follow you as you ran around the corner. Now, on that early morning did you know who was driving that Volkswagen?"

"It was going too fast. . . . And it was dark. How could I know who was driving it?"

Sonny then asked, "Chet, was that the car that Howard Parsons drove you to the bus station in?"

"No! I think I saw a Volkswagen. Howard owns a Chevrolet. He took me to the bus station in his Chevrolet."

"Well, was the car that passed you a Chevrolet or a Volkswagen?" Sonny continued.

"It was a Volkswagen, I said, and it made the next left turn on the street where I was running."

"Did you ever see that Volkswagen before or after that morning?"

Roosevelt answered Sonny's question. "Never. . . . Oh, one more thing, Mister Campbell, I think there were two people in that Volkswagen. When it made that left turn in front of me, I think I saw two people in the VW."

Sonny persisted. "But you didn't recognize who those people were?"

"No. I only saw their profiles."

Ed Wilson spoke up. "I think that's enough for the time being, Mister Roosevelt. We appreciate your cooperative attitude. . . . Oh, by the way do you mind if I call you by your first name?"

"Call me Chet. . . . Mister Campbell does. And he says I can trust you and that you are an excellent lawyer too."

"Well, a rare compliment. Thank you, Sonny. We've got to go now, Chet. I'll be back to talk to you some more tomorrow afternoon. I've got a brief non-jury trial tomorrow morning."

The two lawyers said goodbye and left.

That afternoon, Sonny called Mario Constanza at his room in Henry Ford Hospital in Detroit.

"Mister Constanza, this is Mister Campbell calling you from Hagerstown. Would you answer a few more questions?"

"You guys are getting to be a pain in the ass. What's your question?"

"You remember you told the FBI that you saw the café scuffle from your car?"

"Yeah. And I saw your black killer run out of the place."

"Right. And you also saw a Volkswagen pass your parked car and turn left like it was following Mister Roosevelt?"

"Yeah, that's right."

"Now, did you ever see that Volkswagen again?"

"Maybe. After I saw Howell leave and get into his car and drive away. He had been punching Roosevelt in the café, There was a car that turned the corner ahead of where I was parked and started to come in my direction. That car got behind Howell, like he was gonna follow him. I'm pretty sure it was that Volkswagen."

"Why didn't you tell the FBI all that?"

"Must have slipped my mind. I thought nothing about it at the time."

"Did you line up behind those two cars and follow them?"

"Are you kiddin'? First of all, my car was pointed in the wrong direction. I would have had to make a U-turn. Suppose somebody saw me do that? That would have put me right into a picture I didn't want nobody to see me in. In my business, you gotta be very careful. Suppose I changed my mind and whacked my mark myself that morning'? Anybody who seen me make a U-turn and follow Howell could have talked about my rental car and then that would o' made me an immediate suspect."

"Well, thanks for the new info, Mister Constanza. I may talk to you some more about this."

"Hey, Campbell. Be sure and let the FBI know that I'm cooperating with you guys. I deserve a deal after all I've given you, don't you think?"

"I do, indeed, Mister Constanza. I do, indeed. Bye for now."

At five o'clock, Sonny left the office to go home. He got on the same elevator as Ed Wilson.

"Got something to tell you, Ed."

When they were both on the street, Sonny filled Ed in on the Constanza telephone call.

Ed commented, "Then it is entirely possible that our VW simply drove around the block and when they saw Howell get in his car, the two guys decided to follow him. And they followed him to Plum and Harrison and blew his head off."

"And they weren't following Chet when Constanza first saw the VW."

"Right."

"More reasonable doubt, Sonny. We're looking better all the time."

"Something to think about in bed tonight when I'm trying to go to sleep. . . . Well, see you in the morning, Ed."

"Yup. See you tomorrow, Sonny."

Sonny and Rochelle went out for dinner at a neighborhood restaurant. They talked almost exclusively about the Roosevelt case.

She said, "You know, if Chet had told you that his lover had owned a Volkswagen, I think the case would be over. . . . Lover's revenge for having struck Chet in the face in the café. . . . ***BANG. BANG.*** *You're dead. Nobody slaps my man around like he was a black slave.*"

"That would make things easy. But Howard owned a Chevrolet and still does. Just to make sure, I drove past his house on the way home, and sure enough, there was a Chevrolet parked in his driveway."

"And remember, Chet told you there were two people in that VW. That would make it a conspiracy. . . . Whew! You and Wilson have your hands full."

"Hmm. Hotdogs and beans. Did I ever tell you about the time I ate hotdogs and beans by the light of a candelabra and served by a tuxedoed butler? It was on the Riviera and the hostess was . . ."

"About a hundred times. One of your old war stories."

"You're married to a man of adventure, you know."

"Oh, shut up, and eat your hotdogs."

"Yes, ma'am."

As Sonny was falling asleep, he pictured in his semiconscious mind, Joe's country club celebration. And he saw across the dance floor in front of the punch bowl, Howard Parsons and his new boyfriend. Soon the country club scene disappeared and Sonny fell into a deep and dreamless sleep.

"It is our theory that Roosevelt knew the driver of the Volkswagen and when he saw who it was who was following him, he hailed the driver to a stop. He told him he was in trouble and that a man named Howell might be after him. The defendant was invited into the car and was told that for protection he should secure the shotgun from behind the seats. They circled the block. They saw Howell get into his car and drive off and they followed him.

"We don't know exactly what happened after the Volkswagen started stalking the Howell vehicle, but we have to assume that Roosevelt and his driver friend followed Howell to his house on Jefferson Boulevard where Howell's wife was waiting for him to get home. The defendant and his friend parked outside the Howell house, possibly anticipating what was going to happen next.

"Mrs. Howell will testify that her husband left the house again in the midst of a violent argument over the late hour and her husband's drunkenness. In his state of anxiety and inebriation the victim didn't notice in his rearview mirror that the Volkswagen recommenced its stalking. The defendant was now armed with a shotgun, which would be used by him at the earliest opportunity.

"That opportunity came at the corner of Plum and Harrison where Howell's car was forced to a stop by the driver of the Volkswagen with the defendant jumping out and thrusting the shotgun through Howell's open window. **BANG, BANG** and Howell was dead, his head practically blown off. Roosevelt reentered the VW, which drove off leaving the Howell vehicle to slowly creep along and eventually crash into a telephone pole. Ladies and gentlemen, this was a revenge killing, pure and simple . . . revenge for being punched in the face and being called a nigger and other nasty names some bigots reserve for Negroes.

"As I told you, we will call Mrs. Howell as a witness. We will also call a man by the name of Mario Constanza who was in the rental car parked outside of Carmine's. We will call Mister Timothy Adams, a customer in Carmine's café on the morning of the murder. Then we will call Bucky Livingston, a member of our Hagerstown baseball team, the Suns. Bucky was in the café when the fight between the defendant and the murder victim took place. We will call Detective Steven Berzinski who intercepted Roosevelt with a bus ticket to Chicago in his pocket and conducted the search of the defendant's small apartment. We will call an expert on Volkswagens who's name is James Ryan and was a former Army Sergeant stationed in Germany in the late forties and early fifties. We will also call Mister Howard Parsons who is the defendant's homosexual partner."

Sonny was stunned, not that Hathaway had discovered that Howard Parsons was Chet's sexual partner, but that he would be testifying for the prosecution. What would he say, besides the fact that he drove Chet to the Greyhound Station? Would he lie and say that Chet confessed to the murder? Sonny would remain in a quandary until Parsons eventually was on the witness stand giving his testimony.

Hathaway continued. "So you see, ladies and gentlemen, this is not a complicated case. It is not the first racially motivated murder in this country, and it probably won't be the last. But it was murder. And it was preplanned from the time that Volkswagen started stalking the victim's automobile. And this is where I end my opening statement. At the end of our presentation of the evidence, Mister Wilson's and mine, you'll hear from me again. What I say won't be dissimilar to what you have just heard. Why would it? What I've just said is indeed the way it all happened and Mister Chester Roosevelt is guilty of first degree murder."

Hathaway's statement failed to alter Sonny's confidence in Ed Wilson's ability to bring in an acquittal. Wilson and Sonny obviously knew things that Hathaway didn't know. Sonny left his seat in the back row to resume his duties in other public defender matters.

Judge Piercy asked the traditional question—Mister Wilson, do you wish to give your opening statement now, or do you choose to wait until the prosecution has rested? And Wilson gave the traditional answer—we'll wait, your Honor.

"Very well. Mister Hathaway you may call your first witness."

Hathaway stood in place behind the prosecution table. He remained there throughout the questioning of the witnesses. "Thank you, your Honor. We call Mario Constanza."

The bailiff went out into the hallway. He was there for several minutes, and then returned pushing a wheel chair. A tower, from which hung a plastic bag apparently filled with medication, followed close by and was pushed along by an attendant dressed in white. A tube from the bag was attached to a needle in Mario Constanza's arm.

Hathaway addressed Judge Piercy. "Your Honor, do we have the court's permission for Mister Constanza to testify from the floor in front of the witness chair?"

"Of course."

Constanza was asked to identify himself and was sworn as a witness. Hathaway began, "Mister Constanza, where do you presently reside?"

"Henry Ford Hospital, in Detroit."

"Why are you in the hospital?"

"I was shot, by a party unknown . . . shot in the head."

"Mister Constanza, what was your work, your profession, before you went to the hospital?"

Constanza chuckled slightly, and answered, "I was what you people know as a hit-man."

Several people in the nearly-filled courtroom laughed.

"How long had you been a paid killer?"

"Oh, about twenty years."

"Mister Constanza, did there come a time when you were contacted by a man named Douglas McNamara?"

"Yeah, he called me on my unlisted phone number."

"What did he want?"

"He wanted me to whack a guy."

"Who?"

"Archy Howell, the guy that the defendant in this case killed."

"Objection!" Ed Wilson was on his feet. "Your Honor, everybody involved in this case knows that this witness is denying that he was the one who actually killed Archy Howell and would want this jury to believe that he didn't fill that contract—whacked, the victim as he puts it in mob talk—and we respectfully request that you warn the witness that he is not to shift blame for this killing to the defendant by these gratuitous statements about my client."

"I wholeheartedly agree, Mister Wilson. Mister Constanza, unless you by chance observed the defendant actually kill the victim in this case, you are not to give your opinion on who the killer is. Do you understand me?"

"Yes, your Honor."

"You may continue, Mister Hathaway."

"How much were you going to be paid for whacking Mister Howell?"

"Twenty-five-thousand dollars."

"Did you ever receive that sum?"

"No, because I never killed this Howell guy."

Constanza then testified about seeing the scuffle in Carmine's café and the Volkswagen that followed Chester Roosevelt and circled the block and followed Archy Howell as he drove off.

"What did you do then?"

"Went back to my hotel where I heard on the radio that some other person killed Howell."

"What did you do then?"

"Went back to Detroit."

"Mister Constanza, did you kill Archy Howell?"

"Hell, no. Never saw the guy again after I saw him drive off followed by the Volkswagen."

"Your witness, Mister Wilson."

Wilson stood. "Mister Constanza, were you disappointed when you heard that someone else beat you to the punch and killed Archy Howell before you had a chance to earn your twenty-five grand?"

"Yes. Wouldn't you have been sorry you missed out on some big lawyer's fee to some other mouthpiece?"

Most of the audience laughed.

"Please! I'm supposed to be asking the questions. . . . But I'll admit, that was quite amusing. But to go on, did you ever talk to Mister McNamara again—try to collect the fee for someone else's work?"

"Never. We got ethics in my business. Are you familiar with the word *ethics,* Mister Lawyer?"

Again the audience laughed.

"You think you'll have fun with me throughout this trial, don't you?"

"None of this crap is fun for me, Mister Lawyer."

"Well, we don't need any more of your lawyer jokes. I warn you. Cut it out. You'll force me to ask the judge to hold you in contempt and you may spend an indefinite sentence in the prison hospital."

"Whew! Tough guy, ain't you? I may decide to give you a warning, myself and you know what my business is."

Judge Piercy spoke sternly from his high perch. "Stop it, you two. And particularly you, Mister Constanza. This is serious business we're doing here. Any more of your not-so-funny jokes, and I might decide to hold you in contempt without being asked to . . . get it?"

"Yeah."

"That's *yes, sir.* From this point on you'll have nothing but respect for what we're doing here."

"Yes, sir."

"You may continue, Mister Wilson."

"Thank you, your Honor. Mister Constanza, earlier you told us you were shot by a party unknown, I think your words were. Can you think of any one who might have had a motive to shoot you?"

"Well, when you shoot somebody you want to kill them. When you want to kill them it's sometimes because you want to silence them. The only person who I can think of who would want to keep my mouth shut about anything is the guy who hired me to kill Howell. That would be Mister Douglas McNamara."

"So you believe you were shot so that you would never tell anyone, people like us, here in this courtroom, for instance, that he hired you."

"Right."

"Do you happen to know whether McNamara even knew that the defendant, Chester Roosevelt existed?"

"He must have. All he had to do was read the newspaper or listen to the radio or watch TV."

"So, if you were killed that would remove evidence that any other motive for killing Howell ever existed. McNamara would reap the benefit of your death and reinforce the belief that this was a revenge murder."

"That makes sense to me."

"No more questions of this witness, your Honor."

"Very well. Mister Hathaway, you may call your next witness."

"Thank you, your Honor. We call Edith Beyerly, formerly Edith Howell."

The bailiff went to the door leading to the hallway, opened it and shouted, **"Edith Howell Beyerly is wanted in the courtroom."** Moments later Edith joined the bailiff who led her to the witness stand. Judge Piercy instructed the bailiff to swear her in.

That done, Winston Hathaway started his questioning. "You were once married to the deceased victim in this case, weren't you?"

"Yes, I was."

"Are the events of the morning when your former husband lost his life, still fresh in your memory?"

"I'll never forget any of it."

"Would you recount what you remember?"

"Certainly. He played baseball that afternoon. The Suns lost. They were having an unusual bad streak. He didn't come home after the game. In fact, he didn't come home until almost two o'clock in the morning and he stumbled through the front door and I knew he was drunk . . . very, very drunk. We argued about the late hour without even a phone call, and why he was drinking so much and why he didn't seem to be enjoying our new prosperity. You see, I had just inherited a lot of money, supposedly from a rich uncle I didn't even know I had. He left the house and I ran after him. He squealed his tires and drove off. I can't be positive, but I think I heard a car start up right after that. I discussed that with my present husband who is your investigator sitting over there. He told me I didn't have to be positive . . . that I should just tell you what my impression was. Well, my impression was that I heard a car start up. It wasn't a loud motor. . . . More like a lawn tractor. I went back into the house and went back to bed. I was quite disgusted."

"What's the next thing you remember happening?"

"The phone was ringing and waking me up. It was my brother. In a very solemn voice he told me he had just identified my husband's body at the city morgue . . . that he was shot to death. Of course, I was stunned. Apparently the police suspected it was Archy from the license plate on his car. My brother told me he was sending a good friend of ours to be with me. I turned on the radio, hoping to learn more about the shooting. Not long after that I heard the newscaster say that the police had already made an arrest. By that time my brother's good friend had come to the house to try and comfort me. All I could think to do was to call our lawyer, Douglas McNamara, and tell him about it."

"Did you call McNamara?"

"Yes. He was at my house within minutes. Apparently he had heard about it on the radio, too. My brother also came to the house to comfort and advise me."

"So, you had plenty of people around you that morning to offer advice and to comfort you."

"One too many as it turned out. It wasn't very long after the incident that I learned that McNamara had actually contracted with Mister Constanza to kill my husband . . . all part of a scheme to fix baseball games for a gambling syndicate of which McNamara was a member. Unfortunately, my husband was paid a large amount of money to be a part of that scheme. It's because his conscience got the best of him and he had decided that he was going to expose the whole thing that caused McNamara to want him killed."

"But McNamara's plan never worked . . . Constanza never carried out the murder."

"So Constanza says. In my opinion it was all too convenient . . ."

Hathaway interrupted, "You're not permitted to offer opinions when you testify, Mrs. Beyerly. . . . I have no more questions of Mrs. Beyerly."

Judge Piercy asked, "Do you wish to cross examine, Mister Wilson?"

"If I may, your Honor."

"You may proceed."

"Mrs. Beyerly, have you ever actually heard a Volkswagen start its engine?"

"Let's see, now. I don't recall specifically. I guess I would have to answer no to that question."

"But what you heard that morning in front of your house reminded you of a lawn tractor starting up. Have you ever started a lawn tractor?"

"Once in a while, at our old house where we couldn't afford a grounds keeper."

"Think back to your old house and starting up the lawn tractor motor. Isn't it true that a lawn tractor makes quite a racket when you turn the key to start it . . . maybe as much noise as a full size automobile?"

"Come to think of it, I believe it does. So what I heard that morning could very well have been a full size car starting up."

"Do you think Mister Constanza is lying when he says he didn't kill your husband?"

"I object," said Hathaway. "Calls for an opinion."

"Withdraw the question," said Wilson.

Edith Beyerly spoke up. "But I have good reason to think that he killed my husband."

Judge Piercy stopped her from saying any more. "Mrs. Beyerly what you just said was your opinion and anything else you might say along those lines would be an opinion and is strictly prohibited. The jury is instructed to disregard the witness' last remark."

Wilson said, "I have no more questions to ask this witness, your Honor."

Judge Piercy made an announcement. "Ladies and gentlemen, attorneys and members of the audience, it is rapidly approaching the noon hour. I don't know about you, but I am very hungry. When I pound my gavel in the next few moments that will mean that court is adjourned until one thirty. The jury members may eat anywhere they find a place that suits them. I instruct you that you are not to discuss the case and you are not to speak to either of the attorneys if you happen to run into one of them. I assure you that they will not be offended if you ignore them. They're used to being ignored, except in this courtroom, of course." He pounded his gavel one time and said, "Court adjourned."

At one thirty, Judge Piercy announced, "Mister Hathaway, you may call your next witness."

"Thank you, your Honor. We call Mister Howard Parsons."

The bailiff called for the witness in the hallway and soon returned with him and led him to the witness stand.

"Mister Parsons, you now have been sworn and I will ask you several questions about your relationship with the defendant, all right?"

"Yes, sir."

Parsons appeared to never take his eyes off the prosecution table and throughout Hathaway's questioning he avoided looking at his former lover, Chester Roosevelt.

"Would you describe just what your relationship with Mister Roosevelt was?"

"He was my lover for more than two years."

There was a slight verbal rumbling among the people in the courtroom.

"Where did you meet?"

"At the Washington County Hospital. We both were on the custodial staff there."

"How old are you?"

"Forty-four."

"How old is he?"

"Twenty."

"Did you live together?"

"No, he lived around the corner from Carmine's café . . . two blocks down."

"And you? Where did you live?"

"Oh, about five miles from there."

"You say the two of you were lovers. . . . Where did you do your love making?"

Parsons didn't answer the question for almost a half minute. Finally, he said, "At my house or in my car."

"Ever at his home?"

"Never. He resisted meeting in his home."

"Did you have very many intimate conversations with Chester Roosevelt? . . . In other words, did you get to know him very well . . . I don't mean sexually, but what his likes and dislikes were . . . his fears and prejudices for instance?"

"I think so."

"What were his attitudes toward race relations?"

"He was fearful of white people and resentful of their attitude toward Negroes."

"But you are white?"

"He had a different attitude toward me . . . I think he loved me . . . truly loved me."

"Were you ever in his presence when a white person used racial slurs toward him?"

"Several times."

"Describe them."

"We were in a bar in Baltimore one weekend. A white bully, sitting next to me at the bar, started raising his voice and said—I'll never forget what he said—he said, *Why don't you and your white twink just take your asses out of here you slimy nigger bastard?*"

"What was the defendant's reaction to the bully's statement?"

"He bowed his head at first, saying nothing."

"Then the bully said, *What's wrong nigger, didn't you hear what I asked you?* Then Chester surprised me. He fairly jumped off of his bar stool and attacked the bully, and started punching him with both hands. He was much smaller than the bully and I was sure Chester would get the worst of any fight that would get started, so I threw some money on the bar and literally dragged him out to the street. The other patrons prevented the bully from pursuing us and stopped him at the door. We ran. And the last words I heard were, *You better run, you nigger bastard. I see you in this place again and you're a dead man.*"

"Did the defendant say anything when the two of you ran to safety?"

"Yes," he said, *I wish I had a gun . . . I'd kill that guy.*

Wilson objected. "Your Honor, prior acts are not admissible unless they are clearly relevant."

Hathaway countered, "I will show the clear relevance through my next witness, your Honor."

Judge Piercy responded, "You best do that, Mister Hathaway. If you don't, I will instruct this fair minded jury to ignore Mister Parson's description of this deplorable incident."

"I assure you, your Honor, that I will demonstrate a clear relevance through my next witness."

"Go on with your questions, if you have any more."

"Any other indications you observed in the defendant that would help them know what his typical reaction to racial slurs directed at him might be?"

"Yes, any time, when I was with him, whether we were watching TV or simply out somewhere and he heard a racial slur directed at him or otherwise, he would bristle and say something like, *You just wait, someday that person is going to die for saying something like that.*"

"Oh, I object for the same reason as last time. You can't tell me that Mister Hathaway can make that remark **clearly relevant** by any witness he might call."

Before Hathaway had a chance to counter Wilson's statement, Judge Piercy said sternly, "Objection sustained. Mister Hathaway, let's not have any more of these backdoor statements from your witness. And ladies and gentlemen, I instruct you to ignore this last comment from Mister Parsons, if for no other reason than it might be something that any one of you or even I might have said under the circumstances. Any more questions of your witness, Mister Hathaway?"

"No, sir."

"Have any cross examination, Mister Wilson?"

"Not much, your Honor. Mister Parsons, do you still love my client?"

"No."

"Why not? Did something happen between you two?"

"Isn't it obvious? He's in jail for first degree murder and might be found guilty and executed."

"Is that why you've only visited him once since he's been in the Detention Center, and that visit was more than two years after the murder?"

"Probably."

"So you must have made up your mind early on that you no longer loved him?"

"I guess so."

"And you also must have believed he was guilty right from the first day of the murder, didn't you?"

"I guess so."

"When did you stop being faithful to him?"

Parsons squirmed in his seat. "I don't exactly remember."

"Was it before or after the murder?"

"I'm sure it was after."

"With how many men?"

"I don't remember."

"Or maybe with women?"

"No, not with women."

"Did you attend a party at the Hagerstown Country Club some six weeks ago?"

"Yes."

"Were you in the company of a boy who looks young enough to be your son?"

"I brought a companion with me."

"How long have you known that boy?"

"I don't remember."

"Is that boy one of your current lovers?"

"Your Honor, do I have to answer that question?"

Wilson interrupted and said with a smile, "Never mind. I think you just did answer it."

There was a burst of laughter, mostly from the defendant's side of the courtroom. Chester Roosevelt's head dropped to his chest.

"How old is the youngster?"

"I'm not sure. Twenty-one, I think."

"By any chance, were you with that boy on the morning when the murder of Archy Howell took place?"

"No, I wasn't. I was with Chester."

"How did that come about?"

"He called me and said he was in some kind of trouble. I drove to his apartment and he let me in. He said he would need a ride to the Greyhound Bus Station . . . that some guy by the name of Howell had been shot to death and he was sure the police would think he did it. I asked him if he had done it and he denied it. Then he asked me to take care of his shotgun for him for safe keeping and to tell nobody I had it."

"What kind of a car do you own, Mister Parsons?"

"A 1979 Chevrolet Sedan."

"Did you hide the shotgun?"

"Yes."

"Where is it now?"

"Your partner, Mister Campbell has it."

"No, he doesn't. I have it."

Wilson reached down under his table and pulled up the shotgun that Sonny Campbell had given him. It had a tag marked Defendant's Exhibit A tied to the trigger guard. It also had some lab reports attached to the gun barrel. Wilson asked the judge if he could approach the witness.

"Yes, you may."

"I show you what's been pre-marked as an exhibit for the defendant and ask you to identify it, if you can."

"It looks like Chester's shotgun."

"Had you ever seen it before Chester gave it to you for safekeeping that morning?"

"Yes, sir. I bought it for him as a Christmas gift. It is identical to one I have at home. We wanted to shoot skeet with them, and I would teach him how."

"How is it that you gave it to Mister Campbell?"

"He came to me one day right after the murder and asked me some questions like you're doing know. He asked to look at it and said it might be strong evidence to get Chester out of this mess. Later, his investigator came and took it from me."

"Oh, Mister Parsons, I have one more question. Did you shoot Mister Howell to death that morning?"

"Of course not."

"That's all I have, your Honor."

Judge Piercy made an announcement. "We are in a five minute recess. I want both attorneys in my office right now."

The attorneys sat side by side and opposite the judge who sat behind his enormous desk.

"Let me ask you a question, Charlie. If this is racial rage case, why on earth are you charging this nice young man with first degree murder?"

"Because he had ample time to get control of his rage and talk himself out of intentionally pulling the trigger."

"But isn't that a subjective thing? I mean, our Negroes have been subjected to racial slurs since the slavery days. If one of them turned upon his master because he was called a black bastard, wouldn't that explain his rage and wouldn't that rage last until he got some satisfaction?"

"One would expect his rage to quiet down after a while and he would not turn upon his master."

"I knew you'd have that kind of an answer to my question. Charlie. Our Negroes are still turning on their masters . . . their rage hasn't ceased since they were slaves. And it won't cease until racial slurs are a thing of the past. . . . I'm following your case very carefully and it may be that I'll reduce these charges *sua sponte* to something more in tune with reality. Just thought you should be aware of that."

"You're the boss."

"No, my friend. Justice and fair play are the boss."

"Well, folks, that didn't take as long as I thought it would. I think we have time for one more witness before the end of the business day. Have you got one lined up, Mister Hathaway?"

"I believe I have a reasonably short one, your Honor."

"Proceed."

"Call Timothy Adams."

The bailiff brought Adams to the witness stand and swore him in.

"Mister Adams, where do you work?"

"At the sanitation department."

"Where do you live?"

"Jes down da street from Chet, sittin' ovah der."

"Are you a friend of his?"

"Knowed him since befoh his mama died. He stayed right der even aftah his mama passed. My wife and I kinda looked aftah him for a while. He was a good boy. Smaht too. Good mahks in school."

"Were you in Carmine's café on the morning when Archy Howell was shot."

"Yes, suh. But Chet Roosevelt didn't shoot nobody."

"I didn't ask you if he did. Please, Mister Adams, just answer the questions I put to you. Did you see the scuffle between Chet, as you call him, and another man, a white man?"

"I knowed bettah den to look at a fight between one of ours and a white man. I kept my back to it, till Oscah da cook came out da kitchen and broke it up. He chased Chet out da place and I got out o' der in a hurry aftah dat."

"What did you see after you got outside?"

"Chet was jes turnin' da corner, runnin' like a rabbit down our street to his little place, he was."

"What else did you see?"

"Man sittin' in his car right outside da café and den I saw another car followin' Chet. Little car it was, wid funny little sticks for turn signals."

"Where did you go after you left Carmine's?"

"I walked da other way toward the other corner."

"Did you see anything important?"

"I don't know if it was important, but I saw dat little car again comin' around the block and toward me."

"How did you know it was the same car?"

"Cuz I saw dose little stick-turn signals again when it was turnin' and comin' at me."

"Did you see who was in the car?"

"Nope. Jes dat der was two persons in dat little car. I couldn't see der faces."

"No more questions, your Honor."

"Cross examination, Mister Wilson?"

"Yes, your Honor. Mister Adams, what do people call you?"

"Timmy Adams, most da time."

"May I call you Timmy?"

"Yes, suh."

"Let's take you back into the café. When you were drinking your coffee, were you paying attention to what was going on over in the booths?"

"Not at first. But den came some yellin', but I didn't turn around till dat white man grabbed Chet who was jes tryin' to break up some slappin' goin' on in dat booth. Dey fell on the floor and da white man started punchin' Chet in da face."

"At any time did you hear any bad words about people of your race? . . . Words like nigger, or eggplant, or black bastard, or words like that?"

"No, suh. No words like dat were spoke in dat café dat mornin', not when I was in der."

"And when you got outside and started walking the other way and saw that little car with the stick-turn signals . . . I believe you said you saw it first turning the corner and following Chet and then a second time when it came back up the street ahead of you, and turn and come toward you . . . after you saw it those two times did you ever turn around and see where that car went?"

"No, suh. I jes wanted to git away from dat place and I nevah turned around again."

"No further questions, your Honor."

"Well then, folks, we're going to shut down for today. We'll start again tomorrow morning promptly at nine o'clock. You jury folks assemble in your deliberation room. Our bailiff will check for attendance. Remember, we can't start without you."

Judge Piercy gaveled once and said, "Court adjourned."

CHAPTER TWENTY THREE

With essential persons in place the following morning, Judge Piercy instructed Charles Hathaway to call his next witness.

"Thank you, your Honor. Prosecution calls Bernard 'Bucky' Livingston."

When Livingston was comfortably seated in the witness chair and sworn to tell the truth, Hathaway made a statement that he thought might make the jury and audience more comfortable. "Mister Livingston, you have just been sworn to tell the truth and nothing but the truth."

"Yes, I did, sir, and I will tell the truth."

"If at any time you feel your oath wearing off, let the bailiff know and he will swear you in again."

Most people in the courtroom laughed. Some were perplexed over why Hathaway would make fun of his own witness.

"Now, let's clear the air. Where do you now reside?"

"At the Federal Correctional Institution in Morgantown, West Virginia."

"Why are you living in that minimum security prison facility?"

"Because I pleaded to two counts of perjury and one count of wire wagering fraud. in a federal matter that was tried earlier this year."

"You were once a member of the Hagerstown Suns baseball team, weren't you?"

"Yes, sir."

"Wire wagering fraud means you pleaded guilty to aiding in the fixing of Suns' baseball games, isn't that right."

"That's right, sir."

"You didn't get any prison time for the wire wagering plea, did you?"

"No, sir."

"And the perjury counts mean you did lie about a lot of things in connection with fixing those games, right?"

"That's right, sir."

"I'm quite sure that my opponent, Mister Wilson is going to call you an untrustworthy, out and out liar. Do you understand that?"

"But I'm not a liar any more. I'm being punished for lying. I'm not going to lie in this courtroom."

"We can only hope you won't. . . . Were you in Carmine's café on the morning when Archy Howell was shot to death?"

"Yes, sir, I was."

"Were you with Archy?"

"Yes, we were sitting in a booth and we were both drunk."

"So drunk that you didn't know what was going on around you?"

"I knew what was going on. I saw and heard everything."

"Tell the jury what you saw and heard."

"Well, Archy was also fixing games the same way I was. But his conscience was getting the better of him. I told you he was drunk. He was running his mouth on how he was going to spill the beans on all of us. There was one other player who was in on it and then there was Mister McNamara who had paid us a lot of money. I pleaded with Archy not to tell on us. He got mad and slapped me three or four times. He had me by the shirt collar and he slapped me some more. This black guy . . . that man sitting over there . . . came over and tried to stop Archy from hitting me. Archy said, *Go away nigger, this is none of your business.* The man refused to go and grabbed Archy by the wrist. Archy said, *I said get out of here nigger. This is none of your business.* The man still held on to Archy's wrist, I guess to stop him from hitting me. They tumbled onto the floor and Archy was on top of him and punching him in the face real hard and calling him racial insults like, *You black bastard and nigger, two or three times.* The cook came out of the kitchen and broke it up. The cook told the black man to get out of the café and he got up and ran out of the place. Five minutes later Archy left also. That was the last time I saw Archy alive."

"Did we just hear the truth and nothing but the truth?"

"Yes, sir. I told the truth."

"Your witness."

Wilson asked, "How do you know you just told the truth?"

"What do you mean?"

"You were drunk at the time, weren't you?"

"Yes, I was drunk."

"Mister Livingston, I have interviewed every person who was in Carmine's that morning, and not one of them agrees with you, that there were any racial slurs uttered in there that morning. I've talked to Mrs. Howell who told me that she had never heard her husband use a racial slur in all the time she was married to him. She told me that it was quite the opposite—that Archy was a champion of civil rights. Let me ask you. You played baseball with Archy Howell. Was he a champion of civil rights?"

"I don't really know."

"Did you ever hear him use a racial slur . . . in the locker room for instance?"

"No."

"Or in a bar when a bunch of the white players got together, did he ever tell a racially inspired bad joke for instance?"

"No."

"Were you present when he beat the stuffing's out of a fellow player for calling a black friend of his, a nigger?"

"I heard about it."

"Archy was slapping you around that morning, wasn't he?"

"Yes."

"Why was he doing that?"

"Because I threatened him."

"How?"

"I . . . I . . . I threatened to beat him black and blue . . . till he looked like a . . . a tar baby, if he exposed the rest of us in the game fixing scheme."

"So it was you who was using a racial slur?"

"I guess so."

"And when he had Chet Roosevelt on the floor and was punching him in the face, didn't you silently put words—racial slurs—in Archy's mouth because that's what you would have said if you had a black man on the ground and were beating hell out of him?"

No answer to that question was forthcoming.

"Do you have an answer to my question, Mister Livingston?"

Still Bucky remained silent.

Judge Piercy said sternly, "Answer the question, Mister Livingston."

"I can't."

The judge asked, "Why not?"

"Because it might be true."

Wilson interrupted. "I withdraw the question, your Honor. Best I put this pathological liar out of his misery."

"There will be no name calling in my courtroom, Mister Wilson. Please behave like the kind of gentleman I know you to be."

"No more questions, your Honor."

"Do you have another witness, Mister Hathaway?"

"Yes, your Honor."

"Then call your witness."

"We call Detective Steven Berzinski."

The bailiff came back with Detective Berzinski. Once sworn, he identified himself as a policeman. Hathaway asked, "How long have you been on the force, Detective?"

"Next year, I'll have thirty in."

"How long have you been a Detective?"

"Seventeen years."

"Did there come a time when you arrested the defendant, Chester Roosevelt?"

"Yes."

"How did that come about?"

"After we discovered Archy's dead body in his vehicle, we contacted his brother-in-law, Vern Lewis, who lives out of town somewhere, but works for the City in the Treasurer's office. While he was identifying the body, our medical examiner asked him if he had any idea where Archy might have been that night. Vern told him that he often went to Carmine's to sober up on coffee before he went home. We checked out Carmine's and learned that there had been a fight there between the defendant and Archy Howell. They knew the defendant's name and we got a good description so we put out an all points bulletin on the man."

"Did that pay off?"

"It sure did. I got a radio call from a patrolman that he had spotted a man getting out of a Chevrolet automobile at the Greyhound Bus Station and carrying a suitcase. The man matched the subject's description we had. I told the patrolman to keep an eye on the subject and that I was on the way to the bus station."

"Was the defendant at the bus station when you got there?"

"Yes. He was lined up with other passengers to get on a bus for Chicago when I arrived."

"What did you do?"

"I walked over to the line of people just as the subject was stepping up to get in the bus. I asked him to identify himself. He gave me his right name and then I asked him whether he intended to leave town. He answered, *not anymore*. I arrested him right there and read him his Miranda rights, hoping that he would choose to get talkative."

"Did he?"

"He never said a word until he got to the station."

"What did he say there?"

"He said that he knew why I arrested him, but that he was not Archy Howell's killer."

"Did you ask him if he wanted to talk to you?"

"Yes. He said no. And I asked him if he wanted to talk to an attorney. Again, he said no. So, we put him in the lockup where he continued remaining silent."

"Did he ever consult a lawyer?"

"Yes, the Washington County Public Defender, Sonny Campbell, showed up that morning and talked to him for about thirty minutes."

"Did the defendant then decide to talk to you?"

"No. When Sonny came out of the visiting room he advised us that the defendant was refusing to talk to us. And then Sonny said to me, *personally, I think he's innocent, Steve.*"

Wilson did not object to this obvious hearsay.

"Did you do any more investigation on this case that morning?"

"Yes, sir. We obtained a search warrant from his Honor, Judge Piercy, and went to the defendant's residence and turned it upside down."

"Find anything of relevance?"

"Yes, sir. We found several boxes of live shotgun shells. We took them back to the evidence room at the station for future reference."

"Have you obtained any other evidence which you tie into the case against Chester Roosevelt?"

"No, sir. Nothing."

"No more questions of this witness, your Honor."

"Mister Wilson?"

"No questions."

"Your next witness, Mister Hathaway."

"Call the county's medical examiner, Vincent Catelli."

A small middle-aged man carrying a brief case, was led to the witness stand.

"Mister Catelli, how long have you been medical examiner for Washington County?"

"Fifteen years."

"How long have you been a pathologist?"

"Twenty-three years."

"Would you recite your *curriculum vitae?*"

The witness recited a long list of education and experience.

"Your Honor, may we have a ruling on Mister Catelli's expertise?"

"I hereby determine that Doctor Vincent Catelli is indeed a qualified medical examiner and pathologist and may be sworn as such."

"Doctor Catelli, did you do an autopsy on the body of Archy Howell?"

"Yes."

"What did you find?"

"That Mister Howell was killed by shotgun pellets fired not two feet from his face on the morning of his death."

"That simple?"

"That simple."

"Did you retrieve any of the shotgun pellets?"

"Yes, sir. They're over there on your table in a plastic bag."

Hathaway picked up a small plastic bag and asked for permission to approach the witness.

"Certainly," said the judge.

He walked to the witness stand and showed the bag to the medical examiner. "Is this the bag?"

"Yes, sir."

"I move that State's Exhibit A be accepted into evidence."

"No objection," said Wilson.

"State's Exhibit A shall be accepted into evidence," said the judge.

"No further questions."

"No questions," said Wilson.

Wilson then turned to the defendant and whispered, "Now he'll call a forensic expert."

Roosevelt asked, "Will he hurt us?"

"No way. We've got our ace in the hole."

Hathaway called Doctor Willis Brandt, whose education and experience qualified him as an expert. The doctor was sworn as an expert and a brief questioning process began.

"You examined the contents of all the shotgun shells you retrieved from the evidence room."

"Yes, sir. The pertinent shells are in front of you on your table."

"Your Honor?"

"You may approach the witness."

Hathaway showed Doctor Brandt a plastic bag containing two shells, one still intact, the other empty. The bag also contained several ounces of pellets.

"Until this morning, possession of this State's Exhibit B has been exclusively yours, is that right?"

"I retrieved this exhibit from an evidence locker the day after it was placed there and I've had it in my protective custody since."

"Move to have State's Exhibit B accepted into evidence."

"No objection."

"State's B is in evidence," pronounced the judge.

"Doctor Brandt, did you make a comparison between the shotgun pellets in Exhibit A and the ones in Exhibit B?"

"Yes. They were identical, the shells probably purchased at the same time."

"Your witness."

"No questions."

"Well, gentlemen this trial is moving along at a rapid pace. I congratulate both of you. Your next witness, Mister Hathaway?"

"Call Mister James Ryan."

The bailiff went into the hallway and found James Ryan and brought him to the witness stand. The witness was asked to identify himself and was sworn in.

"Were you once in the United States Army?"

"During the Korean war, but I was stationed in Frankfurt Germany."

"Did you own an automobile when you were stationed in Germany?"

"An ancient Volkswagen—one of those that Hitler had developed for the German population."

"Did the Volkswagen you had have turn signals?"

"Sort of. We called them *Mox Nix* sticks, typical G.I. sense of humor."

"What do you mean?"

"*Mox Nix* is a corruption of the German expression *es macht Nichts* which means it makes no difference. So if you see one of those turn signals pop out of the upper front door area on the right side, the driver may really be intending to turn left. Get it? The signal macht nichts which way the car is really going to turn. It's really an insult to the German engineers who developed the signals, which incidentally lighted up at night when they were made operational."

"Do you know when the *Mox Nix* sticks stopped being used on German Volkswagens?"

"Oh, I'd say in the early fifties."

"Your witness."

"No questions."

Charles Hathaway, who had remained standing, announced in a grand manner, "The State of Maryland rests."

"Do you wish to make your opening statement now, Mister Wilson?"

"Your Honor, it's close to the noon hour. I do intend to make an opening statement, but could we wait till after the lunch hour?"

"I'm glad you suggested that, Mister Wilson. I'm as hungry as a ravenous wolf. Ladies and gentlemen, we will adjourn now and get something to eat. You all know the drill. Don't discuss the case among yourselves and ignore these fine attorneys if you see them anywhere. Be back here at one thirty. Court adjourned." The judge tapped his gavel lightly on its pad.

CHAPTER TWENTY FOUR

Ed Wilson had lunch with Sonny Campbell in a pizza parlor near their office.

Wilson joked, "I'd pay a fortune, if I could have one cold beer with this pizza."

Sonny responded, "Bet you a buck that Judge Piercy is, right this minute, raising a dry martini with three olives to his judicial mouth."

"All's not fair in war, marriage and the courtroom."

"Forget it and drink your root beer."

"I think we got Hathaway by the gonads, Sonny."

"You see how much better trying your client's case with zeal is, win or lose?"

"Oh, hell, Sonny. You don't have to preach your liberal jurisprudence to me any more. I've learned my lesson. I still say, that there are times when making a deal for your black clients is appropriate."

"I never said there weren't such times, but not all the time like they do all over the country."

"Let's drop it, for now, O.K.?"

"Right, my good friend."

"I truly think that Hathaway knows that he's beat. Chester told me he's been watching the faces of the jury. They've been nodding their heads with my presentations and frowning most of the time when Winston Hathaway does his thing."

"That's a good sign of course, but sometimes they'll surprise you."

"Well, I'm gonna put Chester on first. That'll tend to show them we've got nothing to hide."

"That's always a good tactic . . . especially if you really don't have anything to hide."

"We don't, do we?"

"Not as far as I'm concerned. The jury's going to hear an articulate, sincere, young and ambitious, future doctor. You probably won't need any other witnesses."

"Don't be silly. I need to back up every thing I say in my opening statement and every thing Chester says from the witness stand."

"I know that. I was just reinforcing your confidence, not that it needs reinforcing."

"Jeez, this pizza tastes good. Should we order another one?"

"Sure. What we don't eat, I'll take up to the office. They're all pullin' for you up there, you know?"

"They better be. I'd fire the ones who want me to lose. I'm beginning to think that all good public defender's offices should hire no one but liberal Democrats."

"Hear, hear!"

Ed Wilson strolled over to the jury box, carrying no notes and with his head bowed. When he got there he stood still for a moment and then finally raised his head and began slowly to pace back and forth in front of the jurors.

"Ladies and gentleman, I didn't even have to give an opening statement. The court rules say that I could have let it slide. I think you now know where I'm going with the defense in this matter. That's the way it often works when you're positive you have an innocent client. But let's review a few things. First, the motive. Mister Hathaway claims this was a revenge killing—revenge because Chester Roosevelt was slapped around by the deceased and was forced to listen to racial slurs. **Racial slurs? What racial slurs?** The only person on earth who supposedly heard any racial slurs was that drunken speciman of equality and justice, Bucky Livingston, the confessed perjurer who by the time I got through with him, didn't know the truth from the most absurd and damning lie I have ever witnessed. You will hear from the only other people in the café that morning—you've already heard from one, Timmy Adams—people who will tell, and have told you, that there were no racial slurs uttered in that café that morning. So much for motive.

"And for good measure, I'm calling Edith Howell back to the stand to tell you that her deceased husband never spoke ill of black people in the entire time that she knew him . . . and they were high school sweethearts. She will tell you that he actually beat the stuffings out of a teammate for using the word *nigger*. I'm willing to cut Bucky some slack and say that I'm told that when a bigot gets drunk he is fully cabable of substituting his own prejudical phrases for what he thinks he's hearing from somebody else.

"And now I want to talk about shotgun shells and shotguns. Ladies and gentlemen, we've got my client's shotgun right here in this courtroom. And you will hear from a qualified forensic expert who will tell you that as of two days after the killing, that gun hadn't been fired, probably for six months. Doesn't that make the comparison of shotgun pellets irrelevant? Of course, it does.

"Why was Chester Roosevelt going to Chicago? It was because our judicial system has become so one-sidedly prejudicial against Negroes that they often get terrified to think they might get caught up in it—even a Negro whose sole ambition is to one day become a doctor. Think of that. He wants to go from being a custodian in a hospital to one day being a doctor . . . to save lives, not kill people.

"Now, if you think the fact that he is homosexual is pertinent in any way to this case, then we have picked the wrong jury. Remember when the judge asked you to look around this room that was built in 1816? Remember when he quoted an author that this building emanates justice and fair play . . . justice and fair play for **everybody** not just heterosexuals?"

Hathaway objected. "Your Honor, this is beginning to sound like a closing argument, not an opening statement."

"I'm afraid Mister Hathaway is correct, Mister Wilson. Try to curb your enthusiasm. Remember, it's supposed to be just what you intend to prove . . . not what you believe in your heart."

"Yes, your Honor. But I think you just invited me to talk to these fine jurors at the end of this case about what we should all believe in our hearts. In any event, I'm finished with my opening statement."

"You may call your first witness, Mister Wilson," announced Judge Piercy.

"I call Mister Chester Roosevelt."

The defendant, dressed in a wrinkled black suit, white shirt and bow tie, looked a bit like a youthful preacher as he walked slowly to the witness stand. The bailiff thrust a bible toward him before he sat in the witness chair. "Place your hand on this bible, sir." Chester obeyed. "Do you state that you will tell the whole truth and nothing but the truth?"

"I promise I will tell the truth."

"State your name and residence, sir."

"Chester Roosevelt . . . Hagerstown Detention Center."

"Take your seat, sir."

Chester obeyed.

Ed Wilson stood in place behind his table. "How do you feel this afternoon, Chester?"

"Nervous."

Judge Piercy said, "Try to get over that, young man. You have nothing to be nervous about. You're in fair and just hands in this courtroom."

Chester responded, "I'll try, your Honor."

Wilson took over. "Where were you born, Chester?"

"Tupelo, Mississippi."

"Do you have any brothers or sisters?"

"There was just my mother and me."

"No father?"

"I never knew my father."

"Is your mother still living?"

Chester didn't answer at first. He just dropped his head down to his chest. Then he stiffened, raised his head and answered, "No. She died of lung cancer, seven years ago."

"How old were you when she died?"

"Fifteen."

"Who took care of you after she died?"

"I took care of myself."

"Did you have to quit high school?"

"No. I never told anyone in the school that I was alone. Oh, Mister and Mrs. Timmy Adams looked in on me now and then."

"How did you do in school?"

"I had a B average by the time I graduated. It didn't start too well for me but I got a straight A average in my senior year and that boosted my over all average at the end."

"Did you participate in sports?"

"No time for sports. I had to work."

"Where did you work?"

"In the veterinarian business. I cleaned the place up, mostly, but I was able to see hundreds of surgical operations over the three years that I worked there."

"Were you working when you were arrested in this present matter?"

"The only job open to me that was kind of related to my goal in life was being a custodian at the hospital."

"What is your goal in life?"

"To be a doctor, a surgeon."

"How long did you work at the hospital?"

"A little more than two years . . . up until I was arrested."

"What is your sexual preference?"

"It's not a preference. I think I was born with a homosexual tendency. Just like you were probably born with a heterosexual tendency."

"Why did you attempt to go to Chicago on the morning of the Howell killing?"

"Because I'm black and I had gotten into a scuffle with a famous white baseball player who was murdered by someone. I knew I would become an immediate suspect, and I also knew that once a black man gets into the system he's a goner. As it turns out, I was one hundred percent correct. Here I sit, being tried for a murder I did not commit."

"When you were thrown out of Carmine's café that morning and found yourself running for safety to your home, did you realize that you were being followed by a Volkswagen?"

"I saw a Volkswagen, but my street is pretty dark and I didn't see who either person in the car was. I did see it make a left turn in front of me just as I was about to run across the street to the block where my two rooms are located."

"Do you know anyone who owns a Volkswagen?"

"No, I don't."

"Chester, you told us you work at the hospital. Do you work at night?"

"Yes. I want to keep myself free to go to Junior College in the daytime. I wasn't going to school at the time of the murder, but I have got a little more than a full year of credits. I save every penny to pay for tuition and books."

"Chester, how did you get to the Greyhound Station?"

"I asked Howard Parsons to take me there, like he testified."

"Have you seen Howard Parsons since you were arrested?"

"Once. He visited me at the Detention Center some two years after I was arrested. I understand he has a new partner."

"Do you know how old Parsons is?"

"Old enough to be my father. Almost fifty I think."

"Do you long for his company?"

"Not any more. He no longer is one of my priorities . . . especially now that he has a new partner."

"Was he ever in Carmine's café at the same time you were?"

"Many times. He knew my habits. He knew that I stopped in at Carmine's almost every night after the night shift at the hospital ended at midnight. As a matter of fact, he often worked the night shift with me. I met him at the hospital."

"Did you work the night shift on the night before the murder?"

"No, I didn't."

"Did Parsons?"

"No, he didn't."

"When you were still going with him, was he very protective of you?"

"You probably won't understand this because of our sexual relationship, but most of the time he treated me like a son."

"Would he kill for you?"

Hathaway was on his feet. "Objection. Calls for an opinion."

Judge Piercy responded, "Sustained. And Mister Wilson, you seem to be straying from what is pertinent in this case. Kindly get back on a pertinent line of questioning, please."

"Has Parsons ever demonstrated that he would protect you from bodily harm?"

"We were in the grocery store once and I accidentally bumped into a man's wife. The man got very mad and Howard had to literally pull him off of me. Then he started hitting the man and several other men who were standing around had to stop him. Howard might have killed the man if they hadn't prevented him from pounding him in the face."

"Same objection, your Honor. The defendant is offering opinions."

"Sustained. That's enough, now, Mister Wilson."

Ed Wilson apologized. "My fault, your Honor. I'll ask Mister Roosevelt not to offer any more opinions."

The judge reinforced Wilson's statement. "Do you understand why your testimony is objectionable, Mister Roosevelt?"

"I think so, your Honor. I'll try to watch my step from now on."

"See that you do."

"Chester, did the fact that Archy Howell punched you in the face make you angry?"

"No, but it scared me. I thought he was going to beat me until I passed out. I was grateful to Oscar who broke it up and gave me a chance to run away. I guess that makes me a coward. But it taught me a lesson."

"What lesson?"

"To mind my own business."

"I have no more questions of the defendant, your Honor."

"Mister Hathaway, I'm sure you will want to cross examine the defendant."

"I do, your Honor. Thank you."

"Mister Roosevelt, we all heard that you and your homosexual lover owned identical shotguns, purchased at the same time and probably at the same place, right?"

"Yes."

"And how Mister Sonny Campbell's investigator, seized your shotgun, which you placed with Mister Parsons just before you tried to make your escape to Chicago, right?"

"I guess so."

"Tell me something, Mister Roosevelt, how can we be sure that Mister Parsons turned over your shotgun to Mister Campbell and not his own, which he knew hadn't been fired for over six months."

"If you will show me the exhibit that is marked as my shotgun, I will show how I can be sure it's mine."

Ed Wilson picked up the shotgun and brought it to the witness stand. Hathaway joined him there. The exhibit was handed to the witness by Hathaway after he had broken it down and had made sure that there were no shells in its chambers.

Roosevelt turned the exhibit on end with its barrels pointed toward the floor. "You see what is inscribed in tiny letters on the metal that covers the end of the gun butt? *TO CAR-MY LOVE FOREVER.*"

"What does CAR stand for?"

"Chester Arthur Roosevelt."

"I suppose the metal plates could have been switched."

Judge Piercy said sternly, "Please refrain from volunteering testimony, Mister Hathaway."

"Sorry, your Honor. . . . If you knew your shotgun hadn't been fired for six months, why did you take it to Mister Parsons for safekeeping?"

"I also knew that you people would search and find it and I might never see it again."

"Mister Roosevelt, does anybody in your neighborhood own a Volkswagen?"

"I'm not sure, but I don't think I've ever seen a Volkswagen in my neighborhood."

"Who do you know in Chicago?"

"Not a soul."

"How did you expect to get by there?"

"Washing dishes . . . digging ditches . . . walking dogs. I don't know. I've always gotten by, even here in Hagerstown when I was fifteen years old."

"When did you plan to come back to Hagerstown, if at all?"

"When you had caught the real killer."

"I have no more questions."

"Call your next witness, Mister Wilson," the judge directed.

"First, may we have Mister Roosevelt's shotgun placed into evidence?"

"Any objection, Mister Hathaway?"

"No, your Honor."

"Defendant's exhibit is now in evidence."

"Call Mister Randolph Fielstra."

After Fielstra was sworn and in the witness chair, he was asked to give details of his professional background. After almost five minutes of reciting a litany of education and professional experience as a forensic scientist, Wilson asked the judge, "May we have Mister Fielstra certified as a forensic expert?"

"No objection," said Winston Hathaway in a rather sullen manner.

Fielstra's testimony established irrefutably that the shotgun he examined more than a year ago had not been fired for at least six months. Wilson went on to his next witness, a surprise to everyone in the courtroom. He called Douglas McNamara.

"Mister McNamara, where do you presently reside?"

"The Federal Correctional Complex in Beaumont, Texas."

"What are you in for?"

"Wire Wagering fraud, flight to evade being sentenced on admitted federal charges, and soliciting the murder of Archy Howell."

"Whom did you solicit?"

"Mario Constanza."

"Do you know whether he completed the job you hired him to do?"

"He claims that he didn't kill the guy, but what would you expect him to say?"

"I guess our jury will have to decide that one. Thank you, Mister McNamara. I have no more questions. Your witness."

Hathaway took up the questioning."

"Sir, how much did you agree to pay Constanza for the killing?"

"Twenty-five grand."

"Did you ever pay him?"

"He never asked me to pay him."

"Did you ever ask him why?"

"I never spoke to him after the killing, but I figured it had something to do with your arrest of the defendant over there."

"You mean that since Chester Roosevelt had killed Howell, Mario Constanza hadn't earned his money and knew he wasn't entitled to get paid, right?"

"Something like that."

"I object to that little bit of verbal tomfoolery," said Ed Wilson. "Jurisprudence teaches us that an accused is innocent until proven guilty. If anything has been proven in this courtroom, it's that Chester Roosevelt is not guilty. He walked in here not guilty, he sits there now not guilty, and he should walk out of this hallowed hall of justice and fair play, **an innocent man.** Mister Hathaway should not be heard to say things like *since Chester Roosevelt had killed Howell.*"

Hathaway laughed and said, "Talk about verbal tomfoolery."

The judge said, "This time I have to agree with Mister Hathaway. Save that eloquent rhetoric for your closing argument, Mister Wilson. Objection overruled."

"Mister McNamara, Would you have paid Constanza if he had asked you to?"

"Sure. But if he asked for the money that would mean that he probably did kill the baseball player. In the mean time I was satisfied with you guys arresting Roosevelt."

"No more questions, your Honor."

"Mister Wilson?"

"We call Doctor Jack Landsdale."

Doctor Landsdale was eventually sitting in the witness chair and waiting to be asked some questions. Ed Wilson was distracted for a moment and was bending down to talk to Walter Brock.

The Judge scolded, "The witness is waiting for you, Mister Wilson. Are you going to want the Doctor to be certified as an expert?"

"No, your honor. Doctor Landsdale is a veterinarian and comes here today as a character witness."

"I understand."

"Doctor Landsdale, did you once employ this defendant sitting here?"

"He worked for me for three years before he moved on to work at the hospital."

"Do you know why he left you to work at the hospital?"

"I think so. He wanted to be closer to the real thing."

"What do you mean?"

"Well, he started with me as a clean-up person. When he left he had learned to be an excellent surgical nurse. The professional rules do not prohibit a non-credentialed person assisting in a pet OR."

"Did he take a sincere interest in assisting you?"

"I saw him cry once, when we couldn't keep a dog alive, which was hit by a car. Yes, I would say he has heartfelt regard for life . . . for keeping animals alive. We had many conversations about his one day becoming a surgeon. I know he would always be eligible for a recommendation from me, for college I mean, or even for medical school. . . . And now these ridiculous charges. He is morally incapable of killing any living thing."

"Objection, your Honor. That last testimony was an opinion."

Judge Piercey said with a high moral tone. "Yes, it was, Mister Hathaway. It was a sincere, heartfelt opinion and my own opinion is that it is one worthy of the jury's consideration. Your objection is overruled."

Ed Wilson said, with a hint of bravado, "Defendant rests."

CHAPTER TWENTY FIVE

Judge Piercy addressed his remarks to Winston Hathaway. "Are you ready to give your closing statement to the jury, Mister Hathaway?"

"Yes, sir. Thank you, sir." Hathaway stood in place and consulted his notes frequently. "Ladies and gentlemen, Mister Wilson is a very clever lawyer. In the last couple of days he has sold you a bill of goods that even a man from Missouri might be tempted to believe. But don't be fooled. He hasn't fooled me.

"Take the suit off the defendant. Rewrite his sob story about his early life and his difficulty growing up without a father. Take the scalpel out of the junior doctor's hand and replace it with a shotgun. How clever he and his life partner were in exchanging the romantic gift message on the butt of those identical shotguns. But they forgot to get rid of that batch of shotgun shells in Roosevelt's apartment, two of which tore Archy Howell's head off. Just as soon as you find this revenge seeking murderer guilty, Howard Parsons will find himself charged with aiding and abetting the killing."

Ed Wilson stood and opened his mouth as if to pose an objection. Instead he said, "Oh, never mind. I guess I can listen to more of this fantasy." He sat down and said no more.

"You see how clever Mister Wilson is. He's all innuendo and guesswork. To go on. Remember, he never did prove that Mister Bucky Livingston was lying about the racial slurs. All he did was use his lawyering skills to confuse and insult the witness. And the rest of the people in the café were clearly sympathetic to their fellow Negro friend and would themselves lie for him or do anything else to help him get out of the mess he found himself in.

"But the clincher was the mysterious Volkswagen. It was seen following the defendant and only minutes later would emerge again with two people in it, the driver and the defendant, and then last seen following the victim, eventually to his death at Plum and Jefferson. To me it's all as plain as day. Why else would the defendant try to evade arrest and flee to Chicago, some five hundred miles from Hagerstown? A huge guilty conscience drove him to do that, never mind that nonsense about Negroes once getting into the system and not being able to get out of it.

"Ladies and gentlemen, I thank you for your attention throughout this complicated criminal trial. Yes, you're here to do justice . . . justice for the defendant . . . but remember, there's somebody else who's entitled to some justice here and that's Archy Howell. Please don't let him down."

Judge Piercy addressed the defense table. Wilson was leaning in his chair toward Walter Brock who had just come into the courtroom. Wilson was saying something to Brock.

"Mister Wilson, do you wish to give a closing statement now, or do you want a brief recess to collect your thoughts?"

"No recess is needed, your Honor. I'll talk to the jury now."

Wilson stood and walked around his table and over to the jury box. He brought no notes and his head was bowed. He stopped and stood in front of the jury for about ten seconds, still with his head bowed. As he raised his head, he started his speech. "Ladies and gentlemen, you might well have guessed that this is the time allotted to me to tell you what I think your vote should be and why. We lawyers have a name for closing statements . . . a time to . . . *hang out the wash*. Well, I'm not going to hang out any wash this time. I don't feel I have to. With respect for your obvious intelligence . . . remember I helped the court to pick you to be jurors . . . with the greatest of respect, I ask you first to do something. Think back to my opening statement. If you think I have proven all the facts and circumstances I promised I would, then just plug my opening remarks in at this time.

"Now, I want to make a final brief conclusion. I want to quote from the most important witness in this whole trial . . . Doctor Jack Landsdale who has been the one person who spent the most critical time with my client . . . some three years . . . talking to him, observing his demeanor, learning to know Chester's most inner hopes for himself, and seeing him cry when the two of them failed to save the life of somebody's dog. Doctor Landsdale described to you what Chester Roosevelt is. **He is morally incapable of killing any living thing.** For heaven's sake, do the right thing when you cast your vote back there in the deliberation room."

Wilson turned and went back to his seat at the defense table. Hathaway waived the final closing words that he had a perfect right to give.

Sonny Campbell and Ed Wilson sat just outside the courtroom, waiting to hear the alarm bell scream down the hallways indicating that the jury had probably finally reached a unanimous verdict. The bell screamed, but it was a false alarm. The jury had a question. All the official participants of the conduct of the trial were called into place, and the jury filed into their box and took their seats.

The elected foreman stood up and announced, "Your Honor, I believe we are hopelessly deadlocked."

"Don't reveal who's for acquittal or who's for guilty as charged, but tell me what the score is as it presently stands."

The foreman answered, "Eleven to one."

"You shouldn't have a problem if you each talk to that holdout and explain to him or her what your innermost thoughts are regarding your own vote. Go back in there and try again. I fully expect you to come in here with a unanimous verdict. Remember our credo, *Justice and Fairplay.* Keep your minds open to the ideas of others."

That incident occurred two hours after the Judge had instructed the jury. The wait since then was excruciating. Sonny said, "Just think of how anxious Chet must feel."

"I've thought about him. He's really a pretty tough kid. And you know something? In my entire career I never felt better about a case that I tried. I defended with zeal . . . And, oh my, it felt good."

Sonny and Ed talked about nothing in particular for another half hour. Edith Beyerly joined them after the jury had come in to ask their question. She protested, "How could there be one hold out? I wonder if McNamara had something to do with that. He's obviously fully capable of it and he and his syndicate still have a lot of money. I'm going to ask Joe what he thinks."

Finally the bell screamed. Ed said, "That must be it."

The fairly large crowd filed into the courtroom. There were as many Negroes as Caucasians sitting on the defendant's side of the courtroom. The jury filed in and sat in their seats. Judge Piercy asked the foreman if they had reached a unanimous verdict.

The foreman stood up. "Yes, your Honor." He handed a single sheet of paper to the bailiff who took it to the judge. The judge glanced at it for only a moment and handed it back to the bailiff who took it back to the foreman.

The judge asked, "Would the foreman read the verdict?"

"Yes, your Honor. We the jury find the defendant not guilty."

"So say you all?" There was a mumbling chorus indicating that the verdict was unanimous.

The defendant had tears rolling down his cheeks. He put his head on Ed Wilson's shoulder and said over and over again. "Thank you, Mister Wilson. Thank you . . . thank you . . . thank you."

Sonny and Edith approached from the rear. Chester stood. Sonny took him in his arms as a father might. "Next stop, back to college. And then on to medical school."

"Oh, Mister Campbell, I'll never let you down. I promise . . . I promise."

The judge pronounced, "Mister Roosevelt is free to go. This Court is adjourned."

With a smile on her face, Edith had to raise her voice a little to be heard above the courtroom noise. "I never thought it was you, Chester."

Sonny asked Chester if he would mind if he sent Walter Brock along with him to Hoffman's to get him a few decent things to wear.

"You don't have to do that, Mister Campbell."

"Nonsense, that old suit you got on is ready for the scrap heap."

As an aside to Brock, Sonny said, "Take this credit card and Chester over to Hoffman's. Get him a new suit, a sport jacket, four shirts, four ties, four sets of underwear, four pairs of socks and a pair of shoes. Got it? Then bring him over to my house. Rocky and I should be there waiting for you. What time you got?"

"Almost four o'clock."

"Good. School's out and Rocky should be here any minute."

Ed Wilson's secretary, Pat Erickson, showed up shortly after the verdict was announced. Sonny called her aside and asked her to do a favor for him. "Would you make a reservation for two dozen people at Rocky's New York Pizza Parlor on South Potomac. Tell them to expect us around six-thirty. Give them my name and they won't give you any trouble. And go back to the office and tell everybody there that they're invited to Rocky's Pizza joint at six-thirty . . . pizza and drinks on me."

"I'm right on it."

Rochelle Campbell arrived and ran to her husband. "I just heard. It's all over the court house. Do you think he'd mind if I introduced myself and congratulated him?"

"I don't think he'd mind that a bit."

She did more than introduce herself. She gave Chester a hug. He was still weeping.

Ed Wilson grabbed Sonny by the arm. "Hey, Buddy, leave something for me to do, will you? I'll split the bill at Rocky's. Where's he gonna stay tonight?"

"My place. Walter's bringing some new clothes I got him to my house. He'll change and we'll bring him out to the restaurant. He'll go home with us after the party at Rocky's, the best pizza in the world. You and your wife are certainly invited to join us. Hell! The whole gang can come to my house if it wants to."

Walter Brock interrupted. "O.K., Mister Roosevelt, time to go to Hoffman's." The two pushed their way through the crowd, with Chester having to avoid all the congratulatory handshakes and hugs that were offered to him.

Sonny insisted that he and Rochelle go home and change into something casual. Ed Wilson came over to the two of them, "Life's sweet, ain't it, folks? I think I'm gonna celebrate tonight with a great deal of zeal."

Rochelle told Chester that he should wear his new sport jacket. "And wear the blue shirt and leave the collar unbuttoned. The pants from your old suit will do nicely. We're going casual tonight."

"Better listen to her, Chet. She dresses me every morning and never takes no for an answer. I will admit that she's got good taste."

Chester responded, "This is truly the happiest day of my whole life, Mister Campbell." Sonny held up his hand. "Time you stopped calling me Mister Campbell. You'll call me what everybody else calls me, **Sonny.** Otherwise I might not know who you're talking to if you continue with that *Mister Campbell* business."

PART FOUR

Solution

CHAPTER TWENTY SIX

Sonny and Rochelle sat at Smitty's bar. Smitty was talking to them about an issue, which they both, along with many others in town, had been discussing ever since the trial had concluded in Chester Roosevelt's favor.

"I'd ask you two who you think killed Archy, but I'm sure neither one of you has the slightest idea who did it."

Rochelle responded, "You got that right, Smitty. We've talked about it, and talked about it and nothing comes up . . . not a clue. I'd like to think that Howard Parsons is the culprit but the facts just don't support that. He had no connection to Archy and had no motive. But don't fret, either Joe or my brilliant husband here will figure this thing out before they die."

"How's it going with your new boarder?"

She answered, "He's a sweetheart. Doctor Landsdale, the veterinarian who testified for him and probably won the case for Ed Wilson, offered him his old job back right after the trial. The doctor says that Chester could run the business by himself in an emergency. When he's not doing the grunt work or helping in the operation room, he's got a book on veterinarian medicine in his lap, reading and absorbing details about the job."

Sonny spoke up. "You know Smitty, that boy deserves our help. We stole more than two years out of his life, and I firmly believe that society owes him something."

Smitty asked, "You mean people like me owe him something?"

"Depends on how you feel about Negroes being persecuted just because they're black. You realize, don't you, that's what really put him in a jail cell in the first place?"

"Now wait a minute. I was one who in the first place thought he might have done it."

"Because he was black?"

"Yeah, because he was black and was slapped around and subjected to racial slurs. It wouldn't have been the first time that racial rage got somebody shot dead."

Sonny protested. "But there were no racial slurs, and when Archy slapped him around, there was no injury to speak of. It just scared him to death. But that's neither here nor there. What I'm talking about is racial prejudice and profiling in the judicial system. How easy it was to make him a suspect . . . a sure suspect just because he was black. Pop him in a jail cell and forget about him for more than two years and never really ask the right questions about whether they had the right man. Well, we shouldn't pursue this with you any more. I'm just going to tell you that I want you and others to contribute to a fund I'm starting up to send him back to college and on to medical school. You can contribute if you want to, or tell me I'm a liberal so-and-so and ignore it. Smitty, I believe we should give this kid the first break he's had in his entire life."

"You want another beer?"

Rochelle answered, "Bring us both another beer, would you Smitty?" When he was out of ear shot, she said to her husband, "You know, you are a liberal so-and-so. But if you want to succeed with this fund for Chester, you better put me in charge of it. Women know the subtleties of asking people to donate their hard earned money to a cause. You can't club a guy over the head and expect him to feel the same way you do about Chester. When he comes back with our beer, don't talk about it any more. Leave the whole campaign up to me, O.K?"

"You're probably right. Heads up, here he comes."

Sonny slid into a whole new subject matter. "What kind of team do you think we're going to have this year, Smitty?"

"Very strong. The replacements have had a whole season to learn how to play hard ball. I've been down to the stadium, watching the team work out. I like what I see. They're going to fill the stands this year, especially after that fiasco almost three years ago. People have short memories."

Rochelle seemed to be thinking of something else as the men talked baseball. She was composing in her mind a letter that she believed would be effective in getting some financing for Chester's education. She was anxious to go home and get behind her word processor and see what a draft of her letter would look like.

Smitty interrupted her thoughts. "Where'd ya drift off to, Rocky? You look like you're visiting another planet. Come on, you're a hard core baseball fan. Where are you? What could possibly be more important than America's favorite pastime?"

She lied. "I was just listening to you guys and keeping my mouth shut. I'll speak up when you make a mistake. You're right. I probably know more about the game than either of you two jerks."

Smitty challenged her. "O.K. Who's Marty O'Neal?"

"Twenty-two year old short stop who can throw strikes like a pitcher."

"You win. Tell me how I can get a ticket next to you two for the season opener."

She answered, "Leave it to me. I know somebody in the ticket office. And I happen to know about a seat that might still be available. Now, bring us a couple of hot dogs with mustard and relish, will you?"

"Comin' up."

Dear *Mister or Mrs. So and So*,

I'm writing to you about a matter which I think will interest you. I'm sure you'll remember Chester Roosevelt, who was acquitted in a first degree murder trial a few weeks ago. He was acquitted because he truly was innocent, a victim of racial profiling and prejudice.

Chester is boarding with Sonny and me. He got a part time job with a veterinarian within just a few days of his trial. This young man is one of the smartest, most ambitious students I've ever had the privilege of meeting. In his spare time he is monitoring what's left of a biology class at the Junior College. (He was still incarcerated, awaiting trial on the first day of class last January and couldn't begin with the other students.) As he puts it, "By monitoring the part that I didn't miss, I'll have a head start on biology when I start the class in June." As far as we're concerned, Chester will live here in this house until he goes off to a university, somewhere. He is like the son we never had.

And that brings me to why I'm writing this letter. I have no doubt that he will graduate from Junior College in record time, and at the top of his class. His agenda before he was arrested, was to work at the hospital and save every penny to pay for another semester at the College. Our system of so-called criminal justice interrupted that agenda.

Now, I'll be blunt. Sonny and I have established a fund. We have placed a thousand dollars in the fund to kick it off. The fund will help pay for the start of the third year of his education at the University of Maryland at College Park. He will doubtless have scholarship help as well. But this young man needs his first break in an up-till-now life of nothing but undeserved frustration, almost insurmountable obstacles, and suffering the privations of becoming an orphan at the age of fifteen. I'm sure that God has something better than all that in mind for this gifted person.

If you feel you can help with our project, please give your contribution to the fund, preferably by check made out to William Campbell, Trustee of the Education Trust for Chester Arthur Roosevelt. Please open your hearts and your pocket books for the most worthy cause I've encountered in my entire life.

As ever,
Rocky

The money poured in, some from unlikely places. Rochelle was delighted that some of the smaller checks came from Negroes who had somehow heard about the fund. Doctor Jack Landsdale sent a check for two thousand dollars. And there were several startling contributions. Judge John Piercy wrote his personal check for two thousand dollars. State's Attorney Winston Hathaway wrote a check for five hundred dollars. On the ledger line Hathaway wrote *With a Sincere Apology*. Walter Brock gave two hundred dollars and it was no surprise that Ed Wilson gave seven hundred and fifty dollars. And the most startling gift of all came from Joe and Edith Beyerly—a check for twenty thousand dollars.

To administer the trust was, in Sonny Campbell's mind, the most noble endeavor he had ever undertaken. He knew Chester would not disappoint these fine people. He and Rochelle seriously contemplated applying for adoption of the young man. In advance of Chester's graduation from Junior College, Sonny sat down with his soon-to-be son and pored over a University of Maryland catalogue, like any other father and son might do. He was positive that Chester would be able to transfer all of his Hagerstown Junior College grades, mostly As, to the University in College Park. The young man passionately outlined a schedule for his final two years of undergraduate studies. When he did sleep, he often dreamed of a place in Baltimore called Johns Hopkins School of Medicine.

A year and two months had passed since Chester's acquittal. He had completed his final year at Junior College. Rochelle asked Sonny, "Why not? Why not adopt him? He lives with us. We already treat him like he is ours. I think we both love him. He's practically guaranteed to make us proud. And I have a longing to be able to say, *my son the doctor.*"

"What about his sexuality?" asked Sonny.

"What about it? It's not a choice he made. I've talked to him about it. He was born with it. Just like he was born black. Neither one of those things makes a whit's difference to me."

"Nor me. I was just wondering if you had some misgivings about his relationship with Howard Parsons."

"Well, stop your simple minded wondering. Besides, Parsons is a thing of the past. After the way that relationship ended, I doubt whether Chet will even think about a relationship with someone else, boy or girl, until after people are calling him Doctor Roosevelt."

"Boy! You sure know how to put my feelings into words."

"Even after almost twenty-three years you say such a thing. Listen lover, I've been saying what you feel since before we got married, and I wrote those letters to you in Germany."

"I remember. I think it all started on the night I met you twenty-three years ago. In fact, that was probably the reason I asked you to marry me . . . because you could put my feelings into words."

"You want to know something else? . . . I love you . . . I think I fall in love with you every day of our life together. You are a noble man . . . a humanitarian . . . more considerate of others than you need to be . . . and you're not bad looking either. You want to go upstairs?"

"It's only ten-thirty in the morning. But since you can put my feelings into words, the answer is yes, but why bother going upstairs? We're the only people in this house. What do you say?"

She went to him and slowly unbuttoned his shirt. "Promise me you'll keep your mouth shut for the next half hour."

"Mmm. You smell good."

Rocky, are you home?" Chester took off his jacket and hung it in the hall closet.

"I'm upstairs, Chester. There's some mail for you on the hall table. It's from College Park." She was now walking down the stairs. "I almost opened it myself. Hurry. Open it. Tell me the good or bad news."

He ripped the envelope apart and extracted the letter inside. "God bless America! I'm in. I can start in the summer session if I want to. And they're offering me a pre-med scholarship. Where are you going?"

"I'm going to call your fath . . . I'm going to call Sonny. He's still in his office."

Joe Beyerly was on the phone to Sonny that afternoon. He had to wait until Joe was finished talking before he could return Rochelle's call.

Joe Beyerly announced to Sonny, "It was Edith who got my bloodhound's nose to the ground. She wondered how there could have been a holdout when Ed Wilson tried such a perfect case. She thinks there was a little bribery involved. Sonny, you know me. I can't let the possibility of bribing a juror just fade away. I'm determined to find out. I'm going to ask Piercy for permission to talk to the jurors. If I have to eliminate the innocent ones by talking to each and every one of them, I'll do it until I nail the holdout. Then I'll go to work on him or her. If I find out that one of the *Minor League Wagering Team* tried to bribe that jury, I'll have him hauled before Piercy and see how many years we can add to his sentence."

"Are you willing to keep me posted on this investigation?"

"Of course. That's why I called you today."

"Great, Joe. Look, I gotta call Rocky back now. She says it's important."

"What! I'm comin' home . . . **right now.** We've got to plan a celebration at the house tonight. . . . Judge Piercy, Joe and Edith, Walter, Ed Wilson and his wife, Winston Hathaway and his wife. . . . Have I left anybody out?"

"Doctor Landsdale and his wife. That's it. We don't have room for any more."

"Start calling those people. Don't give too many details. Save that for the man of the house."

"Who's that, you or Chester?"

"Me. I'm going to make a speech."

When Sonny got home he kissed Chester on the cheek. "Congratulations, son."

"That's the first time you ever called me that."

"I guess it is. I have to talk to you about that. Let's get this party over first. . . . Here's a hundred bucks. See how much champagne that'll buy. Rocky you call a caterer for *hors d'oeuvres*. See if a bakery can rustle up a cake that says, *Congratulations! We're All Proud of You*—something modest like that. Have we got plenty of champagne glasses?"

Rochelle answered, "I'll ask Edith to bring all she's got . . . then we'll have enough."

Chester protested, "Don't you think you're going overboard Sonny?"

"Look, young man, this is a once in a life time occasion. You've got nothing to say about it. This is more for the parents than for the child."

"I gotta say, for an orphan, I got the greatest parents in the world."

Rochelle spoke up. "We're glad you feel that way, Chester. Nothing could make me happier than to hear that."

All who were invited came except Winston Hathaway. He was preparing for a trial that was to start in the morning. But he sent an envelope with Judge Piercy and that started something. The envelope had a fifty dollar bill in it. Piercy matched the money with an envelope of his own, also containing a fifty dollar bill. On arrival, Piercy laid the envelopes on a glass table near the front door. When Rochelle saw them, she immediately placed a stack of brand new envelopes on the table. Most guests got the idea on arrival. Others were told by word of mouth what was expected of them and they went back to the table and grabbed an envelope in which they placed their contributions in varying amounts.

Conversation at the party was lively. Despite Rochelle's whispered warning that Chester's trial was off limits, much of the talk in the living room dealt with speculation on who killed Archy Howell. Joe's investigation of jury bribery had met a dead end. The holdout had been a woman. He was positive that the she had been approached by the *Minor League Wagering Team* but he was equally positive that no money had ever changed hands. She might have gotten paid if she had been successful in convincing eleven others to vote for a conviction. But she never came close to convincing anybody, not even herself, that Chester had killed Howell. Nobody presented a plausible analysis of who the killer might be. Joe Beyerly was heard to say, "If it takes the rest of my life, I'll find out who the murderer was."

Judge Piercy asked Chester, "When are you expected on campus, Chester?"

"I'm not sure, sir, but the summer session starts in early June. First I've got to find housing . . . maybe with some roommates. That would be the cheapest way to go. Sonny's driving me down there this Sunday and we'll scout the campus and find out what I have to do to get a place to live."

The judge became nostalgic. "It brings back fond memories of my freshman days at Boston College. I still watch all the B.C. football games on TV."

Doctor Landsdale entered the conversation. "Don't we all do that? It's not that we're trying to recapture our youth—it's our innocence we're trying to find again. That's my definition of nostalgia."

Rochelle said, "You know, I never thought of it that way. I think you got something there. Whenever my mind soars back to my little-girl days, it's innocence I'm seeing . . . sometimes to the extent that it makes me want to cry. If only that innocence could persist throughout your life, certainly, the world would be a better place to live in."

Joe Beyerly said, "Well, it's guilt I'm usually searching for. Find the guilty bastards. That's my job. You won't find me crying over lost innocence. But you'll find me laughing at the guilty criminals I find."

Rochelle responded, "Well, I guess the world also needs hardcore investigators like you, Joe. But I bet there was a time that you cried too, about an old memory or two."

Joe refused to admit that that ever happened.

Edith joined the debate. "I caught him crying at a sad movie, one time . . . for what that's worth."

Joe was genuinely angry. "Hey, what is this? *Let's All Make Joe Beyerly Look Like a Pussy* night! I won't put up with that kind of nonsense. You people have your approach to this very tough life we all have to lead . . . and I have mine."

Jack Landsdale interrupted. "I didn't mean to start World War Three."

Edith soothed the veterinarian's concern. "Don't worry Doctor Landsdale, he's really an old softy."

Joe joked. "Only in bed, where it pays off. . . . Hey, Chester. How'd you like to learn how to play tennis? I can start you here in Hagerstown and you can continue when you get to the campus at College Park."

"I don't have a racket, Mister Beyerly."

"That's not a problem. Let me see your hands." Chester showed Joe his hands who measured them against his own. "You see? We got the same size hands. I got a half dozen rackets at home. What's on your schedule for Saturday?"

"Nothing, in the morning."

"I'll pick you up here at eight o'clock on Saturday morning and we'll go out to the Hagerstown Tennis Club. I guarantee you're going to enjoy it. You got the build for it."

"That's very kind of you, Mister Beyerly. I'll be ready to go at eight in the morning on Saturday."

Sonny forced his way to the center of the room. "Time for me to make a speech. You're all here because you've chosen to come aboard a project that is some day going to bring you great returns. This young man is going to break all sorts of barriers to his success, and he's going to do it with your help. On a very personal note, Rochelle and I have discussed thoroughly whether we will try to fill a hole in our lives that we've had to suffer for too many years. We're going to propose to Chester Arthur Roosevelt that he change his last name to *Campbell*. As she puts it, she longs to one day say, *My son, the doctor*. With his consent, of course, we're going to propose to Chet that we adopt him."

Chet was sitting on a couch and holding his head with both hands so as to cover his eyes which were overflowing with tears. Rochelle went to the couch and sat close to him, taking one of his hands in hers.

Sonny picked up his speech again. "Do we have your consent, son, to make it official?" Chester stood, and went to Sonny. He hugged his surrogate father and said softly, "Of course."

There was a burst of applause, which lasted a full half minute.

The following Saturday morning was a very enjoyable day for Chester. Joe Beyerly was right. Chester had the build for playing tennis. He was a natural. They would continue the tennis lessons for three more Saturdays. From then on, Chester was on his own. He was to pick up playing the game on the College Park campus or wherever he was invited by other amateurs to play. On his first break from school, he called Joe Beyerly for the sole purpose of showing off his newly found athletic skill. Joe was truly amazed. "What have I spawned? You ever get better than I am, young man, and I'll run you out of town."

CHAPTER TWENTY SEVEN

There was an occasional dogwood tree still in bloom on the College Park campus. The first building that caught Chester's and Sonny's attention was a red brick church with a tall white steeple. It sat on an elevated piece of campus real estate which helped to show off its grandeur.

Chester said, "I think I'll join that church just so I'll have the thrill of seeing that beautiful Maryland architecture every Sunday."

Sonny observed, "Now there's a unique reason for going to church on Sundays. I'm going to park this buggy and we're going to stroll around the campus. We can stop somebody and ask what a person does about housing. Or if you want to wait until we get home, we can call the registrar's office on Monday and ask them what to do. One thing I want to prepare you for, Chet. You may encounter some lingering heavy-duty racial discrimination, when it comes to housing. But we'll deal with that, won't we?"

"Yes, we will."

Twenty minutes later, they saw two young black men strolling down a cement path. Chester had to run to catch up to them.

"Pardon me, but I'm new on campus. Could you answer a couple questions?"

Both of the men were well over six and a half feet tall.

"What questions?"

"I Just graduated from Hagerstown Junior College. I'll be starting the summer session here. I'm totally in the dark about housing for black people."

The taller of the two said, "You think we'll invite you to live with us, or something?"

"No, I just need information."

"Listen, bro. Your best bet is to ask the white dudes who run this place. We're both on the basketball team and we live together, with all black roommates. Same thing with the white players. You'll be lucky to find any place on campus that you can tolerate."

"It doesn't have to be on campus. Not too far away, though. I don't have a car."

The shorter basketball player suggested, "Grab yourself a newspaper and check the ads. You'll find something. Who's that white dude standing over there?"

"My adoptive father. He just drove me down here from Hagerstown."

The taller player said, "I suggest you don't tell anybody you've got a white father."

"Why?"

"Cuz that makes you neither black nor white. Our people don't like that kind of thing very much."

"That's ridiculous."

"You'll find out what I mean soon enough. Like I said, check the newspapers, bro. We gotta split. We're headed for a practice at the gym. You and paleface over there, can watch if you want. Coach don't mind."

Chester rejoined Sonny. "You want to watch some basketball at the gym?"

"Why not? We're here to get see as much as we can. What did they say?"

"I'll tell you in the gym. We better speed it up. Those guys got long legs."

Before they moved off the campus back onto the highway that would take them home, Chester asked Sonny to drive around and look for tennis courts. They finally found the courts. The saw a dozen white players playing what looked like serious tennis. They parked and Chester got out and walked over to two black grounds men who were replacing a net on one of the courts. The net showed signs of rot and deterioration. "Hi, you guys. Do you happen to know whether these courts are available to all students?"

"Yeah, they are. But you have to sign up for them first . . . over in the athletic building over there. But they got a waiting list a mile long. You can only make one reservation at a time, though. But I warn you, don't expect to feel like they want you to play."

"I never had high expectations of a welcome."

They were now on their way back to Hagerstown. Chester was rather quiet on the trip home.

Sonny asked, "What's wrong?"

"Nothing, really."

"Come on, out with it."

"I was just asking myself why there has to be such a thing called prejudice, even among people of the same race.

"Prejudice is probably the least understood human concept on the planet. Even good people engage in it, know it's wrong, but go ahead anyway. I was

invited to dinner once by a good, otherwise moral, Negro couple and we got
to talking about prejudice. The wife was a light skinned, radiantly beautiful
woman who grew up in the south, the daughter of a prominent physician. She
went to Fisk University, which was established before the turn of the century
and was open to all races. Over time the campus became predominantly Negro.
She was a member of a Negro sorority . . . and that's where prejudice raised its
ugly head. At that dinner table she actually bragged about how her sorority
sisters used to vote no on a girl's application for membership because she was
too black. Negro women who were too black—in other words too Negro
to become members of her elitist sorority, were barred from membership. I
don't know what her motive was in telling me about this deplorable practice
and I never let on to her how disappointed I was in her. But there it was,
she herself, one of the usual victims of racial prejudice, mimicking the usual
white perpetrators of the practice. I never could figure why she thought that
was an acceptable part of her character."

"That's even a better example of what's been bothering me. One of those
two basketball players wanted to know who you were. I lied . . . prematurely
as it was . . . and said that you were my adoptive father. He quickly retorted,
I suggest you don't tell anybody you've got a white father. When I asked him why,
he said that his people . . . meaning his fellow blacks . . . don't like that sort
of thing. To me, that's a perfect example of racial prejudice."

"Yeah. I guess it comes in all varieties and colors. You and I should sit
down some day and see if we can come up with some answers. Right now
pale face is too pissed off to talk about it any more. In the mean time, I have
a notion that you're going to be so busy with your books you won't have time
to suffer because of it."

"Yeah. If one day I have a white dude on the operating table waiting for
me to do something to save his life, I'm going to ask him whether he has any
prejudices against black doctors before I make my first incision."

"And you won't be surprised if even in the operating room the white dude
might say yes and ask for a white doctor to replace you."

"You think it's that strong—white against black?"

"I think it's that strong."

As they pulled into the driveway of the Campbell residence, Rochelle was
at the front door to welcome them.

"I've been sitting on the living room couch staring at the drive way. You
can't imagine how much I missed you guys. I wish you had called me from
the road. I could have had dinner ready."

Sonny said, "Didn't think of that. Why don't you give us time to change and we'll go out for something to eat."

She answered as the three of them went into the house. "That'll be fine. How about a big juicy steak at LJ's?"

"Wanna go top drawer, huh?"

"Why not? We three are worth it."

"O.K., then."

Chester shouted as he dashed upstairs to his room. "**Gang way! Steak at LJ's.** Wowie, wowie **wow, wow, wow!**"

The Campbell family sat at a secluded table at LJ's. "Joe Beyerly called while you guys were gone. Wants to be sure that Chester still wants to play tennis next Saturday morning."

"Do I? Of course, I do. That guy is a terrific player . . . and teacher too."

"Well, give him a call and tell him."

"He also wanted to talk to Chet about Howard Parsons. Says he's not counting that guy out as Archy Howell's killer."

Chester retorted, "That's impossible. That was proven impossible. But I'll talk to him and answer any questions he might have. . . . Pass me the steak sauce, please."

Sonny protested. "If a steak needs steak sauce to taste good, then you shouldn't be eating it."

Chester came back with, "Who's to say a good steak can't be made to taste even better with a little sauce developed seventy-five years ago to do just that . . . make it taste better?"

"Go ahead, ruin a fifteen-dollar steak."

Chester laughed. "First thing I'm going to do on Monday is call the registrar at College Park. I've got to solve the housing problem. And there's a few other details I need to clear up."

"If you're wondering how you should line up your class schedule, they usually have a round up in the gym where you go to desks that have signs with courses named on them that you might be interested in. If they have room for you, you just sign up for the course. They'll check with you on prerequisites, of course."

"As far as housing goes, I've decided I'll take what ever they offer me. I've got nothing to prove as far as race is concerned. All I want is a place to sleep and study. I really don't care what color my roommates are."

Sonny said, "I kind o' knew that's what you'd do, Doctor Campbell. I think I know what your priorities are."

Rochelle smiled. "Wow, that sounds good, *Doctor Campbell—my son the doctor*."

"You know, as trustee of your education fund, we've got to decide how much spending money I should give you."

"Well, I'll say this. At first, I'll need some expense money. But I'm goin' to get a part-time job as quick as I can. I'll probably have some kind of job all the way through medical school."

"Not if I find out that any job you have is interfering with your studying."

"I'll pace myself, without you making decisions for me, thank you."

Rochelle agreed with Sonny. "He's not going to do anything that's going to interfere with his studying. I'll see to that."

As the College Park adventure unfolded, Chester Roosevelt, now officially Chester Campbell, found himself the only black man in a house full of white pre-med students, two of them women. The house lay six blocks east of the campus. It had an elaborate wooden fire escape, which was Chester's favorite place to study, weather permitting.

His grades for his entire time spent at the University of Maryland were near perfect. He was ashamed of a B+ in Comparative Anatomy. The rest of his grades were all at the A and A+ level. He took home scholastic prizes in Quantum Physics and Organic Chemistry.

He didn't neglect tennis. He became passionate about the game and became one of the best players on campus. He would have been asked to become a member of the school tennis team despite his color, but he made it clear that he would refuse an offer to join the team. Playing varsity tennis would detract from his studies.

The time came for him to apply for medical school. At the top of his list was Johns Hopkins in Baltimore, Maryland. This was followed by Stanford in Palo Alto, California. The University of Michigan, in Ann Arbor and Pritsker School of Medicine at the University of Chicago were his next preferences. But he prayed for acceptance at Johns Hopkins. Aside from its reputation for excellence, if he were accepted he would be close to Rochelle and Sonny.

His prayer was answered. He was accepted at Johns Hopkins. The same people who had supported his entry into Maryland University were now invited to a huge celebration at the Hagerstown Country Club. Joe and Edith Beyerly contributed another five thousand dollars to his education trust. When Chester heard about the contribution, he wrote a respectful letter to them in which he promised to pay back the entire twenty-five thousand dollars they had given when it was most needed. He received a response, written by Edith. The gist of her letter was that she and Joe would refuse to accept repayment. She also said that, *After all, were it not for your being falsely charged with first degree murder, Joe Beyerly would never have been offered the opportunity of tracking down Douglas McNamara and Charles Tomlinson and receiving an enormous fee for his success. You owe us nothing except a free yearly medical checkup.*

He graduated from Johns Hopkins with honors. He started his residency in neurology at Henry Ford Hospital in Detroit. There he had heard that Mario Constanza had again fallen into a coma, but this time had not come to. He had died, a sort of end to one of the early chapters in Chester's struggle to reach his lofty goal in the medical world. If Constanza had really fulfilled the contract he had with Douglas McNamara, the truth died with him.

He called Joe Beyerly. "What's up, doc?"

"Did you know that Mario Constanza died?"

"No. He became old news once you were acquitted. Did he go into a coma again?"

"Yep. And he never came out of it. He died more than a year ago."

"I never thought he did it, you know. If he had, he would have insisted on getting paid. The money was the thing. We're still stuck with the mystery of who killed Archy Howell."

"And you have sworn to find out who it was."

"You bet I have. And I'll do it. Just be patient. There's a clue in there someplace. I'll find it. Whoever it was, that person owes you more than two years of your life."

"I don't see it that way. If it weren't for my father taking an immediate interest in me in that jail cell, I never would have met you wonderful people. It became my epiphany . . . a reason why I am where I am."

"You're a hell of a guy, Chester. I envy you."

"And I, you, Joe. You're my kind of person."

"Better hang up now. The last time I cried was when I was twelve years old."

"O.K. Bye, Joe."

As Chester walked down a hall to attend a learning assignment, he thought of that dog back in Hagerstown that he and Doctor Landsdale failed to keep alive. He was certain that in the future there would be many of God's human creatures that he would fail to keep alive and as he walked, he imagined a sort of preview of all those people dying in their beds with their grieving families surrounding them. He suddenly said out loud, **"I didn't mean it. I didn't mean it. I wanted them to live."**

When the neurology tutorial was over for the resident students, Chester hurried to his tiny room in the dormitory across from the hospital. He called the Public Defender's Office in Hagerstown. His father was at his desk.

"Sonny, I've been thinking about something for the past few days that I can't shake myself loose from."

"Sounds important, son."

"I think it might be."

"Do you remember that day when I first met you?"

"Never forget it. The first time I would have a client that I instinctively knew was innocent."

"Thank God for your instincts. There were some facts that I never revealed to you about Howard Parsons. At the time, I didn't want to get him involved any more than I had to."

"What facts?"

"We had a sort of verbal fight that night."

"A verbal fight? What about?"

"I had finally mustered up the courage to accuse him of being unfaithful to me. We were in his bed in his beautiful little cottage."

"I've been in that house. It is beautiful. I always wondered how he could afford it on a custodian's salary."

"He told me that he inherited it from his mother and that practically every penny he got a hold of went to keeping the house up the way his mother had."

"Why did you accuse him of being unfaithful?"

"Because a couple of weeks before, I found a used condom . . . a fancy one . . . a kind he and I had never used, on the floor and half hidden by the bed spread."

"And you waited a couple of weeks to confront him with it?"

"Sonny, I didn't want to lose that man. He was everything to me. Not only a lover, but a good friend . . . and a fath . . . father. So, we had our argument and I got dressed and he fed me some incomprehensible lies about the condom, and said things like *I'll prove to you that I love you and only you.* I left his house in a terrible state of mind and walked all the way to Carmine's and into that mess with Archy Howell."

"Why are you telling me this now, Chet?"

"Because it's been nagging at me for two or three days. I know that you and Joe Beyerly have promised yourselves that you are some day going to solve the big mystery about who killed Archy Howell. And I just want to clear this nagging thing from my mind. I still don't see how it would be possible for Howard to have been the killer from the facts that came out in court. But I just thought you should know everything about what happened to me that night, in case Joe or you, who have better minds than I do about this sort of thing, could see something that I don't see."

"Tell you what I'll do, Chet. I'll talk it over with Joe. As you say, he has a better sleuth's mind than either one of us. Maybe it'll turn out to be the thing that cracks the case. I'll keep you posted. Better yet, Joe may contact you directly if he thinks you've come up with something."

"Sounds good, dad. Apart from all that, how are you and mom doing these days? Still going to ballgames every Saturday?"

"And singing *Take Me Out to the Ballgame* in the seventh inning. What else would you expect from two fanatics like us? . . . Everything's fine with us. And she still loves to say *My son, the doctor.* Bet you're one tired doctor, though. You sound tired. Try and steal a little sleep, will you?"

"Will do, Sonny. I love you, you old coot. Bye until next time."

"Bye, son."

After Sonny hung up the phone, he repeated something to himself that he must have thought a thousand times, usually whenever he realized that he really loved his adopted son and would do anything for him. He compared Chet to himself and the deplorable relationship he had had with his own father. *Everyone urges me to forgive that man. I can't do it. Not because he abused me, but for what he did to my sainted mother . . . used her for a punching bag.*

Sonny spent the rest of the afternoon thinking gratefully about Chester Arthur Roosevelt coming magically into his life.

On a Friday, Walter Brock announced in the office that he was going to play tennis with Joe Beyerly the following morning.

"Do you mind if I come and watch you get beat, Walt?"

"No, I don't mind. I may surprise you, this time. I'm gonna beat that guy some day. The Club opens at eight o'clock. Be there."

"I will."

On Saturday morning, the alarm went off at seven o'clock in Rochelle's and Sonny's bed room. She groaned and rolled over and before she shut the alarm off, she asked Sonny, "Are you up?"

"I'm up, babe. Could I talk you into some tea and toast?"

She groaned again. "I suppose so. Where you going this morning?"

"To the Tennis Club to watch Walter Brock get beat by Joe Beyerly."

"Come on. You don't even like to watch tennis. What's up?"

Sonny answered by telling Rochelle about the call he had received from their son in Detroit.

"I want to talk this new development over with those two investigators. See if they think what Chet told me is important."

"I'll go down and put on the kettle. And after I've fed you, I'm going back to bed."

"I hope you don't dream about Howard Parsons."

"Maybe I'll dream up a solution to this big lingering mystery. I could, you know."

"You know, I still tell everybody that you're a better lawyer than I am. Maybe you're a better detective than Joe and Walt are."

CHAPTER TWENTY EIGHT

Sonny grew weary of watching the tennis match. At long last, Joe Beyerly put Walter Brock out of his misery. The score was more lopsided than usual and Brock had a sour look on his face when the two players were leaving the tennis court.

Sonny strolled out from the spectator seats to meet them. "Great match," Sonny lied. "You got time for a couple o' beers in the club house? I got something I wanna run past you guys."

"You gonna be long winded."

"I got a lot to talk about."

"Better count me out," said Brock. "I got an appointment at noon. Gotta take the car in for servicing."

"Shame," said Sonny. "I think what I got would interest you too. It's on the Archy Howell murder."

"You can fill me in on Monday, in the office."

"I'll do that, Walt. It may be nothing, anyway. Just wanted your opinions, both of you."

Sonny waited in the clubhouse dining room for Joe Beyerly to shower. He was a beer ahead of him, when Joe finally showed up.

A waitress scurried over to their table, and took Joe's order for a bottle of Schlitz before he even got seated.

"Back in a jiffy, sir."

"Well, what you got on the Howell case? You really got my curiosity up."

"I got a call from Chet last week." Sonny proceeded to relate, word for word, what Chester had revealed to him about Howard Parsons.

"Could be important," said Joe.

"It's just that when I first met Chet in the Detention Center, he seemed so enamored of Parsons . . . and when I interviewed Parsons a few days after the murder he appeared to be the same way about Chet. He even cried hysterically over him. And then, more than two years later, when I find out that Parsons had only visited Chet once while he was in the lock up, I started wondering what the hell was going on. And then last week I find out that he was probably cheating on Chet. He claimed to be so in love with him two years before. Chet hadn't seen Parsons again until the day in court when he testified for Hathaway, and he never saw him again after that. Can you make anything out of that?"

"I gotta think it through. I gotta admit, it does sound a little weird. You realize, of course, my boss wouldn't appreciate my hobnobbing with the enemy on this."

"What do you mean, the enemy? We're both officers of the court, aren't we? And besides, the State's Attorney has more reason than the Public Defender has to ferret out the real killer's identity. It's his job. And it's your job too, to say nothing of your promise to all of us at Chet's acquittal party that night, long ago, that you wouldn't rest until you found Archy's killer."

"I did say that, didn't I?"

"Indeed, you did. And that's why I brought this to you. I wanted to tell you about Chet's phone call, face to face. It made no difference to me if Brock heard it, but I thought you were a dedicated man . . . dedicated to solving the Howell mystery."

"I am still dedicated, Sonny. It's just that it's been so long since we had anything to talk about in the case, I had almost given up hope that any thing else would develop. Well, let's get down to business—hang out the wash, as you're so fond of saying in your closing statements."

"What I remember—the facts that are irrefutable—are those two interviews I had with Chet and with Parsons."

Joe followed with, "And what I'm sure we both remember, is that old VW following Archy Howell's car down the road. . . . Everybody in the courtroom remembers that. But we also know that Parsons never owned a VW. . . . He owned a Chevrolet, remember?"

Joe answered, "Yeah, but we're pretty sure, probably very sure, that there were two people in that *Mox Nix* VW when Chet last saw it going around that corner on his street. One of them could have been Parsons."

"But what the hell was Parsons doing at the scene and why would he have a shotgun with him?"

Joe sounded completely frustrated. "That's where we get backed into a blind alley."

"Oh, one more thing we know for sure. Parsons had a shotgun which was identical to the one he gave Chester as a gift. When you give somebody a shotgun for a gift, don't you also buy some shells to go along with it and wouldn't they be the same kind of shells you were in the habit of buying for yourself and in the same gun shop?"

Joe sounded dubious. "Now you're starting to stray from known facts."

"Educated guesses are sometimes as good as so-called known facts."

"If you say so. You're the champion sleuth."

"And it follows, doesn't it, that the murder weapon was Parsons' shotgun—we know it wasn't Chester's shotgun—and that leaves us with Parsons as the killer, doesn't it?"

Joe was still dubious. "You're jumping to conclusions. You still haven't answered the big question—what was Parsons doing out by Carmine's in the first place and how did he even know Archy Howell existed? The only commonality between him and Howell has to come through Chet who didn't even know who Howell was until that very morning in Carmine's."

"They must have both found out who Howell was at the same time."

Joe countered with, "Parsons wasn't in Carmine's."

"He must have been outside, then, looking in."

"Constanza and Timmy Adams don't remember seeing him out side."

"You know, I heard Winston Hathaway once tell a jury that you could parade twenty clergymen before a jury to testify what they saw or didn't see and you'd get twenty different versions of what actually happened."

"You mean Parsons was there . . . but neither Constanza or Adams happened to see him standing there in plain sight?"

Joe answered, "Winston Hathaway would tell you that was possible."

"Now you've really gone astray. I thought we were only going to work with cold, hard facts here."

"Do you know what calculus is and how you solve problems with it? Sometimes you have to use near truths to get to the complete truth."

"Where did you ever learn anything about calculus?"

"In high school. I never got past high school."

Sonny exclaimed, "Amazing! Like Einstein, you're a genius who never got past high school."

"I don't know about the genius part. But what I said about Parsons being there is just a theory. We're going to have to explore that a little further. That's enough beer for me. Edith will be looking for me to walk through the front door any minute now."

"Yeah, Rocky will be looking for me too. Well, now you know all that I know. I suppose the solution will come to you in a dream some night. Do you pay for the beer now or wait for a bill to come at the end of the month?"

"End of the month. I'll chalk this one up to a business conference for my tax return."

The two men went home to their wives.

Rocky asked, "Who won?"

"Who do you think? Walt is going to make trying to beat Joe a lifelong project."

"How about Joe? How's he coming with his lifelong project—finding Archy's killer?"

"He's got some great ideas, but he's not there yet. By the way, did you take calculus in high school?"

"Are you kidding? I was lucky to get through algebra. Why do you ask?"

"He's applying calculus to the problem now. I swear, I sometimes don't know what that genius is talking about."

"Well, you can't argue with his success."

"I suppose you're right, but when? When do we find out who killed Archy Howell?"

"You gotta have a little more patience, lover. You might borrow some from your son. You don't hear him pining away for the answer."

"He's too busy learning about neurology to pine away for anything."

"Not too busy to write, however. We got a sweet letter from him this morning. It's on the glass table in the hallway."

Sonny, read the letter. One sentence stood out. *You know, Dad, Howard Parsons was extremely protective of me. I don't know whether it was because I was black or what it was, really. Even if he was cheating on me, I truly believe he would be capable of killing somebody that he thought had hurt me.*

He walked back into the living room. "Come on, Mrs. Campbell. We haven't been to Smitty's in a coon's age. Let's go down there and wolf down some hotdogs and drink some beer."

"You know, I never knew what they meant by that expression—*a coon's age*—the animal or the Negro. To be on the safe side, I always avoid saying it. You never know when you might really offend somebody."

"Never even thought about it. But you're right, you know, and you won't hear me saying it again either."

"Haven't seen you two in a month of Saturdays. What's new in your adventurous lives?"

Rochelle answered, "Not much, Smitty. How about you? Seems kind of quiet in here for a Saturday."

"It is. I'm thinking of filing for bankruptcy."

The Campbells sat at the bar as usual. "What's the problem?" said Sonny.

"I really can't figure it out, for sure. We are getting a small crowd of fancy boys in quite regularly. But they behave themselves . . . don't go flaming around or hit on any of my regular guys. If they did I'd give them the boot just like any of my baseball crowd who got out of line."

"Must be prejudice, rearing its ugly head," said Rochelle.

"If so . . . if I get any more prejudice, I'm gonna go broke. What do you hear from Chester?"

"That boy, still amazes me," said Sonny. "He writes us on a regular basis. He's getting top grades, but when he starts writing about that neurology stuff, he loses me. And I wish he could squeeze a little social life in between all that residency crap. He doesn't seem to have any friends."

"Speaking of fancy boys, do you remember that pretty boy who you pointed out to me at Joe Beyerly's Country Club party . . . the one you told me was with Chester's former boyfriend?"

"What about him?"

"He's been in a couple o' times."

"You don't say," exclaimed Sonny.

"Yeah. Both times he came in with his small crowd, but then sits at the bar and doesn't seem to want to talk to any of them. He's just there, drinks his Drambuie, and sort o' pouts."

Sonny took the surprising information in and was contemplative for several minutes, while Smitty talked to Rochelle about other matters.

Finally he spoke up. "Smitty, do me a favor, would you?"

"If I can."

"The next time that boy comes in here, call me . . . call me even if it's late at night. And when you see me come in and try to sit next to him, pay no attention. . . . Why do you look so surprised? No, I haven't suddenly switched from Rocky to pretty young homosexuals. It's got a lot to do with Archy's murder." Rochelle started to laugh and didn't seem to be able to stop.

Smitty said, "Behave yourself, Rocky. That boy was very handsome, I seem to recall."

"Very." She started laughing some more.

"I'll call you. . . . That would be something to see—you hittin' on a young handsome boy. Give me one of your cards and write your home phone number on it. I know I lost the one I had."

Sonny couldn't get the subject off his mind. Finally, he suggested to Rochelle that they go home. He would call Joe and tell him about this new development.

Rocky complained. "I was just warming up. I sing when I get a little tipsy, you know."

Smitty complained right back. "I know . . . I've heard you. Take her home, Sonny."

Joe suggested, "When Smitty calls you, Sonny, you call me. I'll drift in there, myself. I want to get a good look at this kid. Don't worry. I won't do any talking. I'll leave that up to you. But you and I should get together afterwards and review what you got out of him while it's fresh in your mind. O.K. with you?"

Several weeks passed before Smitty called Sonny. It was eleven o'clock at night.

"He's here. Came in ten minutes ago with three of his friends. Ordered his usual, Drambuie. Please, Sonny. I can't afford to have an incident in this place. The crowds are sparse enough as it is."

"I'll be very careful not to cause any trouble, Smitty."

Sonny hung up his phone and immediately called Joe Beyerly.

"Smitty just called. The boy just came in with three friends."

"Oh jeez! I'm in bed already. . . . That's alright. I'll get dressed and go right down there. See you there. I won't sit any place near you."

"I was in bed too. I'll get dressed and probably see you when you come in."

The scene at Smitty's was exactly as he had described it weeks before. The boy sat at the bar a little apart from his three friends and was gulping his Drambuie a little too fast. As Sonny walked in, he spotted Joe sitting in a booth fairly close to where the boy sat on a bar stool. Sonny sat down at the bar some considerable distance from the four young men, three of whom appeared to be ignoring Parsons' fancy boy.

Sonny made the unusual gesture of ordering a Stinger. Five minutes later he got a lady bartender's attention, and when she came back to where Sonny was sitting, he told her to take a Drambuie to the boy whose glass sat empty. The bartender placed the fresh Drambuie in front of the boy and turned to point toward Sonny as the man who bought the drink.

The boy acknowledged Sonny and made a gesture of invitation to come and sit next to him. Sonny picked up his Stinger and obliged.

"My name's Jimmy. What's yours?"

"Carl."

"What's your last name Carl?"

"Please, Mister. No last names, if you don't mind."

"I guess it's better that way . . . at least until we get better acquainted."

"What makes you think that's gonna happen?"

"You looked mighty lonely sitting down here. Your friends seem to be ignoring you."

One of the three others overheard what Sonny said. "What business is that of yours, Mister? Anyway, he's ignoring us, not the other way around."

Carl scolded, "Well, we're getting along just fine without any help from you, Barry. Kindly stop bothering us please."

"I must say, you certainly look like a handsome couple. We'll leave you alone, but remember we're your only way home . . . unless of course, your new friend will take you home."

The boy turned to Sonny. "How about it Jimmy, will you give me a ride home?"

"Love to. When do you want to leave?"

"Right now. I'm tired of these people and I'm tired of this place."

Sonny and the boy gathered up their coats. Joe looked up at them. Sonny winked at him and silently mouthed the words *follow us*, confident that Joe could follow them at a discreet distance and not be noticed.

The boy sat very close to the driver's seat, which made Sonny feel a bit uncomfortable. Once underway, Sonny said, "I can't shift if you're going to sit that close."

"Sorry, Jimmy. I was just feeling a bit chilly. I'll be good, now."

"I know another nice bar, if you want to stop there first."

"Couldn't we stop at your place first? That's what I'd like to do."

"Sorry, my friend. How would I explain you to my wife?"

"Oh, so that's the way it is, is it?"

"I think you'll like this place. It's real cozy." Sonny had stopped at the nearest bar which he was sure he had never been in. He thought to himself, *Nobody will recognize me in there, that's for sure.*

A waitress sat the two in a booth and asked what they would have to drink. Sonny ordered for both of them. "A Stinger for me. Want another Drambuie, Carl?"

"Drink nothing else, when I can afford it."

Moments later, Joe walked in. He sat in the booth behind Sonny and Carl. He kept his coat on, thinking that it was less likely that he'd be recognized from having been in Smitty's.

"Well, Carl, tell me what you do for a living."

"To be honest, Jimmy, I'm in between jobs just now. How about you?"

"I work at the hospital . . . an x-ray technician."

"Really! Do you know a custodian there by the name of Howard Parsons?"

"Yeah, I think I do."

"He used to be a good friend of mine . . . a very good friend of mine."

"No longer a friend?"

"Not for nine, almost ten years."

"What happened?"

"He got mixed up in that murder about ten years ago. He testified . . . say, why am I telling you this?"

"We're just getting acquainted. You can tell me."

"You know something. We've got better light in this place than they had at Smitty's. You look familiar to me now. Weren't you at the Country Club party they had for that State's Attorney about ten years ago?"

Joe stood up and took a couple of steps toward the booth in front of him. "Give it up Sonny. He's on to you"

Carl suddenly looked up at Joe.

"I'm Joe Beyerly, Carl. Are you willing to tell us your last name?"

"I'm not willing to say another word, you bastards." Carl grabbed his jacket and started for the door.

"Hold it Carl. Let me give you a ride home."

"So you'll know where to find me again? No thanks." He ran out of the door.

"What'd I do wrong, Joe?"

"Absolutely nothing, Sonny. He made you that's all."

CHAPTER TWENTY NINE

At breakfast, Sonny asked Rochelle, "Have you got Smitty's home number?"

"It's in the telephone directory, isn't it?" answered Rochelle.

"No, it isn't. I'm going to have to go out there and find out what's going on."

Rochelle had to teach at the high school, or she would have gone with him.

He parked his car directly in front of the bar and got out to read the sign in the front door window.

CLOSED
GOING OUT OF
BUSINESS

There was a light on in the apartment above the bar. *Smitty or his wife must be up there,* Sonny said to himself.

He walked over to the entrance to the stairs leading up to the apartment and rang the buzzer.

"Who is it?" said a male voice.

"Sonny Campbell. Is that you Smitty?"

An automatic door opener clicked several times and Sonny went in. Smitty was at the top of the stairs. "Come on up pal. I'll tell you my sad story."

"What happened? Why'd you close up?" asked Sonny as he climbed the stairs.

"I told you a couple o' months ago. I'm bankrupt. Can't keep it open." Sonny reached the top step.

"My God! I didn't think it was that bad."

"Gotta go back to honest work, Sonny. No choice, my friend." Smitty invited Sonny into the apartment. "Want some coffee?"

Sonny nodded his head.

"Into the kitchen, then. My wife's still sleeping."

Smitty busied himself making coffee, as he talked. Sonny usually drank tea in the morning, but under these circumstances he didn't want to be a nuisance and refuse the coffee.

"My customers dwindled down to a precious few. Even when the homosexual crowd stopped coming in that seemed to make no difference. I filed for Chapter Seven last week. Now I spend my days scanning the want ads and trying to run down a job. I bet that answers all your questions, doesn't it? The once thriving *Smitty's Bar and Grill,* went belly up."

"What can I say? Your place downstairs was our home away from home. Do you need any money?"

"Not yet, we don't. But starvation time is on the horizon. Sonny, that's really a noble gesture, an offer to help. But, I'll find a job . . . don't worry about us."

"Just say the word and we'll loan you what we can. O.K?"

"How'd your little project with that boy work out?"

"It didn't. He made me as soon as he saw my face clearly in the light. Joe and I are looking for him. Trouble is he knows that we're looking for him. One thing we found out, though. He's guilty of something. It's my opinion that he's connected to Howell's murder in some way. First he recognizes me from Joe's Country Club party, then he spots Joe who he knows was the investigator for the State's Attorney on the Howell case, and then he runs like hell. We never got his last name. When he was still under the impression that I was on the make, he told me that his first name is Carl."

"How about his buddies? Wouldn't one of them know where he is?"

"We thought of that. But we haven't found any of them either."

"I know that they stopped coming in here after that night when you and Joe were doing your sleuthing."

Sonny choked down the coffee. "Well, Smitty, all I can do then is wish you good luck on your hunt for work. You'll find something. They can't keep a man like you out of work for very long." Sonny stood and offered his hand to Smitty.

"Sometimes, all it takes is a good luck handshake. Can you find your way out?"

"Sure. Let me know if you find anything. I'll stay on the alert for you. Bye, Smitty."

"Bye, Sonny."

Ed Wilson's secretary, Patricia Erickson, tossed the morning paper on Sonny's desk. "How many times have I told you not to do that, Pat. I don't care what you want me to read in that newspaper. It messes up my desk when you do that."

"You mean your desk is not already messed up? It's always messed up. You've got to read what's in there, this morning. It's about Douglas McNamara."

"Sonny grabbed the newspaper and spotted the headline immediately.

Douglas McNamara Released From Prison

He read on.

January 10, 1995. Baltimore, Maryland—Anthony Lacey, United States Attorney for the Baltimore, Maryland District, announced today that Douglas McNamara, who pleaded guilty nine years ago to illegal gambling and tax charges in the United States District Court here, and also pleaded guilty in Hagerstown Circuit Court, to a related Maryland State charge of soliciting first degree murder, was released from the Federal Correctional Institution in Morgantown, West Virginia, yesterday afternoon.

McNamara was a stockholder in the Universal Corporation, which operated out of Las Vegas through the Island of Antigua in the West Indies', Leeward Islands in the Caribbean. He had been imprisoned on a ten year combined federal and state sentencing in the Spring of 1985.

Fellow stockholders, Charles Tomlinson and Mark Greenberg, who each received a one year sentence on illegal gambling charges, were both released in the Fall of 1986.

Sonny's secretary, Lori came over to join Pat Erickson and jokingly scolded her boss for reading the newspaper while on duty.

"I was actually working until Pat threw the paper on my desk." He handed the newspaper back to Pat.

"On your son's case, I'll bet. That case happened ten years ago. It's as cold as herring by now."

"The identity of the real killer is as hot an issue in my head now as it was ten years ago, my dear girl. Remember there's no statute of limitations on murder anywhere in this country."

"You're not due in court until this afternoon. So put your thinking cap on. Maybe this is the day you'll come up with a solid clue, although I doubt it."

"Pessimist. I'd laugh my hind end off if this turned out to be my lucky day."

Sonny couldn't help but think of those horrible days that Chet had to endure ten years ago. . . . *And now that bastard McNamara is out of prison, free as a bird and probably still has his fortune intact.*

No luck for Sonny Campbell on that day, or for the next two months for that matter, but suddenly a thunderbolt struck. Howard Parsons was back in town. He had sold his little cottage shortly after Chester's trial and left town. Now, he was seen by Walter Brock, lurking around a city park known as a pickup point for homosexuals. Brock said to Sunny, "I don't usually come that way, but on that snowy day last week I decided to take a shortcut to work. And there he was, whispering into some poor kid's ear . . . probably a male prostitute."

Sonny exclaimed, "In the dead of a snowy winter, picking up male prostitutes! You know, I'm not the least bit prejudiced against homosexuals, but I can honestly tell you, Walt, that I hate that bastard for what he did in Chet's greatest hour of need in the Detention Center. **One visit in more than two years!**"

Brock asked, "What do you want me to do about this, boss?"

"Go to Joe Beyerly's office and fill him in on the situation. Tell him that I recommend that he arrest Parsons as a material witness in the Howell investigation. Joe will pick the bastard up and bring him to his office for questioning. If Parsons and Carl had a connection to Howell, Joe will find out what it is. I swear he will."

"I believe he will, boss. I believe he will."

It took another week before Joe found Parsons in the park. He was alone sitting on a park bench. Joe, accompanied by a uniformed policeman, approached him, taking him by surprise. Joe asked, "Are you Howard Parsons?" No answer was forthcoming. "I asked you, are you Howard Parsons?" Finally a very weak *yes* was whispered out of Parsons' mouth.

The policeman, with his handcuffs at the ready, said, "Howard Parsons, I arrest you as a material witness in the murder of one Archy Howell."

Parsons stood. "I don't know what you're talking about, but you certainly don't need those handcuffs. I'll come quietly."

The policeman said, "It's the law Mister Parsons. Put your hands behind your back."

The policeman cuffed the potential witness, and the trio marched off to a patrol car, which was parked in a spot unobservable from the park bench.

The patrol car drove to the office of the State's Attorney. Joe Beyerly had driven ahead and was waiting alone in his office.

"Well, Mister Howard Parsons, remember me? I'm the guy who sat at the prosecutor's table throughout the entire trial of Chester Roosevelt. Incidentally, Chester Roosevelt is now Chester Campbell. You remember Sonny Campbell? Well, Sonny and his wife Rochelle adopted Chester almost nine years ago."

"No, I didn't know that they adopted Chester. I guess that's a good thing for him."

"Let me tell you how good that has been for him. In three years he's gonna complete his residency in neurology at a hospital in Detroit. And with high honors, too. You wouldn't recognize the kid you betrayed ten years ago."

"Betrayed! I never betrayed that boy. I loved that boy. I would have done anything for him."

"I bet you would say that about all your little male concubines."

"Why do you say that?"

"Did you love Carl, for instance?"

"Who's Carl?"

"We know that you betrayed Chet—did you get that? **Betrayed Chet**, when you were supposed to be loving Chet and doing anything for him?"

"I did love him and I still would do anything for him."

"Then why the hell did you visit him only once when he was in jail? That's when he needed you the most."

"I couldn't . . . I couldn't bear to see him in that Detention Center."

"And why were you **betraying** him with a sexual relationship with your little pretty boy, Carl? All that time, with Carl, and your beloved in jail waiting desperately for a visit from you."

"I still don't know who you're talking about. I don't think these questions can possibly help you with an investigation into the killing of Archy Howell. What am I doing here, anyway? Aren't you supposed to have probable cause to arrest me for any reason?"

"Probable cause we got, Mister Parsons."

"I can't believe you."

"Oh, but you're wrong, Mister Parsons. . . . Did you kill Archy Howell?"

"I think I need a lawyer. Can you get me a public defender? I have five dollars in my pocket and that's all I have in the world. Indigent, I think you call it."

"Yes, I can. Ed Wilson or Sonny Campbell. Take your choice."

"I know Mister Campbell. I think he would be a good choice, especially since he is now Chester's adoptive father."

"You got it friend. We can have Mister Campbell down here in twenty minutes."

A half hour later, Sonny appeared in Joe's office. Parsons was sitting alone.

"Look, Mister Parsons, before I accept this assignment as your lawyer, I've got to tell you, I don't like you very much. But despite that fact, I will treat you like I would any other indigent person who's under arrest. I once swore an oath to do that."

"I accept you as my lawyer. Can you get Mister Beyerly back in here?"

"Sure can." Sonny stuck his head out through the office door and said, "He's ready for you now, Joe."

Joe came in and sat behind his desk.

Parsons said, "Go on with your questions, Mister Beyerly."

"My last question was a simple one. Did you kill Archy Howell?"

"No, I didn't."

"Did Carl . . . what's his last name, again?"

"Stevens."

"Oh, now you know who Carl is. Did Carl Stevens kill Archy Howell at your request?"

"No."

"Did Carl Stevens kill Howell on his own, without anyone asking him to do it?"

"Now, how would I know the answer to that question?"

"You might have watched him do it."

"Well, I didn't see him do it."

"Where were you when Chester was being slapped around in Carmine's café that early Friday morning?"

"Chester and I had a quarrel and he left my house that morning, some time after midnight. I didn't see him again until he came back to my house around five thirty in the morning and asked me to drive him to the Greyhound Station."

"Is that when he asked you to take care of his shotgun?"

"Yes."

"And you wiped that shotgun down of all fingerprints, didn't you?"

"Yes."

"That was kind of stupid, wasn't it?"

"How so?"

"Anybody examining that shotgun would suspect that Chester shot Howell and wiped the gun clean. Didn't you think of that?"

"But you know from the trial that Chester's shotgun was not the murder weapon."

"Yes, but you didn't know that when he gave you the shotgun for safe keeping, did you?"

"No, I didn't."

"Now, back to my earlier question. Where were you when Chester was being slapped around in Carmine's café?"

"Like I said, Chester and I had had a quarrel. I needed to have a kind word from a friend so I drove to Carl Stevens' place."

"And . . . ?"

"Carl wasn't home. So I went back to my home where I stayed . . . I think until Mister Campbell came to visit me."

"Was Carl Stevens the only friend you could think of that morning?"

Sonny said, "You don't have to answer that question, Mister Parsons. I can't see where it could possibly have anything to do with Mister Beyerly's investigation."

"I withdraw the question, Mister Campbell. Now, another area I think would have some bearing on my investigation. Chester Roosevelt, now Campbell, has told me that you were very protective of him at the time you two were lovers. Do you agree?"

"I suppose so. Yes, I loved that boy very much."

"More than you did, Carl Stevens, for instance?"

"More than anybody else."

"To what extent were you protective of Chester?"

"Very."

"Would you kill for him?"

"I wouldn't kill anybody for any reason."

"Chester seems to think that you would kill for him."

"Well, he's presuming too much."

Sonny spoke up. "I knew this would happen. Now we're challenging my son's honesty. If we're going to do that, I'll have to withdraw from this assignment, Mister Parsons. Mister Ed Wilson, who is the Public Defender for Frederick County, has just hired a brand new assistant. This young man seems to be a very competent lawyer. He's busy this afternoon, but perhaps we can have him put in some overtime and this Q. and A. can be postponed till this evening."

"I was hoping this would be over this afternoon. But I'll stick around till tonight when the new lawyer is here."

"You'll stick around for as long as I say you will. You're still under arrest, you know," said Joe.

Parsons, still handcuffed, was left in the interview room to sweat a little. Ed Wilson's new assistant was instructed to show up precisely at six o'clock PM. Joe and Sonny had a private conference in the law library.

"There was nothing wrong with my being in there until you mentioned what Chet had told me about Parsons being so protective of him. After all, I am the Public Defender for the County of Washington. I got out when I should have gotten out. As it stands now we got two bits of valuable intelligence out of the old bird. He admitted that he was protective of Chet just short of killing somebody for him. And we got Carl Stevens' last name."

"And I got Winston Hathaway to issue an all points bulletin for Carl about ten minutes ago."

"If we get him this time, let's not lose him."

The questioning at six o'clock was superfluous—an hour of meaningless inquiries that went nowhere. The new assistant found himself not having to object to anything Joe Beyerly put to Howard Parsons. Abruptly, Joe said, "You're free to go, Howard."

"Well, I'm glad that's over. By the way, could you tell me what hospital in Detroit Chester is doing his residency in?"

Joe thought, *You son-of-a-bitch. After all the pain you inflicted on Chester you want to try and see him again . . . talk to him again.* "I said, you're free to go. Get the hell out of my sight."

Parsons drove straight to where he knew the man, now known as Carl Stevens to the authorities, was living. He rang the doorbell. A man came to the door, but when he saw who it was he slammed the door in Parsons' face. "You better let me in. I've got something important to tell you."

Through the door, the man shouted, "What could be important after all these years?"

"I just came from the State's Attorney's office. I think they suspect us, both of us."

The man slowly opened the door.

"You can come in for five minutes, that's all. No funny stuff . . . you hear me? Don't even take your coat off."

"I must have answered a thousand questions. They thought they were so clever. They tried to get your last name out of me. They already knew the first name you use when you're cruising I told them your last name was Stevens or something like that. Some name not even close to yours. I think you must have run away from them or something, because they're really focused on you."

"That's a laugh. What about you? Why ain't they focused on you?"

"Never mind about that. I suggest you lay low for as long as you can stand to. If they ever get a hold of you, I don't think you'll be able to hold up to the questions they'll ask you."

"Is that all?"

"I think so."

"Now, get the hell out of my house. I don't trust you as far as I can throw you."

Parsons opened the door and took a step past the threshold. "And don't ever come back here, do you hear me?"

CHAPTER THIRTY

"So much for Hathaway's all points bulletin. It's been two months since we had Parsons in here for questioning. I'll bet you a buck that he was way ahead of us when I tried to trick him into giving us his pretty boy's last name. I thought at the time he was saying *Stevens* like he had rehearsed it in his mind in case we would ask."

"If you say so, Joe," said Sonny. "But I thought up a scheme which may produce a better result."

"I'm willing to listen to anything at this point."

"Let's make a couple of assumptions first. You know, like you taught me . . . calculus . . . remember . . . what you taught me, Joe? Let's say the *Mox Nix* VW belonged to Carl back twelve years ago. We know that Carl, or whatever Pretty Boy's name is, doesn't have a car now. Remember he was looking for a ride that night in Smitty's. So then, he must have sold his VW at some time in the last twelve years. A *Mox Nix* VW is a vintage automobile. Every state in this country has one or more vintage VW car clubs. Where would our Carl have sold his? I'm guessing to one of those vintage club members. You ask, *Which club? There must be hundreds in the country.* I say the nearest one to Hagerstown. You know where the nearest one is? It's in the city of Queen Anne over on the east side of our fair state of Maryland. I looked it up. I've got the address of the Vintage VW Club in the city of Queen Anne, Maryland."

"That's a lot of assumptions," retorted Joe.

"Maybe so, but I'm still going to write a letter to the Club and inquire about *Mox Nix* VWs—whether any of their members bought one in the last twelve years . . . how many members own one and where did they get it and from whom? It's worth the effort. It may surprise you, Joe. And if one pops up that was purchased from anyone in Hagerstown we may have Carl's real name . . . and eventually we'll have Carl, himself."

Vintage VW Club of Maryland
14011 Clancy Court
Queen Anne, Maryland
21657

February 26, 1995

Public Defender of Washington County
100 West Franklin Street
Hagerstown, Maryland 21740
Attention: William J. Campbell

Dear Mr. Campbell:

I have your letter of February 15, 1995. I considered your inquiry important enough to take immediate action on it. I sent a bulletin to all our members, asking them to review the purchasing history of their vintage Volkswagens.

Only one responded that she had bought her auto from someone in Hagerstown. Miss Jane Elizabeth Fortier, whose address is, 324 Mount Holyoak Drive, Queen Anne, Maryland—21658, is the person you should contact. Her letter to me states that she bought her vintage car from one Victor Cantor on December 23, 1985. Mister Cantor lived at 19342 Mulberry Street, Funkstown, Maryland—21734 at the time of purchase. As you know, Funkstown is a suburb of Hagerstown.

She says the car was pretty banged up when she bought it. It had some damage to the right front and many scars from its history over in Germany. She's restored it, of course, and it now looks like it did when those VWs first came out over there in the thirties, flip turn signals and all.

If I can be of any further assistance to you, please don't hesitate to contact me.

Yours sincerely,
Robert M. Brown
President, Vintage VW Club of Maryland
Telephone: (410) 555 1865

"Bingo!" Sonny buzzed Lori. When she stuck her head into his office door and asked, "What's up?" he told her to make a copy of the letter and hand deliver it to Joe Beyerly.

She responded with, "You bet."

He managed to get Joe on the phone despite his busy schedule. "You know whoever invented calculus must have had us in mind."

"What do you mean? You sound joyful."

"I've just read a response to my letter to the VW club. Our man's name is . . ."

"Hold it let me get a pencil."

"You'll have a copy of the letter any minute now. You'll have all the details in ten minutes"

"I can't wait ten minutes."

"I understand. His name is Victor Cantor. At the time he sold the car to this woman named Jane Elizabeth Fortier, he lived in Funkstown. Could be still living there. I'm leaving that up to you to find out."

"Lori better walk in here with that letter in five minutes.

I gotta get started on this. Thanks for the call, Sonny. I'll keep you posted on progress."

"Maybe progress will come a little faster now that we know his name and where he lived."

Joe joked, "And now that you got me on the job."

The next afternoon Joe drove to Queen Anne to look up Jane Fortier. It was near the end of the ordinary business day when he arrived at her home. The house was beautifully constructed and her property was neatly landscaped. He smelled money. He rang the buzzer at the side of the front door. Immediately, the sound of a dog barking could be heard coming from inside of the house. The door opened about a foot and a very attractive woman in her early thirties stuck her head out. Joe could see through the narrow opening that she was restraining a Great Dane by holding its studded collar. "Yes. Are you here on business?"

"Sort of. I'm Joseph Beyerly, chief investigator for the Maryland State's Attorney in Hagerstown. It's about your vintage VW. I thought you might let me take a look at it."

"Oh, Bob Brown told me about you."

"I was surprised to find you at home, Miss Fortier. I'm guessing you don't have to work like the rest of us?"

"That's really none of your business, Mister Beyerly."

"Sorry. You're absolutely right, Miss Fortier. . . . It's none of my business. It's just my investigator's ways showing up again. I'm really very sorry."

"Do you want to come in first? I mean before we go out to the garage?" She was staring intently at his face.

"Best proposition I've had all day."

She laughed and opened the door wide. The Great Dane had stopped barking.

"Can I fix you something? . . . Iced tea, coffee, booze?"

Joe was looking over the furnishings of the interior and after her invitation to fix him something to drink he absentmindedly answered, "Whiskey and water would be nice."

"Wait here."

Moments later she returned with a tall glass, which emanated the sound of ice cubes when she handed it to him. She was staring at him again.

"Do I have a smudge on my forehead, spinach on my teeth, or something?"

"You are a very handsome man, Mister Beyerly. I think I'll join you with that whiskey and water."

"I take it you don't have a husband lurking around here someplace."

As she was leaving again toward what looked to be the dining room where she apparently kept her supply of alcohol, she stopped, turned around, and said, "Mister Beyerly, does this place look like a man is living here? That's why I have the dog. To keep beautiful visitors like you at bay." She turned again and went to fix herself her drink.

He sat on a couch and contemplated what he would do if she carried this bantering any further. *Oh, no you don't, Jimbo. Maybe if I were still single, **but I'm not single. . . . And Edith is the best looking woman that God ever breathed air into.***

Miss Fortier returned and joined him on the couch. She sat a little too close to him. It made him uncomfortable. They finished their drinks and as she was about to say something provocative again, he said, "Time to go to the garage and look at your VW."

She put her empty glass, a little too forcefully, on the coffee table in front of them. "O.K., darling, if that's what you want to do, follow me."

She put on a coat from a hall closet and led him to the attached three-car garage. The garage was full up . . . a Mercedes, a Chrysler station wagon and the VW.

Joe said, "This won't take long. Do you have the pedigree for the Volkswagen?"

"I had one drawn up by an expert."

"What year was it made?"

"1942."

"Did the man you bought the car from come here, or did you go to Hagerstown?"

"I went there. I took a friend along to drive the VW back here after the transaction."

"Was the man you bought it from a young handsome guy with dark hair?"

"Not as handsome as you, but pretty in a swishy sort of way."

They walked toward the car, Joe in the lead. He had a smile on his face.

He looked at the top front of the right door. He didn't know quite what he was looking for, but he saw what must be the turn signals, hidden in recesses on the windshield posts. "Do me a favor, would you, Miss Fortier? Start the car up and turn the lights on and operate the turn signals." She obeyed, hoping there was still a chance to really please this handsome man.

Click, click. Out popped the lighted right signal, then click, click, and then the left one. The lighted signals would be easily seen at night by a car that was behind the VW.

"Well, that's all I wanted to see, Miss Fortier. I've got to be going now."

"Thanks for nothing. If I had known what you wanted I wouldn't have let you in, in the first place."

He pretended not to notice her anger. "I can go right out this side door. I wasn't wearing a coat." She followed him to the door and he left the garage without even turning around to say goodbye. The door slammed as she pulled it shut.

CHAPTER THIRTY ONE

Back in Hagerstown, Joe went straight to Sonny's office on West Franklin Street. He had to wait forty-five minutes for Sonny to return from Circuit Court.

"That's the right VW and Victor Cantor's our boy, for sure," he said, "Isn't calculus a bloomin' wonder?"

"Next stop, his house on Mulberry Street in Funkstown."

"He won't be there, of course. We couldn't be that lucky."

Joe tried the long shot first. He went to the house on Mulberry Street. An eighty-seven-year-old woman was now living there.

"I started renting here when the young man moved out. I saw him only once—when he came back for his ukulele. He had left it on a closet shelf."

"Did he say where he was moving to . . . out of state, maybe?"

"No, but his mail was forwarded to his new address for six months. Then the Post Office stopped doing that."

"You don't happen to remember what the forwarding address was, do you?"

"I never paid any attention to what it was."

Joe went to the Post Office next. He showed a clerk his credentials. "Do you keep records on mail that's been forwarded?"

"How far back?"

"About nine or ten years."

"No, not that far back. Sorry. What's the name?"

"Victor Cantor."

"Wait here a minute."

The clerk came back a few minutes later. He had a letter in his hand. It was from the Maryland Department of Motor Vehicles, and was addressed to Victor Cantor and bore a Hagerstown address.

"But he doesn't live here any more either. We don't know where he lives. Let me write this address down for you. You might go over there and ask around in the neighborhood. Maybe someone will know something."

"Thank you. You've been very helpful."

A woman in Cantor's old Hagerstown neighborhood wasn't very informative. "Vic Cantor moved away from this area about ten months ago. He told everybody he was going to live with his mother—somewhere in Ohio, I think."

Joe called Sonny's home that night. Rochelle answered the phone.

"Is that brilliant husband of yours home, Rocky?"

"That's funny. He says you're the brilliant one. Hold on a minute. I'll get him."

Sonny said with a tone of excitement, "Tell me you located him."

Joe chuckled. "Not yet. The last I discovered, he had moved from here to Ohio to live with his mother."

"But he was back here just a few weeks ago."

"Maybe he was just visiting."

"No, no. Don't you remember when we offered him a ride home, he protested? *So you'll know where I live.* No, he's hiding someplace right here in Hagerstown."

"Right again. But I've still got to go to Ohio and find out whether his mother is still alive."

"Check the Ohio Department of Motor Vehicles or the Democratic and Republican voting records. Oh, listen to me, telling the expert how to find somebody."

"You've got to stop scratching my back, friend. I'm just an ordinary investigator. I'm flying to Columbus, tomorrow."

"And Winston Hathaway approved that?"

"This is still an open murder investigation."

"Well, good luck, Buddy. Call me when you get back. If you really hit the jackpot, call me immediately from Columbus."

"Right. Tell me, are you keeping Chester abreast of our progress in this case?"

"Yes, I am. Are you saying I shouldn't be doing that?"

"Does he know to keep his mouth shut?"

"Of course, he does. Why are you asking?"

"He was once in love with Howard Parsons, wasn't he?"

"You bastard. I'm going to hang up on you now."

Joe took a cab from the Columbus Airport to the Ohio DMV office. He had one piece of small luggage, in the event he had to stay over night. "DMV office please. 1970 West Broad Street."

The taxi driver put his bag in the trunk. "I know where the DMV office is, Mister. Been driving this cab for fifteen years."

He retrieved his bag, paid the cab fare with a generous tip, and entered the DMV office. He showed his credentials at the information desk. "Could you direct me to the Deputy Registrar in charge of licensing?"

The woman at the desk pointed to another woman behind the counter. "But I'm afraid you'll have to wait in line."

"All right with me."

When it was his turn, he again showed his credentials. He knew he would arouse much attention when he said in a soft voice, "I'm investigating a first degree murder case that occurred in Maryland twelve years ago. We're looking for a witness who lives in Ohio. Her last name is Cantor . . . spelled C A N T O R. I don't know her first name. Do you think you can help me?"

"You shock me, Mister Beyerly. First time I've ever been asked to help in a murder case. This isn't a trick of some kind, is it?"

"No trick, Miss. I'm dead serious."

"Wait here. I don't know how long this will take, but Cantor is a rare name. I might be back in a jiffy."

Ten minutes later the Registrar returned with a few pieces of paper in her hands. "I've got three Cantors with drivers' licenses in Ohio. You're a fortunate man. Two of these are men and the third is a fifty five year old woman . . . Virginia Cantor. She lives in Lima. The details, including her address, are on this computer print out. You may have it, provided you sign a receipt that says this is part of an official investigation and will be kept in a confidential file."

"Where's the receipt? I'll sign it."

When the paper work was completed and the receipt signed, Joe thanked the Registrar and went out to the street hoping to find a cab. He looked down the block and thought he saw a main drag. He walked in that direction and soon, standing on the corner, he successfully hailed a cab.

"Nearest car rental please."

He was soon cruising west on Highway 70. He turned north on I-75 and arrived in Lima in record time. He stopped in a station and purchased a city map.

After trying to follow the map for twenty minutes, he said to himself, *she lives on 4812 South Baxter Street. That's just three blocks from where I am now.* At that location, he pulled in behind a Toyota parked in a driveway. He walked up onto a porch of a fairly new house and pressed a buzzer. A woman, whose face matched the one that appeared on the record given to him by the Registrar in Columbus, came to the door. He watched her facial expression closely for any reaction, as he told her he was a State's Attorney investigator from Hagerstown, Maryland.

"Oh, my god! Has something happened to Victor?"

"Not that we know. May I come in for a moment?" He showed her his credentials.

"Why are you here, then?"

"It is essential that we know where he is now living. He is not suspected of doing anything wrong, but we know he is a material witness to a murder. Where is he now living, Mrs. Cantor? You have an obligation to tell me."

She remained silent. Finally, she answered, "I haven't heard a word from him for six months. He hasn't had a phone for years but the last address I have for him is P.O. Box 10, in Fiddlesburg. He tells me that's very close to Hagerstown proper."

"Thank you, Mrs. Cantor. You're a very nice lady. When I catch up to Victor I'll tell him to get in touch with you."

"I have a bad feeling about your coming here, Mister Beyerly. I hope I'm wrong."

"At this point I can't assure you of anything, Mrs. Cantor. I won't know until I talk to Victor."

"Be gentle with him. He's such a sensitive boy. Goodbye, Mister Beyerly."

Joe had not even taken his coat off or sat down. The whole conversation with Mrs. Cantor took place near the front door. He turned around as he said, "Goodbye, Mrs. Cantor."

He drove the few miles to Toledo and turned his rental car in at the airport. He took a flight, first to Baltimore, and then another to Hagerstown. He tried to call Sonny Campbell who was in court and would not be available till the close of business at five o'clock.

He then called Edith and she answered on the first ring. "You know something, Baby. I'm homesick. I can almost feel you in my arms. I can hardly stand it. Homesick and only been gone one day."

"You're gone for a whole day, Monday through Friday, each and every week. You've never thought you were homesick before. Not until now. Well, I wish I had you in my arms now. You better put on a suit of armor to protect yourself when you come through that front door in about an hour. Lover, beware."

The roast lamb dinner she had prepared got ice cold for the lack of eating. Joe and Edith were doing something else, which was far more enjoyable than eating dinner. "Oh, well. I can make you a lamb sandwich if you want."

"That would be fine. I've got to call Sonny, if he's still speaking to me."

"Why would he not be speaking to you?"

"Oh, I said something very, very stupid to him last night and he hung up on me."

"I don't want to hear any more about it. If you two can't get along, then the world will not be a very pleasant place to live in. Call him and apologize before you talk business. You hear?"

"I hear, Baby. And you're right."

"I tried to call you this afternoon, but you were in court. Victor Cantor now lives in Fiddlesburg. He's got a Post Office box for an address. I think we'll find him, now. By the way, I sincerely apologize for the stupid question I asked you last night. Sometimes I don't know my ass from a hole in the ground."

"Apology accepted. No more about that. . . . You want to try and find him tonight." said Sonny.

"I would, but the Post Office isn't open after five. What could we do tonight to find him?"

"You're right, again. Guess I'm a little anxious after all these years. Can I pick you up in the morning?"

"I'll be in front of my office building at nine thirty. I don't want Hathaway to see the two of us together. You understand. The prosecution and the defense are not supposed to mix . . . even outside the court."

"That's nonsense. Does Winston really feel that way?"

"He says he does." . . . Joe suggested, "The Funkstown Post Office on Frederick Road serves Fiddlesburg, you know?"

"That's where we're headed, then."

They parked and both entered the Post Office. On a wall, next to the service counter, were typical brass P.O. boxes. Joe showed a clerk, on duty at the counter, his State's Attorney credentials. "Can you give me the address of the person who rents P.O. Box number 10? This is part of a murder investigation."

"I'll have to get my supervisor. I'm not permitted to give out that information."

After some haggling, the supervisor finally relented and looked up the address for the renter of P.O. Box number 10. He fingered his way down a list. "Here it is, Victor Cantor, 29 Shiloh Church Road, Fiddlesburg, Maryland." Joe wrote the address down on a small, spiraled note pad. "Thank you, sir. You've been very helpful."

As the two men walked out of the Post Office, Sonny made the comment, "That must be out in the boonies someplace."

"Yeah. I wonder if the old Shiloh Church is still standing."

There was no sign of a church in the Fiddlesburg area that surrounded Victor Cantor's address. There was no sign of life at 29 Shiloh Church Road. Joe and Sonny walked up to the small house that was designated number 29. Joe pressed the buzzer at the side of the door. Moments later, the door opened and a familiar face appeared. Victor Cantor tried to close the door again, but Joe prevented that with his foot. He shoved the door with his shoulder and it opened again, knocking Cantor to the floor. Joe remained in the open doorway and spoke to Cantor now sitting on the floor. "Will you come voluntarily or do we have to get a warrant? We really don't need one, you know. You're a material witness to the murder of Archy Howell."

Cantor stood but remained silent.

"Well, are you coming voluntarily or do we get the warrant and call the newspaper and radio and TV stations about what happened here?"

"I'll come with you. Let me get my coat. It's in that closet there."

Victor Cantor sat in the back seat with Joe Beyerly sitting next to him. Not a word was spoken by anyone until Sonny asked, "Your office, Joe?"

"Yeah."

The two men flanked Cantor as they took him to Joe's office on the second floor of the State's Attorney's building on West Washington Street. "Have a seat, Victor. Relax. Make yourself comfortable," said Joe. "We've got a long day ahead of us."

Sonny Campbell didn't say a word throughout Joe's interrogation of Victor Cantor that occurred that morning.

"How did I get to be a material witness to a murder?" Cantor asked.

Joe answered, "Well, it took a long time, but we finally put two and two together and up popped your name and your vintage VW."

"**My what?** What are you talking about?"

"Let me tell you something, son. If you've decided you're going to stonewall this interrogation, I promise you that it's not going to be pleasant for you. It's taken me more than ten years to put you in that chair. It will only take me ten seconds to knock you out of it and mess up that pretty face of yours. **Do you understand me, boy?**"

Cantor nodded his head, his expression clearly indicating that he understood.

"Now let's start with your old VW with the *mox nix* turn signals."

"Look, I'll admit that I once owned an old VW, but what does *mox nix* mean?"

"It means, *makes no difference*. In your case it made a whole lot of difference."

"I still don't get it."

"Never mind. You'll hear nothing but plain talk questions from me from now on."

"If you want plain talk answers, that's what it better be."

"When did you meet Howard Parsons?"

"In 1982."

"How did you meet him?"

"He picked me up in a bar."

"What bar?"

"A place called, *The Raven*. It's in Funkstown."

"A pick-up place for homosexuals?"

"Yes."

"When in '82 did he pick you up?"

"Let's see . . . I think it was January. Yes. January. I remember Christmas music being played downtown a couple of weeks before."

"Did you start seeing him on a regular basis from then on?"

"Fairly regular. I suspected right away that he had another lover. Maybe more than one."

"Why did you suspect you had competition?"

"He would promise to meet me sometimes and wouldn't show up. Other times he would come late to our encounters and then he couldn't perform . . . couldn't get it up, so to speak. I suspected then that he just got out of another bed to crawl into mine. But our relationship continued like that until he, until he . . . until June of 1984."

"You mean, 1982, until Archy Howell was murdered? Is that what you meant to say?"

"No, 1984, when he took me to that party of yours at the country club. He told me that you were the investigator for the State's Attorney. I heard that and I got scared. I never wanted to be seen with him again after that."

"Why were you scared."

"Because of that baseball player."

"When did you first hear of Archy Howell?"

"I didn't know who Archy Howell was until the night he was killed. And I don't think Howard knew who he was, either."

"You're being mysterious, now. Why so cryptic?"

"You said plain language questions. I don't know what *cryptic* means."

"It means obscure . . . ambiguous . . . deliberately mysterious. Does that help you understand?"

"I guess so. . . . Neither one of us ever saw that guy before he was killed . . . shot to death. . . . I think I need a lawyer now."

"Mister Campbell there is a lawyer. Will he do?"

"He's with you . . . working with you. No, he will not do. Nothing more out of me until I have a lawyer sitting next to me . . . one I can trust. Somebody who will advise which questions I should answer and which ones I shouldn't."

"We'll get you your lawyer, but I'll tell you right now that you can't just pick and choose the questions you'll answer, even with a lawyer by your side. It's all or nothing. And if it's nothing, you'll be our number one suspect. You'll have a guilty sign hanging around your neck until someone convinces us to the contrary. Now do you still want that lawyer?"

"Try one more question."

"Who killed Archy Howell?"

"Better get me a lawyer."

Cantor was handcuffed to the chair he had been sitting in. Joe and Sonny left Joe's office, locking the door as they left. Joe intended to go to Winston Hathaway's office, one floor below near the entrance to the building.

As they were walking down the stairs, Sonny said, "Will he be upset when he sees the two of us together?"

"Under other circumstances he probably would be. But when I tell him how much help you provided in finding this guy and getting him to open his mouth, he'll probably kiss you. The unsolved murder of Archy Howell has been hanging heavy around this building for a long time. We're about to bring some relief to Mister Winston Hathaway."

Joe filled his boss in on all the accumulated details of Cantor's arrest and interrogation as a material witness. "We're going to have to take him into Piercy's court and get the judge to appoint someone in the bar to represent him for the rest of this interrogation . . . preferably a lawyer who has an office nearby."

Winston Hathaway leaned back in his leather chair and smiled. "You boys working together on this thing? . . . I suppose Sonny's adopted son was the reason. I always felt bad about what we did to that boy. Why don't we appoint Bob Libner to hold this Cantor's hand for a while? I can smell it in the air. This case is going to be closed . . . and soon. You have my blessing, men. Go to it. I'll have Piercy's written order on Libner's desk in the next half hour."

The scene was set for a continuation of the interrogation. Joe was in charge, sitting behind his desk. Opposite him in front of the desk sat Victor Cantor with his lawyer, Robert Libner sitting next to him. Sonny Campbell sat in a corner of the room, having been introduced on the record as someone who was an interested party who would monitor the proceeding. To one side of the desk was a court reporter who would take down, on his stenographic machine, every word spoken in Joe's office that afternoon.

The record was first oriented with the names of every person in the room and what his function was. Joe asked his first question.

"Mister Cantor, do you know who killed Archy Howell about twelve years ago?"

Cantor looked at Libner who nodded his head, indicating that the question should be answered.

"Yes."

"Who was it?"

"Howard Parsons."

"Would you tell us, for the record, how that came about?"

"I was one of Parsons' sexual partners back when Howell got shot. At that time, Parsons had another partner who he was madly in love with. I suspected there was such a person, but I didn't know who he was."

"Did you ever find out who he was?"

"Oh, yeah. I did find who that bastard was . . . the very night of the killing."

"Tell us how you found out who he was."

"I wasn't supposed to see Parsons that night. But around midnight he came a knocking on my door and came into my place. He was all excited about something. I didn't know at the time what had him so agitated. Anyway he went straight for my zipper. Then he insisted we go for a ride in my car . . . the car that you guys refer to as the *mox nix* VW. He told me to drive to Carmine's café and park in front of the place. The only place I found to park when we got to Carmine's was across the street. Without saying a word to me, he jumped out of the car and dashed down our side of the street, then across the street, and then walked to the front of the café. He stopped and looked into the big window they have there. He kind of stood at the far end of the window as if he didn't want to be seen by anybody in the café. There was another car parked in front of the place but the driver had his back to Howard and probably didn't notice him. He stood like that for almost ten minutes . . . just staring through the window like a zombie. Then all of a sudden he started walking straight ahead at a normal pace like he had been walking all the time. It all happened so fast. First, Howard ran back across the street and got into my car. Then a black guy came bursting out through the front door of the café and turned to his left and started running toward the corner. Howard shouted, "Quick! Follow that man who's running. Catch up with him." I spun my wheels and almost caught up with the man who turned the corner. He was still running and I was just able to turn and follow him."

"After you made the turn, you did catch up with him, didn't you?"

"Yeah, but Howard told me not to stop. Instead, he said to make the next left turn and circle the block, which I did. When we got back to the street that Carmine's is on, I saw someone else come out of the place. This guy was not moving too fast. He was kind of staggering like he was drunk. He staggered across the street and got into a car. Howard told me to turn left and follow him."

"Did you recognize the man?"

"No, but I think Howard did."

"Why do you say that?"

"Because Howard's exact words were, *Follow that bastard. I'll teach him not to mess with my man.* When I heard that I started to understand why we were at Carmine's in the first place. Howard was there to see his other lover. He got to Carmine's window just as this guy—it had to be the drunk who we later followed—just as the drunk was smacking his other lover around. Howard must have seen all that through the window and it put him in a rage."

"Why do you say *rage*?"

"Because of his tone of voice and what he did later on."

"Which was?"

"First I gotta tell you about the shotgun he gave me on my birthday the previous January."

"I'm all ears."

"Howard is crazy about skeet shooting. He wanted me to learn. He gave me this beautiful shotgun as a gift and he bugged me all the time to go skeet shooting with him. It wasn't my bag, but I was happy to have the shotgun for my personal protection. I carried it in my car, fully loaded. I kept it in the space behind the seats."

"Go back to when you started following the man, and tell us what the man did . . . and what you and Howard did after that."

"I guess the man—let's face it, the man was Archy Howell—and we followed him to one of them big, beautiful houses on Jefferson Boulevard. It must have been his home, because all the lights were on. He fumbled with his keys at the front door, but finally let himself in. I turned my engine off and coasted to a stop a ways back where my car was hidden by some bushes."

Interspersed throughout these statements, were Cantor's glances at Lawyer Libner, who, each time their eyes met, would nod in the affirmative, as if to say he was doing fine.

"Howell and his wife started arguing inside the house immediately. They both argued so loudly that you could hear them from where we were parked."

"What kind of things did they say to each other?"

"What did you expect when a man comes home drunk at almost two in the morning? *Where you been all this time? You're drunk again. . . . Yeah, I had a few beers. . . . That's ten times in the last month.* Things like that."

"Did they finally turn the house lights out and go to bed?"

"Hell, no. He came roaring out the front door, got in his car and drove off, weaving all over the place. I started up and followed him again on Howard's orders."

"You say he was weaving all over the place. Did he have any accidents, any collisions, as you were following him?"

"Came close about a dozen times, but there was no collision until he got to Plum and Harrison."

"What collision was that?"

"I want to be careful how I answer that one. It's pretty tricky. . . . We got down there, see. Howard knew where I kept the shotgun. He grabbed it and told me to get ahead of Howell, slow down, and make him stop. I thought he was going to scare the guy. I pulled ahead of him and I thought he was pulling over to the curb but he just kept going until his left front fender kind of scraped my right front fender. He stopped then, all right. He rolled down his window and started to yell at us. I backed up and stopped. He called us names. Howard got out of my car with the shotgun in his right hand. The guy yelled, *You got a gun. Help! He's got a rifle.* But there was no one around to hear him."

"Go on."

"It was quick. Both barrels. He just stuck the shotgun through the open window. And fired two blasts."

"Did you know he was going to do it?"

"No way. I thought he was just going to threaten him. . . . I don't think *he* knew he was going to do it. He never checked to see if the gun was loaded. He never asked me whether it was loaded. He didn't know the window was going to be open. He didn't say anything to Mister Howell, before he did it. And when he got back into the car he said, *Oh, my God! I think I killed him.*"

"He could have killed him, all right. That is, if you're telling us the truth. You've got your story down pat, haven't you? How many times have you rehearsed it in the last twelve years? A hundred? A thousand?"

"I never rehearsed it. This is the very first time that I've said anything about what happened that morning."

"Change a few details and your story would turn into a confession. Your gun. Your VW. You had a perfect motive, if you thought Archy Howell was your competition. That's right isn't it? Didn't you think that Howard was playing around with a famous baseball player? Weren't you jealous of Archy Howell? . . . So jealous of him that you had to take your shotgun and end the romance between him and Howard Parsons?"

"**Stop it. Stop it.** You're wrong. . . . Howard Parsons did the murder . . . not me. If I killed anyone, I wouldn't have said a word here, this afternoon . . . would I?"

"Are you sure that's the way you want to leave this thing? What's your lover going to say when he hears the things you're saying about him? Are you going to get scared when a good defense lawyer works you over and tries to pin this killing on you, you little worm. I don't believe you . . . not for a minute."

Sonny Campbell cleared his throat audibly. He stood up.

"That's right. There's a good defense lawyer, right there, and I'm sure he doesn't believe a word of this cock-and-bull story of yours, do you Sonny?"

Sonny cleared his throat again, and took a few steps toward the office door. Attorney Libner said, "Don't say another word, Mister Cantor. Don't answer another question. These people are not your friends, believe me."

Cantor said, "You're a little late, aren't you, Mister Defense Lawyer? You're probably in with them, yourself."

Before Sonny left the room, Joe surprised everyone by announcing, "You're free to go, Mister Cantor." Sonny stopped in his tracks. "A patrol car will take you back to your house. But remember, if you try to pull a disappearing act again, then we'll know you're the killer. We've got your name and know your habits. If your little house is vacant for twenty four hours, we'll pick you up again in a New York minute. Your neighbors will be our watchdogs."

Joe picked up the receiver on his desk telephone. "We'll need a patrol car and a uniformed driver for Cantor. Take him home and blow your siren when you get on Shiloh Church Road. I want the whole world to be keeping an eye on this twink. Got it?" Joe put the phone back in it's cradle.

"We're going to leave you now, Victor . . . right in this room to wait for your car and driver. Stay close to home, my friend. You'll never know when we'll need you again. Understand?"

The room vacated, except for a very forlorn and frightened witness to wait for his ride home.

Outside the office, Joe took Sonny by the arm. "Let's go to Winston's office. He heard every word that was said. My office has been wired to his since the year one. I hope I wasn't too much of a show off in there. I just wanted to scare him into sticking around till we need him again. I'm really inclined to believe him, weren't you? . . . Well, at least we got enough to charge Parsons and pick him up over in *fruitcake park.*"

Sonny stopped. He looked menacingly straight into Joe's eyes.

"Oh, I'm sorry, Sonny. I still haven't gotten used to Chester being the way he is."

"You mean, you haven't gotten used to him being a doctor, you ignorant son-of-a-bitch. Say *yes* and I won't beat the shit out of you, right here and now . . . and I warn you, if you ever prove your prejudice against homosexuals again in my presence, that'll be the end of our friendship."

Joe started walking again. Sonny followed him.

Joe asked in a very concerned manner, "How's Doctor Campbell doing, anyway? Does he enjoy being a neurologist? I know he must have worked his ass off to get where he is now. Give him my best when you see him, will you, friend?"

CHAPTER THIRTY TWO

"We won't need an arrest warrant, Joe. We got enough probable cause with Cantor's statement. Let's try to get him arraigned before I go on vacation," said Hathaway.

"Where are you going?"

"A little place you never heard of in Michigan. The world's best kept secret. I sail. I swim. I walk for miles. I drink dozens of Margaritas and when my wife's in the mood, which happens there more often than it does here, I make love a lot. Not bad for a sixty-five year old bag o' bones. . . . They tell me that Parsons has turned into a predator . . . hangs out in a notorious park. I didn't know we had places like that in Hagerstown."

"Oh, yes, sir. They've been operating in that park for more than a year now."

"Let that be the first thing on my agenda when I return from Pentwater. We can't have that going on in this town."

"Well, you gotta admit, it makes it convenient for us this time. Parsons is over in that park at least every other day. We're gonna look for him there this afternoon."

"Don't let me keep you. I'm sure you're getting anxious to get over there and get yourself a good place to put your car. I wanna see this guy again. It's been ten years since he told us a bunch of lies from the witness stand. Go get him, Joe."

Joe parked in the shade of a big spreading maple tree. The spot was at least a hundred yards from the pick-up bench. Despite his calculations that Parsons would be on the bench sometime after working hours and before midnight his vigil was nonproductive for more than four hours. He gave up and went home. Exhausted, he went to sleep, fully dressed, on a couch.

Edith gently woke him up at eight o'clock. "What time is it?"

"Ten after eight in the morning."

"Oh, shit! I'll be late."

"No, you won't. I called and explained to Lori you were on a stake-out last night and wouldn't be in until ten o'clock. You need your sleep old man.

Your coffee is on the table next to you, with a piece of toast and marmalade. You've got time to take a shower and change your clothes. I put your lucky tie out for you on the bed. You're sure to make your arrest today."

His head still pounded, despite the hot shower. *My oath to nab this guy has lasted ten years. It's gotten old and rusty. It's time to toss it away. I'll have cuffs on him this very day. I'll call Chester and explain. And the irony, Chester, is that he thought he was doing it for you . . . for your dignity. But that didn't excuse the murder. He showed his evil when he made up his mind that he would let you take the rap for him.*

He dressed and frowned when he had to knot the tie a second time to make the ends meet. She had filled another cup with hot coffee and placed it on the back of the toilet next to the bathroom sink. He brushed his teeth and now he was ready for anything.

He went to the office and greeted everyone with, "Morning folks. Beautiful day." He looked around and saw that word of the impending arrest had leaked out. It was written on all their faces.

It was five thirty in the afternoon. He parked in the same spot. He looked over at the bench. There was a youthful looking man sitting there alone

.Parsons made an appearance a half hour later. He approached the bench and said something to the young man sitting there. He then sat down with his back to Joe Beyerly's car.

Joe strolled casually across the grass towards Parsons' back. He drew his small revolver from a holster.

"Howard Parsons."

Parsons and his companion both look stunned. Joe walked around to face Parsons.

"Mister Parsons, stand up now, turn around, and put your hands behind you."

Parsons obeyed Joe's order immediately. With his free hand, Joe expertly cuffed his wrists.

"You're under arrest for the murder of Mister Archy Howell on May 14, 1982. You have the right to remain silent and you are warned that anything you do say may be used against you at trial. You have a right to have an attorney to advise and counsel with you. If you cannot afford an attorney, one will be furnished to you at no expense. Have you heard and do you understand these rights?"

The terrified predator, almost whispering, said, "Yes".

Parsons' young companion ran swiftly away after Joe told him he was free to leave. The accused went along peacefully but still trembling with his captor. He was led to Joe's car and placed in the back seat, still with both hands cuffed behind him.

Parsons started to speak as Joe started the car and put it in gear. Joe raised his hand as if taking an oath. "I would advise you not to say anything until you have a lawyer to advise you, Mister Parsons."

"I was just going to ask you if Mister Campbell is still in the Public Defender's office."

"He is, but under the circumstances I doubt whether he could legally represent you."

"Why?"

"Because of your prior relationship with his son."

"I don't understand that. I request that Sonny Campbell be my lawyer."

"Weren't you listening? Sonny has an obvious conflict of interest."

"I won't accept anyone else."

"Oh, shut the hell up, Howard. You're already starting to muddy the waters. You're not going to get away with that this time. We've got you dead to rights."

They arrived at the Detention Center and Parsons was fingerprinted and booked. He was placed in a cell by himself. Joe called Edith. "Mission accomplished."

"It was your lucky tie."

"Would you do me a favor, honey?"

"Anything," she answered.

"Call Rochelle and Sonny. I don't have it in me to talk to them today. Say he's in a cell by himself. There are a bunch of inmates in here who would just as soon stone him to death after what he did to Chester twelve years ago."

"Let me throw the first stone."

"To them, Chester's a Martin Luther King, and Archy's killer, a James Earl Ray. Rumors are flying that we've got Archy's killer. Bet you a hundred dollars he doesn't last a month in this Detention Center."

"You're probably right. I'll call Rochelle and Sonny."

Sonny called Chester and informed him of the arrest. Chester managed to get a week off to go home and visit with his parents. On Wednesday, the day after Parsons was arrested and placed alone in a cell, Chester signed the visitors' log. While he was waiting for a sheriff's deputy to bring Parsons to a visiting room, he talked seriously with the head of the Detention Center deputies.

"You weren't on duty when I was in here twelve years ago, were you, deputy?"

"No, sir."

"You know, there may be an uprising in this place and an attempt to take Howard Parsons' life."

"You're Sonny Campbell's son, aren't you? And you're now a doctor?"

"Yes, I am."

"I've already heard rumors that the inmates are planning to assassinate the bastard. Why don't we stay out of it, and just let it happen. Save the city the expense of giving him the gas."

"Is that what you're planning to do . . . just let it happen? You're wrong, you know?"

"Ordinarily, I'd agree with you. But what this guy did, first to Archy Howell, and then to you, Doctor . . . letting you sit in that cell back there for two years. I just can't stomach all that. I say let the inmates have him."

"I want you to do me a favor, deputy. I still know some of those guys. I want you to get the word out that I want them to leave him alone. Let him tell his story. They may change their minds when they hear why he killed Howell. I'm very serious about this. Tell them that, will you?"

"Only because it's you who's asking."

Parsons was brought in, in cuffs and shackles. When he saw Chester, sitting in a chair at a table, he tried to break loose and retreat, but the deputy was holding him firmly by the arm.

In a soft and temperate tone, Chester said, "I'm not here to punish you, Howard."

Parsons stopped his resistance to being led into the visiting room. "I think I know why you did what you did. You probably believe I should be grateful for your responding to the insult to my dignity, but you're dead wrong. Come in here and sit down. I'm not going to make you feel any worse than you already feel."

"Chet . . . I . . . I . . . have to . . . I'm begging you for your forgiveness. I shouldn't have let you take the blame. I should have visited you every day when you were in here It's such a terrible place. I don't think I'll be able to survive in here like you did. I didn't visit you because I just thought I had to put the whole thing out of my mind, including you. I didn't mean to shoot that . . ."

"Please, Howard . . . no explanations. Don't even try. When a person does something and doesn't know why they did it, he can't explain. He mustn't even try to explain. But there are things to be said here."

"What are you going to say? What can you say? You condemn me, don't you?"

"No."

"You should."

"Howard, I loved you, really loved you. I know it wasn't the other way around. You proved that when you were unfaithful to me with that other boy you had. Maybe it was because I desperately needed somebody, **anybody**. Howard, I stopped having anyone to love me when I was fifteen years old . . . when my mother died. You came along and you wanted me. It made little difference to me why you wanted me. I thought you loved me and that's all that counted."

"Chet, I did lo . . ."

"Please, let me finish this. I'm talking to myself as much as I'm talking to you. . . . It was a bad start for the naïve kid that I was. I'm quite sure that I'm over all that pathetic physical stuff. All I want out of life now is to be the best doctor the world has ever seen."

"I'm sure that you're well on your way to meeting that goal."

"Howard, you ask me to forgive you. You've got that backwards. You've got to forgive yourself. You didn't have a bad motive. You thought I would be impressed by this ridiculous, this reckless thing that you did, that is, if you thought at all."

"I'm listening."

"In the months to come, you will have thousands of thoughts about the killing, and me, and God, and dying, and, yes, about forgiveness. I know, I did. I learned to regret the sexual nonsense that you taught me. And I asked myself questions and got very few answers. I was too young. But then my savior came . . . oh, I don't mean God or Jesus. . . . They've always been around. My mama saw to that."

"Oh, Chet. If only God or Jesus could come to me now . . . I would fall on my knees and . . ."

"Please Howard. Let me finish. . . . But after you had become such a huge disappointment to me, and Mister Campbell came into my life, everything changed. He was what I'd really been waiting for . . . since I was fifteen. He was what made it possible for me to become what I am."

"I'm trying to get him as my lawyer. They tell me that's not legal, because of you. Because you're his adopted son, and that makes him have a conflict. He probably couldn't work any miracles for me anyway. I'm not made of the same stuff as you are."

"What's going to happen is going to happen. The only thing you can do, is to make sure, if you're still alive, that you react to what happens in the right way. You've had all the fun that life has to offer a person like you. . . . If you're lucky enough to get out of this mess, you've got to start life all over again. I was lucky. God let me start all over again."

"If I could only . . ."

"I've said all I'm going to say."

"Do I see you again?"

"I doubt it."

"I guess I can't blame you. I once promised to visit you here every week and broke that promise as quickly as I made it. I won't look for you, Chester. For what it's worth, I think I still love you."

"Of course, you'd say that. There's a lot more of me to love nowadays."

Chester buzzed for the deputy to come. The deputy took Parsons by the arm. The first degree murder suspect shuffled back to his cellblock.

It didn't take long for the community of inmates to conspire to take Howard Parsons' life. A few days after his conversation with Chester, he was led by a guard to a visiting cubicle. It was not an ample room like the one provided to Chester for his visit. For that, the head deputy had considered Chester a special case because of his celebrity.

The cubicles were for ordinary visitation by relatives and friends who sat on stools in tiny walled spaces that were separated from the prisoners by thick glass partitions. Communication was by means of telephone devices. Parsons' back was exposed to passers-by behind him in the incarceration half of the cubicle.

A trustee, whose duty it was to sweep up passages in the cellblocks, including the walkway behind the inmates' side of the visiting cubicles, plunged a makeshift shank into Howard Parsons' back as he sat waiting for his visitor to arrive. No one saw what happened. Parsons fell forward. His face rested on the glass partition and looked like a grotesque and misshapen Halloween mask. The trustee calmly resumed his sweeping duties. He was back in the cellblock area before the execution was discovered by Parsons' visitor who arrived minutes later. The trustee was charged with murder on the same day it was committed.

With an air of victory, Joe said, "You owe me a hundred bucks, Edith."

"What for?"

"The inmates got Parsons . . . shank in the back, so I'm told."

"That sounds exciting. Don't expect me to be sorry and sad. I'll spend the hundred bucks on you and Chet and me at dinner tonight. Let's call the Campbells and see if they can eat with us. That'll make five."

"You'll have to check with Chet too. Where do you wanna eat?" Joe asked.

"LJ's, of course, And since I'm paying, how's a nice thick New York Strip sound, with Martinis and big green olives stuffed with blue cheese, before hand? . . . Bottle of Merlot . . . New York Cheese Cake. How's that sound, huh?"

"Like you're amusing yourself with your favorite food."

"I got the feeling there's gonna be a lot of that for us from now on."

"Why's that?"

"With the real killer of my former husband nicely pushing up daisies, goin' out for dinner will probably be the only excitement left in Hagerstown to stir the soul."

"Maybe we'll have to start going to baseball games with Rocky and Sonny. You know what Sonny told me once . . . That they moved here to Hagerstown in the first place to get away from excitement. *Small town lawyer, that's what I wanted to be,* he told me.

I asked him who could o' imagined that some Las Vegas big shots would wanna come here and fix minor league baseball games? Certainly not poor Archy. Certainly not me or Edith . . . or Rocky or you, Sonny. Well, that's all in the past. Hagerstown can go back to sleep now."